I0699946

Copyright ©Nate Fitch 2022
ISBN: 979-8987114506

Author: Nate Fitch
Front Cover and Illustrations by **William Heavey**
Published Independently by NateFitchNovels

NATE FITCH

The Coroner

Kingdom of
Solarno
905 P.A.
Bergine Mountains
The Toterhorn
Faynean Forest
Grimmberg Castle
Aiya's Tears
Cröbátha
Saxis Bay
The Fallow Field
Lazzar Perish
Brinoa
Mont Fich'ette
Turnia
Perthmyre Downs
Gulf
of
Morvano
Cunhalt Glenn
A'mach's Head
Dierganfell Fields
City of Atherheim
Rolhine River
Estavo's Quarry
Gibbet Marsh
Hinterford
Thywick Forest
Cleve Lorn
The Levy
Calitoria
N
E
W
S
Magwyre Knolls
Aelwyd Castle
Sicalla Bay
Butcher's Strath
Marlida Forest

Prologue

She reached the end of the catacomb hall from within the charnel crypt and stopped to catch her breath. A pounding heartbeat filled her skull with a deafening cacophony of rapid rhythmic beating. The sconce above flickered from where she leaned against the wall.

A draft? I am close to the exit.

She thought to herself while wincing from a sharp pain in her thigh,

...just a little further.

As her physiology and faculties returned with the slowing of her respiration, the coroner checked herself for any signs of a potential breach in her uniform's black leathers and wools. As her hands hastily followed her eyes in a frantic search for signs of tears or hemorrhage, a thundering roar echoed in the distance. A ground-shaking force suddenly collided against the subterranean cavern wall from far below whence she came. Dust and debris fell around her.

There was no time to lose. She knew she had to keep on the move or face certain death at the hands of her predators. She reached for a pouch found on the hard leather and steel-plated brigantine and produced from within a small copper syringe. The liquid within the glass vial swirled and bubbled.

As the light of the burning sconce reflected off the glass, vibrant hues of sparkling sapphire danced across the porcelain white thin-beaked mask. With her free hand, she twisted down on the plunger, forcing a long hypodermic needle out from the metal hub housing. Finding the wax-sealed port near her right arm, she plunged the icy large-bore needle into the antecubital fossa.

A pulsating force tapped the plunger against her thumb, indicating the needle had found its mark. A hard, forced plunge drove the cerulean contents of the vial deep into her bloodstream and towards her pounding heart. The drug moved quickly, being drawn closer to the vital organs with each thunderous pound of her heart. Pulling the needle from the arm and shattering the vial against the stone floor of the crypt, the mortalist fell back against the wall in a violent cacophony of spasmodic fits and rigors.

Her body temperature was the first to respond, a soul-chilling sensation followed by the rapid, widespread dilation of the pores of her skin. Beads of sweat began to percolate across her lower back and forehead. One by one, her thighs and biceps muscles swelled from increased blood flow, the muscles contracting, becoming akin to corded steel bands. The diaphragm dropped. The lungs expanded as they filled with increased air volume. The rapid and violent change in her anatomy and physiology from the self-ministered dose of anthemene was as torturous as intoxicating. The situation was dire, and her life was in jeopardy.

The occasion called for an entire vial of the body-altering substance. Twitching and writhing against the wall, the coroner grabbed her head with both hands. The drug had finally started to take hold of the brain and all five of her senses. Sight, sound, scent, touch, and taste. The woman tilted her head back and burst out a blood-curdling scream. The pitch of her demoniac wail started high, but the longer she held the shrill, the tone dropped to a bellowed roar. Her bloodshot eyes opened, pupils blown and shaking like a wild animal. The body-wide aches and pain had dissipated, and only a controlled rage remained. She sprang from the wall and bounded up the next flight of stone stairs.

The sound of clamoring claws and demoniacal howls were closing in on her from below. She drew her pistol from its holster and pressed down on the side lever to break open the receiver. A large-bore brass casing came barreling from the receiver, tumbling, and clanging down the stone steps behind her. The woman reached to her belt and grabbed a heavy grained, thick shell from the bandolier. Quickly, she shoved the red-tipped round into the receiver and gave the firearm a hard flick upwards.

A loud click rang out, and she pulled back on the large steel firing hammer. The entrance was finally insight as the mortalist bounded up the last stretch of stone steps. Crossing the threshold, the floor erupted underneath her sending dirt and stone debris in all directions.

The chunks of exploding stone hurdled at her as she dropped to her knee guards and slid to the side of the crypt's entrance. The center of her back touched the cold stone floor as stone debris and worm-ridden earth soared over her coroner mask's thin, short beak. As the debris cleared, she rose. Using only her quadriceps muscles to stand, the coroner rose to meet the oncoming blow of what hunted her so passionately. Leaping into the air, she landed on the outstretched

tendril of the beasts and darted up to the creature's
head. A backflip and the pull of a trigger sent singed
fur, pus-ridden flesh, and shattered jagged fangs in
every direction.

As she downed one beast, another came
barreling from within the freshly erupted earth. The
woman landed on the balls of her feet and tumbled
forward through the doorway before smoothly
transitioning into a series of somersaults to create a safe
gap distance. Wheeling around in a quickened
pirouette, her eyes caught the huge stone gargoyle
above the crypt entrance. As the creature frantically
searched around the crypt's entrance, the woman
holstered her arm and switched to the spring-loaded
crossbow attached to the top of her steel and leather
arm bracer.

Three successive steel bolts drove a deep crack
into the statue's base. Drawing a rope dart from her
vest, the woman launched the roped ballista at the
gargoyle's base. As the blade became buried into the
stone, the beast within the crypt was drawn to the
sound. It wildly turned and slammed its titanic tendrils
into the stone floor, shattering the stone into pebbles.

A deafening roar erupted from the creature,
sending salivated pus and emulsified bile pouring over
hundreds of rows of jagged fangs.

Come and claim your prey.

The beast lunged from the crypt entrance on all
seven of its tendrils with another ear-splitting roar. The
amalgamated snout of the creature became graced by
the light of the full moon as it crossed the threshold.
Timing her hold, the coroner pulled with all her might
on the tethered rope. The stone gargoyle fell to the

muddied earth with a force that shook the ground, crushing the creature's head and body in a cavalcade of fetid blood and bone, pierced flesh.

The obstructing gargoyle momentarily sealed the door, but a cacophony of howls from within the crypt signaled the arrival of more. The woman looked through the opaque fog that slowly flooded around her. Her eyes quickly scanned the path below, straining to catch a glimpse of the iron gate of the charnel yard. A way was clear. However, the position of her unseen foes had her hesitating to decide. Quickly she twirled to assess the path up toward the holy sepulcher on the hill above. The moon's flaxen rays slowly became enclosed within the fast-approaching blanket of turgescent fog.

As the tumefied smog swallowed the ancient, abandoned church, the notion of seeking any sanctuary from within was lost. The roars below rang out from below the crypt and reverberated throughout the encircling mist. The howls from the entombed beasts had finally been answered by a cacophony of unanimous cries of more from the nearby hamlet. The coroner could hear the thundering clammer of approaching beasts.

Her time was up. With another dexterous handspring down the hill, the coroner made haste to the bell tower in the middle of the dilapidated town. The woman vaulted through broken windows at breaking speed as she cleared empty house after house. As she reached an abandoned warehouse opposite the bell tower, another creature came bursting through the front of the double iron doors.

Time slowed from within her mind at the sight of the lumbering amalgam bounding toward her. Calculating the trajectory and factoring for speed, the coroner fell back and entered a sideways slide.

Dodging the creature's wild lashing, she quickly drew her short coroner's cane from the holster on her thigh and pounded the flattened pommel on the hard stone floor. From within the hollowed interior, a spring-loaded lister knife came jutting out from the opposite end. Two perfectly placed slashes of the lustrous steel blade sent the creature's head soaring from its torso and across the warehouse floor. The headless heap of a rotted carcass slumped to the floor as the coroner sprang back to her feet from the warehouse floor. Rapidly she appraised the warehouse interior for any sign of a quick exit. Spotting a nearby rope pulley, she advanced toward the contrivance and lept up the dangling damp rope.

She climbed rapidly and leaped from the pulley onto the second-story landing. The sound of more could be heard from below, but her eyes remained focused on the open loft door ahead. Her racing mind started to estimate and measure the upcoming gap distance. Holstering her cane and picking up pace, the coroner loaded a rope tethered bolt into the housing of her wrist crossbow. Aiming with an outstretched arm, she held her breath and squeezed down on the firing lever. As it spiraled through the air, the steel bolt shined like a shooting comet under rays of amber moonlight. The steel bolt stuck firmly into the wooden shingled roof of the bell tower's monastery with a burrowing thud. Taking hold of the rope in both hands as she approached the loft doorway, she held her breath and began to count to four.

On the second count of her bounding stride, the coroner bent her knees and sprang into a high arching forward side tuck straight through the second-story loft doorway. As she got to the count of four in her mind, she braced herself for the impending hard impact. Her body barreled and crashed through the rotted wooden ceiling of the dilapidated monastery. Hitting through the center of a weathered wooden beam, the sound of snapping bones and collapsing shingles filled the musty monastery air. Her tumbling body plummeted downward until finally crashing into rows of partially stacked pews and piles of moldy books.

She had multiple contusions, fractures, and a splitting headache from the fall but the adrenaline-infused anthemene rush forced her quickly up to her knees. The massive dose of anthemene she had injected began to work through her wounds as she heaved deep breaths through the reanimation of her wounds.

The sound of cracking bones and snapping ligaments re-aligning from under her taut skin forced a series of writhing grunts before falling forward on extended arms. The pain was over, and her breathing slowed to an even pace. Rising with an amended frame, she felt the ground shake once more as the creatures had caught up with her again. Pounding against the side of the monastery, they meant to bring the wall down through brute force. She scanned the room, her eyes finally meeting a doorway on the far side of the choir.

She pulled her cane and readied the blade again before running and vaulting over obstacles en route toward the tower entrance. The entrance led to a hollow high rise, lined with a narrow wooden spiral staircase as far as her eyes could see. Climbing the tower's stairs, a collapsing stone wall echoed from below and through the tower entrance, followed by the clamoring and howling of more foul beasts.

I won't make it to the top in time.

Looking out from the banister railing to the tower's center, she saw a bell pull dangling in-between next to the center chiming rope. Reaching over the banister, she grabbed the rope, peered upward, and gave it a firm tug. Satisfied with the rope's integrity, she sprang from the stairs and held on tight to her last lifeline. Clutching the thick heavy rope with her legs and one hand, she cut the adjacent bell pull with her cane blade.

The plummeting of tethered sandbags shot the coroner to the top of the tower. Looking below, she could see the heavy bags crushing the skull of another beast. Dozens more tore through the doorway and began to climb up the walls with tentacle-like appendages. As she reached the top of the landing, she jumped from the rope toward the stairwell. A twist of the cane pommel sent the double-edged blade sliding back into its housing before being holstered on her hip.

The coroner then pulled her pistol and reloaded the chamber, this time with a glass tipped round filled with a green viscous liquid. The woman quickly reached into her vest and pulled out two round glass vials from small leather pouches. Throwing the vials down the tower shaft and pulled back on the thick steel hammer while pointing the long octagonal barrel down the shaft. She closed her non-dominant eye, steadied her breathing, and took aim. As the heavy glass flasks met the encroaching creatures, the coroner held her breath and gently pulled back on the trigger. The fiery blast from the steadied barrel sent a specialized round whizzing to meet the glass.

As the green viscous-filled bullet contacted the flask, the entire center of the bell tower shaft erupted in a fiery display of roaring green flames, quickly turning every creature in its path into smoldering green cinders. The emerald flames rained down a haze of pyroclastic fury upon the remaining ascending beasts below, shrieking as they dissipated into piles of burning and writhing scorched meat.

Bullseye.

The desperate act of buying time came at an uncalculated and foolhardy price. The volatile mixture of vitriol and ether vapor ignited an emerald flame so intense that it could bring both tower and town to ruin. The reflection of embers danced across the crimson mirrored lenses of her coroner mask as she witnessed the unfolding chaos she had unleashed. The incendiary madness malignantly consumed beast, wood, and stone with anarchical indiscrimination.

As the structure's integrity began to groan and creak under the corrosive force of the expansive cataclysm below, the floor started to sway beneath her. She looked around in haste, plotting a course for her next stunt. But there was nowhere left to go. She loaded a flint round into the single-chambered receiver of her breech-loading pistol and sent a comet trail of scarlet smoke and flame out over the city towards the far-off fort on the outskirts of town. The last flare trail soared out and fizzled in the distance. The coroner focused her gaze and prayed for the return signal, of a roaring bonfire.

As the green flames rose higher and higher towards the tower belfry, there was still no response from the military installation on the horizon. She reached for her bandolier to grab another flint shot, but her fingers only groped at emptied leather sleeves. The coroner had spent her rounds, and there would be no promised aid for rescue. A pillar of green flames erupted from the side of the tower, sending molten, flaming stone to the adjacent houses near the bell tower.

The thatched roofs soon followed in the spreading infernal blaze she had caused to buy herself time, a moment to still the chaos. As she stood on the belfry railing of the slowly collapsing tower and looked out over the horizon, a single shudder of mortality rose within her. Her raven wheeled over the far-off fortress. The echoes of its shrilling caw reached even her.

Thanks, old girl, but I am afraid this is the end of our partnership. Go home, Vixen, and find yourself a new companion.

From far below the tower, a bone-chilling squeal filled the smoke and fog-filled air. Recognizing the distressing sound, the coroner ran to the opposite banister railing. Leaning over the banister, she gazed down to behold her chestnut colored Solarnian Destrier fighting its way toward her in the streets below.

The destrier bucked and reared as it fought through rapidly encircling pythonic interfused deviations. The horse squealed and groaned as it struggled to reach its stranded and distressed master. The thought of those monstrosities tearing and devouring her horse sent a heart-shattering pain piercing her chest. The coroner choked down a welling of tears as she yelled below to her faithful companion.

"EMILIO! Goddess, damn you horse, get out of here! Save yourself and go! EMILIO! *NO!*"

As she shouted at her mount, the bestial horde swarmed over and engulfed the panicked foaming destrier. She fell to her knees and cried in a trembling, tear-filled rage.

Her screams of heart wrenching pain reverberated throughout the vacuous night air over the flames and carnage below. The last sight she witnessed before dropping to the wooden floor was that of her loyal companion being torn apart and consumed by the horde of bloated slathering beasts. The pain quickly turned to a vengeance thirsting rage.

Rising from the wooden floor of the belfry, the coroner began to assess her remaining stock and gear. Formulating and finalizing the details of her last stand, the coroner began rigging her chymiac vapors and salts with the remaining alkahest and brimstone chargers she had. Before she could descend from the fiery collapsing bell tower and avenge her horse's death, a sudden whip on her ankle from behind sent the coroner to her belly.

Flipping over onto her back, she could see the visage of a smoldering, half-charred beast clinging to the side of the shaft entrance toward the middle of the belfry. The corrosive ichor from the flagellated appendage began to singe the leather of her knee-high boot and gaiter, burning through till the Kreiger steel plating of her shin guard was exposed. Acting quickly, she grabbed ahold of a nearby banister railing with one hand and reached for a throwing knife with her other. But her hand only groped more empty pouches.

She unholstered her other cane, and with a push of a button, a spring-loaded steel rod shot from the weapon and split the head of the burning creature in twine. But just when she thought she was safe, another climbed up behind it and lashed out, snatching her other ankle. As the beast jerked and writhed, it pulled on her with all its remaining might. No longer a desire to feed but motivated through a pure lust for death and carnage.

The tower swayed once more before a crashing sound from below signaled the start of the tower's collapse. The giant heavy brass bell chimed with the swaying of the building, the reverberations jarring both coroner and beast alike. As the bell tower started to tilt, the weight of the pulling beasts began to take its toll on the thin wooden banister railing. A hissing crack of wood sent a splinter over the ocular of the coroner's mask. Looking up, she could see the start of cracking in the wood. She closed her eyes and focused on her breathing. She began to slowly count down in her head from within the stillness of her mind. One by one, the cacophony of stifling background noise washed away all noise and sound from around her until nothing was left but the beating of her heart. Silently she began to pray.

> *Goddess Myrina, Selenestic Mother of sorrows*
> *and Dianastic mother of mercies. Hear my*
> *prayer and grant me courage. I face the gates*
> *of evil, and death blows her furious horn.*

The beam cracked once more as the coroner slowly opened her eyes.

"This is for my horse. You cyclopean, grotesque, swine-sarding cunt!"

A sudden snap of the banister rail sent mortalist and monster plummeting to the central fire chasm of the tall bell tower. As both woman and monster slide into the fire, the Mortalist drove her blunted cane deep into the beast's skull as the sound of the dying creature became engulfed in a roaring rupture of emerald flames. The bell rope slid against the charred and chipped wood floor until finally snapping taut with a loud crack. As the rope pulled down, a single toll of the brass bell rang out across the burning hamlet under the mist-shrouded light of the harvest moon.

Across the moor, the tiny flickering of a signal fire began to take shape. As the raven dove down and wheeled over the fort, its caws grew louder and louder over the sound of the fort's garrison started to rouse at the sight of the rising and roaring green flames engulfing the hamlet on the other side of the Perthmyre Downs. The women of the guard emerged from their barrack, bunking in armored coats and tricorn hats, to see the commotion from Lazzar Perish. The garrison's captain came from her lodging and walked the castle's outer bailey, a spyglass in hand. As she assessed the hamlet, her face grew pale in shock at the sight she beheld in the lens.

"By the goddess."

Uttered the wide-eyed captain, her skin crawling with chills. Dropping the glass, the captain of the guard whirled around and braced herself on the battlement. Peering down from the crenel, the captain shouted to the courtyard below.

"LIEUTENANT!"

A younger woman came running from the barracks into the courtyard, confused and half-dressed. Placing the yellow and blue tricorn hat upon her loose untidied flaxen hair, she looked at the battlement with bewilderment at the commotion around her. With her sheathed broadsword and sword belt clutched in hand, she shouted back up to her commanding officer.

"YES, CAPTAIN!"

The captain pointed to her rear and shouted below, hoping all would hear her command.

"RALLY TO ARMS! MAKE FOR LAZZAR PERISH!"

The lieutenant gave the captain a hurried salute and echoed the order to the guardswomen of the garrison.

"RALLY TO ARMS AND MAKE FOR LAZZAR PERISH! SOUND THE HORN AND SOUND THE DRUMS! TO ARMS, DAMN YOU! STRIKE THE BANNER!"

The sound of horns and battle drums rang out from the fort as the women of the Turnian Guard dressed for battle and made ranks. Crossbows and spears leaped from the weapon racks behind the garrison's quartermaster station. As the gates opened, the captain began to lead the forces toward the forsaken Lazzar Perish riding atop her white war courser. As the garrison troops marched to the beat of drums, the green flame roared over the horizon. Pillars of smoke from the hamlet's comprehensive fire rose high in the abyssal twilight sky until they almost covered the face of the low-hanging harvest moon. As the garrison troops encroached the village's borders, the path behind became quickly enclosed in a rapid envelopment of dense fog.

The garrison captain gripped the reins tightly as she halted her troops on the outskirts of the hamlet. Peering through the overgrown bramble and overgrowth surrounding the path to the front gate, her eyes caught a glimpse of something bounding from the outer wall of the village and into the tree line. As the mysterious entity darted out from the shadows of her periphery, the white stallion reared and whinnied in fear.

Pulling back on the reins to still her spooked mount, the shrieks and shouts of terror erupted from the rear ranks like a flash of sudden lightning. In a state of confused panic, the captain ordered her soldiers to stand their ground and fight their lives.

As the sounds of battle commenced outside the village, the collective screams of horror were soon drowned out and smothered by the clanging of the great bronze bell of the tower. The tolling continued to ring over the burning city as a lone raven's croak echoed across the mist-shrouded moor.

"A mortal man is nothing more than flesh, blood, and bone. The saw, and the blade, allow us to observe this putrid and defiled anatomy underneath the light of objective truth. But a rotting corpse has no life to grant them a subjective voice.
So, young Coroner.

Grant them this resurrection."

Coroner Antonio Dispacci,
Anor 545 P.A.

=Act I=

The Inquest
Of
<u>Ms. Abigail Lengelhaus</u>

Ms. Abigail Lengelhaus

Occupation: Village Blacksmith
Born: anor 880 P.A.
Murdered: anor 905 P.A.

The Village of Glengloam calls upon the Crown for the
service of a Royally Appointed Coroner to hunt down
the assailant and bring them to justice.
The Order assigns Resurrectionist Paolo Reveré the
submitted inquest.

*This is the coroner's 228th inquest in his 21 years of
service to the crown.*

Village of Glengloam

<u>The March of Brinoa</u>
Kingdom of Solarno
20th hour of the 75th Day
In the Season of Empyripas
Anor 905 P.A.

The Sheriff of Glengloam walked out from the snow-covered cabin and inhaled the cold night air deeply. A quick couple of strikes of flint brought the torch held firmly between his legs into a burst of roaring flame. The wind roared off the tall peaks of the Birgine Mountains, which loomed far off to the north of the village. Towering, jagged peaks disappear into the cumulous clouds above. Though they were leagues away, the howling gale still could be heard from down into the valley of Grimm's Glenn.

Pulling his thick woolen tartan sash around his shoulders, the Sheriff adjusted his black tam on his head and made his way down the steep slope toward a small stone hovel. Every step was treacherous out in the knee-deep snow of the Glenn, but the seasoned mountain dweller navigated it with ease. Arriving at the stone hovel, the Sheriff drew his blade from its scabbard and used the tip of his service saber to push the heavy wooden door open. Kneeling over the corpse in the corner was the feared man in black. The raven of Calitoria. *The Coroner.*

It wasn't the bone-chilling winds that sent shivers rippling down the spine of the seasoned and hardy master of the night guard. Nor was the constant threat of enemy invasion from the northern realms over the Birgine range gave the old man unsteady knees and

23

a lump in his throat. The raspy breathing of the masked man echoed throughout the darkened stone room. Hot steam-infused breath seeped from the brass pores of his raven-beaked mask, as it could be seen from the doorway though he kept his head low and focused. The Sheriff felt a bolt of quivers ripple down his right arm toward the hilt of his saber as his aged ears picked up the low murmuring and half-mutters of the shadowy figure from within the stone house.

"Ecchymosis on the larynx… broken hyoid…"

The raven-clad man continued in his mumbled speculations and fixated ravings,

"…damp behind…though dry in the front…"

Quick but gentle, leather-clad hands jutted out from under the thick, heavy cloak draped over the man's broad shoulders. Diligently and methodically, the shrouded man caressed the blood-stained linens of the red-haired corpse. Starting at the neck, he worked his way down, handbreadth by handbreadth, feeling every portion of her ice-cold ebony skin through the dirty wool. The Sheriff felt a sickness wrench his stomach. What this man was doing was improper, disrespectful, and foul. The shrouded man reached the ankles of the corpse and suddenly stopped in his assessment. A low grunt from within his hideous mask.

A flick of his wrists sent the wool dress and petty coat beneath soaring over her chest and head. Even though the darkness of the hovel cast a shadow over the body, the Sheriff knew what lay bare for the gods. Exposed indecency. The sound of deplorable squishing came from in front of the crouched man in black, and the Sheriff finally had enough of the mockery happening before him. Slamming the saber's tip onto the stone floor of the dark hovel before bringing his torch in to lighten the room with bright orange and red hues. The raven-clad man stopped in his task. Another low grunt came from within his mask.

"That is enough, Master Coroner," the Sheriff burst with a heavy Brinoan accent. "I won't let you defile this poor dead woman any longer. You dishonor her family name with such foul actions!"

As the Sheriff proclaimed his disfavor, he swung his saber about the home entrance. Slowly the Coroner turned his head until both of his ruby red lenses lit up from under the wide brim of his black capotain hat. The torch light danced off the transparent glass as the Sheriff eyed his own reflection. The harrowing visage brought his boastful speech to a stuttering stammer. It was unnatural. Not being able to see a man's eyes. Only the bright glow of two blood-red crystals cut through the shadows like demonic starlight. The harrowing visage brought his boastful speech to a stuttering stammer. The Coroner rose from his crouched position and turned his torso towards the Sheriff. The Sheriff struggled to peel his gaze from his own reflection. Breaking his trance, the Sheriff's eyes wandered downward until he caught a glimpse of the torchlight reflecting off the collection of strange instruments. Steel implements of various designs lined the peculiar, armored vest the Coroner was donning.

His mouth dropped to admit a gasp that never came. Instead, only a faint wheeze came crackling through the cold night air. The Coroner rose from the ground and swung his cloak behind both shoulders. Pressing his hands tightly together, the Coroner pressed his fingers between each other to tighten down the leather from his gloves to the skin below the surface.

"Close the door, Sheriff." Barked the masked man as he placed a silver-coated instrument back into the thin leather sleeve found on the front of his brigantine vest. "You are tampering with my crime scene."

The mustachioed man released a croak in response before exploding into a cacophony of ravings in his native Brinoan tongue. The Coroner paid no mind. He turned to the body of the murdered young woman who lay strewn on the hay-covered floor below his feet. The Coroner eyed her face one last time before cocking his head toward his rear to speak to the bothered Sheriff of Glengloam.

> "Sheriff McTavlash, would you kindly set down your torch and come give me a hand with the corpse?"

Sheriff McTavlash stopped abruptly in his rantings, undecided on if he was more angered by being cut off in the middle of his complaints or by the baffling request from the Coroner.

> "I beg your pardon, Master Coroner? Do you find me *a div*? Or *a gommy*? What in the bloody hell do you want to do with that body that body that you need my help?"

The Coroner sighed heavily, growing irritated by the local constabulary. With each passing second, the Sheriff remained in the room.

> "I am not fluent in Brinoan by any means, Sheriff. But I am positive that *div* and *gommy* mean the same thing. Now, I need your assistance in lifting her up to this table so that I may carry out the resurrection. So, would you kindly help lift her up here or would you like to report back to your alderman on why his Sheriff is being hauled back to Calitoria in chains. On seven counts of obstruction?"

The Sheriff ruminated on the Coroner's words with heavy mumbling and groans in Brinoan before slamming his lit torch into the empty sconce on the wall and shutting the door behind him.

The two men lifted the young woman's corpse onto the warped and aged wooden table in the tiny hovel. The Coroner then walked to the door, picked up two medium-sized leather bags from the ground, and shook the heavy snow from the top before returning to the table. After requesting more torchlight from the bewildered Sheriff, the Coroner opened his bags and started his ritualistic removal of their contents.

Various scalpels, forceps, lancets, and other medical instruments were laid out neatly across the table next to the blue-hued corpse, as were several opened glass jars filled with a colorless fluid. As the Sheriff returned with more lit torches, the Coroner christened his resurrection by taking shears and cutting the deceased dress and petticoat off to reveal her contusions and lacerations under the concentrated light.

The Sheriff grew angered again, demanding answers on the necessity of the act.

"I have limited time, Sheriff McTavlash, to perform this resurrection. The blood in her veins has already coagulated and rigor mortis has set in. Now, if you would please fetch me the village magistrate so that they may record my findings I would be most grateful."

Upon returning, the door opened, and two people entered the now overtly lit hovel.

The Sheriff entered first, followed by a woman in the uniform of a magistrate with black and white hair. The Coroner looked up from the body and gazed at the Magistrate through the ruby-red lenses of his oculars. The sound of raspy and labored breathing could be heard from within the long beak of his mask as the Coroner thought to himself in silence.

Tall in stature. Dark complexion. One eye was blue, and the other bright amber. Fine, straight hair as black as coal with strands of gossamer white. This Magistrate couldn't be any more Brinoan. A woman of this pure of stock, well, I hope she speaks the common tongue.

The polychromatic eyes of the Magistrate moved from the Coroner immediately to the deceased young woman lying on the table. Tears began to well up in her tear ducts as she eyed the corpse before her. The Sheriff and the Magistrate exchanged a few words in Brinoan before they said their formal goodbyes. With the departure of the Sheriff, the Magistrate removed a small portable writing desk from the satchel, which hung from a thick leather belt across her midsection. Grabbing a quill from within, the Magistrate pulled a bottle of ink from another pocket and held it above the flickering flames of the nearby torch.

"I shall be ready in a moment, Master Coroner." The Magistrate fixed her eyes on the ink bottle as she spoke common tongue forcefully through her thick Brinoan accent.

> "I apologize for my ink being frozen, but it will be ready in a moment. Would you like this unabridged or in shorthand notation?"

The Coroner scoffed at her question and chose to answer it with a question of his own. He believed in the comforts of formality and decided to learn the young woman's name before they began their duty together.

> "What is your name, Magistrate?"

Pulling the bottle from the flames, the Magistrate looked at the Coroner with wide eyes and was momentarily silent before providing an answer.

"Magistrate Tamritha MacHauser, Master Corner." The Magistrate bowed her head as she announced herself officially to the masked man in black.

The sound of heavy breathing from within the beaked re-breather reverberated off the stone walls of the hovel as the Magistrate returned to an upright posture. The Coroner only replied with a slight nod before returning to his instruments.

The silence brought a slight twitch to the Magistrate's cheek. After another moment of silence, Magistrate Tamritha could no longer stand the lack of respect from the masked man in not granting her the same courtesy.

> "You are Resurrectionist Paolo Reveré, are you not? The infamous Coroner who brought down the Butcher of Heinkult twenty years ago? My da and ma told stories of you when I was a wee lass. I didn't think Flayskins worked in the field as long as you have, if you even are the same man from da's stories."

The Coroner took the long flaying knife from the table and held it lightly between his fingers. Twirling the blade gracefully, the Coroner kept his fixated on the flustered Magistrate.

> "If you are going to annotate in shorthand, Magistrate Tamritha, I would prefer Esthesian shorthand instead of Arclovian."

Tamritha's nares flared as she stared down the Coroner with fiery eyes. The Coroner lowered his head and placed one hand on the abdomen while his other hand steadied the scalpel blade. Right before the tip of the cold steel instrument touched skin, he pulled up on the handle and returned to a standing posture.

> "Magistrate Tamritha, have you ever seen the viscera of a fellow person? Are you familiar with the sight and scent of blood?"

The Magistrate's face changed from a healthy color to an intense shade of pale as the blood drained from underneath. Slowly she shook her head, signaling to the resurrectionist that she had never been exposed to such sights.

"Splendid," the Coroner responded while returning to his focus, "If you are to evacuate the contents of your belly, please do so outside. I can't stand the sound of retching. It ruins my line of thought."

The sharp edge of the scalpel pierced the skin with ease, cutting a path from the sternum to the pubic bone as the Coroner moved his hand with swift precision. Setting aside the scalpel, he placed both hands inside the abdomen and pulled back the window. The sound of wet sheering and oozing tearing filled the small hovel like a danse macabre orchestration. Thick red blood congealed around the edges of the incision before pouring over and splattering onto the wooden table upon which the body lay. Grabbing a pair of forceps from the table, the Coroner began the first notations of his resurrection.

"There is one large laceration to the victim's right flank, approximately two fingers in length and one digit in width. The laceration was made with an upward thrust as to place the tip of the blade into the victim's rib cage and puncture the heart. Initial speculation was that this wound was the mortal blow to the victim and so a mid-planar incision was made to the victim's abdomen to assess the flank, which has been found. Please note, Magistrate, that upon inspection of the internal flank tissue that the blade used was non-serrated."

Magistrate Tamritha wrote furiously with hopes of keeping pace with the fast-talking and fast-cutting, Coroner. As the resurrectionist confirmed his suspicions, he set aside the lister blade and reached for the adjacent heavy bone saw. Placing the saw on the distal edge of the sternum, the Coroner quickly began to see the breastbone in half to inspect the heart.

As the thick flat bone cracked and splintered from the serrated blade of the saw, Magistrate Tamritha started to feel weak in her knees and dizzy. Shaking her head with a solid determination, Tamritha gripped her quill tighter and continued in her annotation of the resurrection. Upon sawing the rib cage in half, the Coroner set the saw aside before grabbing the ribs with each hand. After a sudden, violent pull, several ribs broke in half with a loud snap.

As the broken ribs fell outward, a set of lightly blackened lungs lay bare to the warm air of the hovel. A still, lifeless heart sat snug between the two pink organs, although four times the size Magistrate Tamritha would think a heart would be.

"That heart is large, is it not? I mean, even for a Brinoan."

The Coroner scoffed again, impressed by the Magistrate's inquisitive mind and lack of vomiting at this point in the resurrection.

The Coroner reached over to the table and grabbed a long thin steel bistoury from the side of the table. Taking the sharp end of the instrument, he drove the device through the tissue, which forced what seemed like a bottle of blood from within.

"You have sharp eyes for someone ignorant of gross anatomy. What you are seeing is not the heart, but a sack of thick tissue that lines the organ. We call it the pericardium. It swells like this if the heart is damaged from within, filling the space with fresh pumped blood. The victim was stabbed in the heart by a long blade. It pierced the heart with precision, poking a hole and then releasing the blood into the chest and abdominal cavities. This was a clean puncture, made by a still hand. A hand of a killer that has done the act a thousand times by the judge of this yawing."

Feeling the sinew between his gloved fingers, the Coroner froze and fell silent. Tabitha stood like a statue. Her mind filled with angst in anticipation of what the Coroner would say next. Placing the bistoury down softly, the Coroner once again began softly muttering to himself.

A hand that has done this a thousand times before. She bled out like an animal at the slaughterhouse. The Coroner responded to the revelation with a muffled exclamation.

"This wasn't a cold murder," he said softly. "This was a *mercy killing*."

As he continued murmuring to himself, the Coroner finished his resurrection by cutting out selective organs from the deceased. First, he removed the victim's gall bladder, then bone marrow was extracted from the lumbar vertebrae. Finally, the Coroner used a small mallet and a chisel to excise a piece of the brain stem before cutting out one of the victim's eyes. Each organ removed was promptly dropped into one of the four opened jars he had laid out before the resurrection. Upon finishing, the Coroner laid the instruments down and sealed the jars. As he finished, he broke the long silence between the Magistrate and himself with a string of questions.

> "Tell me, Magistrate. Did you know this woman? This Abigail Lengelhaus?"

"Yes, everyone knew Abby. She was our village blacksmith."

The Coroner nodded in confirmation, "did Ms. Lengelhaus have any enemies here in the village? Or from any nearby villages?"

The Magistrate took a moment to search her mind before answering.

> "No, Master Coroner. Abby was a great smith and kind person. She had no enemies but did have a line of suitors wanting her hand in marriage. Even though Abby was faithful to Reba and had no taste for men, her business made her too much gold for most of the men in the area to go without wanting a hand in it. Fights broke out over this at the tavern every weekend since the summer of her flowering."

The Coroner lifted his head up as Tamritha spoke, flashing his blood-red oculars from under the long stiff brim of his capotain hat. Intrigued by this newfound

34

information, the Coroner made the magistrate repeat what she had informed him.

"Are you saying Ms. Lengelhaus was tribas?"

"Of course, she was tribas, everyone here knew she was. Do you not have tribas in the capital, master coroner?"

The Coroner scoffed angrily and barked back at the Magistrate, "Of course we have tribas in the capital, don't be an imbecile. My shock isn't directed at Ms. Lengelhaus's choice in bed partner. I am more so flustered in the fact that I wasn't informed of this detail during my initial inquest with the local gentry."

Thrusting his fist into the table, the Coroner then fell silent again as he returned to the confines of his mind. After a moment of thinking, the masked man looked at the instruments that lay soiled on the table below him. His eyes caught a glimpse of the wide cleaving blade.

Slowly, the Coroner looked back up to the Magistrate.

"Does your village have a butcher?"

His voice penetrated through his re-breather in a low groveling timbre as he asked his question, which brought a shiver to Tamritha's spine.

Quickly she responded, "Yes, of course we have a butcher. His name is Struben. Struben MacRund. He is also the village hunter and tanner!"

The Coroner wiped his hands on a rag before pulling his heavy wool cloak back over his shoulders. Turning back around, he faced the Magistrate and pulled his leather gloves tight against his hands before cracking his knuckles.

"Go fetch me the Sheriff and have him ready the horses. I am going to go pay a visit to this Struben MacRund."

Cunkalt Glenn Pass

The March of Brinoa
23rd hour of the 75th Day

The wind howled as the horses climbed the steep highland pass, blowing snow and hail in every direction. The elevation gave the windchill the bite it needed to cut straight through the thick wools of the Coroner's cloak and uniform and freeze him to the bone. The eponymous Kreiger steel splints that lined his brigantine vest and shin guards should have brought his remaining core heat low enough to finish the job, but they remained warm as he was told they would in these conditions.

The Kreiglanders were known for their metallurgy. The hearty giant people north of the Birgine Mountains had kept the riddle of their sacred steel secret for over a thousand years. If it wasn't for the neutrality of the craftsman's guild in their lands, allowing them to sell their steel during times of war with the Kingdom of Solarno, Paolo knew he would freeze to death on that highland pass.

Sheriff McTavlash stopped his long-horned and heavy-haired Hylan Coo at the next overpass on the ridge and turned in the saddle to address the frost-covered Coroner.

"Struben's Cabin is up at the peak of this next ridge. We should leave the Hylan mounts here and approach on foot, so we have something to ride back into the village once we finish. No need to tie 'em up, they won't go anywhere."

The Sheriff dismounted the giant bovine beast, as did the Coroner. Lighting a torch, the Sheriff led the way up the narrow, snow-covered pass until a single log cabin appeared. Smoke billowed out from the stone-stacked chimney. Struben MacRund was home.

A series of three loud knocks rang out as the oversized Sheriff banged on the crooked wooden door of Struben's cabin. A high-pitched voice answered the knocking in Brinoan with what Paolo believed to be a request for a moment. The low thudding of heavy leather boots on dry wood flooring echoed from within before the door swung open to reveal a wild-looking man staring at the two visitors through a tangled, unkempt mess of beard and brows.

Struben MacRund stared at the Sheriff with intense polychromatic eyes. The blue and the amber were swirling with a fiery mix of anger and bewilderment.

"McTavlash!" Howled the butcher while keeping his eyes fixed on the Sheriff, unaware of the Coroner standing off in the shadows of his porch. "What the bleeding fuck are you doing here this late?"

While the butcher was focused on the sudden arrival of the Sheriff, the Coroner used the opportunity to eye the suspect and drink in his features.

Although his beard was coarse and covered his entire face, Paolo could see faint signs of bruising and swelling on Struben's lips and cheeks. A swollen and blackened left eye was also visible under his thick eyebrows. These were not damning on their own, as Brinoans were known for drunken brawls. But it wasn't looking suitable for Struben the Butcher. The two men carried on in their native tongue as the Coroner waited patiently for his introduction to the unexpecting man.

"Calm down, Struben. This isn't a social visit. Would you mind letting me and my companion in here and out of the cold."

As the Sheriff finished talking, he moved to his left and turned his shoulder to point his attention of Struben to the resurrectionist standing in the shadows.

The visage of the man clad in raven's black sent the butcher stammering and staggering backward before tripping over a small wooden stool. The trip sent Struben hurdling to the floor and crashing into a small cupboard, sending pots and cups to the floor with a loud clash. The Coroner slowly walked through the open doorway, his riding spurs ringing and clanging with each step of his heavy leather knee-high boots. Paolo kept the blood-red lenses fixed on the butcher. The light from the small wood fire flickered, danced off the crystal, and reflected off the crazed man's miscolored eyes. With each passing moment that Struben stared into the red lenses, the wider his pupils dilated before no color was visible.

Struben struggled to form words, only stammering loudly with acute wheezing exhales through pursed lips. A trembling pointer finger lay at the end of Struben's shaking hand. Breaking eye contact with the coroner, Struben shifted his feral gaze to the Sheriff of Glengloam.

"You bring this demon into my home,
McTavlash! You wish to curse my humble
home with this monstrosity!"

The outburst shocked Paolo, as Struben had chosen to
yell it in the common tongue instead of his native
Brinoan.

The Coroner looked around the small cabin for
anything that would rule out or rule in, Struben's
involvement. The house was fundamental in its layout
and furnishings. If Paolo had found himself inside the
cabin without any context, he would have no way of
knowing who the occupant was by trade, as there were
no signs of the man's business in the home. Paolo could
not see a single sign of a butcher's workshop save for
the simple oakwood longbow and quiver of iron-tipped
arrows hanging by the fireplace.

"I hear that you are the village butcher, Mr.
MacRund. Is this true?"

Paolo finally broke the silence with a simple question,
standing firmly between the fallen man and the Sheriff
blocking the doorway. Struben's eyes darted around the
cabin wildly, which Paolo noticed at once. Hoping that
his eyes would land on a clue spot, the butcher finally
stopped eyeing the room and fixed his gaze on the
Coroner.

"Aye, that is true. What of it, Flayskin?"

Paolo brought his left leg around and slowly moved
around the cabin.

40

Placing his arms behind his back, the Coroner surveyed the back room and bedroom area in silence before returning to the two men near the front door.

"Do you work from this cabin, Mr. MacRund?"

The Coroner's voice was low but echoed loudly with resonation through the rebreather's inner chamber. Each uttering sent quivering whimpers from the battered beard of the downed man.

"I do, my butcher shop is around back. I have it locked up due to the snowstorm."

The Coroner stopped once again and turned to face Struben, his riding spurs clanging against the rigid heel of his boots.

"I would appreciate it if you would allow me to inspect your workstation, Mr. MacRund."

The Sheriff left the doorway and approached the still-floored Struben.

Bending over, the Sheriff grabbed the butcher by the lapels of his worn wool coat and picked him up to his feet. The three men made their way around the back of the snow-covered cabin under the light of Sheriff McTavlash's torch. The blizzard had died enough during their time indoors that Paolo's oculars could absorb light properly.

With the return of his night vision, Paolo felt more comfortable than before. A quick turn of a skeleton key forced the heavy iron lock to give way from the iron loops fixed on the heavy barn doors. Struben unwound the thick iron chains that held the double doors in place and tossed it off to the side before opening them up inwards into the slaughterhouse. Upon entering the butchery, the stale, ripened air collided with Paolo's rebreather.

The packed incense from within the beak's inner chamber rapidly began to ignite and smoke. Filling the Coroner's nostrils with the sweet aroma of smoked chocolate and crushed vanilla. His chosen scent. Only one thing triggers the incense from within a coroner's rebreather. The lingering smell of death. Paolo stayed his hands, unsure if his mask was picking up the scent of slaughtered bovine, swine, and fowl. Or if something more sinister had occurred within the confines of the blood-seeped shack.

There was only one way Paolo would determine if the death scent was from a man or a beast. Reaching toward his pouch-lined brigantine, Paolo popped the latch on a round leather case and flipped back the hard lid. A palm-sized brass flask returned with his hand, with intricate embroidery and scrollwork on the metal. Removing the cover, Paolo poured the flask's contents into the palm of his gloved right hand.

"What is that Master Coroner?" The Sheriff rumbled while bringing the torch light closer to Paolo.

Turning to spot the torch, Paolo brought his exposed hand to his chest and took a sidestep away from the Sheriff.

"Don't take another step toward me, Sheriff McTavlash! This is a chymiac powder, and it is highly flammable and combustible."

As the Coroner barked at the Sheriff, McTavlash wheeled backward like a reigned horse. Spooked by the words of the Coroner, he immediately started apologizing and quickly backed away. Once at a safe distance, Paolo brought his hand back out from under his cloak and slowly opened his fingers to reveal the glistening white powder from underneath. As the torchlight flickered, the powder radiated under the warm rays of the flame.

"This is a combination of the chymiac salts, saltpetyr and salerite. Coroner's call it by a different name, Spirit Grains."

The Sheriff stared at the radiating powder in wonder, his mouth gaping as his eyes dilated at the sight of the magical appearing powder.

"What is it used for?"

Paolo took the powder and began to sprinkle it around the room. Over tables, instruments, and troughs.

"It will bind to the blood of man and emit a glowing light that is only visible under the vermilion crystal lenses of my oculars. Indicating that Mr. MacRund is indeed our killer."

The butcher grew angered by the Coroner's accusations, "What? What are you saying? You think I killed someone?"

Paolo ignored the man's question and continued applying the spirit grains to the slaughterhouse floor.

Finishing the last of the spirit grains, Paolo turned back and closed his eyes. After taking a few tiny breaths, Paolo opened his eyes and panned the room slowly. After a few moments of scanning, Paolo finally spotted the faint glowing white rays from under the central table in the middle of the room. Approaching the table, the Coroner knelt on the ground and closely inspected the faint blood spots.

Paolo reached his hip and pulled a collapsed steel device from a leather holster strapped to his thigh. Taking the two pieces in each hand, the Coroner pulled them apart until a soft click sounded from the center of the steel cane. Using the tip, the Coroner shifted the dirt around the most prominent glowing white spot he could find. Pooled around the bottom of a wooden bucket. Digging around, something surfaces from under the earth that stops the Coroner in his search. Reaching down, Paolo grabs the single thing that seals the fate of the butcher of Glengloam.

> "Were you one of the many suitors madly obsessed with Ms. Abigail Lengelhaus. Were you not, Mr. MacRund?"

As the Coroner waited for a reply, beads of sweat began to pool on the brow of the panting Struben MacRund. His heartbeat raced so quickly that Paolo could hear the erratic beat from where he crouched, not a few paces from the butcher.

The lack of an answer was starting to annoy the Coroner, who waited patiently for Struben to confess. A confession would be easier than what awaited him back in the Praetorium. The screams from the dungeons still gave him restless nights from when the time he spent as a novitiate in his youth. Haunted him so

44

profoundly that he never once in his time in the field wrapped irons on a suspect before hearing a confession.

> "I don't know what you are talking about, Flayskin! Finish taking your look around and get sarding lost. The both of you!"

Struben raised his cracking voice, strained to give a sense of intimidation through a wave of overwhelming anxiety and primal fear.

The Coroner rose from his crouched position and slowly turned around to face Struben and Sheriff McTavlash. Fixated between his pinched fingertips, the Coroner held a single strand of long hair aloft. The light of the Sheriff's torch flickered just enough to reveal the color of the hair to be auburn. The Coroner kept his gaze fixed on the now shivering Struben, noticing the copious sweat pouring from the man's temples and dripping onto his exposed shoulders.

> "Care to explain to me, how I found a strand of her hair in a hastily cleaned pile of the victim's blood?"

The low croak of a descending raven from the night sky echoed out over the snow-covered cabin as Struben blinked uncontrollably in disbelief at the single strand of hair in the Coroner's hand. Allowing the frazzled butcher a moment for his stressed mind to catch up, Paolo removed a small glass vial from his vest. Using a pair of steel forceps, he placed the hair within for chymiac phlogistic examination later.

The sound of flapping wings and the sudden thud from a landing bird on the shack's roof snapped Struben out of his addled stupor. Like a cornered animal, Struben raced toward the far-right wall. In an act spurred on by fear and lunacy, the desperate Struben chose to rush toward the various cleavers and blades hanging from the wall in a poor attempt to arm himself. As his hand grasped the frigid wood and iron handle of a large butcher's cleaver, Struben turned his head to see a sailing glass vial hurdling toward his chest.

As the glass shattered against his sternum, a whirl of purple vapor filled the air surrounding him. The bitter fumes were heavy and acted quickly on his senses, bringing his nares and mouth to a biting, numbing sensation. His eyes grew restless as the world around him began to grow hazy. Sound slowly faded away for Struben as the room started to spin before finally going into sudden darkness.

The sound of jingling riding spurs on the soft dirt floor was the last thing Struben MacRund remembered before his entire world dissipated into nothingness.

Village of Glengloam

The passing of the blizzard from the night before brought a bright morning. The sun breached the high peaks of the eastern ridge and bounced off the frozen surfaces of the piled snow mounds that half-buried the small, isolated mountain village. Though there were no fields to till or livestock to tend to save for the small lingering few kept in small hovel-side barns, the entirety of Glengloam Village was awake and gathered around the Alderman's cabin.

Murders in small communities were always the worst inquest to take, Paolo thought to himself as he awaited the Alderman's council with the local gentry. It was customary to present the forensic findings of the inquest to the Alderman so that the locals could discuss how to handle their own local justiciary formalities before signing off the killer's life to the crown.

There was the matter of finances owed to the family, electing a new community member to take the position of the newly convicted, and of course, the issue regarding property and any outstanding debts needing to be collected. Paolo had seen the same song and dance for the past twenty years as a resurrectionist in the field. The bureaucratic formalities were a necessity, a necessity he understood and respected. He would never stand in the way of these proceedings or interfere, just as he expected the good people of the village not to interfere with his investigation in turn.

The ever-rising roar of the gathered crowd outside the cabin was the reason for the seasoned Coroner's current sense of unease. Gathered crowds always seemed to slow boil the longer the accused remained in the community. Common and decent folk never took too kindly to the mindless massacre of their own lot. Especially in a case such as this, where the woman killed was one so loved by the community.

These angered and emotional few would soon become infectious, their passion spreading from one to the next like wildfire. Paolo braced for the forthcoming and inevitable transition from an upset crowd to a bloodthirsty group. When the mob mentality was in full force, things would get ugly.

Coroners had a reputation throughout the land. A particular ill importance that was equally steeped in peasant superstition. A fulmination of hushed whispers between fear-stricken locals over their darker nature and foul tidings.

It was warranted. Paolo had learned early on in his profession that if you dawn the disguise of the carrion bird, you then spend your days shrouded by the darker recesses of man's anxious and paranoid mind. Raven, Flayskin, body snatcher. These were some of the more common obscenities he had been called to his face and behind his back. The arrival of a coroner to any township or village was enough to turn the entire community into a ghost town.

A flightless raven brings the creeping melancholy.
Blood and bone, and festering malady.
Pray to keep ye' children and keep ye' spouse.
Or find the raven outside ye' house.

Or so the Cudwytchian nursery rhythm goes.

These fears kept the public in line and cooperative when the fear was still fresh. When the killer is still out there, a wolf amongst unaware sheep. This all changes when the wolf finds itself in the snare trap set by the cunning carrion raven. Once the sheep realize that they are now as much a wolf as the beast pinned to the ground, now that's when the masses are swiftly reminded that only one individual is allowed to dispense justice in the wilds of the kingdom.

The Alderman banged his small worn gavel against the block of his desk. Demanding order from the council and the roused villagers from outside the town hall. The crowd was reluctant but calmed enough to hear what the elected leader had to say.

"Now that we have concluded the official justiciaries and common practice following the presentation of evidence from Coroner Paolo Reveré, I now move to agreeance on the release of the accused murderer Struben MacRund over to his custody. Now are there any members who object?"

As the Alderman announced his intentions to release the prisoner, a louder uproar from the crowd erupted from the village square outside. Torches, wood axes, pickaxes, and fists jutted forth from the rising mob. All shouting in unison in Brinoan, one singular phrase.

"CEARTA BERGMANN!"
"CEARTA BERGMANN!"

The chanted phrase was one that Paolo had heard before, neigh on twenty years ago. He was not fluent in Brinoan, but he knew the meaning of that phrase.

Miner's Justice

These people not only wanted him to pay for his crimes here in town but also demanded ancient rites from a more barbaric time. The splitting of the long bones with mining picks and sledgehammers while the person is still alive is not to kill a man. Cruel to the core but set the tone for how the ancestors of the Brinoans handled their justice in darker days.

As the Alderman rose from his seat to try and quelch the rising fire from within his community, the sound of breaking chains echoed out from the other side of the village square and pierced Paolo's eardrums like an arrow.

Swinging his head around, Paolo spotted the source of the sound. A group of men and women had shattered the chains holding the mining equipment storage shed shut and had begun to disperse the heavy picks and heavy hammers amongst the crowd. The slow boil had finally reached an apex, and the people were now in a frenzy. The captain of the guard looked to her guardswomen of the Brinoan home militia and drew her basket saber from the scabbard, shouting orders to defend the cabin front.

It only took the passing of a moment for the hardline to be formed in the snow. The invisible line separating guardswomen and angered mob. Raised crossbows were pointed at the first line of axe and hammer-wielding villagers, with a row of shield bearers in front and a pike wall to the rear. For a platoon of twelve highly trained women, they looked menacing in their matching red coats, feathered tricorn hats, wool mouth coverings, and black iron armor. But Paolo knew as well as the captain of the guard that twelve Brinoan guardswomen stood no chance against fifty bloodthirsty miners. The waiting game thus commenced. Was sacrificing a dozen or more people to exact revenge on one butcher worth it?

Paolo used the standstill in the square to his advantage and approached the bench of the Alderman and his small council of elders. Keeping his voice low, calm, and collected, the Coroner stated his case and made his illusionary request to the committee.

"Alderman and council of elders. I beseech you to release this prisoner under my custody at once. The longer Struben MacRund stays in this town, the more dangerous the environment grows for your citizens."

Paolo reached over the table, snatched the unfolded parchment bearing the seal of his order, and slammed the paper down in front of the Alderman with a loud bang from the palm of his hand.

"Sign the inquest form, Alderman. Now."

Looking to his peers, the Alderman received only nods of agreement from his council. Taking the quill from the inkpot before him with a quivering hand, the Alderman signed over the prisoner to the Coroner. He then handed the folded parchment back to Paolo while gazing outside at the rising tensions in the street.

The crowd slowly started testing the guardswomen with slow and sudden advances toward the shield wall. The tension building in the taut bowstrings of the crossbows echoed in response to their testing of the guardswomen's fortitude. The Alderman's cabin door swung open from the wingless raven's forceful heel kick. The mob members in the front looked up to spot the Coroner clearing the doorframe with the prisoner Struben in chains. As the Coroner came into view of the crowd, the entirety of the village went as silent as the grave.

Paolo's riding spurs were the only thing to reverberate off the little exposed walls of the cabins and hovels surrounding the village square as he descended the stone steps before the captain of the guard ordered her guardswomen to stand down and make a hole for the Coroner. The guardswomen jumped to a new formation, quickly clearing a space for the Coroner to walk with his prisoner.

Paolo remained still and eyed the crowd for a moment. Taking a slow inspiration, he hoped for the mob to stay calm until he locked the prisoner in the rear of his wagon. All eyes of the village were fixed on him as he took his first step from the steps and onto the snow-covered cobble road of the town square. Paolo slowly walked forward. The prisoner Struben held firmly by his side.

As he advanced forward, the crowd moved right and left of him to create a path but remained at reach length, which gave the Coroner an uneasy feeling. Step by step, the Coroner silently made his way to the rear of his black wagon of wood and iron. The back of the cart was nothing more than a small prison cage for transportation. Paolo reached the door and turned toward the crowd before reaching for his small key ring

52

hanging from his belt. As his fingers hooked through
the iron loop, a large bald man pushed through the
crowd and began to advance toward the Coroner, a
large rock-splitting hammer in his right hand.

> "Why should we let this little raven from the
> big city dictate how we dispense our justice. I
> say we do away this outsider and make Struben
> pay for what he has done the way our ancestors
> did before us!"

The crowd roared in agreeance with the man's words.
Words that Paolo did not understand nor care to find
out.

The chants returned as the man raised his arms,
holding the large rock splitter high toward the sun. The
mob continued to cheer and chant as the man slowly
turned back toward the Coroner, but their cheers and
jeering were short-lived. A spray of bone shards, brain,
and blood washed over the gathered mob, followed by
the concussive blast and black smoke from the hands of
the Coroner. The giant Brinoan rabble rouser fell to his
knees in the blink of an eye. His head was blown clean
from his body. An eyeball bounced off the shoulder of
a middle-aged woman in the crowd before she caught
the organic debris in the palm of her hand. Her shrieks
filled the murmuring square.

As the man demanded blood from his brothers
and sisters in arms, he failed to notice that Paolo had
drawn a weapon from the harness strapped to his back,
concealed by his long wool cloak. The Coroner's
blunderbuss. The firearm was unique only to the Royal
Order of Coroners, as the archivist who tinkered and
toiled in the Fabrinarum of the Praetorium were the
only individuals in all four kingdoms who knew how to

craft black powder. It was the ultimate tool in a field operative's arsenal. Able to strike sheer panic-inducing fear in both peasants and warriors alike. The 50-caliber slug made short work of the man's head, sending the crowd and the guardswomen reeling backward with a ripple of bewilderment and fear.

Paolo lowered the blunderbuss before pressing a long thin lever on the side with his thumb. The firearm receiver broke open, sending a spent soft brass casing sailing into the cold mountain air. Reaching his brigantine, Paolo drew a fresh slug shot and slid it into the receiver before closing the block with a quick upward thrust and loud clanking click.

"NOT ANOTHER MOVE!" Roared the Coroner raising his firearm into the air and pointing it forward,

    "ONE MORE PERSON APPROACHES ME, OR THE PRISONER, AND THEY WILL BE PUBLICALLY EXECUTED FOR HIGH TREASON AGAINST THE CROWN! GET BACK!"

Paolo took a step forward as he shouted at the crowd forcing the entirety of the mob to quickly move to the far side of the town square. He hated raising his voice. Paolo despised executing peasants. Especially when they had every right to demand blood for blood.

Although he sympathized, he also knew the reality of a mob that ran unchecked. The Coroner was there in the city of De'Lorme fifteen years prior when an angered crowd revolted against a fellow resurrectionist.

He had watched a dear friend from the academy get torn into pieces, drawn, and quartered. Not by horses but by the hands of bloodthirsty men. Paolo knew he had survived 18 years in the field by removing his sympathy and empathy and treating most situations like a fight for survival.

The crowd responded with motion, but it wasn't until after he settled his nerves that the realization of the language barrier set in. Paolo looked up toward the steps to the captain of the guard, who stood as frozen and afraid as the rest of the villagers below.

"Captain," Paolo slightly turned his shoulders toward her direction, which brought a slight spastic jerk from the woman's musculature as she shook her head in response. "You speak the common tongue?"

The captain of the guard shook her head in agreeance once more, too afraid to utter a word unless asked.

"Relay what I said to these villagers to them in your own native tongue. Tell them I am going to lock the prisoner up in my cart and be on my way. And that the crown will send financial compensation to the family for the death of the man I shot. I'll waive his treason considering the collective emotional state of the village. If everyone else remain calm and I go unmolested in my duty."

The captain agreed and belayed his message to the crowd. Only silence answered in response. Paolo turned back toward his cart and approached the prisoner Struben who lay on the ground in a puddle of his urine. After unlocking the cage and opening the door, Paolo was loading the prisoner into the cell when he was interrupted by the shouting cries of a young woman in tears. Paolo swiftly turned, his blunderbuss held firm and outright at the sounds of the shrieks and approaching boot steps, only to find the end of his barrel pointed in the face of a young woman clad in the garb of a tavern maid emerged.

Her blue and amber eyes swelled with tears as she reached out toward the Coroner and his prisoner. As she spotted the octagonal steel barrel held toward her, she stopped in her tracks and fell to her knees, continuing to weep uncontrollably. The Coroner lowered his firearm and then promptly returned the weapon to the harness on his back before pulling his cloak back over his shoulder. The young woman continued to sob and shout incoherent rantings through a swollen windpipe.

"Master Coroner…plea…please…I beg of you."

Paolo knelt before the young woman and grabbed her by the shoulders, hoping to bring her back to her feet. But the young woman refused.

"No…you…you don't understand… it's not fair! This animal! What he did to my beloved Abby! My wife!... he must pay for what he has done… he must… I DEMAND JUSTICE!"

Paolo closed his eyes from behind the one-way lenses of his oculars and sighed heavily at the pleas of the young woman before him. A sharp pang struck his hardened heart like a tiny bolt of electricity as he gave the girl a moment to speak her mind and confess her

56

soul. It was the most challenging part of the job. The aspect his doctori never covered adequately during his time in the academy. Most think that taking a life is hard. Any soldier who met the enemy in open battle can tell you otherwise. The clashing of men on foot and horse, the fight to survive. Kill or be killed. Taking a life isn't difficult. Not in this savage world. The harsh reality comes from the intimacy of facing the evils that senseless death brings in its wake. The ripples in the still pond were twice disturbed.

The Coroner told the mothers that they had lost their daughters and informed wives that they had lost their husbands and even children and that their parents would never be coming home. He had been a shoulder to cry on, a punching bag to let out aggression, and had doors slammed in his face. Paolo had never truly learned how to become numb to the pain of intimacy.

True isolation from mankind is what leads men to become monsters, a lesson he remembered hearing as a novitiate upon entering the Coroner's academy at twelve years old. Soon after, both of his parents were murdered before his eyes.

Paolo gave the young woman a moment but then chose to leave her to her pain. If she wasn't going to stand before him and hear reason, he would make better use of his time by getting on the road and as far away from this town as possible. Turning his back from the young woman, a familiar voice shouted out from the Alderman's cabin.

"Coroner Paolo Reveré!" The voice of Magistrate Tamritha echoed out over the silent crowd, drowning out the sobs of the collapsed woman in blue.

"You owe her an explanation! You owe her that
much. You can't just ride from town and expect
this to all go away."

Magistrate Tamritha ran down the steps and quickly
moved to the sobbing woman's side.

Taking a seat beside her on the cold cobble
street, Tamritha placed her hands into those of the
woman in tears. Kissing her forehead and whispering
words of comfort in their native Brinoan. The
Magistrate shifted her focus back toward the Coroner
as soon as she calmed the widow Lengelhaus. Paolo
stood frozen in place, his back toward the two women
on the ground, remaining silent.

"Will you say nothing? Will you offer her no
other comfort in her time of mourning? My Da'
was right, you are just a Flayskin. Human
bodies are nothing more than carcasses to you.
No different from this butcher here. Damn you
and may the umbress take you!"

Magistrate Tamritha Rose from the ground and started
striking the back of Paolo's shoulder, hoping to get his
attention. The Coroner allowed two hard strikes before
whirling back around and snatching the wrist of the
Magistrate. Paolo then pulled the Magistrate close to
him, speaking into her ear so that his words only fell on
her ears and her ears alone.

"You think this comes easy to me? The death,
the pain, the tragedy of it all? You think I enjoy
watching innocent, good people suffer? You
may be the most academically educated
member from this frozen shithole of a

58

community, but you truly are the imbecile I believed you to be when we first met. Still your tongue and cease this foolish pageantry at once, or else more people will be hurt this dawn."

Paolo eased up on his grip of the Magistrate's arm and pushed her back from his embrace.

"This man will face justice, Magistrate. I justice so terrible that you could not even begin to conceive a thought close enough to the truth of what horrors he will endure. What you don't understand, and what you can never understand, is that the burden of death for both the victim and the killer falls on one person and one person alone. Me. I will condemn this man to the great corpse road, and the weight of his death will be stacked heavily upon my scale. A measure the goddess will surely punish me for when I have finally seen the last of my days. You want justice, justice you shall have and justice you did receive! Go now and comfort your friend. Go return to your happy quiet lives, in your quaint mountain village."

The Magistrate began to shed a single tear before more formed and followed. Paolo lowered his head to the ground so that his wide-brimmed hat covered his face as he said his final remarks.

"Go be young and careless, live and love freely. Be safe and happy. The way you deserve and are promised, for it is bittersweet and short lived. Let this taste of evil be the last you hopefully taste. For the sun will rise tomorrow and you move onward with your life. I have a different path, a path of misery and death. Just focus on supporting your loved ones. And leave the hunting of monsters to me."

With his final words, Paolo locked the prisoner cage and rounded the wagon's side toward the driver's bench. As he grabbed the reigns and gave them a light tug and a click of his tongue. His dray horse nickered and started to drag the heavy snow-covered cart slowly through the thick snow before breaking through and advancing down the road.

The winds began to pick up once more as a blizzard started to pick up from the southern slopes of the Birgine mountains as Paolo rode out of sight of the small mountain village.

And was gone.

A Report of Inquest

To All and Sunder,

I hereby find Struben MacRund guilty of the following verdicts,

One count of
Felonious Manslaughter
and
One count of *Necrophilia*

Currently enroute to the capital city of Calitoria, for trial and subsequent execution.

Penalty recommended is *castration*, followed by *death by crucifixion*.

Signed:

Res. Paolo Montalba Reveré, Я.Ѳ.Ҁ.

The Arbiter's District

City of Calitoria
Kingdom of Solarno
21st hour of the 81st Day
In the Season of Empyripas
Anor 905 P.A.

The tolling of the Astrolaborarry clock tower reverberated off the gilded rooftops and moonlit white marble buildings that towered over the wide empty cobblestone street as a single horse-drawn cart rattled its way up the winding city road. It had been a long journey for the man seated on the driver's bench and the whinnying black dray horse that pulled the large black iron and wood box cart up the road. Sitting in the rear of the cart, closed within jet black iron bars, sat a third-party member of the long voyage.

This person, a man both shackled and writhing in his cramped prison, had grown louder and more obnoxious in his protests for the past three days of travel. Howling with rage, the shackled man rambled on and on about wrongful accusations, misplaced evidence, and blatant village conspiracies that had made him out to be the innkeeper's killer. He had no part in it, and if the nice man in the black raven uniform let him out, he would do his best to help track the natural killer down. First, there was denial, then guilt in his actions, followed by the anger-filled outburst, then finally pleas of bargaining and cries of desperation.

It had been like this for the entirety of the voyage. At any point, the white raven-masked man in black wool and leathers could have stopped the vehicle along the road to gag the pleading soul imprisoned in his gaol cart but instead, he had learned to drown out the noise by taking his mind off the task at hand. There was no doubt that the iron-bound individual had killed the innkeeper. He had the evidence and witness accounts to prove it. The man was doomed to a cruel fate of disembowelment and crucifixion.

The driver felt it was more of an act of mercy to let the poor wretch spend his final moments with the freedom to scream at the night air.
Rather than suckle on a piece of dirty, spittle-drenched cloth. Onward, the cart rolled down the cobblestone path. The sound of grinding from the metal rims and the turning of creaking spokes reverberated off the various darkened frosted windows that lined the street.

It was nearly the hour of evenfall in Calitoria, and the entirety of the city was virtually silent. Only the far-off sound of various howls and jeers could be heard from ten penny lane to the south. Not a single soul was out in the Arbiter District, except for the night watchwomen, whose torchlights could be seen in various alleys and atop the high walls and stairwells lining the upper districts of the beautiful capital city.

It had rained the night before. The man driving the cart was sure of it. From spraying foamy water from the smaller puddles to the splashing of filthy, muddy water from the larger pools as the cartwheels rolled through them, he deduced it must have been quite the deluge. The wind had also picked up after they entered the city, and soon there was a noticeable chill. The man kept one hand on the reins while using a now freed hand to pull his heavy, black-wool cloak around his shoulders to cover his chest and legs.

What I wouldn't do for a smoke from my pipe, thought the man as he gave the reins a quick whip forward with both hands. The season's change was near, and the night temperature had already steadily dropped.

Great billows of thick white steam could be seen from the various sewer grates and covers that lined the street sides and the middle. As the cart approached a cross street, the man pulled the reins to the right and steered the horse around the corner. A giant rat crawled up from a nearby sewer grate and scuttled quickly across the road before darting into another sewer grate on the opposite side.

The rat catchers and mudlarks should be lining their pockets this night, thought the man as he watched the giant rodent scamper across the path as his cart passed. A light appeared up the road, and a lantern wielding night watchwoman came from a billowing column of steam. She moved to the right side of the street and stopped to hail the man in the cart as he approached. As he pulled up on the reins, the coach swiftly halted.

The night watchwoman was clad in the typical vestments of a Solarnian Custodi. The only difference is the color of her justacorps coat. The color of a custodi's uniform was that of the ruling nobleman of the land. In this case, the colors were that of the high king of Solarno, a vibrant royal blue with elaborate gold buttons, cuffs, and lapels. Underneath her coat was a brightly polished iron breastplate, ornately adorned with the coat of arms of the House of Romero. A thick leather guige was strapped around her chest and back that bore a heavy wooden and iron crossbow underneath a medium-sized heater shield.

A simple steel broadsword hung from a scabbard buckled to her belt, strapped around her waistline, keeping the heavy wool justacorps tightly tailored to her armored figure. Boots of finely crafted Turnian leather hid underneath tightly strapped shin guards, same for her leather gloves, which had been covered by polished iron arm guards almost hidden underneath her button-cuffed gold sleeves. Adorning her head was a hooded coif of iron chainmail and a top that was a matching blue and gold-trimmed, felt tricorn hat which bore the badge of her post on the right side. Hoisting the lantern up, the guard eyed the man in the cart before addressing him.

"Good evenfall, Master Coroner,"

She said while giving the masked man a small salute. The man nodded in reply, returning the small courtesy in return.

"Good evenfall to you as well, Custodi,"

His voice was raspy and coarse as he gave his response. The salerite-soaked cloth lining the inside of his mask had almost faded out, and the stifling sweet odor of the chemical had finally taken its course on the man's throat. As he finished his greeting, he reached up and tipped the wide brim of his black felt capotain to the guard. The red lenses of his oculars tended to spook most people, so he did what he could to help avert the wide-eyed gaze of others. His gesture, it seemed, had done the trick. He watched as her boots passed by the wheel axel toward the couch's rear. The guardswoman rounded and held her lantern up to the bars to inspect the now silent prisoner.

> "I see you have a brought carrion for your
> fellow ravens, Master Coroner.
> I'm sure your peers at the Praetorium are
> wheeling overhead in waiting."

She began to chuckle at her own joke while the man gave out a slight sigh to himself. Suddenly the prisoner lunged forward like a caged animal and grasped the bars with both of his shackled hands. Pressing his dirt-covered face to the cold iron bars, he began to shout in his thick Brinoan accent at the now startled guardswoman.

> "Please, Custodi, I am innocent! I never would
> kill anyone, please, you must help me! Help
> save an innocent soul!"

She took a step back from the bars and reached for the hilt of her broadsword. Hearing the commotion, the man in black leaned over the side and addressed the guard in a stern but soothing voice.

> "Custodi, come now. That won't be necessary.
> The fool is doomed for the cross beams, and
> they act out like beasts when the end draws
> near. Go about your business. I have a delivery
> of carrion to make."

"Right," The now disgruntled Custodi responded to the fright by giving the iron bars a quick jab with her iron gauntlet, which sent the prisoner flying back to his cold hard bench seat with a howl.

"That's enough out of you, scum. Save your breath for the chamber."

She pulled the tip of her tricorne hat back down and gave the side of the cart two taps from her fist. The coroner returned to his seat. Picking up the reins, he whistled and whipped them forward, sending his dray along the path. The prisoner lunged for the bars again as the cart rolled down the street, crying out to the Custodi in desperation before snapping back into an outburst of rage as the cart rounded the last turn and disappeared into a column of opaque vapor billowing from up from the street side sewer grate.

As he reached the top of the steep incline of the street, the cart pulled up to a great black iron gate that separated the main road from the courtyard of the building ahead. Pulling up to the front of the entrance, the man looked up and beheld a silhouette of an excellent amber moon that loomed behind the central glass cupola tower of the building. As he gazed upward at the xanthous celestial body shrouded in twilight, a murder of ravens suddenly flew overhead.

Croaking and shrilling at one another, the blackbirds fervently beat their wings against the wind as they made their back to the aviary within the second tower of the building. From behind the man's neck, a jet-black beak poked through from underneath the folding of his cloak, no doubt awoken by the croaking of his brothers and sisters flying overhead. Blinking its sleepy eyes, the raven shook its ruffled feathers and rose to take flight. Before leaving, the blackbird gave her master a friendly peck on the side of the man's mask. He watched as his avian companion began flapping her wings and taking flight and continued to watch in envy as she passed above the ornately decorated wrought iron gate to join the others in flight.

The moon was intoxicating to gaze upon that night. Its fragmented heavenly beams of white and flaxen hues caressed the rooftop and statues as it reached out to the damp cobblestone path and grass of the courtyard grounds. The man eventually dismounted the side of the driver's bench and approached the large gate that had halted his horse. As he passed the side of his no-doubt-tired dray horse, he gave the mare a loving pat on the neck. The mare whinnied and nickered at the touch of his leather-clad hand, turning her head to give the thin man a nudge with her nose.

"Good girl, good girl. We are almost done for the night. I promise, just give me a few moments more."

He spoke to the horse with the same affection a soldier would give a brother in arms. He produced a bright red apple under his cloak and fed it to the mare, who gobbled the fruit up quickly. Leaving the horse and cart, he turned to approach the gate but was halted by a sudden and loud 'pop' from his right knee.

"Bloody perfect,"

He whispered with closed eyes. Shaking out the cobwebs of his battle-worn joint, the man tried to ignore again the toll his profession was taking on his no longer youthful frame.

As he walked, the heels of his boots hit the cobblestone with a heavy clop. He could feel the heavyweight of the blackened steel shin guards hidden by the equally damp black canvas gaiters, both fastened at each knee-high black leather boots. The layering of his uniform was crafted and designed to be both practical and combat effective, but at times like these, they just felt exhausting and cumbersome. He approached the gate in as much haste as he could muster, ignoring his internal pains of hunger and sleep deprivation for only a few more moments.

A tall wrought iron black gate closed the path to the walled-off courtyard. The timeworn iron egress bore a decorative plate on its façade, depicting his order's ancient and respected crest. On either side of the double swing doors were tall grey stone columns crowned with intricately carved stone statues.

The statue on the right column was that of the founding coroner, Beniamo D'Lorm. Syr D'Lorm stood both tall and proud in his raven armor of yore, holding a giant two-handed sword between his legs and cloaked in a feathery cape. At his feet was a lit brazier and below that was an iron plaque engraved with his name and reason of importance in hammered brass lettering. The other column featured a statue in the likeness of a man known as the father of the contemporary coroner field, Girolamo De Silica. Gone is the knightly armor of Syr Beniamo's age. Instead, Girolamo is clad in the more modern uniform of light leather armor under a wax-coated wool cloak. A raven sat perched on the wide brim of the statue's capotain hat. One hand gripped the pommel of a cane, and in the other, he grasped a thick tome, which the man could see another raven perched upon. As he looked upon the towering visage of each notable man, he observed that both statues had started to show their withering to the passing of both time and seasons.

"I suppose not even the two of you could solve the riddle of time. We must all succumb to the same fate, whether by brotherly deceit or the ever-changing leaves. Humbling."

He reached the boiled leather brigantine underneath his cloak with a single gloved hand. The field brigantine of his uniform was specially crafted by the master quartermasters of his order, not only lined with special Krieger steel splints, but also fitted with several rows of various fastened pouches, sleeves, and specialty cases. Each of these adornments was filled with varying tools of his professions. Numerous neatly lined leather sleeves, each filled with small ornately decorated glass vials, hard black leather pouches containing brass coated glass flasks of powders, and square button-closed cases filled with neatly packed metal instruments, the front of the coroner's heavy protective vest. As he passed from pouch to pocket, he could feel the fraying and cracking of leather.

It wasn't just his knees that had started to pay the price. His gear was also beginning to show signs of age. Finally, his fingers found what his mind was searching for. He pushed on a small brass latch of the hard leather case and quickly flipped open the hard leather lid. From inside the case, the coroner drew a palm-sized lantern, and with his other hand, he threw back the left side of his long thick woolen over-cloak, revealing a broad leather holster strapped to his thing and belt.

A metal cane of brass and steel making was within the holster, collapsed at the middle by a brass hinge. The coroner drew the collapsed cane from its holster and flung it open with a quick flick of his wrist until it locked in place. Now the complex instrument was a full-length device of superior craftsmanship and one of the most essential tools of his trade. He unscrewed the round pommel of the cane, and in its place, he screwed the lantern on tightly. He produced a small glass vial with a cork stopper from a separate pouch on his brigantine.

Within the vile was a small white piece of wax paper, wadded up in a ball and twisted close at the top. He popped the cork stopper and retrieved the paper ball from inside. Tearing away the paper, he poured the contents into his opposite hand after placing the cane under his arm. A small damp clay ball, red and white coloring, rolled out into his palm.

He quickly opened the latch door of the palm-sized lantern, turned it over to dump a withered black ball of ash onto the ground from the inner glass housing, and turned back over to place the new one in its place. The man shut the latch, pushed a small plunger on the top to produce pressure, and gave the cane a quick flick downward with his wrist. As the lantern came to the end of its pendulum swing, a faint crackling came from within, followed by a sharp hiss. Soon an amber light as bright as torchlight lit up the shrouded ground around him.

"Ah, that's much better,"

He said to himself as he reached toward his belt to produce a small key ring under the light of his pommel lantern. The keyring possessed three iron skeleton keys. He selected the critical bearing the crest of his order and slid it into the keyhole at the center of the gate crest. Turning the key, the mechanisms within clinked and rattled until there was a final clunking sound.

With the great gate now unlocked, the man opened one side thoroughly, followed by the other, before returning to his cart. He slid the cane into a metal tube by the driver's bench and climbed up and rode his cart before stopping to close the gate behind him. As he pulled his cart around the courtyard to the front of the towering stone building, the Astrolaborarry tower began to chime again, signaling the top of the hour. With each tolling of the great bells, the dong of the bell grew louder and louder over the silent city encased in the twilight.

"How fitting," said the coroner loud enough for his prisoner to hear the words through the thick leather, brass, and porcelain mask covering his face,

"...right on time."

The Praetorium

<u>City of Calitoria</u>
Kingdom of Solarno
22nd hour of the 81st Day
In the Season of Empyripas
Anor 905 P.A.

The coroner unlocked the gate of the gaol cart and swung open the single barred door with a heavy hand. Looking inside, he could see the prisoner sitting slouched over and lifeless on the hard wooden bench seat. He raised the cane and lit the cage's interior, keeping a firm grip on the weapon in case it was a rouse. The lantern's light revealed purpling on the man's neck and foam on the corners of his mouth.

"Shit. You have got to be kidding me,"

the coroner grabbed the man by his shackles and pulled him down from the cart to lay him on the cobblestone street. He placed the tip of his cane on the prisoner's neck and, after a few moments, detected only a weak threading pulse up the semi-hollowed cane shaft. It had become clear to the professional that the prisoner tried to take his own life by choking himself on his restraints in his final moments. A ridiculous act the coroner had seen many times before.

"Oh, no, you don't. I didn't listen to you bitch and moan for three days for nothing. You are facing the queen's justice."

The coroner put his boot on the prisoner's chest and produced from his vest a wax-sealed vial containing a murky and viscous xanthous tincture, followed by a brass hypodermic needle. Filling the syringe with the substance, he bent down, replaced his boot heel with his steel-clad knee, and jammed the hypodermic needle into the left side of the man's neck. The hypodermic needle punctured the prisoner's jugular vein and passed deep until near the heart's left atrium. The coroner then jammed the syringe's plunger and watched the viscous liquid slowly drain into the prisoner's bloodstream until the glass tube was empty. He pulled the needle from the man's neck, stood up to switch his knee back to his boot heel, and began to count. The prisoner's eyelids shot wide open, and he began to writhe on the street as if he had been struck by a lightning bolt.

The coroner removed his boot heel and watched with cold eyes as the man's muscles contracted and contorted with such violence that it was visible from beneath the skin. A loud crack, like the sound of a bullwhip, rang out in the courtyard. It was soon followed by a second crack and a grown man's shrilling ear-piercing scream.

The prisoner had palsy so severe it had broken the bones in both of his arms. He turned over and painted the cobblestones with projectile vomit, continuing to cry and whine between bouts of vomiting. The coroner shook his head, returned the syringe to its proper place within the leather case on his vest, and turned to lock the gate back up.

"What have you done to me?!"

The man had finished writhing and vomiting. Crawling, the prisoner dragged his convulsing frame through dirt

74

and bile toward the boots of the coroner. As he pulled himself across soiled cobblestones, the prisoner shouted vulgarities at the cloaked man in between howls of torturous pain.

> "What have you done? I was dead! I took my own life, but now I am back. It isn't fair! What sort of black sycrassal craft have you done? What foul wytchecraft and sorcery have you done to me? You better fucking answer me, black feather?! Have you damned my very soul?"

The coroner finished locking up the cage of the coach, ignoring the guilty man's obscenities. Putting away the gaol key, the man extinguished the flame of the portable lantern and returned the device to a vest pouch. The prisoner spasms and strained as he lifted his head to see his sad reflection in the bright scarlet crystal of the coroner's ocular lenses.

> "Those eyes, those red eyes of umbryssal evil. It's unnatural. All of it, you and your ilk are all touched by the void. I demand a right to a fair trial in a chamber not run by flesh-devouring creatures born of both men and fowl!"

The prisoner looked up to the moon above and shouted out to the heavens,

> "Goddess above, oh great heavenly mother, save me from these foul and evil conjurers of dark arts!"

Sighing again, the coroner approached the man. A sharp blow from the cane to the back of the prisoner's head sent the shackled man hurdling back toward the cobblestone. Though a thickened stream of blood ran down from the man's head, he had remained conscious.

> "That's enough. If you keep this up, I will tack on disturbance of the peace and sedition to your charges. Am I clear?"

The coroner reached down and grabbed the man by his wrist irons. As he pulled the man up by the iron cuffs, the prisoner's arms bent in unnatural directions, filling the night air with more screams and howls.

"You should have thought of this before trying to take the easy way out,"

Muttered the coroner as he pushed the man forward up a small path towards a black iron door.

> "I just don't understand. I was dead, and now I am alive. How could this be?"

"You weren't dead," The coroner could no longer take any more of the man's intoxicating ignorance.

> "Yes, I was," replied the prisoner, "I felt a warming sensation. I was calm! And finally, at peace!"

"No, you weren't. You imbecile. You only put yourself to sleep by momentarily cutting off your air supply. Once you lost consciousness, you removed the blockage by dropping your arms and started breathing

76

again. The warm, calming sensation you are describing wasn't the afterlife. It was you urinating on yourself."

The man looked down and observed the trail of a damp bright yellow stain down the length of his breeches and hose. He began to lightly sob once again,

> "This is more wytche trickery! You did this to me!"

The two men stopped at a large red door at the end of the path. A metal plaque on the door read, The Tablinum. Arriving at the door, the coroner gave the prisoner a slow glance,

> "Are you implying that I, a court-appointed officer of the Queen's law, pissed your breeches?"

The prisoner only could look at his captor in shame before nodding his head in defiance.

> "That's it. I am adding sedition to your indictment."

The coroner reached out and opened the door, corralling the prisoner into the room ahead. They walked down a short hallway before entering a large, brightly lit chamber. Sconces lined the columns along the stone walls of the chamber. An extended counter of intricately decorated wood was on the far side of the room. The coroner guided the prisoner to the counter. Behind the desk stood a shorter man in similar garb to the arresting coroner but albeit with some variations.

He wore no hat, but his head was covered by a simple wool hood attached to a long black wool gown draped to the floor. As they approached the desk, the robed coroner leaned forward and spoke loudly at the arresting coroner.

"Name, Order, inquest number! Loud, slow, and clearly! If you would, please."

Paolo slid the matte black badge from its brooch housing pinned to his cloak. He held the badge aloft in view of the cantankerous archivist and began his announcement.

"Coroner Paolo Reveré, of the Most Worshipful Branch of Steel. Inquest number one, zero, one, nine, nine, eight, seven, nine, nine, one."

The robed coroner reached up to his mask with a slender, gloved finger, flipped a brass magnifying lens apparatus in front of his red crystal lenses, and then craned his neck down to an open-faced tome that lay on the desk below him. He perused the long list of inquests that filled the pages with his finger until finally arriving at the right one. Slowly the robed coroner reached out with his opposite hand and lightly grabbed a feathered quill pen from a small wooden stand, and with his other hand, he opened a bottle of ink.

Lightly and methodically, the robed coroner dipped the quill in ink, dabbed the sides on the inside of the bottle, and began to write notations. As the archivist pressed his quill to the crisp parchment pages of the tome, the two coroners began their long-winded exchange of judicial information.

"Right, Coroner Paolo of the Order of Steel.
You will be noted as the arresting coroner for
this filed inquest, submitted by the Lord
Hawkshaw of the March of Brinoa on behalf of
the people of Glengloam Village. What is the
name of the indicted prisoner?"

"Struben MacRund." Paolo nodded while confirming
the man's question.

"What is the standing of Struben
MacRund?"

"He is of the peasantry class."

"What is your official indictment as it will be
presented before the Royal Court of Pleas and
the Chamber of Arbiters?"

"I have found the indicted Struben MacRund guilty of
felonious homicide and necrophilia."

"Has the felon been issued any partial verdicts
from the arresting coroner?"

"I have charged the indicted Struben MacRund with
partial verdicts on counts of fleeing from justice,
obstruction of justice, disruption of peace and trespass
against the commoner, suicide, and sedition."

Paolo ended his partial verdicts with a heavy sigh. The
archivist steadied his writing hand and stopped in his
documentation. With an upward jerk of his beak, the

archivist quickly peered upward at Paulo with a cocked head,

> "Did I hear you correctly, resurrectionist? You have assigned the partial verdict of sedition on this man? You have evidence that this man was conspiring against the crown through starting public outrage?"

Paolo cleared his throat, "This man declared that I, a royally appointed coroner on duty for her majesty the queen, was practicing wytchecraft and necromancy as well as urinating on his trousers. Now that I think of it, he was trying to convince the masses that all of us in the Order were guilty of these heinous acts."

The robed coroner took a moment before standing up from the wooden stool beneath him to lean over the counter and inspect the trousers of the prisoner,

> "This man publicly accused the entirety of the Order, of urinating in his trousers?"

There was a slight pause from Coroner Paolo before replying,

> "No, archivist, that action he only accused me of. He was accusing us all of practicing wytchecraft and necromancy."

The archivist took another long silence before dipping his quill back into the ink bottle and returning to writing in the book.

80

"I will document your partial verdict, resurrectionist Paolo. Resurrectionist, I must warn you that all indictments documented here and within must be presented to the chamber of Arbiters by the arresting coroner unless out on another inquest for the crown."

"I am aware, archivist."

Paolo replied with a smile hidden in secrecy behind his beaked mask.

"One last question, resurrectionist, before the transferring of the prisoner. Were you able to obtain a verbal confession from the indicted prisoner?"

"There was no confession from the indicted, either written or verbal."

The archivist nodded in confirmation of Paolo's response before finishing his documentation. Upon completing the final notations, the robed coroner put away his quill and closed the bottle of ink before turning in the wooden stool and pulling on a long rope that hung from the wall. Far below them, the faint sound of a bell could be heard.

"Take the prisoner down to the right and prepare him for transfer. Good evenfall, resurrectionist!"

Paolo returned the nicety to the archivist and started to lead the prisoner down past the counter to the right side of the chamber hall toward a large, caged holding cell. Paolo opened the iron-barred door and led the shackled Struben into the rectangular caged room before shutting the door behind them. He walked Struben to the middle of the room and then proceeded to walk around to the front of the bound prisoner.

The coroner removed the key ring from his belt and used the second key to unlock the iron cuffs from around Struben's wrists. Paulo took the iron cuffs and folded them neatly together before returning the irons to a leather pouch on his belt. While the coroner seemed distracted, Struben, in a last an act of desperation, lunged forward with his head at Paolo. As soon as the broken man lunged, the resurrectionist quickly turned his body to the side and held out the tip of his boot. Tripping over the coroner, the man hurdled toward the stone floor with outstretched arms hoping to break his sudden fall. Landing on his wrist, the poor wretch of a prisoner had forgotten he had broken his arms not long before.

As his wrist contacted the ground, a sharp broken bone came piercing out from the man's flesh and linen shirt sleeve. The coroner shook his head in pity as Struben writhed once more on the ground, shrieking, and howling like a crazed hound while clutching his bleeding and a broken forearm.

"Why do they always do that?"

Said the coroner, half expecting the attack from his prisoner.

"We need a better system of transferring prisoners. Should I add assaulting a royally appointed crown servant to your indictment?"

The wooden door creaked and then swung open violently against the great bulging iron-clad forearm of a person wearing black iron armor, a long black cloak, and an iron helm shaped like a raven. The iron-clad brute bent over to pass through the doorway. After the first had cleared, they were followed by another massive person in a matching uniform who also ducked to enter the cell.

Each coroner stood two spans high, weighing about three stone apiece on Paolo's quick estimation. On their left shoulders were strapped two Ecranche shields, like those worn by jousting knights, bearing their branch insignia. The two hulking coroners belonged to the Branch of the Shield. Coroners of Shield Branch were known as Martials.

When not out in the realm searching for groups of murderous bandits and mercenaries, the martials oversaw running the interrogation dungeon of the Order. The first martial bent at the waist to inspect the bleeding prisoner before addressing Paolo,

"Is this your handiwork, *flayskin*?"

The muffled voice booming from inside the iron helm was the most baritone voice Paolo had ever heard come from a woman's throat during his time in the Order. As much as he wanted to, he couldn't rightfully take credit for the damage to poor Struben. No matter how much respect it would gain him in the eyes of the Order's brawniest members.

"No, sadly, it is not," said the resurrectionist dolefully. "These injuries have been brought about by the prisoner's own volition."

The second martial let out a heavy expiration in disappointment, followed by a light head shake of disappointment at Paolo's answer.

"Figures." Grunted the out the large woman clad in black iron. Bashing her gauntlet into her thigh to force the leather tight between her fingers.

"We will take it from here, *flayskin*," Said the first martial while the second reached down with an anvil-sized hand and grabbed the wide-eyed Struben by the back of his linen shirt.

Paolo watched as the two martials retreated through the door with the sobbing Struben. The tormented screams and wailing could be heard echoing up from the lower dungeons located further down the winding stone staircase.

The last vision Paolo had of his prisoner was Struben's round unkept face turned a ghoulish shade of pale as he heard the shrilling screams of the tormented souls below. A sound so blood-curdling, he had once again wet himself as the second martial shut the door and locked it behind them. Paolo left the transfer cell and began making his way back through the Tablinum. The resurrectionist stopped at a clerk counter near the middle of the chamber and pulled a small leather notebook and pencil from his vest. While going over his notes in preparation for the trial of his prisoner, the red door swung open with a ferocious bang.

The heavy iron wrought door slamming against the stone wall forced the man to whip around and reach behind his cloak to the blunderbuss, which sat nestled in a form-fitting leather holster on his back. From the hall, a blood-soaked man flew forward, propelled by an unforeseen force. A whirlwind of chains and limbs skid

84

across the dimly lit chamber floor before coming to a stop. Following the now ragged man was another coroner.

Paolo eyed his peer, and from the garb of the coroner, he could tell they were fellow resurrectionists, although they donned a black felt tricorne hat instead of the more common capotain worn by most other branch members. Paolo removed his hand from the stock of the blunderbuss, closed his notebook, and returned it and the pencil to its proper pouch before moving over to the unconscious and limp prisoner sprawled out on the chamber floor. Before he could move to pick the man up, a woman's voice barked out at him angrily from behind the mask of his colleague.

"Step away from that pile of trash. The prisoner is mine."

Paolo nodded in agreeance and took a step back from the man who had regained consciousness and began to hungrily gasp for air. The other coroner hastily walked toward the prisoner with a fully extended cane held firmly in her hand. As she approached the man, she snatched the man by the irons and pulled him to his feet before sending him collapsing to the ground with a vicious blow to the abdomen with the pommel of her cane.

"I warned you!"

She said before picking the man up again by his neck with her gauntlet-clad hand.

"If you groped my backside one more time,"

another blow to the abdomen from her cane sent vomit and blood gushing from the man's toothless and yellow-stained mouth.

> "Then I wasn't going to hand you over to the martials in one piece!"

With her final words, she wrapped the side of the heaving man's face with a mighty blow from her cane, sending his last remaining tooth hurdling across the floor before finally bouncing off the side of Paolo's boot.

The outstretched hand of the prisoner twitched in synch with his erratic breathing before finally falling limp. The woman was still visibly angry but must have known that any more acts of aggression would be the end of her tenure and revoking her badge. She bent over and placed the cane length behind her knee guards to catch her breath before leaning against the stone wall for support.

Paolo tilted his head and could observe a grimy handprint on the lower end of the woman's cloak and knew immediately what had sealed the imbecile's fate with his colleague. The woman turned her hand towards Paolo and noticed his gaze. Quickly she regained composure and launched herself off the wall, holding the tip of her cane out to the now retreating Paolo.

> "It's one thing to be treated like a common street whore from this sack of shit, but from one of my own!"

He could sense a slight tremble in her voice and immediately felt ashamed of his actions.

"No, no, please. I apologize. I was merely observing the situation. I didn't mean to demean you by any means."

Paolo tried to make up for his uncouth act as best he could, but the woman remained rigid.

"Listen, what I did was in bad judgment. I can sense you have had a rough experience here, and I, too, have had a long three days with a prisoner. I haven't slept or had a meal, and I am sure you haven't either. Again, I apologize."

The woman finally 'et down her guard and returned to leaning against the wall to catch her breath before turning back to Paolo.

"No, you are right. It is me that is being the stubborn ass here. I can keep my nerves under a lot of stress and scenarios, but the flagrant sexual degradation is where I draw the line with these peasant-bred animals."

She gave the man once over before checking his pulse with their cane,

"Oh! Thank the mother, he is still alive."

Paolo let out a slight nervous laugh at her discovery,

"you say that like someone who has delivered cold carrion before."

"I have."

The woman holstered her cane and picked the man up by his raggedy, blood and mud-soaked sleeves. Paolo watched as she dragged the man toward the indictment counter. He wished to offer the woman aid with the unconscious man. Still, Paolo hypothesized that she would likely see that gesture as an insult to her capabilities as a fellow coroner.

Looking past her, he noticed the archivist was also watching the scene from behind his tall counter in rigid awe. She approached the counter, dropped the man before the archivist, and started to recite her information to the archivist without waiting on them to initiate the process.

"Coroner Atrionna Forsythe. The Worshipful Branch of Resurrectionist. Inquest number…"

The small, robed, bookish archivist scrambled for quill and ink as she ratified off her inquest report numbers. Paolo gave a light chuckle at the wild-natured spirit of his mysterious colleague.

"Come on, come on, bookkeeper. I have had a long day, and I am tired. Keep up!"

She continued in her report as Paolo stared at his peer, scoffing at the brashness of her professional demeanor.

Atrionna Forsythe, he thought to himself, *I don't think I have ever met her before. The name doesn't sound familiar. She must be from one of the younger classes below me. Her voice did sound young. And Brinoan. Explains the temper.*

He chuckled again at his last thought and turned for the door. As he made his way back outside to the courtyard of the Praetorium, he could see a cart pulled off to the side and behind his own. Making his way through the coaches, he returned to his dray horse and took the mare by the reins. Together they walked to the stables on the other side of the campus.

When they arrived, Paolo insisted on leading his horse to her stable so he could remove her harness and bridle, brush her coat and mane, and finally say goodnight to her. After departing from the stables, Paolo walked through a set of double doors and made his way to the quartermaster workshop to turn in his equipment report and inspect his weapons. The quartermaster at the workshop window sounded too young for Paolo's liking.

The high-pitched and soft boyish voice drew a sense of hesitancy on whether he should hand over his cane and firearm to the young lad.

> "I don't mean to be rude, young quartermaster, but what is your ranking here at the workshop? If you don't mind me asking."

As he questioned the youth, he held his belts and holstered weapons close to his chest, like a mother coddling her babe.

> "I do not mind, master resurrectionist, not at all. I am a humble novitiate quartermaster who graduated from academy not too long ago."

Paolo cocked his eyebrow at the boy's response, "if you graduated, that means you have survived 18 seasons this year?"

"Correct, sir."

Did I sound like that as a novitiate? This lad sounds like a boy no more than 14 or 15 years.

As Paolo stood clutching his weapons, the sound of a person clearing their throat came from behind him. He turned to see the hostile colleague from the Tablinum, also with gear and weapons.

> "My apologies, I will be done shortly. I was making sure that a quartermaster, higher than the rank of novitiate, was present in the workshop."

"Oh, of course, sir, Master Quartermaster Tomlin is here. He is in the back, at the forge. Would you like me to get him?"

> "No, that is okay. If there is a master quartermaster in the shop, that will suffice."

Paolo then placed his weapons and instrument cases on the counter while the novitiate reviewed the list. Afterward, he reached down and brought up his chymiac cases and apothecarium satchels. As they finished the list, he stood patiently as the young quartermaster reviewed the lists.

> "Oh, master coroner Paolo, sir. It says you are due for a mask inspection and cleaning, sir. We will need you to leave that with us overnight, sir."

Reluctantly the coroner agreed to the request. Mask inspection and cleaning were only done every two decades, a sharp and harsh reminder of how much time he has spent in the field. Paolo reached up with both hands and unbuckled the mask before pulling the oculars off first and setting them down on the counter. He then unbuckled the brass fittings and removed the beaked re-breather. The leather ring of the salerite basket came peeling from around his lips, showing also the cloth was ultimately bone dry. He stretched his mouth and shook the cool night air from his face.

It had been almost a month since he had removed his mask, and the sensation of cool air can become an alien experience if one spends too much time hidden behind a mask. Paolo handed the novitiate the beak of his mask, pulled up his hat, dropped the tight leather hood from his head, and let loose his shoulder-length peppered brown and grey hair before returning the capotain to the crown of his head.

The woman behind him shifted in her stance, a sound he could hear even more evident than before. The young coroner thanked Paolo and returned the bin of his gear to the back of the workshop.

He turned from the counter, threw his saddlebags over his shoulder, and picked up his black satchel bag from the floor.

"Have a pleasant time off, *master coroner*."

Said the still masked coroner from before. He said nothing in response, only tipping the brim of his capotain to her as he left the workshop and started his long walk back to his loft in the city.

As he walked down the damp cobblestone
streets of Calitoria, the Astrolaborarry clock tower rang
out throughout the city. Signaling the top of the
twilight hour.

The moon was now high in the night sky overhead,
gracing the entirety of the city in its heavenly glory. As
the wind picked up and the chilled night breeze shifted
the humid sea air around, he could feel the pain in his
knee return.

*The end is near, old friend. But when will it come? I
can't see myself becoming a doctori, but I didn't see
myself dying in the field this soon. Where has the time
gone? Where has it gone?*

Paolo reached the steps of his building and nodded to
the night watchwoman, trying to hide the dread of
climbing the seven flights of stairs on the way to his
floor. As he ascended each floor, his grip on the
banister railing tightened until the bronze skin of his
knuckles was a pale white.

Opening the door to his home, he staggered into
the main chamber and gave himself a moment of
respite before neatly putting away his things. When
nothing was left to put out, the old coroner made
himself a hot bath and filled the tub water with a bag of
healing salt from the apothecarium.

He got undressed and slowly lowered himself
into the brass tub before quickly drifting off before he
had a moment to scrub his skin with the brush in his
hand. The sound of the wooden brush handle dropping
to the floor was the last sound his raven heard before it
was followed by the loud snoring of a week-long sleep-
deprived man.

92

The Grand Hall

Paolo sat on a wooden bench at the foot of the immense statue of the goddess Myrina. The giant stone statue of the goddess filled the entirety of the cupola tower, and her crescent moon-crowned head also served as the secondary aviary of the order. Ravens wheeled high above him, the silhouettes casting shadows on the marble floor below him as they cut through the sunlight shining through the glass roof of the dome skylight high above.

He enjoyed the undisturbed tranquility while reviewing his notes before delivering his inquest statement in the Court of Common Pleas. Every once in and while his neck would give a sharp jolt of pain when he turned his head too quickly while reading the page, but that would happen after spending the night sleeping in a metal tub.

After he felt satisfied in reviewing his notes, he put the papers in the leather satchel bag attached to his belt and began to make his way back to the workshop to pick up his equipment from the quartermasters that he had left there the night before.

Waiting his turn, Paolo finally approached the window of the workshop. The window opened, and Paolo was greeted by a coroner that sounded much more seasoned by the tone of voice, which felt welcoming to the resurrectionist.

Statue of the Goddess Myrina
Mother of Mankind

"Name?"

The quartermaster spoke in a harsh gravely tone while opening the logbook on the counter in front of him.

"Resurrectionist Paolo Reveré", Paolo replied in a chipper tone.

> "Ah, yes. The *old-timer*. On record, you have one standard-issued, breech-loading, fifty-caliber blunderbuss with a rifled flanged barrel. One standard-issued cane with resurrectionist modifications, and finally, one field-issued salerite re-breather with vermillion crystal oculars in standard resurrectionist beak design. They have been recalibrated, re-aligned, cleaned, and ready for pick up. Sign, here, here."

The quartermaster turned the record book around on the counter toward Paolo and held his pencil out for the coroner to take and sign. No hand took the pencil from the quartermaster, who, after trying to initiate the process of gathering Paolo's equipment, grew disgruntled and turned to face the blank face of the man before him.

> "I said sign here, here, and here, dammit! I don't have all day," barked the old quartermaster.

> "What do you mean by *old-timer*?"

Asked Paolo in a hushed voice while leaning in over the counter. The quartermaster withdrew into his window at the advancing resurrectionist,

> "Listen, buddy, I am married, so take a step back from the counter and sign the damn book."

Paolo stayed persistent in his inquiry into the man's comment,

"you said, *old-timer*. You called me that, why?"

"Because you are," Snarled the quartermaster back at Paolo. He took the pencil from the cantankerous quartermaster's hand. The old man continued as he gathered Paolo's gear from the bins lining the wall next to him.

> "No, you are an old-timer. You sound like an old man behind that mask of yours. I am still young."

The quartermaster placed the heavy holstered blunderbuss on the counter and gave a hearty raspy chuckle at Paolo's comment.

> "Ha, ha. I am, but age and titles such as old-timer differ when you consider the branch the coroner you are addressing is in. Yeah, I may be older than you by years, but you see, I am a quartermaster in the branch of chronicles. An archivist. We archivists are the bookkeepers, tinkerers, craftsmen, and librarians of the order. You aren't an old-timer in the branch of chronicles until you are at least in your late sixties to seventies."

Paolo sank back behind the counter and pontificated on the words of the now heartily chuckling quartermaster finishing up preparing his things.

"So, what you are saying, is that age is relative to sub-profession in this line of work?"

The quartermaster slung up his holstered cane and mask onto the counter and slid them across the counter to Paolo.

"I am saying to you that I have been doing this job for almost forty years. And if all my time as a quartermaster has taught me about your other types, is that two decades as a resurrectionist means one of two things. You are one tough son of a bitch, or you are great at what you do. Maybe even both. But you are one of the few I have met that has made it to your re-breather getting fixed and cleaned. So, stop whining and take the title as a badge of honor, you' prissy. NEXT!"

Paolo moved to the side and allowed the coroner behind him to collect their things.

He slowly put his gear back on, pausing here and there to think about what the old quartermaster had said. No matter how he spun it, he couldn't figure out how to take the news of what the man had said. If it was a title of pride or a shameful insult. Paolo left the workshop and began the long route back to the rotunda to await his case presentation. As he climbed the stairs past the Librarium, he stopped to look at the various oil paintings that lined the coroners' walls from years ago.

As he reached the second story, he then gazed down the long hallway that led to the lecture halls of the Academy. The statues of previous chief coroners from throughout the ages lined the sides of the ornate red-carpet runner in the middle of the hall. He made his way down the hall and gazed at the statues of the men and women who had led the order through ancient and turbulent times. He observed the plaques at their feet, noting their birth and year of death.

Most of them never lived past thirty-five years of age and had made the rank of chief no less. Here I am at neigh on forty, and I am still slogging it through the filth of the kingdom's backwaters. Reaching the end of the red-carpeted rug, the door to the lecture hall opened, and from within, a score of second-year academy students came pouring into the hallway. If he had to guess, every one of them had survived no more than thirteen seasons. They quickly formed groups of close friends and began to discuss the content of the last lecture, anatomy it sounded like. He loved anatomy as an acolyte. It's what drew him to the calling of being a resurrectionist.

Paolo tried to think back on his youth, from when he was just a waist-high orphan who was shepherded into this bloody and scary business because he scored high on some exam, he was forced to take at the orphan hall. But as hard as he tried, the memories fell through the cracks of his mind like water poured over coarse sand.

They seemed like a lifetime ago. As he stood reflecting on the past, the present, and the future, the sound of a door opening behind him forced him to turn around and inspect the source of the commotion. From the doorway came a coroner clad in the uniform of an archivist, although she wore a tricorn hat on her head instead of the typical hood.

I must be getting old. He thought in silence. *I do not get this new tricorne hat trend that seems to be popular now.*

The archivist first looked down the far side of the hallway before turning and looking upon Paolo.

"Oh, excuse me," said a female voice in a soft tone, "you appear to be a resurrectionist, are you not?"

"I am," He replied, placing his hands behind his back, and nodding at the woman. The archivist moved from the doorway and clasped her hands together while giving a small bow of her head.

"Perfect. I have been scouring the entirety of this place looking for a member of your branch, and I cannot seem to find him. Maybe you might know where he is?"

Paolo returned the bow in likeness, although hesitantly. Unsure of her goal, Paolo cleared his throat before responding to her inquiry.

"Maybe, I mean, I am not that great with names as I used to be but give me a try. Whom might you be looking for?"

Moving her clasped hands to her backside, the archivist lifted her chin into the air. She spoke clearly and confidently. An air of pretension

wafted from her presence. A pretension most
common among members of her branch.

"I've been asked by the chief surgeon to fetch a
Coroner, Paolo Reveré. Would you know a
resurrectionist by that name, perchance?"

Paolo chuckled at her question, "why you are in luck. I
do happen to know that individual."

"Great!" laughed the archivist with a sigh of relief, "do
you happen to know where he is?"

"He is standing right here. Paolo Reveré is me. I
am whom you are looking for."

She dropped her welcoming demeanor and crossed her
arms across her chest.

"Well, you could have led with that, couldn't
you? I have been climbing up and down stairs
like a bloody hooligan just to have the person I
have been sent to fetch just stand here and play
silly word games with me."

It was the second time this week that Paolo was
passive-aggressively scolded by a female colleague. He
began apologizing like before but was stopped by a
solid upright hand of the tempered archivist.

"Save me the sorry speech, dearie. I just want to
get you to your destination so I can return to my
research. I have things to do myself, you know.
We archivists don't live and breathe solely to

100

serve the other branches. Come now, follow me. Come along."

She waved Paolo through the door she had come from at his continuing protest.

"Listen, I appreciate it, but I know how to find the chief-surgeons office. I can navigate there myself."

"Who said anything about the chief surgeon being in his office. Are you assuming? I hope you are not assuming anything because you know what assuming makes you?"

"I don't understand, Chief-Surgeon Houmpherdine is always in his office. Where else would he be?"

The archivist stopped in the hallway and crossed her arms again, this time fidgeting her fingers as if to hold back a slap from her right hand. She took a deep breath before speaking once again. In the meantime, Paolo braced himself for what he expected to be a typical Solarnian woman explanation.

"Well, Chief-Surgeon Houmpherdine is no longer Chief-Surgeon. So, I will let that slide as you are no longer in the loop on who the chief surgeon of your branch is. I don't mean to come across as rude, but if I were a resurrectionist, that might be something I would want to catch up on."

The news of the chief -surgeon's death came as a complete shock to Paolo, forcing the stout man of thirty-eight years to stumble backward and catch himself on the wall behind him. The sight of the coroner taking the news harshly forced the woman to take a more relaxed stance in his presence.

> "I am sorry if that was new information to you. It appears that Chief Surgeon Houmpherdine was close to you. I just didn't think anything of it, being that he was an older gentleman and one of the last members of the old guard."

Paolo scoffed at her comment about the old guard before regaining his composer.

> "How did he die? If you don't mind me asking."

"I do not mind, not at all. From what I hear, the previous chief surgeon slowly died from decrepitude before suffering a sudden bout of apoplexy. He died in his sleep at home surrounded by friends and colleagues."

The coroner smiled behind his mask at the thought of his old mentor, his father figure, dying in peace in his own bed at home. But was saddened at the thought of not being at his side in his final hours. He held a moment of silence for the passing of his beloved mentor and thanked the archivist once more.

> "Okay, so who is the new chief surgeon, and where are we headed?"

"The new chief surgeon is Galini De'Medi, and he is located in his new office, which is back in the flesh pits,"

Answered the woman quickly as she returned to making her way down the hall. Paolo shrugged off the stiff knee to keep pace with the woman, his mind racing with questions.

"Did you say De'Medi? Where is Medi? I have never heard of that place. Is he Solarnian?"

The woman stopped at Paolo's question, whipping around, and digging a sharp outstretched hand into the center of the coroner's leather brigantine.

"What made you ask that kind of question?"

Her voice remained stern but fell to a hushed whisper as she responded,

"I am not sure where the new chief surgeon is from, but he looks different from the two of us. Now, Chief Surgeon Galini is an old academy friend of mine. He is brilliant and a very kind man. But don't be alarmed or say anything stupid when we reach his office."

Paolo was taken aback by what the archivist was saying.

He looks different. What could that even mean?

"Okay, thank you for the incite. But if chief surgeon Galini is in uniform, how could I know what he looks like anyway? Unless you imply, he looks akin to one of those haunting silver skinned Rholhynians."

As the words left his mouth, the archivist stopped once again, but this time struck Paolo across the beak of his mask before shoving a finger up in his oculars, "there you go again, with the words and the moving of the mouth. Do not say that again, and do not imply that the Chief Surgeon is a Rholhynian.

There are very few things that upset Galini but insinuating that he is from the Kingdom of Rholhynia will most definitely imbalance his humors. You understand me?"
Paolo shook his head in agreement, removing the archivist's slender boney finger from his face.

"Who are you?"

Was all that he could utter in response to one of the most bizarre hallway conversations and strolls he had ever been a part of in his life.

"Archivist-Librarian Luiza De'Maichi, why do you want to report me to the Grand Archivist?"

"Ah, so you're from the village of Maichi? That explains the temper, I suppose."

The two coroners continued down the winding hallways of the Academy until finally arriving at the laboratorium for gross anatomical dissection. Librarian Luiza unlocked the door with a key from her key ring and led the resurrectionist through the darkened, white-tiled surgical room.

104

The sunlight from the hallway windows provided enough light absorption for the vermillion crystals of their oculars to navigate the pitch-black room with relative ease, being that their oculars were designed to give coroners almost near-perfect vision in the dark.

They navigated around countless porcelain-coated steel slabs, each supporting a partially dissected human corpse that the current academy class was studying their anatomy. Even though the room was lined with packed ice blocks from the northern march of Brinoa, the lingering scent of dead flesh was triggering the ignition and burning of the aromatic incense packed intensely in the wired mesh chamber within his beaked re-breather. His nostrils were filled with the pungent smell of pine needles and sea salt, the only memory he had of his early childhood. After moving through two more rooms, they finally arrived at a locked door bearing a plaque that read Chief-Surgeon Galini de-Medi, on its front.

Librarian Luiza stopped and knocked on the door before unlocking it with her key and gesturing to Paola to enter the room. The resurrectionist nodded his head toward the archivist and bid her thanks and goodbye before the door was shut and locked behind him.

The Flesh Pits

Of the Praetorium
9th hour of the 82nd Day

As Paolo stepped further into the room, he looked at the desks to the right and left. Scrolls and papers lined the tables, each bearing scribblings and writing in strange nomenclature and symbols, most of which he had never seen before. On the cupboards above the desks were ancient tomes with titles and dates written in Solarnian dialect from at least six to seven hundred centuries ago.

As he passed, he looked down and noted strange drawings of humanoid anatomy that seemed almost alien. This filled his inquisitive mind with numerous questions regarding the nature of the chief-surgeons research in this dimly lit room tucked away in the bowels of the flesh pits. As he gazed at a drawing on the table to his left, Paolo noticed a phrase written in hasty penmanship hidden below the picture he was studying. With a single finger, he reallocated the top sketch to reveal the words below, *The Brume*....

> "Good day to you, Coroner Paolo Reveré. It is nice to finally meet one of my most experienced field resurrectionists."

The voice came from above Paolo, and when the Resurrectionist picked his gaze up from the desk, his eyes kept glancing ever upward until they met face to face with the tallest man Paolo had ever seen.

The Chief Surgeon towered over the native Solarnian by a reasonable span of the Resurrectionist's arms. Paolo estimated that he had to be taller than the largest martial he had met. The sheer eminence of his superior's height forced Paolo to stagger back slightly, if only in natural reflex to being towered over.

He finally realized what the archivist was getting at earlier about how the chief surgeon did not look like the rest of them.

He only wished she would have specified. Even though Paolo had staggered backward, the tall and slender chief surgeon took no apparent offense in his subordinate's behavior. Paolo quickly ushered a forced apology, something he found himself doing an abundance of in the past twenty-four hours since his return to the city. The chief surgeon held his hand up and informed the Resurrectionist that he took no offense.

> "I am used to the reaction by now, trust me. I understand I am taller than most individuals you have met. Unless you have completed several contracts in the borderland country of the realm, I suppose others of different anatomical composition or proportion can be alarming."

Paolo noted how soothing the man's voice was. As the words came from the surgeon's mouth, they washed over his troubled mind like a warm tide. He was reassuring and comforting, almost to the point where Paolo was no longer bothered by the man's looming presence.

> "Have you?"

The chief surgeon asked in a slow, monotone voice.

> "Have you spent much time in the borderland country in your long tenure as a resurrectionist?"

"Yes, Chief Surgeon, I have. I have completed inquests from Kreighorn to Ngwenithen. I know much about navigation and customs for both the March of Turnia and the March of Clevelorn. I am even fluent in both old Turnian and Cudwytchian dialects."

The chief surgeon tented his fingertips together and leaned upright at Paolo's response.

> "Interesting, that is very good to hear, Coroner Paolo. I am very pleased to hear this. You are the perfect man for the task I have."

As the chief surgeon finished his sentence. A queer noise came from the dissection slab in the center of the observation pit behind him. The noise was soon followed by a peculiar rattling noise like someone's hand started to shake metal instruments on top of a metal tray. The noise intrigued Paolo, who tried to lean around the Chief Surgeon to see what could be causing such an alarming sound. But before he could keep his eyes on the dissecting table, the chief surgeon began talking again.

> "What do you know about Lazzar Perish, Coroner Paolo? Does that name sound familiar to you?"

As he asked his question, he craned his large frame
downward once more as If you eclipse the table behind
the man and force the coroner to look solely at him.
Paolo desired to know what lay behind his superior, but
when the chief surgeon said the hamlet's name, it
snapped the Resurrectionist out of his inquisitive
stupor. The name Lazzar Perish harkened nothing but
an overwhelming sense of dread from the seasoned
veteran.

> "Yes, Chief Surgeon. I know of Lazzar Perish. I
> know the history of that rotting place, at least. It
> is a colony of the damned. Some believe
> spiritually, while others believe physically. It
> makes no difference to me. Lazzar Perish is
> filled with nothing but squaller, filth, and
> human degeneracy. The populace comprises
> leecher-women and bandits, who only provide
> the kingdom with inbred children that grow up
> to become body snatchers and bone grubbers
> for the eastern Rholhynian church they so
> preciously covet."

The chief surgeon fixed his red lenses on t"e
Resurrectionist, choosing to remain in his bent-over
posture as the man spoke about the forgotten and
shunned perish. Paolo stopped in his response to gauge
the chief surgeon if the answers he was providing
pleased his superior.

> "Go on, Coroner Reveré. I am intrigued by how
> much you know of such a quaint and forgotten
> village on the outskirts of our great kingdom.
> Please, continue."

Paolo cleared his throat and was about to continue when from behind the Chief Surgeon came a different sound than he had heard before. A loud banging noise rang out from behind the chief surgeon. It sounded like someone had dropped wet mud on the table, followed by a cacophony of horrendous hissing and bubbling before something akin to a mouth blowing bubbles in a pool of water came from underneath the tarp covering the cold porcelain slab. Paolo jerked both his eyes and his head to the table at the bottom of the observation pit, but the long lanky chest of the Chief Surgeon swallowed his vision once again, followed by the long beak of his mask.

"Go on, Coroner Paolo. Focus on me for a moment more and tell me all you know."

Paolo snapped his eyes back on the looming man who now was so close to him that it was forcing him back toward the desk behind him.

"I know Lazzar Perish is a place where no coroner is welcome, and neither is the Lord Hawkshaw of Turnia. Hence, no inquest of homicidal slayings is ever filed from there, and no resurrectionist has been sent there in over two hundred years or more."

The Resurrectionist had finally provided the chief surgeon with precisely what he wanted to hear. As the words finished pouring from Paolo's mouth, the chief surgeon rose from his hunched position and pulled his long slender fingertips apart.

He slowly removed a single scroll from within his cloak and handed the parchment over to Paolo for

110

inspection. Paolo took the scroll from his superior's hand and turned it in his hands, searching for the wax seal of the sender. As he quickly rolled the scroll over, his eyes beheld a purple broken wax seal bearing the pressed seal of the coat of arms of the Viscount of Turnia along with the name Von Eckstein buried in ribbon underneath the crest. Paolo opened the scroll and began to read its content. As Paolo read the contents, Galini turned and made his way down the several steps into the observation pit and stood at the side of the porcelain dissection table.

> "I don't understand, chief surgeon. This is an inquest submission to our order for the investigation into multiple accounts of homicidal slaying, multiple accounts of aggravated rape and cannibalistic assault, multiple accounts of stolen children from surrounding farming villages, and the mass slaughter of livestock and poultry with signs of buggery."

The words came trembling from his mouth as he read them. It was the most appalling list of public trespasses he had ever read aloud throughout his career. Mass murder, rape, cannibalism, the kidnapping of children, and bestiality? This was most disturbing if it was indeed true, but the evil of this magnitude was unheard of in their age. The gravity and levity of the words written on the paper the coroner held in his hands were almost too much to comprehend, even for a seasoned veteran like Paolo Reveré.

> "Chief-Surgeon Galini, this is signed and submitted by the Viscount himself. I cannot

possibly fathom that all of this is coming from
one place, even a place with a bad history like
Lazzar Perish.”

The chief surgeon gave no reply to the worried
Resurrectionist, only stood in momentary silence.
Suddenly the silence was broken by a different voice
from the tall thin man. No longer was it soothing and
calm, but now was echoing throughout the tiled
chamber in a booming monotonous tone.

“Please tell me, Coroner Paolo, what is the date
forged on the bottom of that document?”

“It was dated almost a full three months, chief surgeon.
It’s been almost a month since I arrived at the order.”

“Precisely,” Boomed the chief surgeon.

He turned from the table and took a step to his right. A
small instrument table stood at the foot of the table,
covered by a single white cloth. The chief surgeon
threw back the fabric to expose a fresh supply of
recently cleaned and sharped resurrection instruments.
He beckoned to the Resurrectionist to approach
the table opposite him, an order Paolo followed without
question. As he descended the steps and rounded the
chief surgeon, Paolo gazed at the dissection slab in the
center of the chamber and beheld a white sheet, soaked
with through and saturated with an unnaturally colored
viscous liquid upon initial inspection appeared to be
luminescent.
What lay underneath the cloth was at least
shaped like a human body, but its shape was unnatural,
lumpy, and writhing more like some insect rather than

a man. Paolo did as he was told and got into position. The chief surgeon reached over to the instrument tray and pulled the long dual-edged lister blade from it. He reached out an empty palm toward Paolo.

"If you have any spirit grains on you, please hand me the flask from your vest."

Paolo reached into one of the pouches on his brigantine, produced the small brass flask the chief surgeon had requested and placed it firmly in the man's palm.

The chief surgeon turned from the cloth and opened the lid of the cannister with the tip of his nail at the end of a long slender thumb. As soon as he tilted the flask over and began to pour the white powder onto the edges of the long white-lustrous blade, whatever lay beneath the spoiled cloth began to violently contort and writhe with a ferocious bout of spastic palsy that Paolo had ever seen.

"This is the moment of your final test, Coroner Paolo, do not fail me."

Before the coroner could question the intent and nature of the chief surgeon's words, the tall thin man pulled back the cloth to expose a creature so abhorrent and vile that it completely captivated the eyes and mind of the veteran coroner. Whatever this horrific amalgamation was, it was at one point a man, or part of a man, this Paolo could tell by the noticeable anatomy alone.

"Tell me what you observe, coroner. I want every detail, both calmy and orderly", boomed the chief surgeon, whose eyes remained fixed on Paolo. Paolo briefly closed his eyes and took a moment to center his thoughts before opening them once again and starting his inspection.

"The creature of unknown origin is approximately one span in length and one cubit in width at the widest portion. It has one intact appendage, which appears to be homologous to a right arm. Several orbital appendages are pulsating from the surface of the creature's flesh. These appendages appear to have a central iris and react to light and sound, indicating they are some sensory organs homologous to an eye. There is abundant hair growth wherever there. It isn't obvious signs of tissue necrosis or cankers. Sporangiophore growth is noted interspersed in the hair growth and flagella-like appendages. I can appreciate numerous druse bodies all over the mid-section of the, surrounded by undulating sores of black bile and pus. A cacopathy of cymose bules is present on both exposed fragments of bones along with severe mortification and mass hyperdentition covering large portions of the upper squamous tissue linings."

As the coroner finished observing the creature, the chief surgeon turned the handle of the dissection knife and presented the blade to Paolo.

"Take the blade and plunge the tip deep into one of the orbital appendages, Paolo."

The coroner took the blade's handle and drove the powder-coated tip deep into the most immense orbital growth he could find the fastest. As the scalpel

114

pierced the writhing and hissing mass, a hissing sound like beef on a hot pan rang out in the observation room. The various orifices lined with rows of sharp teeth opened, letting out an ear-piercing shriek as the blade burned and singed its tumor-like eye. As the creature screamed, the individual teeth could be seen writhing and wriggling in its foul cankerous and pus-filled pits of hair and bone.

Despite this, the coroner remained ever methodical and ever surgical in his technique. The waves of screams and terror washed over him like a rock in a sea storm. Finally, the mass of alien tissue ceased in its movement and fell silent and still on the table. The surgeon requested the blade back from the coroner, which Paolo returned promptly to his hand. The chief surgeon cleaned the blade's edge on the damp cloth from the watering bowl on the instrument tray and placed the scalpel back in its place.

> "What I am about to share with you and what you have seen and performed in this chamber will never leave this room. If I hear even the slightest hint of a rumor on what has transpired here today, you will have dire consequences. The fate of the very realm relies on the complete subterfuge and secrecy of this knowledge. Do I make myself clear?"

Paolo nodded in silence, for he was still coming to terms with what he had just seen and done moments prior.

"Over three months ago, I dispatched one of my best field agents to this Lazzar Perish. She was to investigate the root cause of all the madness expressed in the inquest submitted by the Viscount. I agreed with all the initial assessments you provided on the document. It seemed outlandish, absurd, and implausible. But it came from a high-ranking nobleman and couldn't be ignored. To the depths of an unknown abyss, I sent Mortalist Wilhelmina Strense. Both blind and alone.

A month passed, and I heard nothing from the mortalist. Finally, after another fortnight of waiting, her raven returned to the Praetorium. The bird was covered in blood and bore a leather pouch filled with a lump of writhing flesh and a single note. The note read spirit grains, and the words Burn followed. I didn't know what to make of it at first, so I have spent the time since then locked away here in research. Pouring over everything we have in the Annals of the Archivum, trying to solve the riddle on the potential source of this abomination.

But three months have passed, and yet no sign of Mortalist Wilhelmina. I fear for her life, specifically that I sent her to her doom out in the border country. As tragic as her loss is and as foolish as my initial assumption, we have sworn an oath to the kingdom, the queen, and the people. Whatever this is, it must be stopped. So, I won't make the same mistake again. My mistake was sending in a mortalist when this is a job for Resurrectionists."

Paolo looked up from the pile of horrors at the surgeon's words and met oculars with his superior.

"But sir, if you want me to go to Lazzar Perish, I will. Just answer this one question. Where did this come from if she only sent you a lump of flesh?"

"Coroner Paolo, this was the pound of flesh that
Mortalist Wilhelmina sent us."

Paolo looked down in utter amazement at the lifeless
tissue on the slab,

"This is mutagenic?"

The chief surgeon replied with a silent nod,

"Precisely, I need you to pick up where she left
off. We must get to the bottom of this!"

The two continued to discuss the details of the
strange case at the desk, the surgeon providing every
ounce of information he had obtained in his research in
the Archivum. Soon they both departed the office of
the chief surgeon.

The door closed behind Galini on their way out,
and the surgeon locked it with a turn of the key. The
room was once again still and silent. Underneath the
soiled cloth came a horrible cacophony of demoniac
crackling and repugnant gurgling. The mound of black,
bile-riddled putrefaction began to come alive and move
once more.

The Council Chamber

The trial of Struben MacRund was over in less than an hour. The martial leading his interrogation had announced to the chamber that MacRund had confessed to his crimes after an injection of black henbane, an application of the fork, and twenty minutes of strappado before finally breaking in between bouts of cacodaemoniacal madness brought about by the immense torturous pain of his guilt-ridden and melancholy mind. As the martial gave her testimony, Paolo could not help but remain fixated on the twitching and whimpering Struben.

The prisoner was on his knees and locked into a pillory on the center stage of the chamber, illuminated by the piercing skylight high above the ceiling. All who broke the Queen's common law were brought before the Council of Five Arbiters in the same manner, shackled and humbled before the crown and goddess.

Here, criminals were to face supreme justice for the realm's most reviled crimes, that of slaying your kin and kith. As Struben kneeled before the Council, his spasmodic palsies, burst of light sobbing, and incoherent ramblings under hushed breath were becoming intolerable.

Before turning the chamber floor over to Paolo for his delivery of prosecution, Arbiter Sechenov of the Worshipful branch of Shadows called a bailiff over to the chamber center and assisted the accused with his melancholic demeanor. A fast and hard ministration of the bailiff's iron-clad fist to the prisoner's temple alleviated Struben of any more residual henbane in his humors as his trembling frame went stone-cold limp in the pillory, followed by a faucet of blood.

Arbiter Sechenov promptly nodded thanks to the bailiff for his medical assistance rendered upon the prisoner before motioning to Paolo to commence his delivery of prosecution in a now silent chamber hall.

Paolo gave his prosecution, methodically recanting every detail of his inquiry and investigation. The seasoned Resurrectionist performed his role flawlessly, reviewing every facet of the case with surgical precision. From the witness reports, scene of death analyses, the resurrection report, and the phlogistic lab results of the victim's lacerated flesh, Paolo left little to no doubt for the Council that Struben MacRund had murdered his wife's brother.

After giving the prosecution, the Council briefly discussed the partial verdicts before Chief Coroner Bellarmíne rose from his chair to render upon the accused the ruling of the Council. Struben MacRund was found guilty of felonious homicide and was sentenced to death by crucifixion at the Kingdom's penal fortress of Fawrgrave Gaol in the far-off providence of the March of Clevelorn.

The other arbiters gave their unanimous in-favor response in sequential Order down the bench, and upon reaching the final arbiter's agreeance, the Chief brought the gavel down and sealed his fate to death.

The echo of the gavel rang in Paolo's mind as he watched the bailiffs collect Struben from the pillory and carry the lifeless body off and out of the chamber hall. Paolo knew what awaited Struben. The horrors of crucifixion will haunt a man until his dying days if looked upon just once. Paolo had been to the Great

Corpse Road in eastern Clevelorn March. He had seen the rows of thousands of wooden crossbeams that riddled the Gibbet Marsh. Each is decorated with the gutted and flayed bodies of men and women.

Each had been found guilty of murder in this chamber, all sentenced to rot in the elements like animals. Whatever spurred those wretched fools to commit such fateful misdeeds was intoxicating enough to drown out the reality of such a fearful fate. To become nothing more than rain-soaked carrion for the ravens of Clevelorn.

Quickly the coroner shook himself free of his wandering mind and made his way out of the chamber to make room for the following coroner and their prosecution. As he made the long walk down the chamber hall, Paolo was passed by a familiar presence.

The coroner he had met the night before was making her way into the chamber. She gave him a quick bow in silence as she passed by before continuing down toward the low bench. As she approached the Council, one of the arbiters rose from their station to address her.

"Coroner Atrionna Forsythe, I am pleased you can join us today."

Paolo immediately knew by the cold tone of the arbiter that the woman speaking was Chief-Resurrectionist Myria Montessorí, head of the Worshipful Branch of Steel. Paolo also understood by the arbiter's tone that she was, in fact, not at all pleased to see Coroner Atrionna.

"Chief-Resurrectionist Montessorí"

Coroner Atrionna kneeled in reverence before the arbiter and remained kneeling,

"The honor is mine, and I am humbled to hear such a praise from you, madame arbiter."

"Indeed. Rise, Coroner Forsythe. Rise and inform your superior and the rest of the Council why you have wasted our precious time this noonday hour."

Atrionna rose from her penitence to witness the two bailiffs enter the side door of the chamber carrying a lifeless body wrapped and bound in white wool sheets between them. Atrionna remained silent as they laid the wrapped corpse on the docket at the base of the pillory before finally addressing the Council after clearing her dry throat.

"I do not understand, madame Arbiter."

"He is dead, Coroner Forsythe. Since you are a badge pinned Resurrectionist of the Worshipful Branch of Steel, I would hope even that information would be apparent to you. This is simply embarrassing and outrageous, Coroner Forsythe. This is the third prisoner of your short career you have brought in that has died before the martials can obtain a proper confession. By the mother's mercy, you conduct yourself like a barbaric animal. Be it your Brinoan blood or not, this will not become a chronic problem. Do you understand me, Coroner Forsythe?"

Paolo quietly opened the chamber door and showed himself as silently as he could. As he opened the door, the thundering echoes of Chief-Resurrectionist Montessorí's scolding rant filled the marble-floored hallway before being silenced by the closing of the tremendous heavy double door.

Since reaching a more seasoned station in his career, Paolo found the disciplinary hearings of younger Resurrectionists quite entertaining.

But now that his chamber trial was over, he had no more time to waste this day. Paolo quickly made his way from the Council Chamber to the council clerk window at the far end of the long corridor. Approaching the counter, he reached up and gave the frosted glass three wraps with the back of his gloved hand. There was a short silence before the sound of a creaking chair could be heard from the other side of the glass sliding window.

The window slid open slowly to reveal a short and slender coroner, whose long white beak of their mask barely peaked over the opposite countertop. Clad in the thick, black-dyed wool robes and a hood pulled over their mask, it was hard to tell which branch this coroner served.

Paolo leaned over the counter and through the window opening to spot the matte-black iron badge keeping the cloak pinned around their shoulders bore the crest of the Worshipful Branch of Chronicles. Below the shield was a rectangular nameplate that promptly informed Paolo that the petite colleague standing before him was, in fact, an archivist.

Paolo raised his gaze to find that the Archivist was looking back at him with their magnifying opticals still attached to the oculars of their coroner mask. He remained to lean forward as he addressed the Archivist,

122

"Keeping those monoculars on when not reading cannot be good for the eyesight."

"My eyesight is already *sardin'* poor!"

A high-pitch groveling squeak lashed back at Paolo from the throat of a very, extremely old-sounding man. Paolo chuckled at the Archivist's comment and leaned back from the counter while they reached for an inkpot and quill with slightly trembling hands.

"I am assuming you are here to transfer coinage, are you not?"

Paolo confirmed his intent with the old man as he reached into a pouch on his brigantine to produce a small leather coin purse and his notebook with pencil. The old man gave a heavy grunt and a groan as he struggled to move the sizeable brown leather record book from the desk behind him and onto the countertop below the window. Opening the large leather book, the Archivist pulled up a wooden stool and sat down with a long-winded sigh before adjusting the dials of the magnifying opticals on his mask.

"Name, branch, inquest number"

Paolo opened his notebook and slid the pencil from the leather cover.

"Coroner Paolo Reveré, Worshipful Branch of Steel, inquest number one, zero, one, nine, nine, eight, seven, nine, nine, nine, one."

The old Archivist slid the quill across the dusty page
with the grace of a skilled artist as he filled in the
various lines and boxes.

"Final verdict of the inquest?"

"Guilty of Felonious Homicide, guilty of all other
partial verdicts. The sentence passed was death by
crucifixion."

> "The Lord Hawkshaw of Brinoa will be
> informed by raven of the verdict. I am sure the
> people of Glengloam Village will be pleased to
> hear that the Queen's justice was promptly
> dispensed by her noble and righteous arm of the
> law."

Paolo relinquished a hushed scoff in response to the old
man's words,

> "Yes, I'm sure they will revel in the news that
> their one and only village butcher killed their
> one and only village blacksmith."

The old Archivist continued to write while Paolo
rambled on in his brief lamentation.

> "I don't know, think of me what you will, but
> sometimes when I am riding out to these
> peasant villages and townships, I just hope that
> the killer isn't a man for once. In our city, there
> are craftsmen by the dozen. There are only a
> few out there, though, in the Hintergreen and
> wilds. Why can't the culprit be a wild and feral
> beast for once?"

124

As Paolo finished his question, the old Archivist placed his quill in the inkpot and slid a medium-sized wooden chest closer to his station.

"Young man, if wild and feral beasts were stalking men in the country, this organization would be an entirely different order. When I was a young archivist, I had heard many a tobacco tale told over tavern tops while down at the old Cavalier Tavern about the various night-haunts from across the realm. The Cudwytchians of Clevelorn with their forest-dwelling urlagores, or the Turnians with their fang and clawed vermodens. It's all merdo, my boy. Excuse my Solarnian."

Paolo lowered his head and laughed.

"No, you're excused. I understand what you mean."

The Archivist produced a keyring under his cloak and opened the heavy iron padlock on the front of the wooden chest.

Opening the chest revealed the neatly packed and organized treasury of various coinage. Rows of golden crowns, silver scepters, and copper crescent moons glistened from the chest interior as the old man reached for the quill and ink.

"The Royal Order of Coroners request seven-pound sterling scepters and nine copper crescents as tax levied from the Village of Glengloam of the March of Brinoa. You received the amount paid in full, from the village alderman, did you not?"

Paolo pulled open the coin purse and counted the coins within, after which he handed the brown leather purse into the outstretched hand of the Archivist. The old man weighed the purse with the palm of his hand, and once satisfied with the weight, he poured the coins onto the book's pages, counted them for good measure, and neatly placed them in their respected slots.

> "The reality is not a truth most men want to hear. The only monsters and beasts that prowl the dark crevasses of the land is man himself. Now, for your inquest and arrest, you, Coroner Paolo Reveré, are owed the amount of two-pound sterling scepters and two copper crescents."

Paolo continued documenting the filed inquest number and transaction in his notebook. If this had been any other day, in any other year, he would have agreed with the old man.

But after his eyes beheld the abomination from the flesh pits, it was better to let the old man's word dissipate in silence. Finishing his documentation, he answered the senior Archivist's next question before it was asked by the man.

> "Just hand me half and put the rest toward my room and board fees, please. It's dangerous to be about Calitoria with that kind of coin in one's pockets."

The old man handed over the coroner's wages back to him in the brown leather purse and placed the rest of it in an envelope. Sealing the envelope with wax, the

Archivist was halfway through writing the post address before letting out a sharp cackle in delight.

"Ah-ha, I see what you did there. Very clever, young man, very clever. To think, a rogue or ruffian attacking a uniformed coroner on the street over silvers and coppers. What a delicious thought. With that complete, is there any other service I may provide you with Coroner Paolo?"

Paulo returned the coin purse to the same pouch on his brigantine from whence it came while pondering on career and age again.

"Yes, Archivist, there is. After seeing my career file there, would you say I am old for a resurrectionist?"

The Archivist returned after placing the book on the opposite desk and adjusted the dials on the magnifying opticals.

"Old? How difficult do you find it to relieve yourself while standing at the pot?"

The Archivist placed his hands on both his hips as he waited for the Resurrectionist to reply. Paolo stared in silence back briefly before stuttering out a reply.

"Well, I meant career-wise. But to answer that oddly specific question, I have absolutely no issues relieving myself."

The Archivist gave out another sharp cackle at Paolo's nervous response.

"Well, you aren't old then! Regarding career-age? That's bullshit too. Just do your duty to the crown, and the divine mother will guide your destiny."

Paolo thanked the Archivist, tipped the brim of his hat, and turned from the counter to put away his notebook and pencil.

Problems with relieving yourself, he thought to himself while snapping the closure shut on the pouch for his personal ledger. *I hope I am cut down in the field before anything like that happens. Sounds intolerable.*

Before Paolo could take a step, the counter window slid open again in a rattling fury. Paolo quickly turned to be greeted by a different robed archivist. This one had the voice of a young woman.

"Are you Coroner Paolo Reveré"

The young Archivist sounded slightly out of breath as she requested the coroner's identity.

"yes, I am. Is there something I can assist you with, Archivist?"

"I have a message for you."

She reached across the counter with an outstretched hand and handed Paolo a folded piece of parchment.

Paolo took the parchment from her hand. Turning it over, he could see the small envelope enclosed behind a melted red wax seal. The seal bore

128

the stamped crest insignia of the Worshipful Branch of Steel, his branch. He quickly thanked the Archivist for her service before opening the sealed parchment.

The women bowed in return and shut the frosted window behind her. The sound of her receding footsteps faded before finally being silenced by the opening and closing of a heavy wooden door deep within the clerk's office. He broke the seal and opened the folded parchment to find a neatly scribed message in rich black ink.

Cr. P. R.,
Please report to the Fabrinarum
at your earliest convenience.
There you will meet with
Chief-Weaponsmith Evangelo Torcello.
There you will be properly outfitted
for your upcoming inquest.
-C.S. Cr. G

It was a queer message from the Chief Surgeon, as no coroner besides quartermasters were allowed into the Fabrinarum.

The Archivist who held the rank of Quartermaster was a peculiar lot, cursed with a special touch of genius that bordered on madness. Their entire career was spent toiling and tinkering away in their subterranean workshop, leaving only the young novitiates and doddering or cantankerous elder members to man the Cage on the surface floor of the Praetorium.

Very few were allowed to pass the gate and venture into their hovel, so whatever clandestine agreement the Chief Surgeon had arranged with this Chief Weaponsmith Evangelo must be coming from an entity of the highest-ranking. Paolo folded the parchment back up and began to make his way to the Fabrinarum. Paolo had arrived at the central rotunda of the Praetorium, passing through the main hallway archway and descending the grand stairwell.

The Noonday sun shone through the crystal glass windows of the cupola above to illuminate the central rotunda's black and white marble stone. The gentle rays of the sun's incandescent light graced the side of the giant statue of the sword and crescent moon-wielding goddess, who stood looming over any who would gaze upon her from both floors of the Praetorium. High above, the immense murder of order ravens circled the head of the Goddess Myrina.

Some sat perched on her arm, others on the great stone raven which sat perched on her giant right shoulder. As the ravens flew in concentric patterns high below the glass ceiling, their immense murder would blot out the sunlight as they passed in front of the light. Forming brief moments of darkness. Paolo descended the second flight of stairs behind the great statue of the goddess, which led to the front of the statue's base. Glancing at the white marble ground, he observed that the three hallways to his remaining cardinal directions were marked by three large crest insignias hewn into the marble floor with black marble tiles and silver inlay.

The hallway to his left was stamped with the badge of the Worshipful Branch of Shadows, bearing the sigil of a horned serpent coiled around a straight-bladed dagger dripping with venom.
The great steel doors down that hallway would lead to Apothecarium and Order greenhouse, where the Mortalist Apothicarians would prepare all the plants, herbs, toxins, and alkaloids used in the coroner arts.

To his south, he observed that the hallway floor bore the crest insignia of the Worshipful Branch of the Shield, the sigil of a roaring bear head. The heavy iron and wood doors would lead Paolo back to the Tablinum dungeons, where Martials practice their torturous trade of confession acquisition and manage the subterranean holding cells. Finally, to his right was the crest insignia bearing the badge of the Worshipful Branch of Chronicles.

The sigil of the open tome with quill beneath crossed hammers informed him that the red-painted double doors would lead him to the dwellings of the lifeblood of the Order, the Archivists. As he walked over the sigil, Paolo looked down and read the inscription on the shield crest. Written in metallic banded in-lay, the words

TOTUS QUAD VINDRAS

Paolo quoted the inscription first in old Solarnian, then muttered the words in the common tongue.

"For the Race of Men."

Paolo scoffed before continuing muttering to himself.

"Fitting that their crest would quote the dying words of our founding member. Syr Beniamo would roll in his grave if only he saw what had become of his founding branch 900 years from his timeline."

The Resurrectionist passed through the red doors and continued down a long hallway before arriving at a junction.

Ahead were the doors to the Archivum, the ancient and grand library of the Order. To the right were the lower lecture halls of the Academy, as well as the Officarium of Scribes. Paolo turned sharply left and made his way to the Order's stable yard and Fabrinarum. Passing through a set of double doors, he had arrived at the narrow hallway which led to the stables and workshop entrance. The hall was filled almost wall to wall with fellow coroners.

Rows of black capotain, tricorn, and slouch hats covering white raven-beaked masks filled his view as he tried to navigate his way to the Cage's entrance. Pushing past the line of fellow Resurrectionists and other coroners who were either returning or departing, he had finally arrived at the access to the Cage.

Approaching the door to the Cage, Paolo overheard the sound of two familiar female voices. The voice of the woman who was speaking the most he recognized as the Librarian from earlier, while the other was that of the fellow Resurrectionist who recently most likely just finished limping away from a Council hearing with no pay. As he passed the two women, he could read that these two women were close, most likely friends from Academy.

"Don't you two have work to do?"

Paolo's sharp interjection forced the Librarian to stop mid-sentence while the one known as Atrionna pushed herself off the wall with a slightly alarmed demeanor.

Before either of them could produce any rebuttal to Paolo's rhetoric, he left them in the hallway, scoffing and muttering before shutting the door to the Cage behind him. The coroner approached the counter and banged on the iron bars of the sliding window until a quartermaster appeared from around a wooden shelf behind the counter.

> "Hello, cage-keeper, I am Coroner Paolo Reveré. I was recently informed that I was expected here."

The Quartermaster sat down the tools in their hand and moved around the shelves in the back and out of Paolo's sight.

After a series of metal doors opening and closing, followed by the sound of keys cranking open heavy padlocks, the entrance to the right of the cage window opened with an ear-piercing noise of metal grating on stone. The cage-keeper then appeared from the doorway and beckoned Paolo to follow them through the open door.

The Resurrectionist stepped through the iron gate entrance and waited for the Quartermaster to lock the door behind them before setting off down the narrow corridor ahead. To his left, Paolo could see the expansive interior of the Cage.

Wooden shelves lined with various tools of the coroner trade, all cataloged and tagged with thread-bearing bits of parchment tied to canes, firearms, masks, armor pieces, and the like. More Quartermasters toiled inside the Cage at the various workshop tables as the ringing of small hammers filled the room and poured out into the narrow hall. The two coroners continued down the aisle, Paolo in close tow behind the cage-keeper until they reached a widening in the corridor that led into a storage room.

Bins, boxes, and sacks lined shelves and could be found stacked neatly on the floor, all labeled with various strange symbols. If Paolo had to make a hypothesis on the origin of the peculiar ideograms, he would speculate that this was some form of shorthand symbol writing that the Quartermasters had created and then perfected over the centuries.

The warehouse had three doors, one to each side and a final entry on the far side of the room. The room to the right had a steel placard hanging above the doorframe that read stables. The placard, over the top of the far side doorway, read receiving docks. And finally, the door on the right bore a large overarching steel placard that bore the words,

TES FORTICUX

Paolo read the words in his mind in the common tongue, *the foundry*.

"Follow me. We're going this way."

The Quartermaster said while stopping and pointing to the door on their left with a thick gloved finger.

"Also, do not, at any point, wander off. Stay close behind me. Touch nothing, no matter how tempting. Everything in here can, and will, kill you. Just keep your hands to yourself and your eyes focused on me. The last thing I want to do is spend the rest of my shift scraping up Resurrectionist off the floor."

The brawny apron-wearing Archivist sounded as cantankerous as the Quartermaster he had spoken to recently. Paolo started to think it was a part of their recruiting process for becoming Quartermaster. With a silent nod of agreeance from Paolo, the two men made their way toward the door on the left.

The Fabrinarum

<u>Under the Praetorium</u>
12th Hour of the 82nd day

As the Quartermaster turned the key within the lock, the latches within the thick iron doors clanked and finally gave way with a pounding thud. The Quartermaster returned the key to his apron pocket and opened the heavy iron door enough for the two men to pass through. The connecting hallway was more expansive than the previous one and dark as the abyss. Not a single torch or sconce lined the long and wide hallway. The Quartermaster shut the door behind them before the last inking of light was absorbed into the vermillion crystals within his ocular lenses.

With the door finally sealed shut, the room transitioned from dimly lit to entirely illuminated with a scarlet tint. It had always amazed Paolo, the borderline supernatural capabilities of the vermillion crystal.

A single minecart shaft was in the center of the flat declining hallway, which the two men moved around and hugged the wall as they descended the side of the cart path.

"Not a fan of torchlight, I take it."

Paolo broke the silence between the two as they continued to descend the dark, cold, and damp stone corridor. The Quartermaster only grunted out a sharp response,

"Torches are fire, the fire ignites saltpetyr and brimstone salts, ignited saltpetyr and brimstone salts explode, explosions kill novitiates and dipshits. The death of grunt labor decreases productivity. And gets you yelled at. So, no torches. Does that satisfy your obnoxiously inquisitive mind?"

Paolo only remained silent in response to the man's reply. His guide's course nature was starting to get on his last nerve.

Finally, the two men reached the end of the hall and arrived at a set of even taller and thicker iron doors. The Quartermaster walked around a parked minecart and called out to a novitiate sitting next to a large wooden wheel connecting to a chain pulley to open the doors. The young novitiate hopped up from his stool and hastily began to turn the wheel with all his might.

The grinding of hidden gears and rattling of heavy iron chains began reverberating off the corridor walls as the immense iron doors slowly gave way and opened outward from the two coroners. Paolo could see the makings of a great cavern as the doors opened. They crossed the threshold and entered a large, caged platform held within a steel scaffold tower. A small door enclosed the two men within the cage.

After another loud bellowing shout from his guide to more novitiates below, the sound of more gears and chains rang out in the cavern hall as the platform was lowered down to the ground floor of the foundry. Paolo looked around him in astonishment at the various stalagmites and stalactites that lined the walls and ceiling of the great hall.

Hewn into the stone walls were forges of blackened iron. Smelters twisted and snaked around anvils and water troughs as the sound of heavy hammers rang out like a carefully orchestrated symphony. These men and women were no mere tinkers and toilers, they were musicians, and their song was the shaping of steel and iron. Exiting the cage, Paolo followed his guide through the foundry, glancing around to absorb the wonderment of seeing how every asset and tool of their trade was crafted. They passed armorers benches, where Quartermasters sat pounding small plates of burnished steel into leather brigantine vests.

Workbenches were lined with lustrous steel rods hammered and shaped into cane components. Grinders spun, and sparks flew as Lister knives were shaped and sharpened for dissecting flesh and bone.

The two continued past great iron kettle smelters that, when tipped, would pour its pyroclastic contents into great iron ammunition presses. Bullets of every size lined the adjacent workbenches, from 175 grain to half-stone canon shot. Kegs of brimstone salts, and saltpetyr salts, sat on wood and metal racks, ready to dispense the exact measurements needed to press the brass firing caps of the various firearm rounds used in the field.

It was indeed a wonder to behold, and Paolo wished he could stay and observe everything around him if the time permitted. Passing from the foundry, the two men entered the adjacent craft hall. There were more benches, workstations, firing parlors, and other weapon and armor testing stations. As they rounded the rows of shelves lined with bins containing mixed metal and leather parts and components, Paolo began to hear the shrill sound of a distinct voice from the other side.

138

"No, no, no. Don't touch that. I want you to attach the screw blade to the opposite side of the bracer. WHY? Because I said so. Can't you see that the distal radial protuberances and the ulnar distal ulnar protuberance are inversely arranged from the central fulcrum? ARE YOU BLIND!"

With the final shout from the mouth of an apparently crazed individual, a wrench came hurdling through the air over Paolo, forcing the resurrectionist to duck his head in reflex. The tool clanged off the stone floor as Paolo turned to see where the commotion was coming from.

A tall and, almost alarmingly, slender coroner stood looming over a cowering novitiate gripping a wooden stool in fear. Paolo noted the man's queer uniform, which was extensively modified from the standard archivist uniform worn by most quartermasters. His robes were altered, hemmed, and tailored to expose more of his slender forearms.

Though none of his skin was told, as it was forbidden while a coroner was on duty, he barely met uniform policy. His only protective layer was a long-sleeved linen undertunic and thick leather gloves. He wore a leather vest, which was the oddest sight, which was lined with rows and rows of queer and peculiar instruments the like of which Paolo had never seen.

Pencils and chalk could be seen crammed and tucked in various locations, as well as different small books he had strapped into custom-made leather belts that hung from his waistbelt and even strapped to his thigh. His hat was a tall stovepipe capotain with an upright turned brim over his left eye and banded with what looked like a women's garter belt. Tucked into the garter belt was another short thick book and more coarsely sharpened pencils of various lengths. As the cowering novitiate, which Paolo assumed to be his assistant, moved their backside toward him and the cage-keeper. The ranting and raving quartermaster was forced to turn to maintain eye contact with his target of verbal abuse.

As the madman came into full inspection, Paolo could see that his coroner mas was missing the left ocular lens. Paolo could easily see an almost glowing, bloodshot, and spasmodically twitching fiery hazel eye as it darted around at such a speed that it almost made Paolo motion sick. The man continued in his ravings.

> "If we crafted this contrivance following your idiotic design, the blade's length would produce a perpendicular impact point with canceling translational and rotational forces at the sliding pivot point, which is AFTER THE IMPULSE has been factored in, might I add. The percussion center on this blade design would not be at the tip, but at one-third of the length creating…."

The man suddenly stopped in ravings mid-sentence and snatched a pencil from the apron of the cowering novitiate, who jolted back in fear at the animalistic ferocity of the now muttering madman.

He fell to the hard stone floor and started using the stones as his personal parchment, scrawling across the ground a cacophony of letters, symbols, and numbers, all while enshrouded in a myriad of sputtering gibberish and cackling. Finally, he wrote the

140

number 120, circled it, and jumped to his feet with
arms held high.

"HA, HA! LUXOS! It's genius, genius, I say!"

The man whirled around, grabbed the terrified novitiate
by the shoulders, and pulled them up to their feet
continuously.

> "Margaretta, you are an absolute genius. This
> design is perfect. Why would you ever doubt
> yourself? I would never have selected you from
> the sea of degenerate mouth-breathers if I
> thought you were some sniveling, cowering ball
> of disappointment! NO! you knew that I would
> conclude that the percussion center would be at
> the optimal distances for both linear velocity
> speeds and rotational velocity to maintain
> proportional elastic properties! Therefore, the J-
> hinge must be calibrated to dispense the
> contrivance at 120 degrees! My sweet, sweet
> Margaretta never doubts your bright young
> mind again. Now run along and get yourself
> food, whatever meal is appropriate depending
> on the hour and position of the celestial bodies."

The novitiate was equally confused as she was
stunned at the absolute showcase of mood polarity the
man had undergone. The poor girl could only stammer
in response before the man turned around to notice her
standing before him and shooing her off with both
hands to return to deep thought. As the novitiate
hurriedly passed, Paolo and the cage-keeper tried to
hold back either tears of joy or tears of sadness.

The cage-keeper stepped forward to announce their arrival to the mad man.

> "Chief-Weaponsmith Evangelo, I have brought you that Resurrectionist you wanted to see, sir."

Paolo could not help at let out a low laugh at hearing what his guide had just said. This stark raving mad man is the commanding officer of the entire Fabrinarum? This is an absolute lark.

The cage-keeper sharply turned to acknowledge that he had heard Paolo's laugh but turned back to his commander and bowed before leaving Paolo with his new host. The resurrectionist stood in silence, waiting for the man to acknowledge his presence but was only met with a cold shoulder and the hushed whispers of what sounded like mathematical equations coming from the hunched over chief-weaponsmith as he continued to study his scribblings. Growing tired of waiting, Paolo slowly approached the man but ensured to keep at least an arm's reach away before loudly clearing his throat.

Chief weaponsmith Evangelo did not budge from muttering his mathematical incantations but did finally offer a reply to Paolo.

> "Margaretta, could you please run-up to the Apothecarium and fetch me more anthemene salts. I am running low, and there is far too much work to be done for sleep to get in the way now."

Paolo was not shocked to hear this, as Evangelo elicited all the signs and symptoms of a man addicted to anthemene salts.

"So, Chief-Weaponsmith Evangelo, you are
happy with the work of the novitiate?"

The question seemed to draw the man out of his stupor
and force him to turn and face Paolo. His exposed
bloodshot eye scanned Paolo wildly, dilating,
constricting, and oscillating between the two states
before finally blowing out to a broad black pit.

"You, my good man, are not my assistant. YOU
are a resurrectionist, not a Quartermaster! Who
let you down here?"

Paolo remained firmly planted and unphased by the
twitching chief, establishing an immediate report that
he was not a novitiate, by rank, or by emotional
fortitude.

"You did. Chief Evangelo."

Paolo gave a sharp, calm, and firm reply, ensuring not
to make any sudden movements. The weaponsmith
eyed him again, but his pupil returned to a standard
size, and the furrowed brow above it relaxed in tension.

"Oh, why didn't you say so. Well, welcome to
the foundry, coroner… whatever your name is.
Wait, who are you again?"

"Coroner Paolo Reveré, resurrectionist."

The man cocked his head, and his gaze turned upward
as if lost in momentary thought. He began to mutter

again before snapping out of it and meeting the eye of his guest once more.

>"Ah, that is right. Paolo Reveré, the Resurrectionist. You are Galini's new man for the job. How wonderful to finally meet you."

Evangelo approached Paolo with an outstretched hand, and the two men shook hands.

>"I apologize if I had kept you waiting, but I am very behind on these prototype weapons for Shadow Branch, and I have been working on it for seven days straight without rest."

"Seven days? Without sleep?"

The sound of Paolo's wholesome concern forced Evangelo to look back at him again from his equations.

>"Well, what day is it, again?"

"It is the 82nd day of Empyripas, around noonday."

The man's exposed eye darted in thought before snapping back to Paolo.

>"Oh, nope, my apologies, I was wrong. It has been eleven days, but if that Margaretta can get back here with my anthemene, we can finish this up in no time, and I can move on to those rotational saw designs. Ha, ha."

Paolo was utterly astonished at the sheer fact the man standing before him wasn't dead, let alone in a

144

catatonic comatose state. Anthemene was a powerful substance used in life-threatening situations in the field to enhance the performance of a coroner.

This man used it to doodle equations on the stone floor and tinker in his workshop. It was intolerable and offensive, but there was nothing that Paolo could do about it is that he was heavily outranked by the chief weaponsmith. Taking a deep breath, Paolo shrugged off the offense and moved to finish his business in the foundry.

> "I was told to come to see you about some alterations to my equipment and gear for the inquest I am about to embark on. Can we conclude that business so I can be on my way and let you get back to your stargazing, Chief-weaponsmith?"

Evangelo squatted down to the floor and drew more strange glyphs on the ground while continuing to mutter before standing up, tucking the stolen pencil into free space on his vest, and beckoning Paolo to follow him.

> "Ah, yes. Of course. You resurrectionist and your toys. Come with me, Coroner Paolo. I have something you will love."

Paolo followed Evangelo down the second great hall until they had both arrived at a blue iron door bearing a plaque that read the private laboratorium of the chief weaponsmith. A key was produced, a lock was opened, and the two men entered the brightly lit chamber. The room was filled with desks, tables, tools, benches, and supplies. But something drew Paolo's attention to the center, something so outstanding that it made everything else disappear in his periphery. On the table in the center of the room, resting on a wooden stand, was a blunderbuss, the likes of which Paolo had never seen.

The sight of beholding the weapon froze him in his tracks, and his stunned reaction was not lost on the Chief-weaponsmith, who moved around the opposite side of the table in preparation for a showcase. The firearm was crafted from nothing other than that of Kreiger steel, the most precious metal in all of V. That much was apparent to Paolo.

The metallic sheen of the barrels, receiver, and trigger guard could not be mistaken for anything other than Kreiger steel. The forearm and comb were constructed from hardy Cudwytchian oak, which he could also tell. The exact design of the firearm exuded such a profound sense of mystical craftsmanship and design.

Paolo slowly approached the table of the gun to get a better inspection.

> "I see you have taken notice of my little slaying machine, Coroner Paolo. It brings me joy to know that it was able to catch even a resurrectionist tongue."

"What is this?"

Paolo uttered in a state of bewilderment.

> "This, my friend, is a firearm. But it is not your typical blunderbuss or blundercanon of the Order. No, no, no. This firearm is the future of the Order. This is my greatest work and the

146

exclamation mark I shall leave on the world when I shed this mortal coil."

The weaponsmith paused for breath before giving his long-winded breakdown of its features.

"As you can see, this is a 4-span long firearm, similar in the overall design of the stock standard blunderbuss but with numerous modifications. Instead of the blunderbuss break-action, breech-loading receiver, this is fitted with a falling block, breech-loading receiver with a side lever trigger guard. The striking hammer is still present but notes two striking hammers, one on each side. That is because instead of the single, large-bore barrel of the blunderbuss, you instead of two octagonal, large-bore, over-under barrels with a single bead pin site."

Paolo found himself almost alarmingly aroused by the complete breakdown of the firearm's vast list of specifications. Clearing his throat, Paolo motioned toward the gun and requested if he could pick the weapon up and inspect it. Evangelo gleefully agreed and unhooked the two latches that kept the gun in place on the stand. Paolo first gripped the forearm with his right and then the comb with his left.

The wood felt smooth in his thin leather gloves as he effortlessly lifted the large hulking weapon off the stand. Kreiger steel was the most precious metal in all realms, mined and crafted in the Kingdom of Kreiglan, far over the northern Birgine Mountain range, which separated the two kingdoms. Kreiger steel was light in weight, which was what most coroner armor and weapons were crafted from, except the armor of the Martials.

As he inspected the intricate design of the firearm, Paolo humbly requested that the weapon-smith walk him through the load and reloading process.

> "Of course, there is a small shooting parlor here in my laboratorium if you would like to test its bite yourself."

Paolo fervently agreed and followed the chief weaponsmith to the small, single-laned shooting parlor. As they approached the stall, Evangelo kicked a wooden trim level with his foot which spurred into motion a series of gears, cogs, and rope to raise up a platform carrying a white statue bust of the famed Solarnian composer Senoré Vivalto Tocatta. On the counter was an ornately decorated wooden box, which Evangelo opened to reveal a red felt inlay with freshly crafted ammunition rounds in neatly spaced rows. He reached into the box, pulled out two lead slugs, and handed the ammunition to Paolo.

> "To load the weapon, pull down on the side-lever bar. The long metal bar below the comb also acts as your trigger guard. Right, excellent. This will drop the fall-block and open the receiver up so that you can properly load the firearm."

Paolo pulled down on the slender steel bar with a quick thrust of his right hand, sending the block down and dropping the receiver forward slightly to reveal two large vertical holes. The lead ammunition was more

148

prominent in circumference than typical blunderbuss
rounds and felt four times as heavy.

"What kind of ammunition is this?"

Paolo asked while rolling the finger-length lead ballista
in-between his fingers.

"Standard-issued rounds come in 175 grains for
the resurrectionist's blunderbuss. On the other
hand, this firearm fires a 350-grain cylindrical
round."

Paolo could only chuckle as the words left the
weaponsmith's mouth.

"You jest, this will surely break my wrist.
Firepower like that is for brutish martials, not
resurrectionists."

"I never Jest when it comes to ammunition, master
Paolo. And never worry about bodily harm or
kickback. The reverberation suppression of Kreiger
steel coupled with the Cudwytchian oak wood was
chosen specifically to reduce recoil and maximize
suppressive fire while maintaining an attacking
advantage on your foes."

Paolo slid the first round into the top receiver, before
loading a second round into the bottom chamber.

"Now, pull back up on the side lever to bring
the fall-block up and lock the receiver in place.
Good, now pull back on both hammers until
you hear a click and feel the dual triggers lock

in place. Excellent, now my lad, you are ready to fire. Now, you can fire from the hip or point and aim the weapon for mid-range accuracy of over fifty yards. I recommend aiming at Senoré Tocatta's head there, fire when ready."

He slowly raised the firearm to his cheek and took aim down the pin sight, controlling his breathing. Paolo held his breath at the top of his exhalation and squeezed the trigger. The large hammer came down in a flash of controlled sparks before a loud concussive blast came booming from the behemoth weapon.

The statue bust of Tocatta erupted into a cloud of white smoke and debris, leaving nothing but a few pebbles and a piece of nose lying on the platform down the parlor lane.

"That was dead-on accurate. Also, I didn't even feel a thing!"

Paolo was awestruck by the performance of the firearm. Pulling down on the side lever, the fall-block dropped and sent two spent brass caps flying out the back of the now exposed and smoking receiver.

"This is genius, Chief-weaponsmith, purely genius."

Evangelo reached over to a second box and opened the lid with a flick of his wrist.

"Oh, Paolo, there is more."

"More?"

Evangelo retrieved a slender, rectangular, metal box with a flanged edge on one side.

> "Go ahead and squeeze in the forearm grip until you hear a click, then slide the forearm backward toward you."

Paolo did as he was instructed, and as the forearm grip slid back on the tracks, two hidden crossbow arms shot out from an unobtrusive metal housing below the second barrel, followed by the snap of a thick metal wound bowstring. Paolo could not believe his own eyes at the intricacy of the design as he eyed the crossbow attachment with widened eyes.

Evangelo held the top barrel steady as he slapped the metal box into the base of the crossbow until there was a secondary click.

"Cartridges are loaded into the crossbow housing through the bottom, don't worry about obstruction. The forearm slide has a cut-out on the underside, preventing that from happening. Now set the crossbow with a bolt after loading the cartridge, pull back on the forearm slide, and notice the arms come with you. Now once you hear that clunk, the bowstring has been hooked. Now push the slide forward until the bowstring is taught. Don't worry about the bolt. They are automatically fed into the track with a separate internal mechanism. When ready, you aim the weapon and squeeze the forearm grips inward to release the bolt. Reloading is just as simple as repeating that process."

The chief weaponsmith kicked another lever with his boot to reveal a second statue bust. Paolo took aim, and after squeezing in the forearm grip, the cracking noise of the bow twang rang out as it sent a steel bolt hurtling towards the statue bust. The bolt landed directly square in the forehead of the figure, splitting the stone head in half and tumbling to the floor below. Paolo was brimming with a gleeful smile under his mask. This was indeed a marvel of a firearm.

"What have you decided to call this thing, chief weaponsmith?"

Evangelo closed the boxes and returned to the center counter. He bent down, replaced five cases of the various specialty ammunition, and placed them on the counter.

"It is called the Hamherbuss."

Paolo smirked at hearing the name.

"Clever, the Turnian word for the gavel. Correct?"

"Correct. Because sometimes, my lad, when faced with certain circumstances in the field, a coroner must know when to drop the gavel. Cruel men must be met with cruel fates. Is it not the gavel of the arbiters who signals such executions of justice? So, I felt it was a fitting name."

"I couldn't agree more, Chief Evangelo."

Opening the wooden boxes for Paolo to inspect, the weaponsmith began to review his field-issued equipment checklist for Paolo's mission.

152

"Now, I have provided you with five standard ammunition types. You have 300-grain mord rounds, flint, fume, shred, and my favorite, glass-tipped vitriol rounds. You will be provided with two cases of sixty rounds each and four cartridges of Kreiger steel crossbow bolts. The size of the Hamherbuss is substantially larger than your blunderbuss. As such, you have been fitted with a new holster and brigantine rigging system tailored to your most recent measurements to save time. Of course."

Once again, the weaponsmith reached under the table. Returning, Evangelo laid a new black leather brigantine with freshly crafter leather pockets, pouches, and sleeves. Paolo noted the modifications that the large waistbelt was sewn into the brigantine, and there were two thigh holsters, each with their own thigh belts to keep everything close and snug. Chief weaponsmith Evangelo continued in his listing.

"You will also have the standard-issued field ammunition crafting kit, including a specialized brass cap press, which has already been mounted to your cart. The bullets, try not to spend them all. The bolts, try not to lose, any, as a matter of fact. Kreiger steel is expensive. Also, try not to forget that the Hamherbuss is a prototype weapon, so whatever you do, do not lose that firearm. Take it to your grave if you must. Are there any further questions you might have for me?"

Paolo pressed in the forearm slide, returned the crossbow to its housing with a thundering click, and then began to assess the weapon one more time.

"Yeah, I have one more question for you, chief. Can you load the end with silverware?"

The Great East Road

The cart rolled down the cobblestone street of Calitoria's Gate District on the route out of the city. The sun was high in the blue sky, painted over with whisps and streaks of gray clouds. The resplendent rays of the sun pierced through the darkened clouds and reflected off the golden rooftops of the cityscape. The city's white stone and marble walls illuminated the entirety of the Lux Pugna Basin, turning the saltwater of the basin into an aureate beacon of hope and prosperity for all travelers and sailors to the great capital city.

Paolo passed hordes of merchants and commoners, who crowded the city's cobblestone streets in droves. He had never liked departing on an Inquest in the middle of the workday, and if this was any other Inquest, he would have waited till evenfall to leave the city when the streets were most still. But this was no ordinary Inquest, so Paolo and his dray mare had to suffer through the narrow city streets with as much haste as possible.

As the cart turned the final corner of the main road, he passed the last checkpoint and finally departed through the opened colossal golden gates of the city. The entirety of the Royal Bridge was as congested as the main road of the Gate District. Thousands of merchant wagons were backed up as far as Paolo could see, along with a spattering of rickety hand carts and one-horse carts of various peasants around the realm.

Paolo did not envy the city gate guard, as he had noticed the increase in peasants applying for citizenship. Some unknown event had spurred a migration, be it an increase in taxes or population increase. The reason was anyone's guess. Paolo did find it curious that most of the peasants and commoners waiting in line in the city were either Turnian or Cudwytchian. He also found the exodus interesting in that most of these people had little more than their infant children and one traveling bag, which gave him the inclination that times appeared more desperate than he had previously thought.

Passing Arrow Island at the far side of the Royal Bridge, Paolo gave the reins a whip and whistled as the cart started the steep incline up the path.

The Lux Pugna Basin was an immense water-filled crater with a mixture of salt and fresh water. From the Basin Climb path, you could look out and see the entirety of the vast caldera. At least, that was the current theory of how the Lux Pugna Basin was formed. Calitoria sat perched atop an island in the center. Surrounded by a thin, almost invisible crevasse that lined the entirety of the island. A prodigious waterfall, filled with saltwater from the Gulf of Morvano, poured over the eastern basin edge. The cascade was regulated by a league-long dam of white stone known as the Levy. The structure was a marvel of engineering, acting as a dam and a transport of ships bringing trade from other kingdoms.

Ships would enter a partially submerged lock and, through a system of chain pulleys and water wheels, be lifted out of the sea and lowered down into the basin below. This system was imperative to the sustainability of the capital, as, without this structural marvel, Calitoria would be isolated and without trade. The Levy was an ancient structure constructed long before man's arrival to the abandoned island city. No 'ne knows who engineered and built such a colossal structure. The same stood for the City of Calitoria itself.

The crevasse surrounding Calitoria Island's edges had also been recently discovered to be artificially carved out. After scholars and engineers had explored the pit, they found that the basin's water which flowed under the city fell into colossal brass pipes.

These pipes dove deep down to subterranean hot springs. The heat and pressure of the hot springs then pumped the water throughout the city in a separate system of brass pipes and conduits, creating an intricate artificial and natural plumbing system. An entire aqueduct system had also been discovered, leaving the royal engineers confounded. When Paolo learned of this, he was as equally impressed as the scholars and engineers. Paolo reflected that whoever, or whatever, preceded men on the continent of Vetosa were far more advanced in their understanding of structural engineering.

And whenever these ancient ones departed or expired, they took their methodologies along with them. Before the cart reached the top of the basin, Paolo looked out over the city one last time to appreciate its beauty and grandeur.

Far down below, Calitoria sat and radiated with an aura of golden beauty. The Basin Climb peaked over the side of the basin in the center of the Rholhine River waterfall, and after a few more fathoms, the cart left the paving stones and transitioned onto the hard dirt of First March Road.

Far off on the horizon, Paolo could see the eastern border of the North Millwood Green. As his eyes shifted from tree line to skyline, the clouds were also undergoing their own transition. The light grey clouds covering Calitoria were moving towards an ominous shade of obsidian black. There was a storm ahead, and it would make the back half of the trip intolerable for both man and horse.

The far-off lightning flash could also be appreciated hovering over the southeastern horizon of Clevelorn. Paolo was at least thankful that he was not heading in that direction and further hoped that the eye of the storm was moving away from Turnia and staying within the borders of Clevelorn March. The Coroner kept a quick traveling pace, ensuring not to overwork his Brinoan Black this early in the trip. Slowly but surely, the cart moved closer to the eastern tree line of northern Thywyk Forest.

He had reached the first fork of the road by sunset. A large wooden post bore two arrow-shaped signs. The right bear the words Old Solarno, and the left bear the name March of Clevelorn. The cart stayed left and kept on till evenfall. The forest's borders, regionally called the North Millwood Green, came upon them as the sun was slowly going down over the horizon. Paolo hesitated momentarily in his decision to keep traveling onward or stop and camp at the edge of the forest but eventually decided to push on through the night. He wanted to hopefully make it through the North Millwood Green and cross over the Hinderford by dawn.

This would put him on track to reach the first Turnian town of Oberndorf by the following evenfall, barring no interruptions. As the moon peeked over the horizon and illuminated the forest, Paolo could see the curling oak trees surrounding the eastern road on either side as it winded through the Millwood.

He reached into his brigantine and took out his tinderbox. Paolo opened the small brass box, retrieved a striker, and put the tinder box back. The striker ignited flames as he swiped the tip across the side of his boot heel. He lit the lantern hanging by the driver's bench and shook the striker till the flame went out. The warmth of the lamp would be his only comfort on the long road ahead and through the abyssal darkness of the forest.

The night air temperature rapidly plummeted the deeper into the woods the cart traveled. Paolo pulled his cloak as far forward as possible, providing enough protection from the elements. The clouds eventually covered the moonlight, and soon after, the rain started. The Brinoan Black dray horse gave out a loud whinny. The hot steam from the mare's nostrils could easily be seen in the frigid night air.

> "I know, old girl, I know. Konstantina, you have my sympathies, for I am miserable as well. But we are needed and must make haste. So, let's endure this together, and I promise I will make it worth your while."

The horse nickered 'n response and shook the drizzle from her mane as she cantered on down the road, her hoof beats keeping in rhythm with the spinning of the wheel spokes. As they continued down the Great Eastern Road, Paolo began to feel the heavyweight of sleep encroach on his consciousness.

The combination of frigid night air and the lulling sound of the cart's wheels was starting to numb his mind and senses. Paolo struggled to gain control of his eyes, and right before he dozed off on the driver's bench, a familiar noise roused him from the intoxicating pull of sleep. The echoing croak of a raven sounded overhead, and soon his feathered companion joined him after landing on the dashboard of the cart. The blackbird spread its wings and gave out two baritone croaks before tucking its wings back. The raven pecked at the steel knee guard fastened over his trousers.

The sharp, shrilling ding of the bird's beak on the metal armor piece reverberated through the tall oak trees around them, forcing Paolo to sit up from his slumped posture and adequately address him.

> "Nice of you to join us, Corvax. Your timing is impeccable, as per usual. Right on time to enjoy this lovely weather, we are having this evenfall. Cold and rainy, your favorite."

The bird bobbed its head as Paolo spoke, gazing at him with its right eye and then changing to its left. After he finished speaking, Corvax hopped forward and began pecking his knee guard again, increasing the frequency of beak taps as if demanding something from the road-weary Coroner.

> "Oh, you want something. You can't expect to get paid for showing up late on the job, Corvax. We have been over this. You want dinner. You show up on time. It's not that hard."

Corvax spread his wings and let out a series of shrills at his keeper in disagreement.

"Hey, I didn't make the rules. Go shrill at someone else. Okay, fine, I will give you a bite of bread. I can't have you making all this noise. You'll draw too much attention to us."

Paolo reached behind him and slid open a small wooden latched window behind his head. As he turned to look inside for his full rations, something on the road forced his horse to rear back and let out a blood-curdling squeal. Paolo whirled around on the bench enough time to see something standing in the middle of the road.

"Holy Goddess and Mother!"

Paolo reached down and snatched the reins from the dashboard. He pulled back on the reins with all his might and kicked down on the brake with his left boot. The collective efforts of Paolo's driving forced the spooked horse to violently rear and bring the cart to an almost crashi'g halt in the middle of the road. Rearing back, Konstantina got both iron-shoed hooves of her forelegs down hard on the road. As the horse became level again, Paolo rose from the driver's bench and beheld the object of their sudden stop.

It was a little girl. And as the horse stamped its large, feathered hooves at her feet, she didn't move or flinch a muscle. The Child only stared forward with a glassy-eyed stare. Paolo immediately hopped down from the driver's bench and ran to the Child in the middle of the road.

"Child, are you alright? By the Goddess, I could
have killed you. Child? Are you alright?"

His words were as calm as he could make them, even
though the adrenaline was still fresh in his humors from
the incident. As he questioned the Child, she remained
unmoved and unphased, only staring off down the road
with both hands clasped together as if in prayer.

Paolo told the Child to stay put and returned to
the cart for a quick inspection before pulling his cane
from its holster and flinging the instrument open to its
entire length. Quickly he lit the small pommel lantern
and replaced it on the cane for more lighting. Even with
the bright light from his cane, his vermillion lenses
could only see so far through the thick surrounding
woods on either side of the road.

Before returning, Paolo loaded a vile of ether
vapor into the side housing on the end of his cane. A
humane precautionary, only in case the illumination of
his true visage was too much for the Child to bear in
her current state. He returned from the cart to find the
girl had turned around in the road and was now facing
east. The moon had finally peaked from the clouds,
only slightly, but enough to provide a little light on the
pitch-black road. As he slowly walked up, Paolo
observed the skin of the girl's feet and legs displayed
patches of black mortification and dried blood.

Her gown had been torn along the back, with
multiple deep lacerations as if someone had taken to
her with a lash. As he assessed her wounds from a
distance, he felt his stomach drop in his belly, followed
by the welling up of fiery anger. Seeing enough, he
moved around the girl and slowly kneeled before her,
so they were on eye level. Her face was as gruesomely
disfigured as her legs and back.

Cracked lips, bloodshot eyes, and deep bruising of both eye sockets indicated that she had been violently beaten across the face and neck. Paolo could also deduce that it had happened recently, within the past six to eight hours. As he assessed her injuries in silence, ravens sprang up from the treetop and rang out a cacophony of croaks and shrills. From the cart, Corvax joined his brethren in both flight and song.

Paolo looked back to see them wheeling far off down the road.

"Run, mi' lord. Run. They are coming."

The Child finally spoke. Her voice was dry and cracking in the wind. Her eyes remained glassy and frozen behind the pitch-black bruising of their crushed sockets. He reached out and grabbed her shoulder with a warm hand and asked the Child who was coming. The little girl slowly raised her slender porcelain-white arm in response. Extending a boney, trembling finger, she pointed down the shrouded road and parted her cracked, blood-caked lips.

"The *monsters*."

Her statement was as peculiar as it was alarming. What did she mean by monsters? Thought Paolo as he kneeled before the child and began a hurried assessment of her health and capacities.

Placing a soft gentle hand on the pale child's shoulder, Paolo assessed the cold vacuous windows of her eyes.

"Monsters? What mon…"

As the words left his mouth, a sharp and sudden noise rang through the forest. It was from some beast, but a beast Paolo was not familiar with. A howl, but a groan that seemed to match that of the wolf and a whinny of a stallion. First, there were only one of these braying howls. But soon after, it was met by three more. A pack? Whatever these beasts were, they were moving in on their position at a tremendous speed. The snapping of fallen branches echoed as Paolo snatched the little girl off the ground, placed her over his shoulder, and made for the rear of the cart. Paolo rounded the coach and made for the iron cage.

He opened the latch and swung open the cage door. He figured she would be safe inside, but as he turned her around his shoulder and her eyes met the destination, the little girl became overcome with rigors and let out a blood-curdling scream. Paolo tried to calm the Child, but the sight of the iron cage had broken all the Child's fragile faculties. Her cry was met by more braying howls from a distance. Their position was compromised. Failing to calm the Child with words, he squeezed the trigger of his cane.

A blast of ether vapor coated the face of the Child, and within seconds she was unconscious from the sedative. Asking forgiveness from the Goddess, Paolo laid the small Child inside the iron cage, shut the gate, and locked the cage with a key. He knew that whatever was coming, be it man or beast, nothing could break the steel bars of the gaol cage.

Paolo extinguished his lantern and holstered the cane to his thigh. Drawing the Hamherbuss, he pushed down on the lever and dropped the falling block. Paolo removed the mord rounds from the chambers and slid the ammunition into the sleeves on his belt. He drew a flint round from his belt and loaded it into the top chamber.

He locked the receiver in place, raised and aimed the Hamherbuss into the air, and pulled the trigger. A thundering crack from the drop of the firing hammer sent an arc of blindingly bright red flames and smoke sailing into the air. As the flare soared down the forest road, the vermillion crystals of his oculars hummed with latent energy. Paolo could now see the forest as if the sun was illuminating the woods.

"Come, Child. Let us now behold your so-called monsters."

Paolo cranked open the receiver of the Hamherbuss once more, sending the spent brass cap sailing to the mud. Quickly he placed two more rounds into the chamber, slammed the side lever up, and pulled back on both firing hammers. The sight of the soaring flare not only brought illumination to the dark woods but also a more familiar sound, albeit still faint.

The Coroner grew weary of the suspense of what was approaching. Paolo closed his eyes and steadied his breathing, focusing all his conscious power on the slow pounding of his heartbeat. As the thud of his heartbeat grew deeper in tone, it was as if all time and space suddenly stopped around him. The sound of the wind and the rain ceased to exist, as did the birds and the rustling of leaves. The more he focused, the more sounds he eliminated in his mind until there was only the sound of blood pumping in his chest and air in his lungs.

All coroners were trained on the technique of honing, a heightened sensory method that utilizes deep focused meditation to eliminate distractions. Now that

he was in a honed state, the Coroner directed his
hearing toward the familiar sound.

"Bloody…fuc…oroner…find the…. She must be…."

As the voices entered his consciousness, he began to
build a profile of his targets.

*Men, four of them in total. Three are Solarnian in their
early twenties. The other I, hmm, I cannot say.*

From the sound of the shouting men, he expanded on
the surrounding noises. He could hear the clamoring of
metal plates and the clinking of steel weaponry.

*They are donning steel plate armor, chainmail, and
leather. Steel swords in wooden scabbards. It could be
knights, but more likely mounted soldiers.*

Next, Paolo moved on to their mounts. But all
he could hear was the same braying howl as before, but
with the addition of a bone-chilling gurgling noise
when the creature breathed. The sound was growing
louder, even in his honed state. They were drawing
nearer. Slowly, Paolo returned his faculties to a normal
state. The cacophony of noise had always hit like a
flood of water on his mind as he returned to reality.
Shaking his head, the Coroner turned around and
grabbed his mare's reins. Rubbing the inside of the
barrel with his forefinger, Paolo lightly rubbed the
inside of the mare's nostril.

"I know you hate gunpowder, Tina, but there
might be more of it soon, so better prepare
yourself now, girl. Don't need you getting any

166

more spooked. Now listen, if anything happens to me, I need you to turn around and head for the city. You hear me, girl?"

The horse snorted while shaking out her mane before tapping the beak of his mask with her nose.

"That's my girl, now take the cart and head off the road."

Paolo turned back as his horse cut off the road and made it for a thicket of oak trees. After a few moments more, the rays of torchlight pierced through the tree line as several men clad in armor came riding around the corner and down the road at Paolo. The Coroner walked down the road towards them to close the distance and hopefully make his cart less noticeable.

The mysterious men in armor approached Paolo at a thunderous pace before rearing their mounts and stopping before him. The Coroner assessed the strange beasts the men were riding with slightly frightened curiosity. They were horses or some form of an animal that was related to the horse but at the same time could be related to the wolf. From the feathery dark brown fur coats to the broad-set jaw filled with razor-sharp fangs, these saddled mounts loomed over the Coroner like some form of canid beast.

The longer he stared at the beasts, the more unnerving their visage became. Eyes of solid ochre and long pink tongues hung from widened panting jaws. Large snouts with widened nares, equine legs with thick hooves, and peaked ears made up the creature's horse-like qualities. Paolo remained calm and even keeled.

His training forbade him from expressing anything other than stoic while wearing the coroner uniform. No matter how frightening or bizarre, they stood before him.

The men were lined and mounted three abreast across the road with a fourth armored man out in the front. Paolo took him to be in charge. Their armor was worn as expected. Steel plate armor with chainmail lining, which Paolo could now see that it was as black as his uniform.

The tunic that hung over their breastplates bore a strange sigil. As with their bestial mounts, this was one more thing the Coroner had never seen.

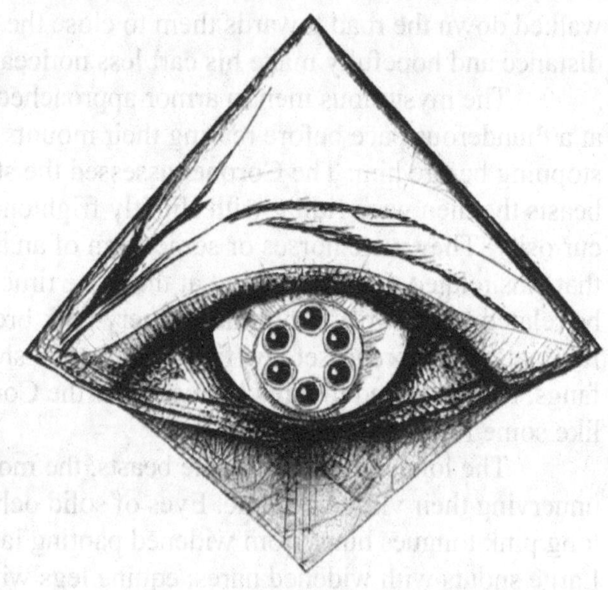

The Polycoric Eye

A red outlined diamond on a black field and a red eye in the center with six red pupils. It was like the Polycoric eye of legend, but Paolo had only heard of such a sigil in books, no one was known to wear such a symbol. Especially one with ties to ancient, vile gods long forgotten by man.

Of the four men, three shared Paolo's relaxed decorum. The man to the far back right of Paolo was behaving a little more fidgety than Paolo was comfortable with. The man in the front of the group held up his torch and looked down to inspect the Coroner.

The steam of his breath jutted from the pores of his helmet visor like stovepipes as the man sat in the saddle in momentary silence. The visored man gave his wolfish mount a spurred kick and rode the creature toward the Coroner. The hot steaming breath of the beast washed over Paolo as the man pulled back on the reins to halt the animal directly in front of him.

"A single raven in the woods. Without his cart
or pony. Are you lost, little raven?"
His voice was almost inhuman.

Course, jagged, and deep. The words came echoing from within his pig-snouted helm in bouts of choking gutturals as if suffocating on each syllable. Paolo kept his eyes fixed on the man while ensuring his peripheral sight contained the concerning man on the end.

"Strange to find a wandering coroner. On foot.
But your business is your own. Such is ours."

The more words that sputtered out, the more stream came spouting from the pours of his helm. They lingered heavily in the cold night air, like the morning fog that rolled off from the moors. As the vapor reached Paolo, the incense in the mask started to ignite. The scent of birch wood and sea salt began to waft toward his nose from within his beak.

"What exactly *is* your business?"

Paolo's question caused the armored man to sit up in his saddle. As he shifted, clanking chainmail in steel echoed in the night air.

> "A runaway came this way. A slave. One of ours. We have been on her heels for hours now. Tell me, Coroner of the Queen's law, have you seen our runaway slave?"

The Coroner rubbed the grip of his firearm with his thumb, thinking carefully of his next move.

> "I don't recognize your sigil. Or your station. Declare yourselves, and I will think about my answer."

The man on the end reached down and gripped the wood handle of his longsword. The sound of tightening leather on wood rushed into Paolo's ear.

> "Tell your man to stay his hand. Or I will."

The armored man gave a guttural chuckle and leaned forward in his saddle.

> "Or you will what, master raven?"

As the man finished his question, a small cry came from the tree line. The girl had roused from her sedative state and started to whimper. As soon as the girl's cry came into the audible range of the men, the helmed man shot bolt upright in his saddle and gripped his reins tightly. Paolo moved before the man's mount and raised his firearm until the barrel leveled with the creature's snout. The knight relinquished the grip on his reins and chuckled once more.

> "Put away your toy, little raven. And hand over our slave. Or we will kill you where you stand. And feed you to our Rholhynian coursers."

"I say we just kill the bastard now."

The man at the end of the line finally showed his true intent and began to unsheathe his long sword. The combustive blast of the Hamherbuss rang out through the silent forest with a thundering crack as a lead slug sent pieces of brain, flesh, steel shrapnel, and bone spraying in every direction. A blood-drenched sword gripped within the hand of a severed arm hit the muddy road. Followed by the blood and tissue drenched, half-decimated torso of the rider. The carcass of the knight came crashing to the earth in a cavalcade of clanging metal and gurgling slops of butchered flesh.

The bestial courser looked to see their master in pieces. The eyes of the mount ignited like ember as it let out a ferocious whinnying howl and turned to charge at the Coroner. Another thundering crack rang out as the creature was blown almost in half by the second mord shot, sending bits of blood, skull, and spine hurdling into the woods. The Coroner was quick in his reload, rapidly popping two more rounds into the chamber. Raising and pointing the loaded firearm, Paolo spoke once more to the helmed man next to him.

> "Now, see, I warned you to tell them to stand down. I am done with warnings. Now tell me your names and stations or meet the same fate."

The helmed man pulled back on his reins and wheeled his courser around the opposite direction, grunting and cursing loudly. He rode up to the other armored men and stopped to bark orders at them.

> "Kill the raven and bring me back the girl. Or don't come back at all."

The helmed man spurred the wild courser and took off down the road. The other two men looked at each other with shared frightened expressions before facing back towards the Coroner.

Their eyes reeked of fear, and their heartbeats were palpable even at Paolo's distance. The one motioned for his sword but second-guessed his action and rested his gauntlet on the bridle.

> "We don't have to do this, Lawrence. We can just go back. I don't want to die over some stupid child. Did you see what he did to Jacobi? Blew his sarding body entwine with that contraption!"

The one boy's fear appeared to give courage to the other, who eyed the corner with a look of a hunter tracking a potential prized game.

172

"Go back to what, Kolby? We are third-born sons of lesser lords. This is our one and only opportunity for glory and lands. You heard the Order. I say, fuck this bird beak. His weapon might be powerful, but he can't take us both."

Lawrence spoke with the heroic stupidity of a young man, a young man with a death wish.

Paolo pitied them and hoped that they saw reason before actions led them both to an early grave. Before Paolo could have a chance to speak sense to them, the boy named Lawrence reached for his sword handle and gripped the wood with a steeled fist. Two shots rang out, and the boys rolled off the back of their wolfish mounts.

The carcasses of the coursers lay in the mud, twitching and headless, blood pulsating from the exposed arteries. Paolo reloaded and approached the boys, who lay in heaps of plate and chainmail, gripping and licking their wounds. The Coroner reached down with one hand and pulled the one called Lawrence up to knees, keeping the barrel of the Hamherbuss pointed at his chest. Spitting, the boy laughed in a shrill cackle at the sight of the Coroner.

"How about you put away that weapon and face me like a real man. You coward. Plus, why do you even care what we do with peasants and their brats? Her mother got to lay with a noble-born lord, but that sniveling shit had to go and cause a fuss. So, we did what we had to do to keep the rabble down. No one will weep for a broken whore and her broken whelp. You have no authority to bring us justice, raven. We are protected by birthright."

The Coroner threw the young man back down into the mud and holstered the firearm.

"On your feet, boy, quick. And pick up your blade."

The once smiling and cackling youth ceased in his reveling. Turning as pale as milk, Lawrence looked at his friend.

"Just let us go, master coroner. He didn't mean what he said. Honest."

The other tried to reason, but all Paolo could think of was a severely battered and broken little girl in his cart, and his blood was once again starting to boil. Paolo pulled tightly on his leather bracer and gauntlet so that the tips of his fingers were snug and the leather taut on his hands.

"I said, on your feet. Boy. Pick up your steel."

Lawrence rose with newfound confidence and grabbed the steel sword lying below him in the mud.

He gave the long sword a few twirls in his hand before slowly advancing on the Coroner's position. Paolo stood upright and planted firmly in the mud, awaiting the boy to make the first move. Lawrence looked back at his friend and turned to face the corner. Paolo swiftly advanced in the few moments that the young man was turned. As Lawrence turned his head, a crushing blow from Paolo's right hand shattered the young man's nose.

Blood erupted from his face, and he reached to cover his nose. As the boy's hands rose, Paolo grabbed his right hand and disarmed Lawrence of his longsword. Delivering a multitude of swift jabs sent the young man to his knees, gasping for air. A final thrust to the broken nose from the Coroner's knee sent Lawrence flying onto his back, rendering him unconscious.

"No, I don't think so. You haven't learned your lesson yet."

He reached toward his vest and drew a syringe of henbane from a leather pouch.

Taking a knee, Paolo grabbed the young man by the breastplate and pulled his limp head up from the mud. The Coroner drove the needle deep into the jugular vein and the plunger downward with his thumb. In seconds, the once unconscious Lawrence sprang alive and began to writhe and scream in agonizing pain. Paolo only tightened his grip on the young man's breastplate, jerking him around until the boy was forced to see his reflection in the lifeless crimson lenses of the Coroner's mask.

"Who harmed that little girl? Tell me who and why someone would harm little children. Why are you enslaving children? Answer me!"

With each question asked, a crushing blow from the Coroner further concaved the shattered crater of a broken nose. Each crushing blow added an exclamation mark to the series of unanswered questions Paolo demanded from the screaming young knight. Paolo had become gripped in anger and began to drown in his bloodlust and fury.

"You like to harm children? Do you? You like to make them watch as you defile their mothers, their sisters. Do you feel like a man now? Does that make you a chivalrous knight? ANSWER ME!"

The young knight was long past dead as the Coroner delivered blow after blow with his gauntlet-clad fist. Paolo had driven his nasal bone-deep into the skull and into the young man's brain moments ago but was blinded by pure rage to see what he had done. The sound of retching and vomit from Kolby brought Paolo out of his rage-induced interrogation.

The Coroner looked down to see that his fist was striking nothing but bone and tissue-drenched earth. Paolo rose from his knees, panting heavily from within his mask, his head swirling from the adrenaline. Kolby wiped the vomit from his mouth and started to run from the Coroner, making a break for the tree line.

Paolo looked up and began to make chase after him. Through the thicket of the forest and in the dead of night, the poor Kolby stood no chance of escaping the Coroner.

With the ability to see in the dark, Paolo quickly closed in on the boy, and with a quick toss of a throwing dagger, it sent the armored young man hurdling toward the bramble patch before him. Kolby turned in the mud and the thorns, tears running down his dirt-covered face. The blade had severed his spine, and the boy had lost control over his legs. He tried to crawl away, screaming in terror at the sight of the approaching corner. Paolo's vermillion lenses reflected a blood-chilling crimson red under the wide brim of his hat.

The drenched beak of his mask was dripping with thickened droplets of blood as a melting candle drips wax. Paolo drove the heel of his boot into the shoulder of the trembling youth, pinning him to the forest floor. The Coroner bent down and slowly pulled the young man up till his face was near the tip of his beak, his friend's blood dripping onto his forehead.

"Tell me everything."

Kolby wept as he confessed his deeds to the Coroner. The young knight spoke of the numerous atrocities he and his knightly Order had committed in both the Marches of Clevelorn and Turnia. All of it was done in the name of their Order, the so-called Knightly Order of the Cult of the Personiphi. When Paolo questioned where this Order was from, the young knight did not have an answer.

He and his friend Lawrence were recruited into the Cult as the Order needed noble-born sons to carry weight throughout the realm and protect them from persecution.

"The enslaved people. Where were you taking them?"

"Um…ah, I don't remember."

"Think carefully."

Paolo took the tip of his cane and pressed a button on the side of the shaft. The seven hypodermic needles of the blood leech shot from the hollowed brass tip and plunged deep into the pectoral muscle of the young knight. Kolby screamed in pain and grabbed the shaft of the cane.

> "LAZZAR PERISH! Lazzar Perish. That's where we were taking them. Please, master coroner, make it stop. Please, stop!"

The hamlet's name pierced Paolo's conscious like a bolt through his brain and echoed on as his mind raced in thought. This was no mere coincidence. What did these bandits and their slaving have to do with the pound of writhing flesh he saw back at the Praetorium? There were too many missing puzzle pieces to obtain any form of a clear picture formed just yet.

Paolo stood and adjusted his gloves once more. The sound of paw pads caused his ears to prick up from under the leather and linen hood. The Coroner looked up and saw multiple sets of reflecting eyes through the tree line ahead, each with marching sets of sharp canine teeth.

> "I've told you everything, master coroner, I swear it. Now please, help me. I can't feel my legs."

Paolo cocked his head and slowly bent back down towards the injured knight.

> "That little girl, the one you and your knightly friends left motherless and an orphan. The mortification has set in on her right leg. Did you know that? It will need to be amputated soon if she is going to live. But what kind of life is there for a peasant girl with only one leg? What

chance of survival does an orphaned child with one leg have in this realm?"

Kolby started to sob once more until the sound of growling wolves greeted the two men from the tree line behind them. The knight froze like a statue, gripped in fear. The realization that they were no longer alone in the forest washed over him, turning his skin a lifeless shade of pale.

Paolo kept his eyes fixed on the young man, driving the can deeper to induce a little more blood loss from his trapped prey.

"I would say that little girl has the same chance of survival as a crippled gimp of a man who is pinned down to the ground under the weight of his heavy steel armor. And surrounded by hungry wolves. See, now pay attention, pay attention, brave Syr Kolby. Look at me and hear my words. This little predicament you are in, to me, is true unadulterated justice. Pure justice. That immense fear has seized you, the realization of your fragility. You are alone, abandoned, and forgotten. Crippled and unable to protect yourself. And now the wolves are closing in. I say, Syr Kolby, this is the most proper execution I have ever condemned a man to in my entire career as a coroner."

"NO, no, no. Please, you can't leave me here! Master coroner, please. I am a noble-borne son, from a prominent noble house! This isn't fair!"

"I'll be sure to let the Child know of what you deem as fair, Syr Kolby of the Briar Patch. Now try to keep your voice down. The wolves of Clevelorn only grow

more emboldened when their prey squirms and bleats.
They can sense the fear.

Reva noxi, brave sir knight."

Paolo wiped the blood from his beak, turned from the
young man, and started to make his way back through
the forest.

The wound he had created on the knight's chest
started to ooze and hemorrhage with fresh blood, the
scent of which was beginning to excite the hungry pack
of canids. The wolves slowly moved in on the helpless
knight, encircling his writhing body as he tried to crawl
through the bramble patch towards some form of
safety.

Paolo had almost reached the road when the
sound of blood-curdling screams rang out through the
woods before being drowned out by the barking and
howling of the frenzied feeding pack. The Coroner
made his way up the road and found his horse and cart
near where he had left them.

The sound of his approaching spurs drew a gasp
from the Child, but as he opened the side cabinet door,
his eyes caught hers through the back window. The
construed view of the Coroner through the rear window
was enough to calm the Child's frazzled nerves. Paolo
could hear her breathing come to an even pace as her
small head dropped out of sight, and the Child returned
to her wooden bench seat. Paolo opened and began to
rummage through bags and drawers, which seemed to
calm the Child's frazzled nerves.

He found a clean corpse wrapping cloth and
commenced to clean his armor and leather of the blood,
not wanting to scare the Child more than she already
was. Satisfied with his job, the Coroner shut and
latched the side cabinet door, approached his horse, and

allowed the loyal beast to sniff the blood-soaked rag. Stroking the thick mane of his mare, he soothed her as the horse became familiar with the scent.

"You did a great job, old girl. A damn fine job. I am in your debt once again."

Konstantina responded with a whinnied nicker and brushed her snout against his beak before craning her neck around and nodding towards the back of the cart.

"Always the selfless and noble steed. I know. I will bring the girl up. But let's get this cart back to the road first. Shall we?"

He grabbed the reins gently and guided the horseback to the road, although not perfectly centered, but enough to As he rounded the back of the cart.

Paolo could see that the little girl was wide awake. He opened the iron cage and picked the Child up gently into his arms. Carrying her to the bench seat of the cart, he held her close and whispered into her ear.

"You need not fear the monsters anymore, Child. You are safe now."

Climbing into the bench seat, he sat the Child on the cushion next to him and wrapped her up in his cloak.

After maneuvering, the cart was out of the tree line and back on the road. As they made their way down the road and through the forest, the moon sank over the horizon with the dawn rising.

Paolo again felt the weariness of sleep as they finally passed the last of the Millwood but quickly shook himself of the exhaustion. Looking down, the Child was soundly resting against his side. No longer gripped in fear by the wolves that surrounded her in the dark of the forest. She was safe and would be for the rest of the journey.

=Act II=

"The land, once brimming with golden shafts of wheat, now lay barren. A sickness had taken hold of the people, and the very soil itself. Turnia, our once beautiful agricultural country, was nothing more than a graveyard of windmills…

And rotting corpses."

—Martial Reinhorn
Von Blickensdorf, ROC

Oberndorf

<u>March of Turnia</u>
Kingdom of Solarno
21st hour of the 88th day
Anor 905 P.A.

The remaining journey to Turnia March was thankfully uneventful. As the sun rose and they continued through the northern borders of Clevelorn March, there was no further sign of ruffians. Wherever these slavers were, they had longed departed by the time the Coroner and his cart passed through forest and dale. Paolo did have to stop and make a minor repair on one of the rear wheels. The sudden halting of the night prior had stripped the metal from the felly rim and spokes.

Paolo assessed the damage and was able to hammer it back together with ease. The two were back on the road in no time. The rain had picked up, as did the wind. Luckily the Coroner had packed an extra waxed cloak in his luggage, which he promptly gave the child for the soiled one and wrapped himself up before the storm worsened. Paolo wished he could provide more for the child, not only a change of clothes but in warmth and freshwater. Nothing would bring her parents back.

That was a brutal reality that no amount of charity could mend. Paolo harkened back to painful memories as an orphan in his childhood. He knew he had stepped out of the boundaries of his station and

leaving the corpses of those noblemen on the road
would bring a whirlwind of internal and external
investigators as soon as they were spotted by the first
merchant on the eastern route.

But it was an injustice he could not and would
not stand for. First, the two crossed the Mycine River at
the Hinderford, then continued till the fork of the
Procession Road. A mighty storm hovered over the
City of Aberheim off in the distance, as did a colossal
murder of ravens.

The great mass of blackbirds wheeled over the
city and Bonegrubber village to the west of the city
walls. Paolo had never seen such a gathering of ravens
in the wild before. They reached the second fork and
turned north. By the moon's first light, the cart rolled
over the Ankhlotter Ford and crossed the mighty
Rholhine River. Passing over the long wide stone
bridge, Paolo once again tried to get the child the talk
as his previous attempts were fruitless.

> "What is your name, child? If you don't want to
> tell me anymore, I understand. But will you
> give me the courtesy of your name, at least? So,
> I can call you something other than child for the
> remainder of the trip."

Paolo's Cudwytchian was rusty, but he stayed
persistent.

> "Diffynwyd."

The girl replied after a long pause, keeping her eyes on
the road and her head buried in his side.
Paolo smiled under his mask, happy to have at least a
name.

186

"Diffynwyd. After the flower. It's a beautiful name. Nice to meet you, Diffynwyd. My name is Paolo."

"I know. Your name is here, below your black metal birdy."

Paolo looked down to see the child was holding the matte black broach, which housed his badge of office.

"You read letters?"

The girl nodded her head slowly.

"Mam taught me. And numbers."

The memory brought tears from her eyes, and she buried her head back into the side of the Coroner. Paolo pulled his cloak in tighter and let the girl cry her tears in peace. The cart passed the long stone bridge and cut through a wide path in a slight stretch of trees before finally gracing the wide-open and flat agricultural country. Giant windmills, farm fields, streams, and orchards filled the scenic view of the expansive and fertile March of Turnia as the cart came to the top of a small hill. Down below was the fishing and farming community of Oberndorf, which would be the Coroner's first stop. As the cart rolled along, approaching the quiet village, the numbing grip of exhaustion hit the middle-aged man like a pound of bricks. It had been almost three days without sleep, minus a quick nap here and there.

The warm beds of the inn were a welcoming thought to the Coroner. The wheels passed from dirt road to cobblestone as the village square drew near. Paolo leaned upright to stretch his aching back and steered the horse toward the right side of the roundabout. They had finally arrived at the second largest building in Oberndorf, the Carp-Angler Tavern and Inn. The bright lights of multiple fire spits showed through the frosted windowpanes of the inn and danced across the damp cobblestone street as the cart passed the front of the inn and toward the adjacent livery.

Paolo pulled his cart into the stables and was met by a dreary-eyed stable boy. The Coroner tended to his horse against the wishes of the young lad. After he was satisfied with Konstantina's conditions, he went to pay the lad in coppers. As he pulled back his cloak to reach for his coin purse, the eyes of the stable boy were drawn to the Coroner's holstered cane and firearm. The light of the lantern and the moon reflected off the polished Kreiger steel of both weapons. Paolo counted three coppers and looked down to find the lad enamored by the various instruments and vials strapped to his brigantine and belt.

The Coroner closed his waxed cloak and coat and thrust the coins into the hand of the boy, who was snapped out from his trance at the feeling and sight of hard currency.

> "Thank you, Master Coroner, much obliged.
> But I barely did anything. I should be paying
> you."

The young lad's Turnian accent hit the vowels with comical eccentricity as the lad struggled to converse with the Coroner in his best common tongue. Paolo continued to grab his bags before helping the child down from the cart and setting her on the straw-coated stable floor.

"The money isn't for what you have done. It is for what you will do. I must rest, young stable master. While I rest, you will tend to my steed."

Paolo grabbed the last of his necessities and locked the cart with various keys. The Coroner then approached the stable boy and kneeled to meet the lad in the eyes with his own. The brass tip of his white beak almost touched the dirt-covered nose of the stable boy as Paolo lowered the tone of his voice.

"And if anything happens to my horse, you will answer to me. Do we have an understanding?"

The stable boy leaned back at the freighting reflection of himself in the opaque crimson lenses of the Coroner's mask. A stammering yes sir came piping out from the boy's tensed throat. Paolo nodded in response and made for his bags.

"You take more care of your mount than your friends, master coroner. That is for sure. I won't let you down. You will receive the best care for the horse, Master Coroner."

Paolo stopped in his tracks and slowly turned back to the boy, the heel of his boot scrapping off the cobblestone as he pivoted.

"My friends? You mean to say, other coroners?"

The boy whistled and hummed as he fetched a pale of freshwater for the horses, nodding cheerfully at Paolo in response.

> "Oh yes, master coroner. Two of them. Clad in all black like yourself. Except they were the largest people, I had ever seen. Like giants, they were. Like the giants in the tales, my nanna tells me. Paid me less than you did, less generous, but let me do the stable work. Big logs they had for weapons too, just like giants!"

Paolo left the stable boy to his ramblings and began to walk back toward the inn. Martials? Here in Oberndorf. I wasn't informed of this in my debriefing. Maybe they are here on other business. Bandits, most likely. The inn was crowded with a mixture of travelers and locals. Traveling merchants, fishermen, bards, farmers, and members of the town guard all crowded around tables and countertops. The sounds of merriment, smoking of clay pipes, and the clanking of cups filled the tavern. All was normalcy until the door shut behind Paolo, and the many eyes of the room glanced over to view the new arrival. Table after table, a wave of silence fell over the room until only the bard, and his minstrel band was left making noise. Soon even they, too, fell in silence. Whispers and hushed voices began to erupt from various corners of the room.

> *"A black one here?"*

> *"A raven, Goddess, have mercy."*

"Murder? In Oberndorf?"

"Dark tidings on our land, Mother, preserve us."

Paolo had heard it all before. The sound of beads pricked his ears. Looking down to his left, the Coroner saw a thin woman was clutching her prayer beads. She rubbed the small pendant in the shape of the Goddess Myrina fervently while muttering her prayers in hushed tones. The Coroner walked from the door to a long counter near the entrance, his spurs echoing throughout the silent tavern. As he cleared the doorway, many patrons rushed for the door and filed out. Only the town guard, a few locals, the band, and the drunkards remained. Paolo picked up the small brass bell from the counter and gave it a ring. A door opened behind the counter, and a portly man wearing a red stocking cap emerged. His bushy eyebrows rose to reveal two warm eyes that widened as he beheld the Coroner.

"Good evenfall, Husbor. How are the beds?"

The man blinked twice before his plump cheeks turned a bright shade of scarlet, and his eyes softened. His large mustache rose as a smile appeared on his rosy, red face.

"Ha, ha! Paolo. Paolo, my dear friend. It is good to see you. It's been long, too long. What brings you to our humble town of Oberndorf?! Business? Did Vortöker finally kill his son-in-law? Ah, I knew it. Not to name any names or point fingers, but it was bound to happen. That lazy fool of a swineherd."

Paolo leaned against the counter and raised his hand to try and stop the old innkeeper, but it was in vain.

> "Oh, pardon me, what am I doing. You need a bed, rest, drink, and food. Let me get Gennota. GENNOTA! Wife, come at once. Master Paolo is here. Make the room ready for our special friend."

From the bottom of the stairs behind him came the clamoring of pots and silverware followed by the loud shrilling sound of a woman yelling profanities at her husband in Turnian. The sound of clogged shoes on wooden stairs could be heard before Gennota emerged through the doorway. She was a small woman in her late thirties, much younger than her husband. The lady of the inn had a head of gold flaxen hair tied up in a bun and held in place with a wooden cooking spoon. Her slender frame donning a soiled apron over a weathered blue dress with white stitching. She stood and continued to scold her husband over various concerns before she turned and presented the Coroner with a soft smile and eyes as warm as her husband.

> "Paolo, it is so lovely to see you, dear. I will make a bed and bring up warm water and bowls. The room will be exactly how you like it."

"Wait, Gennota. I need two rooms."

The Coroner reached down between his legs, pulled the child up, and set her on the counter. At the sight of the child, Gennota gave out a harsh gasp. Quickly she embraced the child in a warm motherly fashion before turning to Paolo with a stern and horrified look.

> "Who could have done such a thing to such a precious being?! Paolo, you tell me right now! I will hunt them down. I swear on the Goddess. Has she had food? Look at how thin she is. This just won't do. I will feed and bathe her at once."

Paolo lowered his head,

> "Don't worry, I took care of that. Listen, the child's name is Diffynwyd. She only speaks Cudwytchian. I found her on the eastern road. She was alone in the middle of the North Millwood Green. Being hunted down by knights bearing a strange sigil. They were out slaving, and she escaped."

Both the innkeeper and his wife gasped at the news. The women hugged the child while Husbor only shook his head.

> "Slaving? That is awful. Her mother and father have been hauled to the capital to be sold on an auction block. I don't care if it is blasphemous or illegal. I curse this new queen for passing that despicable law. No man should sell his brother in chains. It is unnatural. Brings curses and other damnable things upon the land."

Paolo was quick to reply to the women's words.

"She's an orphan. The knights killed her mother
when she tried to stop them from forcing
themselves onto her."

Gennota's eyes grew damp, but she collected herself
quickly and took the child upstairs for a bath.

Paolo grabbed his bags and followed Innkeeper
Husbor upstairs. The Coroner's guest room was large,
the second largest next to the innkeeper's room. It had a
writing desk, a fireplace, a dining table with a chair, a
small wooden tub, and a bed. Paolo started
immediately to unpack his things, starting with his
weapons, which were placed next to his bed next to the
nightstand.

While unpacking and removing his armor,
Paolo began to prod the innkeeper for information
regarding the martials he had heard about from the
stable boy.

"Your son, Knap, told me about how some
martials came through here recently. Know
what it was about?"

Husbor was placing fresh candles in the brass
candelabras around the room when he stopped to
twiddle with his mustache while deep in thought.

"Oh yes, the martials. Big brutes, black armor.
They barely fit into the door, those two. Ate
half of my larder and drank twice as much. A
man and a woman they were, partners they
called each other. Found it strange, but your lot
has many strange titles and words."

194

Paolo sat at the dining table and laid the Hamherbuss
on a cloth sheet along with his leather weapon cleaning
kit. The Coroner took a fine-toothed brush and started
brushing the firearm barrels when he grew impatient
with Husbor's long-winded ramblings.

> "Husbor, please. What were they doing? Did
> they ask any questions or say where their
> destination was?"

"Hmm, well, now that I think about it, they did ask
questions. They had many questions about the roads in
Turnia. Which were safe and which were dangerous. If
I had heard any news about missing women or children
in the surrounding villages. And if any armored men
had come through these parts. I found these all strange
and informed them I had not. The only news I have
recently considered strange is that the town guard
hasn't received their conscripts from training at Fort
Fermyre and that a Sarella was seen walking the
northeast road to Lethelheim."

Paolo stopped cleaning and looked up at the innkeeper,
who had finished lighting the candles in the room and
stoking the fire.

> "A Sarella? Walking the road to Lethelheim?
> How come by you this news?"

"A merchant from Kreighorn village, bringing fish and
gourds, spotted her on the road. Offered to give the
physician a ride, but she humbly turned him down.
Proclaiming that she was on her way to Lethelheim
and, after that, to Lazzar Perish. Can you believe that?
A physician summoned to that forsaken place."

Paolo reached up, took off his wide-brimmed hat, and set it on the post of the bed. He unbuckled the belt straps of his mask, first unfastening the top two buckles. Keeping one hand on the beak, Paolo pried the oculars off with his other hand and set them on the table.

Removing the oculars first allowed his eyes to adapt to the new dimmer room. Then Paolo unbuckled the bottom two straps and removed the re-breather. The leather basket that held the salerite cloth had formed an adhesion to the skin around his mouth, and he had to use the warm rag to help pry the strips from his skin.

After setting the mask down on the table, the Coroner reached up and pulled back the black leather and linen hood. A mane of gray and black peppered hair tumbled to his shoulders as the hood fell back across his black wool cloak. As he finished, Gennota arrived just in time with his fresh clothes and warm water, setting the bowl down in front of him and smiling.

"Paolo, it is a shame you are forced to wear that hideous bird mask. You are a handsome man. Maybe if you could showcase your face, you would have found yourself a nice person to settle down with."

The Coroner smiled and thanked the woman before cleaning his face and wiping his eyes with the fresh hot water.

"Where is Diffynwyd? Do I need to tend to her wounds again? I treated them on the road and

196

saved the leg from festering, but she will need fresh bandages."

"The child is safe, and I have already seen to that. I first bathed the child, gave her fresh clothes, and fed her three courses of pork and potato stew. She finally succumbed to sleep while trying to shovel down the fourth bowl, poor thing. I put her to sleep with the other children before coming in here. I will be right back with your meal, Paolo."

Paolo thanked the women and rose from the table to set his mask on top of the nightstand. He took off his waxed cloak and draped it across the chair, followed by his waxed overcoat. Buckle by buckle, Paolo unfastened the straps of his heavy brigantine vest and then the thigh buckles of his two holsters.

Undoing the large thick buckle of his waistbelt, he removed the entirety of the newly crafted harness and placed it in the dresser in the corner of the room. The Coroner felt lighter in weight and less constricted in his breathing after removing the heavy body armor and gear. Paolo was also surprised that his lower back was free of the usual knotting and dull pain he was accustomed to.

You are more than a genius, Chief Evangelo. You are a savior.

He removed his knee guards, Kreiger steel gauntlet, and leather glove with a bracer and placed them in the dresser with his other arm. Gennota and Husbor returned with a large meal of stew, bread, and fish, along with two pints of ale. Paolo returned to his chair and thanked the two for the hot meal.

"Husbor, thank you for the hospitality. But I
have one more favor, and I hate to ask."

Gennota handed the Coroner his silverware and placed
a warm hand on his shoulder.

"Paolo, don't even say the words. Of course, I
will look after the girl."

Husbor rubbed his mustache after setting the mugs on
the table before Paolo.

"The road is no place for a child. She will be
happier and safer here with us for the time
being."

Paolo took a bite of stew and wiped the corners of his
mouth.

"I will cover her lodging for the duration of my
absence. And this isn't a permanent
arrangement. I will return for her."

"You owe us nothing, master coroner. You saved that
poor thing from certain death. It's the least we can do to
help. As much as I would love to take her into our
home, the child is bound to you now, Paolo Reveré.
You were meant to rescue her in those woods. The
Goddess ensured that. I promise you."

The Coroner drank from his flagon and let the
truth of the woman's words sink into his soul. He had
never thought of becoming a father. His life had been
his career and nothing more. But what kind of father
would a coroner make? He thanked the couple for a

198

final time and bid them a good evenfall. As he finished his supper, Paolo continued to think about the reality of his situation.

Before the dawn's first rays, he would be back on the road and gone before he could say goodbye to the child. This thought led him to ponder further the potential horrors that awaited him in Lazzar Perish. The Coroner took his bath and readied himself for bed. He slept in the comfort of the inn while the fire roared in his room.

When the last crack of the dying log snapped, Paolo opened his eyes and checked the time on his chronorrery. The outer dial of the device showed a slender hour hand pointing at the gap space before the pictograph of a rising sun, indicating it was hour zero of the new day. He rose from his bed and started his morning exercise routine, followed by stretching.

Limbered and ready for the day, the Coroner dressed and assembled his armor and weapons. The cold morning air was kept at bay under the layers of his black wool and leathers. A fresh salerite cloth in the beak of his re-breather filled his nostrils with the sweet chemical scent that helped clear his mind. Paolo walked past the stable boy, whom Paolo could see was in a deep slumber. He quietly chuckled at the loyal innkeeper's son.

Stayed with my Konstantina all night, good lad.

Paolo dropped a silver scepter into the boy's cap on the wooden stool and approached his horse. He handed an apple to the horse and caressed her snout lovingly. He backed the wagon out of the stable and climbed into the driver's bench before giving the reins a light whip.

The cart began to roll down the cobblestone path and out of the small village as bakers and farmers emerged from their homes to start their workday. From the doorway of the inn stood a little Diffynwyd, her eyes looking out the small clear glass of the door, watching as the black cart of the Coroner rolled past the last house and turned out of sight.

The Fermyre Moors

<u>March of Turnia</u>
16th hour of the 89th Day
Anor 905 P.A.

The black coroner cart rattled through the mist-shrouded cart path heading north through the eastern border country of Turnia March. Rows of flaxen wheat stretched as far as the eye could see to the west. However, Paolo could only see the ever-expansive wet and rolling marshland of the Perthmyre Downs to the east of the cart path. As his cart drove through hill and dale of Halych county farmland, he passed over the covered bridge and curved westward to the borders of the Anorheig county farms. Crows sat perched atop various scarecrows of the intercalated gourd and wheat fields of Anorheig farms. As he watched them wheel and hover over the west side of the cart path, it seemed oddly peculiar to Paolo how the carrion birds avoided the marshland to the east. Rain began to fall once more. The storm clouds that Paolo had hoped would stay south had crept up the northern border of the realm over the night and through most of the day. A towering windmill became visible on the northwest horizon, and the crossroads to Lethelheim soon followed.

Arriving at the crossroad junction, a weathered and delipidated wooden post sat half-sunk and tilting in the muddy marsh ground ahead of his coach. A sign pointing northwest read Lethelheim, while the sign pointing northeast read Fort Fermyre. Paolo sat on the driver's bench of his wagon, staring at the splintering boards, deep in thought over which direction to take.

If I go northeast, I could investigate the strange news that Husbor spoke of. But that would take me off course from Lethelheim. Hmm, this is a tough choice.

A lightning bolt lashed out over the northeastern horizon, snapping the coroner out of his stupor as the flickering discharge lit up like sunlight in his oculars. The coroner flicked the reins and guided his horse to the left side path towards Lethelheim. The coach rounded the small hill where the windmill stood and continued past more farm fields and streams.

An outline of some wreckage came into view as the coach came up over a low-rising knoll. Paolo gave the reins a rugged feel before clicking the roof of his mouth. The horse nickered in response before changing pace from trot to canter until the wreckage became clearer in view.

A merchant's wagon lay torn in two, not twenty paces off the side of the mire-side road. As they arrived, Paolo whistled and brought his cart to a stop to closely inspect the scene. Spilled barrels of grain, barley, and oat with torn bushels of wheat shaft lay scattered around the half-smashed and shredded wood of the wagon.

Whoever did this wasn't after the merchant's crop, that is for sure.

The coroner walked around his cart and gave the horse a quick stroke of her mane before approaching the roadside to inspect the scene further. He drew and extended his cane while his eyes scanned the nearby marsh. No noise could be heard except the creaking of the windmill's sails.

The coroner walked down the road, keeping his gaze fixed upon the road. He had walked just shy of a fathom but saw nothing more than the expected tracks of horse hooves and wagon wheel markings on the freshly muddied road.

How peculiar.

Thought the coroner as he began to retrace the events leading back to the roadside wreckage.

The merchant traveled along the road, staying near the center and most likely traveling at average speeds to make the targeted destination in time.

The coroner stopped in his recanting and bent down toward the road. He was at the precise moment the tracks indicated a sharp veering from the road and into the marsh.
Something forced him to the left side of the road, but what? He looked at the horse prints, and to his surprise, they had disappeared entirely from the road.

He veers left because something takes the horse. Paolo searched nearby for more clues, stopping, and rising back to his feet.

First, the coroner assessed the nearby roadside. Tallgrass and reeds jutted out from the ankle-deep marsh water as he stepped down from the road and inspected the vegetation. A series of bent and broken reeds and grass informed the coroner that he had found where the horse landed.

Beyond the broken grass, an extensive oval outline could be seen in the marsh, followed by a series of deep borings that appeared as if something had dragged the animal deeper into the swamp. The coroner stepped down into the bog; the weight of his step drove both gaiter and boot deep into the wet ground.

Paolo circled the small crater toward where the head of the horse would have been and reached up toward his pocket-covered brigantine. His hand returned from a leather sleeve with a palm-sized and ornately decorated brass flask with a paper label on the front.

The title read Spirit Grains, with neatly scribed cursive letters. Popping the top lock of the flask and removing the sealed lid, he turned the flask over to pour the white powdered contents into the palm of his opened, gloved hand. Paolo began to sprinkle the spirit grains around the area underneath.

As the finely ground powder touched the surface of the marsh water, a sizzling reaction between particles and water began to unfold. The spirit grains had found traces of spilled blood, and the chymiac response lit up like burning flames through his vermillion oculars. The grains had confirmed his suspicion, and the tracks show that whatever attacked the horse had dragged the bleeding animal deep into the fog.

He turned his head and peered into the thick mist of the moors beyond him. For the first time in his long career, Paolo could not see into the unnatural turbidity of the lingering bog vapor. The mist from the moors gave the seasoned veteran a feeling of purposeful tampering. A coroner relies on their artificially heightened senses to detect and survive in

the field. As ridiculous a notion as it was, he couldn't
help but consider the possibility.

> *This heavy brume is unsettling. I should be able
> to see right through, but my lenses are as
> helpful as my own two eyes.*
> *There is something more happening here;
> something is changing the nature of the marsh.
> Maybe I should have turned toward the Fort,
> but maybe not.*
> *Riding through this mist would only get me
> killed.*

The coroner closed the flask and returned it to
his vest pouch before turning back toward the road.
Paolo searched for animal prints on the road, but there
was no sign of bear prints or wolf tracks. Paolo found
broken wheat shafts on the opposite side of the road.
Bending downward to his knees, he investigated the
disturbed soil and found something that had him utterly
confounded.

Boot prints?

The coroner thought as he observed the finding with
the tip of his cane.

> *These prints are a standard 6 span length.
> Narrow at the arch, and at the ball of the foot.
> This is a woman's boot. Heavy heeled with a
> flat center. A woman with heavy-leathered
> boots. There is only one post in the realm where
> a woman could obtain boots of this specific
> issued cobbler's mark.*

The coroner rose and followed the boot prints from the field to the road. The tracks stopped three paces from the veering of the wheels off the main road. His mind raced as he calculated both attacker and target trajectories and speeds.

The logistics were sound, but the implication of the scenario had the coroner unsure of his findings. Paolo returned to the site of the wreckage and hastily searched for more insights. He inspected the broken fragments of wood and the side paneling of the wagon. His gloved hands ran along the panel to uncover five unnaturally deep-bored grooves. He stopped midway and noticed that the distances between the markings were almost in line with the fingers of his hand.

His cane poked and rummaged through spilled grains and torn cloth, but no sign of flesh or bone. The coroner poured more spirit grains around the bench seat, but no chymiac response occurred.

> *The horse is brought down and then forcefully dragged off. The attacking entity returns for the driver. The attacker destroys the wagon, attempting to seize the merchant, but fails. Whomever this individual is, they must have escaped, but where to?*

As Paolo finished his assessment, his cane sunk deeper into the marsh than it had the last plunge. He gazed downward to observe a sunken footprint in the bog. The tracks continued from the swamp back up toward the road.

Quickly the coroner pursued the impressions back to the road and towards the rear of his cart. He stopped at the final clear boot print and looked upward from the road.

> *The windmill. The merchant must have made it inside or died trying to get in.*

Paolo returned to his cart and slid the brake down over the wheel. Lighting the lantern by the driver's bench to warn other riders of his parked coach, Paolo pulled his firearm and began to make his way up towards the creaking cyclopean windmill. The path toward the windmill entrance was evident, as the fleeing merchant had left a trail of broken wheat in his wake as he ran in fear. One set of boot prints was visible in the freshly damp soil, but the coroner maintained his guard as Paolo slowly approached the windmill door.

He reached down toward the door and gave the handle a push but was met with resistance. Someone had barred the entry from the inside. He closed his eyes and focused his hearing on the inside of the mill. All he could hear was the grinding of wheat and the churning of gears. A swift hard kick from his boot sent the windmill door sailing back into the belly of the building.

Wood fragments and dust soared into the air as Paolo bounded inside, the Hamherbuss at the ready and aimed. He scanned left and then right before gazing upward. Upon the small second-story floor landing, Paolo could see the outline of a crouched and cowering person.

> "I am Coroner Paolo Reveré, a Resurrectionist of the Royal Order of Coroners. Whoever you are, please come down from there and let me inspect you. You are safe now."

As Paolo finished his introduction, an ear-splitting shriek rang out outside the windmill. The coroner took his eyes off the person above and ran back toward the entrance to look across the fields.

"DUS VAREMODEN! DUS VAREMODEN MERE! EENSHATTS!"

The cowering man had sprung from his hiding and began to shout at the coroner in Turnian in agonized terror. Paolo ignored his insult but found his singular noun of peculiar importance.

"Varemoden? Dus eshtach Varemoden, mena eggherfoon?"

Paolo replied in his best Turnian, but the Turnian man fell to his trembling knees and began to sob. The merchant grabbed the sides of his head, gripped his long hair between his fingers, and trembled in fear as the sounds of shrilling howls rang out once more over the fields outside.

Paolo fixed his eyes on the door, growing steadily impatient in waiting for an answer. The sudden departure and shrilling of crows from the gourd field caught the coroner's attention. He pointed the barrel of the Hamherbuss toward the gourd field and narrowed his vision. The rising of crows on the horizon drew his attention to the rapid parting of wheat to the southeast of the mill. Something was moving at incredible speeds through the field and toward their position.

"VAREMODEN! AH! DUS MERE!"

The merchant continued to shout in between low sobs. A sharp squeal and whiny from a spooked Konstantina rang out from the north. The coroner knew he needed to move quickly and return to the coach before his horse took off in self-preservation.

Paolo turned and holstered the Hamherbuss before hastily ascending the ladder to grab the merchant. The Turnian put his hands up towards Paolo, demanding to stay in the windmill. The disgruntled coroner grabbed the man by his coat lapels before hurling him towards the floor in a single toss.

Paolo jumped down, picked the man up from the ground, and threw the flailing and cursing merchant over his shoulder before drawing his firearm and heading back towards the doorway. Paolo descended the hill and made toward the rear of the cart.

The coroner ripped open the rear gaol cage door and threw the rattled merchant inside. Shutting the door, Paolo whistled loudly and slapped the side of the coach. Konstantina reared back with a loud whiny before launching into a full gallop down the northern road. Paolo quickly turned and gripped the comb of the Hamherbuss in anticipation of his mysterious foe.

Off in the far distance, the clang of a brass bell thundered over the empty fields. The bell from the Selenestic Sepulcher of Lethelheim was signaling the sundown. Paolo then turned his head to see the setting sun on the western horizon. The bell tolled once more. Shrieks and howls answered the tolling of the distant bell, growing louder as the violent tossing of wheat and gourds became visible from south of the windmill.

Paolo quickly scanned the territory and searched for the better ground to fight on. The third and final bell toll echoed over the horizon, but no bestial howl answered this time.

A sudden, blood-chilling silence fell upon the fields and the moors around him. The last dying strands of daylight started to recede back toward the west and away from the coroner as the sun dropped below the peaks of the Western Turnian Ridge. As the sun migrated toward the mountain range, the mist over the moors started to roll westward. Paolo looked down at the low moving waves of heavy fog as they rolled over and collided with his thick leather boots.

As the coroner turned his head eastward to inspect the bizarre oddity, he was halted by a sudden disturbance behind him. A faint ceasing of sound was all it took to make the hair on the coroner's neck stand on end. The consistent and familiar creaking sound of the slowly spinning windmill sails had abruptly stopped.

The light of the rapidly fading sun cast long stretching shadows from behind him. He moved his gaze to his left and beheld the shadow of the windmill. From atop the windmill, he could spot the cause of the disturbance. Something sat perched on the roof of the cyclopean structure and was watching him on the road.

Paolo quickly turned and raised his firearm but was met by the bounding leap of a secondary creature that had silently crept upon his position. The coroner drove the barrel of the Hamherbuss into the cymose-ridden torso of the leaping attacker and pulled up on the trigger.

The mord shot blew through the snarling fiend with an absolute reckoning, sending gnarled entrails splashing in every direction. A sea of ghastly shrieks rose in response to the concussive blast of the firearm. From both field and fog, they came. An onslaught of amber-eyed attackers came bounding and sprinting towards Paolo's position from every direction.

210

The varemoden.

The first to lunge at the coroner met the decimating blast of the second mord shot from the Hamherbuss. The sanguineous debris caught the eyes of another, forcing the beast to cover its eyes and bellow. As the varemoden wiped at their eyes, Paolo slid back on the forearm of the Hamherbuss and reached for a box canister on his belt. The crossbow sprang from the housing as Paolo slapped the box of bolt ammunition into the weapon.

A menagerie of brain and bone erupted from the creature's split skull as Paolo sent a steel bolt whizzing through the air. Pumping the slide and setting a second bolt on the track, the coroner took aim and fired at an oncoming third varemoden from the fog of the moor. The bolt caught the beast in the shoulder, sending a severed arm sailing through the air and into the shallow water below.

The varemoden wildly contorted and brayed before Paolo, turning to gaze at its lost appendage. As the bestial woman turned, Paolo drove another steel bolt into the back of her skull. The headless corpse of the varemoden collapsed into the shallow watery grave, her legs twitching before finally falling still. Crows wheeled ahead and rained down a symphony of high-pitched cawing from behind Paolo.

Quickly he turned to see two more varemoden spring out from the wheat field and onto the muddied road. Sharp claws jutted out from torn leather gauntlets and boots. The jaws of both women began to twitch and contort under quivering gnarled flesh. The sound of cracking bones and snapping tendons could be heard as their faces swelled and mutated. What was once a woman's face was a harrowing fusion of wolfishly bony protuberances erupting with innumerable rows of jagged, sharp teeth.

212

Paolo drove two more bolts into the beasts and sent them barreling back into the wheat field from whence they came. He pushed the release button on the forearm slide and dropped the emptied canister into the mud below. Returning the crossbow to its housing from within the forearm of the Hamherbuss, the coroner pulled down on the side lever and began to load the weapon with two more rounds.

A flurry of wheat and beast exploded at the coroner, sending both Hamherbuss and Paolo soaring in two different directions. The jarring blow from the newly mutated varemoden had forced the air from Paolo's lungs. His vision blurred, and a deafening ring echoed through his ears. Gasping for air, the coroner rolled to his back to behold the varemoden bounding toward him on the offensive.

Paolo tucked and braced his knees to his chest, catching the breast of the beast with the soles of his heavy leather boots. Launching the creature from him, the coroner transitioned into a forward roll. Paolo drew the cane from his side as he rose and pulled the lister knife from the pommel.

The varemoden quickly recovered and lowered itself into a quadrupedal stance. Slowly the beast circled him, growling and snarling while bearing its repugnant rows of mutilated fangs. Paolo kept his gaze focused on the creature's fluorescent amber eyes, keeping a firm grip on the handle of his blade in anticipation.

A sudden breeze blew from the east. As it passed, it caught and blew the coroner's waxed cloak, forcing the cloth to wave in the wind. The sudden motion of black fabric was enough to draw the feint, and the creature sprung from all fours toward him. Paolo turned his body until parallel to the leaping beasts and plunged the thickened razor-sharp dissection blade deep into the varemoden's skull cavity. The force of Paolo's strike drove the instantly lifeless creature straight into the muddy road.

As the amber eyes rolled back in the skull of the revolting abomination, he quickly reached into his vest and drew a three-span steel hay-saw. Rapidly the coroner sawed his way through the neck of the beast, keeping a knee firmly planted into the creature's back.

The bone saw made quick work of the rotting, odious, polypus flesh and soon had cleaved its way through the putrefied vertebral bone of the spine. As the teeth of the saw reached mud, the winded coroner pried the head of the gruesome predator from its twitching torso. Rising from his knee, the coroner held the severed mishappen head aloft. He peered deeply into the amber eye of the horrendous monstrosity and revealed the truth of the merchant's so-called varemoden.

The aromatic incense in his beak was ignited and burning intensely within the iron mesh housing from within his beak. This finding and his other observations during the fighting proved his initial inclination toward the creatures' origin.

These were women once.

The coroner thought in silence as he observed the impaled head and the other carnage strewn around him about the moor.

And not just any women. By the looks of these torn garments and embossed brass buttons,

...Proves my boot theory.

214

I would think these guardswomen belonged to the 1st Turnian Defense Regiment. Stationed at Fort Fermyre. But what in the goddess's name had turned these young soldiers into mangled amalgamations?

Paolo was snapped out of his internal observations by the familiar croaking of a raven.

Corvax.

The call of the coroner's raven came from the northwest of his position. As Paolo turned toward the call of his raven, he began to hear the distant sound of horse hooves followed by the creaking of coach wheels. Soon on the horizon of the remote road, his eyes beheld that of his black coroner coach. He also could see that someone was sitting on the bench and was driving his cart toward him. The coroner furrowed his brow in contempt at the unsettling sight.

Konstantina, you better have a damn good reason for letting a stranger drive my cart.

As the cart slowed, Paolo could see that the person driving his coach was a woman. She wore a black wool mantle draped over a long white scapular gown and tunic, held tight to her waistline via a thick black belt. Leather cases, satchels, and pouches hung from her belt, as did a set of surgical instruments. The delicate instruments of a chirobarbist. Covering her head was a black linen veil tied by a cincture over a white linen coif. The coif came up over her mouth so he could only view a pair of vibrant emerald eyes below thin black eyebrows. Her hands were covered by white linen gloves that rose high into the sleeves of her mantle.

A small patch of visible skin was the same olive shade as his own, from which he could deduce she was Solarnian. Her distinct uniform was that of a Seralla, of which she must have been the one he heard about back in Oberndorf. The Sarella eyed the coroner from the cart with a stern look of disappointment. Her eyebrow was cocked as she surveyed the carnage around the moor and on the road.

> "You fool. You hacked and slashed these creatures with all your martial prowess, but it will all be in vain if you do not purify the remains with fire. Quickly you imbecile, pile the bodies and set them ablaze."

The Sarella set down the rains and climbed down from the cart. Hiking up her mantle and tunic, the physician began to gather remains of nearby varemoden and set them within a pile.

> "Are you going to watch me do it or help? Quickly, master coroner, we don't have much time!"

Paolo helped the Sarella gather the bulk of decimated beasts into a pile by the roadside in silence. When they had finished their labors, the Seralla approached the mound and stopped. Raising her hands toward the moon, the physician began to recite a Selenestic incantation in old Solarnian.

As the Sarella continued in her invocation, she reached toward her belt and produced a small glass vial. As the moon's light graced the flask, the liquid

216

inside became irradiated, glowing vibrantly with swirling white light. Paolo was ensnared in momentary bewilderment at the sight of the concoction, as he had never seen a liquid react simply to exposure to a celestial aurora.

The Sarella continued until the completion of the ancient devotion, and upon finishing, she doused the corpses with the mysterious tonic. As the drops rained down upon the butchered remains, the mass of dead tissues began to violently writhe and squirm.

"Master Coroner, a striker if you would please. Send this cursed flesh back to the Umbryss from which it came."

He drew a striker from his tinder box and lit the end with the back of his boot. Tossing the ignited contrivance onto the pile set the entirety of the stack into a rapidly spreading and awesome inferno. The bonfire consumed the acrid viscera, reducing the maddening mounds of perversion into nothing more than smoldering embers.

The unholy wailing from the gnawing and mashing maws of the creatures as they turned to ash sent chills down Paolo's spine. The Sarella bowed her head and remained silent. Before the last licks of the crackling flames rose, the vermillion lenses of Paolo's oculars picked up a sight that almost made him shudder in recoil.

From the pile, he could see a faint aura of blackened smog crawl forth from the tissue and dissipate into the thick vaporous mist of the moors. Paolo blinked rapidly and shook his head, believing the sight to be a byproduct of his concussive blow from earlier. But the smog still oozed from the mound and

dissipated until the last ember fizzled out under the
light of the irradiant moon.

>"You saw it, didn't you? From the scarlet
>crystals of your oculars."

Paolo slowly turned toward the Sarella, who remained
fixed with hands clasped and head bowed in reverence.

>"Forgive me, Sarella. But I don't know what I
>saw. But I have questions of my own. What
>form of chymia did you just perform? And how
>did you know what I saw through my lenses?"

With her right hand, the Sarella made a sweeping
figure of the Crescent Dianasis, and slowly raised her
head to meet Paolo's eyes. The emerald eyes of the
Sarella lit up like starlight within the reflection of his
vermillion lenses.

>"Return with me to Lethelheim, Master
>Coroner. And I will share with you everything I
>know."

Paolo jumped into the cart without a moment to lose.
The entirety of the inquest had taken a sudden and
sharp turn toward the realm of madness. Good women
turning into foul and hideous monstrosities? How could
that even be possible? If the Sarella had answers to
these baffling anomalies of the natural world, then
Paolo would see to obtain them.

>The two barreled down the muddied road,
leaving the broken and destroyed merchant wagon, in
the blood-soaked marsh behind.

218

Lethelheim

<u>March of Turnia</u>
20th hour of the 89th day
Anor 905 P.A.

The town of Lethelheim was not but a league from where the Sarella had returned to pick up Paolo. As the black coroner coach pulled into the town, Paolo could see that the furthest and most isolated settlement in Turnia had fallen into tarnished dereliction. The uneven, pitted roads of the town had become overrun with thickened gnarled bramble and abnormal saprophytic weeds. The buildings lining the town square were of equivalent senescence in their immediate presentation upon arriving.

Boarded windows and shut doors could be seen in every building and home as the coach entered the town gates and traveled down the potholed and weathered cobblestone path. The coroner and the Sarella sat in silence as they passed through the silent ghost town of Lethelheim. Paolo looked around at the pitiful sight of squalor and filth of the town's state of dismal disarray. The fields that lie adjacent to the thatched roof homes were littered with the fly swarmed rotting remains of bovine carcasses.

As they continued past the town square, the coach passed the first patches of town vegetable fields. Here the coroner could see mold-covered gourds and ergot-ridden shafts of wheat jutting scarcely from the yellowed abandoned field.

Progressing onward, they passed the blacksmith's forge and dilapidated tithe barn before finally crossing the outskirts of the town proper and towards the village green. There were numerous questions Paolo had for the Sarella but chose to save them for a more appropriate time.

A radiating pain shot through his side and across his chest with each heavy dip of the coach wheels along the pox-scarred road, and it was enough to still the coroner's tongue during the remainder of the trip. The moon hung low behind the looming sharp stoned Selenestic Sepulcher sitting atop the church hill. Below the Sepulcher hill was a more minor hill, surrounded by a ring of trees.

Through the trees, the coroner could see a two-storied building and connecting small house, which he recognized as the rectory. The Sarella instructed Paolo to head toward the rectory and that there would be a driveway that he could pull the cart into when they arrived.

Beyond would be Selenestic Sepulcher which was their destination. The village green was barely a green. Paolo felt the open field appeared more like a charnel yard. Monoliths of various sizes dotted the yellowed decadence of the field along with the random assortment of piled box coffins and bodies wrapped in soiled linens.

The Sarella looked over to spot the coroner's fixed gaze toward the harrowed display of irreverent desecration.

> "I have been doing what I can to help the poor people of this town, but my efforts have proven to be fruitless. Two days past I ran out of assistance for helping with the deceased. It was a personal tragedy to lose those two young boys."

The coroner only looked at the converted graveyard with an emptied, listless stare hidden behind his mask as the coach pressed on toward the rectory hill.

"You should have burned the bodies. The mephitic air will only bring about more death. You more than anyone else should know that."

His words fell heavily on the discouraged Sarella, but the coroner lacked the empathy to offer a heartfelt apology or words of comfort. Buzzards and crows wheeled over the exposed bodies strewn over the field. Above the blackbirds swirled and churned tenebrous storm clouds, which crackled and hummed with a sporadic horizontal display of electrical discharge.

The cart passed over the small hillock and through the rusted iron gate of the Sarella's Rectory. Paolo could see a two-story brick building standing behind, followed by the towering sepulcher atop the adjacent knoll. Bringing the coach to a stop, the Sarella climbed from the driver's bench and made her way around the harnessed horse toward the rectory door. Unlike the Sarella, Paolo was slow to move from his seat.

As the coroner attempted to move, a sudden pain seared from his right side and shot through the entirety of his core. His vision blurred as a splitting aura exploded from within his skull. His respirations slowed, becoming erratic in nature before dropping to a harsh wheeze. His windpipe stiffened as he clutched at his chest with trembling hands.

Reaching out toward the turned Sarella, Paolo struggled to descend the driver's bench. His heart pounded within his chest as he continued to gasp in deep rhonchus breaths.

The coroner spun and fell backward as his legs gave out from underneath him. His body landed in the dampened dirt of the cart path with a heavy crash. Paolo controlled his autonomic physiology as much as possible as his trembling gloved hand reached toward his vest. His groping fingers finally landed on the exposed brass plunger of a sleeved syringe below his field aid kit. As he yanked the brass device from its sleeve, the Sarella rushed to his side and dropped to her knees to assess the fainting coroner.

"Lung…my … lung. Pierce my…with…."

His vision blurred and began to fade. The last bit of strength in his grip faded from his quivering fingers as the brass syringe slipped to the inside lining of his wool cloak.

The sound of the Sarella's voice became washed out by the sporadic pounding of his heartbeat. As his faculties shut down, the coroner faded into a deep tranquil serenity.

"Master coroner."

The physician shook the unresponsive Paolo in desperation before reaching into her satchel and scrambling for instrument kits.

"Master coroner. You can't die on me, not now!"

The dark crevasses of a man's subconscious can reveal many twisted and tormented obscurities once

222

suppressed from the light of his conscious mind. As
Paolo descended deeper into his mind's twilight façade,
the many faces of his fulminating fears took shape
before him. For an eternity, he fell through a torturous
abyss, a void filled with hundreds of rotting faces.
Faces of the men and women he had sentenced to rot.

Eviscerated and maimed. Criminals he had
condemned, fated to be slowly consumed by the carrion
crow while helplessly bound and nailed to the wooden
beams of their horrific sky grave. He saw them all.
Their hollowed, sunken, and eyeless faces upon those
splintered wooden beams, forever festering in the acrid
fumes of the expansive Gibbet Marsh.

Paolo could only sputter out feverish ravings as
he writhed in the endless void until a blood-curdling
shriek of the most unholy cacodaemoniacal nature
ruptured from the deep. He covered his ears and
answered the cacophony with a series of roaring
fulminations of his own. Demanding an end to the pain,
the sound ceased, and a warm sensation washed over
him from below and above.

The coroner opened his eyes and found that he
was standing upon the Great Corpse Road. The bodies
of thousands lay exposed and strewn upon the tipped
crosses lining the long dirt road. Paolo gazed to each
side of the road, scanning from right to left. He looked
and beheld the strung corpse of Struben MacRund.

As his eyes met the pecked and mutilated
Struben, the eyes of the crucified man snapped forward
and slowly rolled toward him within their sanguineous
sockets.

Paolo recoiled in horror before noticing that
every head of every strung corpse was also gazing
down upon him. One by one, the sun-dried and
eviscerated corpses freed a single arm from the rusted

spikes embedded in their withered palms and pointed down the long dirt path. His eyes followed where their hands pointed, and as the coroner gazed down at the horizon, he could see an isolated outline of Fawrgrave Gaol. No sooner than his eyes beheld the looming structure did the fortress structure start to move.

The building came closer and closer as if possessed by some unforeseen force that was drawing upon his fears towards his position. The portcullis opened, and his eyes beheld a maddening scene of demented atrocities that sent the man falling backward in a fit of raving distress.

Emoc sah eramthgin eth!

The words from the corpses rang out in his ears as the coroner began to writhe in a state of gripping madness. Finally succumbing to the pain, he screamed toward the black sky as the road swallowed him from below.

The Rectory

Paolo launched upright, profusely sweating and in bewildered agitation. His eyes took a moment to adjust to the torchlight of the dimly lit chamber. He wiped the sweat from his forehead and swung his legs over to the side of the sanitarium bed he found himself on. Breathing in deeply, a sharp pain radiated from his side.

> *Well, I'm not dead. But these broken ribs won't do.*
> *Wait…*
> *Where is my mask?*

Paolo rose from the sweat-soaked bed and searched for his boots and other gear, but his things were not in immediate sight. Paolo could feel the damp chill within the windowless stone room as he stumbled through the chamber, searching for his belongings.

His legs were stiff as if the controlled motor movement of walking was a new concept to his gross lower musculature. The coroner collapsed face-first into a single wooden chair in the corner of the room. His agitation grew exponentially as his patients thinned to a nonexistent state. Growing weaker in his struggles and panicking at the lack of a protective uniform, the coroner cried out for his recent travel companion.

"SARELLA!"

His words reverberated off the chamber's stone walls
until swallowed by the silent vacuous void of his dimly
lit prison. He slumped from the chair to the stone floor
before turning over and propping himself up against the
cold stone wall. His ears pricked at the sudden creaking
of a wooden door outside the room.

      The echo of heeled boots followed, and finally,
the door to his room opened to reveal the physician.
She carried a silver tray with a scarce supply of food
and a filled wooden cup in her hand as she entered the
room and closed the door behind her. As she turned
from the door, her emerald eyes first scanned the empty
bed before moving to find the broken corner on the
floor and slumped against the wall. Hurriedly the
Sarella placed the tray down on a small stand by the
door and rushed to help Paolo to his feet. The physician
helped him to his feet while berating him for his
actions, her tone calm with an undertone of vexing
hisses.

> "Fool of a man! I spend hours mending your
> wounds, use more of my scant supply of
> bandages and medicines, and the first you do
> upon waking is hurl yourself to the floor like
> some child—shame on you, Master Coroner.
> Lie down and let me assess my work. Quickly
> before you are taken by grippe and agues."

Paolo struggled to break free from her grip but
eventually complied with the physician. He sat on the
edge of the bed and allowed the Sarella to observe her
stitching before finding the energy to speak.

"Where are my things, Sarella. I need my
belongings."

The coroner's voice cracked through an aired windpipe
and dried tongue as he spoke.

"Please, Sarella, my equipment. Do you
understand the gravity of the position you have
put me in? I am a coroner. I cannot be in the
field without my protective equipment. I need
my mask."

"They are here, stop bellowing like a child."

After scolding the agitated coroner, the physician
remained silent as she removed the soiled bandages
around his chest and reached toward the bedside cart.
Paolo quickly eyed the physician as she reached for
fresh bandages and stilled her hand with his own.

"Sarella. Save your bandage supply for the
people of Lethelheim. Get me my equipment,
now."

She pulled free from his grip and began to curse in Old
Solarnian as she left the room quietly. Paolo quickly
made his way toward the tray of food and water. First,
he gulped down the cold fresh water and replaced the
wooden chalice before grabbing the meager amounts of
chicken breast and freshly baked bread loaf.
Like a starved beast, the coroner tore into bread
and fowl as if it were his life's first and last meal. The
Sarella returned with two black leather bags as he
finished the meal. Paolo helped the physician by taking

the giant suitcase from her hand. He placed it on the
bed before opening and removing its contents.

> "I know of your Order's customs, Master
> Coroner, and you are not at risk of being
> exposed to any mephitic source. We are far
> underground, in the catacombs of the rectory."

Paolo remained silent as he removed his protective
equipment pieces from the bag. Finally, he found what
he was searching for so passionately. Paolo removed a
brass syringe from a button-enclosed leather case and a
short thick glass vial. He paused in his actions to
address the physician.

> "You, um, you carried me from the courtyard to
> this room?"

The Sarella scoffed at his question and folded her arms
into the oversized sleeves of her mantle.

> "I served as a combat healer in the King's army
> after completing my academic studies. A
> physician learns quickly how to maneuver
> heavy men in plate armor and chainmail toward
> the back lines. You were not too bad."

Paolo loaded the vial into the inner housing of the brass
syringe. Pausing, Paolo gave a sideways glance toward
the Sarella. A faint smile could be seen through strands
of black and grey hair.

> "Well, thank you. And thank you for treating
> my wounds. But I don't have time to let my
> body heal naturally. I'm getting too old for this

228

rough business as it is. Now stand back, and whatever you do, don't touch me, or intervene. Better let this next part take its course, eh."

Before the Sarella could say a single word, Paolo drove the large-bore hypodermic needle deep into the brachial vein of his right arm. Pushing the plunger down, a quarter of the vial's contents rushed into his bloodstream. Paolo drew the needle from his arm and tossed the device onto the bed, grimacing and grunting as the anthemene began to take effect.

"I hate this part."

Body temperature is always the first to drop, then followed by a sharp rise until sweat begins to percolate from the dilated pores of the skin. As his heart rate and breathing rate increased, Paolo collapsed to the side of the bead and lowered his head to the ground. Panting heavily, he could feel every muscle in his body contract and swell in size. Loud consecutive snaps and pops rang out in the chamber, and the coroner let out a suppressed groan. The Sarella watched in terrified curiosity as the once broken and bruised ribs on Paolo's side began to quiver and snap back into place.

Once the bones had adjusted, the bruising rapidly dissipated before her eyes. The regeneration was complete. Once the last bruising had healed, the coroner fell into the bed. His muscles twitched as he choked and gasped with newly reformed lung tissue. The increase in oxygen was also taking a toll, but he quickly adjusted and steadily rose from the floor. His body felt twenty years younger, but not to let it get to his head. The seasoned coroner knew the momentary rush was fleeting, and he would return to his aching self sooner than he would like. He pulled the pieces of his uniform out and assembled them before himself on the bed. Grabbing a fresh linen shirt, the coroner began to dress and gear up in both his leather and steel.

"I.... have never seen anything like that."

Whispered the awestruck Sarella.

"What form of substance can have such a profound effect on the body's anatomy and physiology. It even mended your skeleton."

Paolo strapped and buckled both holsters to his thighs before reaching for the two portions of his coroner mask. He first strapped and buckled his rebreather before attaching his oculars. The coroner reached toward the bedpost and grabbed his black leather capotain hat. He placed the wide-brimmed hat snuggly over his form-fitting hood and turned toward the Sarella.

"The substance is called Anthemene."

"Anthemene? I have never heard of such a tincture before."

Paolo slid the collapsed coroner cane into the left holster before holstering the Hamherbuss to his right side. His various vials were remeasured and refilled and placed within their unique sleeves and pouches along the front of his new brigantine.

230

"It is kept within the Order, and only members of the Order have access to it. I am no apothicarian, Sarella, but my humble understanding is that it is a mixture of both alkaloid and chymiac salt. The plant is grown within the Order's greenhouse, and the salt is harvested in the caverns deep below the Praetorium. The two ingredients have been within the Praetorium for centuries, but only recently have the Order's brightest archivists and apothicarians combined the two ingredients to make such a tincture. A great little cure-all. Yes, it can mend wounds, but it is mainly used as an enhancer. The anthemene increases every humor of the body, acting on anatomy, physiology, and cognition. We can move faster, strike harder, think quicker, and sustain more bodily harm than a regular man. Endurance, both physically and mentally, is enhanced as well as reflexes. One can go days without sleep while on the substance. The bolster to sensory perception is also helpful in the field."

> "Surely, there are side effects. Men were never meant to reach towards the power of the gods."

Paolo began to walk forward but abruptly stopped at hearing her question.

> "The side effects of too much anthemene, from what I have been told, is death. First, the compound takes a toll on your mind. Turns the user into a crazed fiend, reducing you to your basic animalistic needs. Then the toll on your cardiovascular system reaches its peak, and your heart ceases to beat. This is just hearsay and proper precautions from the lips of the

chiamist. I have never heard of any coroner taking more than half of a vial at a time."

Paolo started for the door but abruptly stopped once more and turned toward the Sarella.

"By the way, what is your name?"

"I am Seralla Augathina de'Sicalla."

As she formally introduced herself, she bowed her head toward the coroner, who bowed in return. Rising, the coroner tipped the brim of his capotain and returned the courtesy of a formal introduction.

"My name is Coroner Paolo Reveré, a Resurrectionist. Again, you have my gratitude. I also thank you for respecting my Order and bringing me indoors and underground before unmasking me. Now, what can you tell me about what is happening in Turnia? You seemed to know more about those creatures than I would have guessed."

"I know what you are, Master Coroner. We may come from different orders within the realm, separated by the crown and the faith. But a physician knows how to spot her equal from within your Order. Only a resurrectionist would rely on their own medical knowledge in order to foolishly try and save themselves. Now, follow me and keep up. Maybe you can aid me in my research."

The physician moved around the coroner and beckoned him to follow her. Paolo smirked from behind his mask

232

and pulled his cloak around his shoulders as he followed in tow behind the lamp carrying Sarella. She turned right from the entrance and proceeded down a long stone hallway. As the two descended deeper into the catacombs of the Rectory, Sarella Augathina filled the coroner in on her status.

> "With the waves of fleeing peasant immigrants into the capital, the Serallas was placed in charge of treating the sick. As we began to lend our aid to the people, we kept hearing of strange disturbances in the far east of the realm. In both Turnia and Clevelorn marches. The melancholy and the forlorn spoke of night haunts and demoniac beasts terrorizing the border realms. We brought this news to the Superior Surgeon Canoness, and a council was summoned. After the Selenestic Convergence, the Auguritical Abbess chose me to carry out a sacred mission. To travel to the town of Lethelheim and investigate the disturbing rumors and lend my healing aid to those conflicted by the scourge."

The two had descended deep into the catacombs. The walls had been lined with sarcophagus-filled alcoves when they first began their descent. As they progressed further through the gossamer-lined, antediluvian labyrinth, the cavities were soon replaced with piles of ivory skulls of the long-entombed dead. As the two rounded a corner, Paolo could observe at the end of the short hall an iron-bound wooden door. Sarella Augathina stopped in front of the door and began to search for a key.

"So, we appear to be on similar missions from our orders. Although the Royal Order of Coroners receives its intelligence from a corporeal source. I, too, was sent to Lazzar Perish to investigate the mysterious circumstances."

Sarella Augathina pulled from a pocket a rusted iron key fixed upon a white rope. Before unlocking the door, she stopped to address the coroner.

"I will not tolerate blasphemes, Master Coroner. Believer or not, the will of our Selenestic Mother does guide us all. Sarella and coroner alike. It was a mistake to assume that one who dons the guise of her sacred raven would be more reverent of our Goddess."

The coroner apologized for his offense while the Sarella made the sign of the Crescent Dianasis with her right hand before turning to unlock the door. Paolo followed the Sarella into the chamber and beheld a makeshift field laboratorium. Around the circular room, Paolo observed piles of books, filled beakers, phlogistic scopes, alembics, and trays of blood-stained dissection instruments.

The Sarella had brought down four long wooden tables into the catacomb antechamber. Three of the tables were aligned around the walls of the room, while the fourth sat in the center. The various books and equipment were strewn around the tops of the three radial tables, whereas a sheet covered the center table.

The Sarella waited for Paolo to enter the room before proceeding to shut the door behind him and lock it. A key lock, a padlock, and a slide lock ensured the two were utterly imprisoned within the stone antechamber. The outline of a corpse could be seen lying under the crimson, and xanthous stained cloth draped over the center table.

As soon as Paolo spotted this, he knew why the Sarella had sealed the two within the room. Candles and sconces were lit around the chamber from the flames of her lantern until brightly lit. Paolo moved to the table to his right and shifted through the numerous sheets of parchment paper. Drawings of deviated anatomy along with quill scribbled notes filled the entirety of loose leave pages all around the table.

Heavy glass jars lined the far side of the broad wooden table, each filled with carefully dissected organs submerged and floating amidst faintly xanthous solutions. A book on anatomy lay open next to an empty ink well and dried quill.

The pages revealed to him that the Sarella recalled the anatomy of the heart and its great vessels. As Paolo reached to turn the page of the book, the organs within the jar began to slither and throw themselves against the sides of the heavy jar. Boney protuberances sprouted from crowning orifices along the surface of livers, hearts, and brains.

The arachnid appearing flagellations of the fetid tissue struck the lids of the heavy jars in tenacious unison, trying in vain to break themselves free from their watery prisons. Paolo stepped away from the table upon observing the cavalcade of nightmarish horrors found within the jars.

"They are antagonized by the presence of the living."

The Sarella stood on the opposite side of the center table as Paolo turned his head to acknowledge the words of the physician.

"I can see that. How did you harvest such pristine specimens without provoking a mutagenic response in the organic tissue?"

> "They are submerged in a solution of blessed water and alkahest."

The coroner turned back to observe the jars once more under the light of the sconces and candles of the room.

> "Impressive. How did you know to use alkahest?"

He asked in a piqued curiosity, further inspecting the reactionary organs in their jars.

The Sarella moved to pull back the drapes with a single hand, keeping her eyes fixated on the coroner as he studied the specimens.

> "The Serviticle Sarellahood of Ecclesial Physicians has their recorded chronicles of times past, and ages long forgotten. Curious, Master Coroner. How is it that we remember histories that our corvial brethren seem to have let fade into antiquity? Did the coroners send a resurrectionist into the forsaken Lazzar Perish to die a vainglorious death? Or were you sent to dispense the justice of the Goddess upon those that desire to spread misery and anguish upon the realms of men?"

236

Sarella Augathina threw back the soiled linen cloth to reveal a partially dissected corpse of a half desiccated regimental guardswoman. The portions of exposed flesh were enveloped under a web of oozing and fetid vesicular decrepitude. Patches of animalistic fur jutted forth from the boiled mass of tissue, spanning the length of her half-rotted and oil-saturated corpse.

The collection of anatomical deviations that lay shackled to the table before Paolo was akin to the fiends that had attacked him on the road in the moors. Although, while under the bright torchlight, Paolo was able to better observe the anthropomorphic intricacies of the semi-human abomination.

His eyes were immediately drawn to the head of the beast, which appeared to be an amalgamation of canid, ursid, felid, and finally, human, craniofacial configurations. He bent closer to the table, further observing that the boney protuberances comprising the gnarled and fleshy snout were not spliced or grafted.

These were only tumorous outgrowths of the underlying natural formed osteology of the face. Sarella Augathina allowed the coroner to momentarily observe the specimen in silence before continuing to address him.

> "If you are to vanquish these monstrosities, you must be better prepared. I was told by the Abbess that my arrival to cursed Lethelheim would be alleviated by the arrival of a great winged raven. If you are my winged raven, then Goddess preserves my soul, as you are as clueless as that raving merchant you sent here in your carriage."

Sarella Augathina turned and grabbed a scalpel and forceps from the table behind her. Paolo watched as the Sarella cut a piece of flesh from the creature and pinched the sample between the teeth of the steel forceps.

She transferred the tissue sample into a clay bowl and sat the forceps down. Handing the bowl to the coroner, she then asked Paolo to perform the phlogistony on the tissue sample. He took the bowl from her with hesitated contempt, unsure of the hidden undertones of her motivations.

> "You want me to conduct phlogistics on this tissue sample? But we use phlogistics to confirm an act of homicide."

Sarella Augathina moved past the coroner and pulled forward the kiln, alembic, and phlogistic scope she had confiscated from Paolo's carriage earlier and then pulled out a wooden stool from under the table. She beckoned to the coroner toward the seat, inviting him to initiate the chymiac process.

> "Your orders phlogistic scope differs from the model we use in the Sarellahood. I have a scientific inclination that the phlogistic bodies of this tissue sample will prove to you that there is something more supernatural at work here. Now, please, apply your trade."

Paolo now understood her motives and scoffed at the physician's reasoning. Although he found her fanatic ideologies farfetched and benign, he held a deep desire to know more about the truth of the Varemoden.

"Before we can properly conduct the
phlogistony, I need a sample of the specimen's
ichor. The aether piston of the device needs
properly harvested ichor from one of the four
premeasured organs of aether of the deceased or
the chymiac reaction won't properly work."

Sarella Augathina reached into her mantle toward the
satchel hanging from her leather belt. From within the
leather belt, the Sarella produced a brass syringe
containing a murky pearl liquid and handed it to the
coroner. Her emerald eyes shone with prideful
contempt in the torchlight of the chamber.

"I know what is needed for the procedure to
work, Master Coroner. You were incapacitated
long enough for me to read from the collection
of books you carry with you in your traveling
library. I measured out the weights of the eye,
the brain stem, the bone marrow, and the gall
bladder. I assure you they weighed four grains,
four crowns, four gills, and four pounds,
respectively."

Paolo took the syringe from the physician with a scoff
of surprise before clearing his throat. He loaded the
ichor syringe into the phlogistic scope's aether piston
before shutting and locking the device. Paolo sat the
ceramic bowl on top of the table and took a seat on the
wooden stool. To initiate the phlogistic process, he had
to first heat up the portable iron kiln.

"I need to reduce the tissue to its four
perceivable humors first. Now, normally we
conduct this on traumatized tissue collected

from the murder victim as those fibers will elicit the purest distillation of all four humors. So, whatever you are hoping to find in this test, well, I wouldn't get my hopes up."

As the tissue began to bake within the kiln, it slowly converted into a pile of charcoaled ash. The coroner took the ash from the kiln and carefully placed them into a stone mortar. Using a pestle, the coroner ground the charred tissue ash into finely ground dust within the stone bowl.

After the grinding, Paolo dumped the ash into the glass beaker of the alembic and then poured a measured amount of alkahest solution in with the particles. He lit a fire under the alembic with a striker and waited for the liquid inside to percolate. Slowly, the solution rose to a steady boil within the round glass container. The condensation of the percolated solution began to move through the connecting glass tube. Slowly, the concentrate dripped into the collecting beaker.

The concentrate dried under the heat of the second flame, leaving a small pile of a crystalline particulate in the wax paper of the second beaker. Paolo removed the waxed paper and pulled forward the Phlogistic scope closer to him. The apparatus stood a span in height made entirely of brass, steel, and glass. At the base of the device was a brass-flanged circular disc. Here, Paolo sat the crystalline particulates in the center of the brass dish. On either side of the observation plate were two cylindrical pistons of different sizes.

The right piston was an upright brass tube with a thin-glass housing with a single rod plunger known as the fire piston. The fire piston oversaw producing a measured amount of light equivalent to sunlight. This light from the fire piston was projected onto a focusing mirror that would then focus the light through a spectral lens wheel that would then shine upon the particulates.

From his vest, the coroner drew out his chronorrery. As Paolo checked the inner Auroric dial of his chronorrery, the hour hand of the device pointed to the late dayspring hour.

> "I was incapacitated for that long? My chronorrery shows that it is late dayspring on the 91st day."

The coroner grunted and mumbled under his breath at the minor annoyance as he measured out the proper amount of concentrated brimstone light needed from the fire piston. Pushing the plunger down slowly, the wick within the piston ignited with a bright white flame. The light reflected off the focusing mirror and down into the spectral lens dial. Paolo took his left hand and gripped the second piston device, the aether piston.

This was a larger brass tube with two-piston plungers at the top. First, Paolo pushed the right plunger inward. A tiny droplet of the dark ichor dripped from the syringe hypodermic tip and landed on the particulates below.

After the ichor had been added, the coroner pushed the left plunger down, which forced a minute gust of air onto the particulates. As the air caressed the dampened crystals, his left moved carefully toward the spectral dial. His slender gloved finger located the notched wheel of the dial, and slowly he rotated it until it reached the sepia lens.

"We eliminate the traces of the first humor,
blood."

As the light pierced the pile of particulate powder, the phlogistic body of the specimen's blood produced a combustion reaction followed by a cloud of scarlet smoke.

"Second, we remove traces of the second
humor, yellow bile."

He gave the aether plunger the second ministration of ichor as well as a secondary gust of air. His finger rotated the dial once more, this time to a blue lens. The cerulean tinted light shined down upon the particulate, and as the second phlogistic reaction occurred, a billow of xanthous fumes fizzled outward and upward from the smoking damp pile until dried once more.

He repeated the process once more with a yellow lens to eliminate the third humor, that of phlegm, which brought forth phlogistic combustion producing a blue vapor from the particulates.

"One last humor, black bile. Are you sure you
want to do this? Without victimhood, there
cannot be black bile present in the humors."

Sarella Augathina closed her eyes and slowly nodded her head. Paolo could see that from within the sleeves of her mantle, the Sarella clutched something within the palm of her hand. He turned back to the phlogistic scope and repeated the process one last time. As the scarlet lens fell into place within the dial, a beam of penetrating crimson light shot through the particulates.

As the phlogistic reaction hissed and popped from the particulates, a black and grey smoke began to slither out from the crystalline powder. Paolo recoiled backward on the stool, his eyes blinking rapidly at the sight of the writhing viscous bodies that began to squirm their way toward the crimson light source.

The sconces and candles within the chamber started to flicker as more than black bile erupted from the grains within the dish. Within the view of his vermillion lenses, Paolo could see that the bile itself radiated with a faint purple glow, the likes of which he had never seen in all his years as a resurrectionist. Fixated on the peculiar finding, he was snapped out of his astute observation by a violent eruption of rattling from the table behind him. Paolo turned to see that the corpse on the table had begun to twitch and contract with seismic force within the iron clasps that held it pinned to the wooden table. As the coroner rose from the wooden stool, Sarella Augathina began uttering incantations in old Solarnian.

Her voice started low, but as she progressed in her recitations, it increased to a thunderous timbre. The body on the table shuddered a final time and then fell still. Paolo moved from the table slowly and advanced toward the gap space between the table and the wall, gazing at the continuously rising billow of smog from the phlogistic scope reaction. The tenebrous pollution moved to the wall and coalesced with the shadows of the room.

"What in the name of…"

uttered the coroner as he gazed upon the slithering darkness that rapidly encapsulated the stone of the chamber around him.

The Sarella threw back her mantle and revealed the artifact that she had concealed from within her sleeves. A selenestic rood of pure silabar was clutched in the right hand of the Sarella as she ordered the coroner to stand back against the wall.

"GET BACK! STAY FREE OF THE WALLS!"

She shouted at the coroner before focusing her lustrous fetish back on the writhing corpse on the table. At the sight of the silabar rood, the body on the table began to writhe once more. As it contorted and twisted, the face of the amalgamated creature let forth a howl of agonizing pain as it tried to tear free from the iron shackles. Paolo could see that the smog had started to blow out the firelight of the chamber as it swept and engulfed the stone wall in a blanket of abyssal twilight.

As the darkness reached the door from both sides, it was as if the coroner and the sarella were swallowed within the ever-expansive umbrage. Suddenly the body on the table ruptured with thousands of skittering insects that poured out from the flesh and over the sides of the table.

Sarella Augathina held her silabar rood aloft and continued in her incantations. The room began to reverberate with unforeseen energies, throwing instruments and pages from the tabletops and onto the floor.

Some hidden force wants out of this antechamber, thought the coroner as he braced himself on the nearby table and pulled out his cane from its holster.

244

The door rattled on its hinges as the physician continued in her prayer. The pins of the hinges flung outward and finally gave way. The iron banding crunched inward and broke the wood of the door into splinters and flew into the catacomb hallway outside within a vortex of both shadow and faint echoing yowling.

As the shadow tried to free itself from the confines of the antechamber, the eyes of the Sarella burst into white flames. Slowly she rose from her feet into the air of the room, her words echoing in a fulminating timber of both divine retribution and wrathfulness.

"YA'QAH VAH ANRAH NUH'NQO-TATH WAHNU UCH'EIDA!"

As her words pulsated against the stone of the antechamber, the fleeing umbral remnant was sent hurtling to the floor. The silabar rood began to glow in her sun-kissed hand before finally emitting an incandescent ray of celestial light. Paolo shielded his eyes from the sight of the glowing fetish. The intensity of rays forced the vermillion lenses of his oculars to rattle and hum with latent energy.

"MHM' YAHWI RA'IJO NUHN AHN CPHI'OCH MHAN DELITH SAMY'CHI!"

Howling and shrieking came from both corpse and shadow. The amalgam shook and rattled until the sheer intensity of the incantation began to produce an acrid reaction from the rotting flesh.

Smoke and bubbles erupted from the amalgamated fistulas as the corpse gushed from the table in a gory display of atrocious and repugnant putrefaction. As the decomposition raged, the wooden table became consumed in the bubbling acid and collapsed under the weight of the corpse.

The shadow entity boomed with a noxious force before dissipating into a faint breeze. The physician fell to the ground and collapsed forward onto the stone floor. Sweat fell from her brow as she gasped for air through her black linen veil that covered her mouth and nose. Paolo went to help the Sarella up but was sent flying backward by a sudden explosive force that came from the doorway of the chamber. The shadowy tenebrosity returned, though this time, it had taken form. A towering figure of a female, cloaked in phantasmic obscurity, rose from the floor. The amber eyes of the mist-shrouded giant looked down upon the panting Sarella Augathina with a fiery gaze of curiosity and hatred.

> "There you are, Moon Priestess of Myrina. You have done well in keeping yourself hidden, but I now know where you skulk and hide. Your pitiful incantations to an even more pitiful goddess cannot stop what has been set in motion."

The voice that poured forth from the obscure vapor was that of a gurgling hiss.

As it spoke, it made the hair on Paolo's neck stand on end, and his skin crawl. The malevolent shade reached out with an arm of smoke and grasped Augathina around the chest. The Sarella twitched and cried in pain as the umbral clutches of the giant remnant picked her up into the air. A wave of smoke sent the Sarella soaring through the air and into the far chamber wall. The sinister giant cackled in delight at the sight of the fallen physician.

> "Soon, the ritual will be completed, and the entirety of your pitiful race will be consumed by the formless one. We will watch in contempt as your race turns on one another, butchering and killing until no man remains. Your agonizing cries will reach the heavens, but no answers will come. Then you will truly know the weakness of your pathetic Goddess, as she watches from on high, the genocide of her even weaker creation by their own hands."

As the voice continued, Paolo rose from the ground and studied the apparition carefully. He pulled from his vest a small vial of eosphorus powder and a vial of brimstone salt in each of his hands. *This ought to work, I hope.* As the entity was focused on the Sarella, Paolo slowly moved to its flank and lowered himself behind a tipped-over table. Under the safety of cover, he slowly and carefully pulled the stoppers of both vials and mixed the salts together within one vial.

Paolo then slowly reached for his small flask of acrid azotite and poured a small amount over the combined salt mixture. Placing the cork stopper back over the vial and returning the other supplies to his vest, the coroner clutched the vial in between his gloved hands and shook the precipitate until he could feel a faint warmth from the within the thin glass. As the chymiac reaction raged from within the vial it began to emit a radiating glow that pierced through the gaps of his gloved fingers. He peered from behind the

248

table, checking to see if Sarella Augithina was at a safe distance from the gloating apparition. As he eyed the physician, Paolo saw his window of opportunity and sprang from his hiding spot and bounded toward the amber-eyed shadow. Despite his positional advantages, a shadowy appendage lashed out from the umbral figure and wrapped itself around the torso of the coroner.

The tendril lifted Paolo into the air and squeezed the Coroner tightly. Struggling to free himself, Paolo slid the thin vial up the sleeve of his undercoat. The murky feminine face ceased in its gloating and pulled its gaze from the downed Sarella to inspect her ensnared prey. The glowing amber eyes of the shrouded figure darted to Paolo and widened as they beheld his visage.

> "What do we have here? A lone Koratok. Hmm, interesting. Not the Koratok we remember, but a Koratok, nonetheless."

With each guttural hiss that lashed forth from her forked tongue, she pulled the struggling Paolo closer to her amber eyes for closer inspection. The glowing amber eyes from within the feminine outlined mist seemed to pierce through his vermillion lenses and gaze into the coroner's soul. Widening her jaw, the entity let out a series of demoniac cackles before turning back to the Sarella, still struggling to regain her strength.

> "So, the sniveling priestess thinks you are her carrion savior. HA! Faithless and lost, your Order has become a hollow husk of its former glory."

The eyes moved to gaze upon Paolo once more.

> "We do not fear you, right hand of Myrina! Whispers have reached even our ears, of the truth about the once fearsome Koratoks. How even the flightless murder of the mighty Brinax have lost their penitence. Tossing aside the sacred covenant with your creator in favor of finding comfort in man's newfound natural philosophies. You are pathetic. Weak, in both will and mind. We will break you just as easily as we have broken this pathetic priestess."

The umbral appendage tightened its grip around Paolo, who grunted as he struggled to fight himself free of the cackling shroud. From behind the shadow and down the catacomb hallway, a noise pierced through the cackling laughter of the malevolent umbrage. The noise was the echoing reverberations of a raven's gurgling croak, louder and deeper in timbre than any raven that Paolo had ever heard.

The shadow slowly turned, its eyes darting wildly as it frantically searched for the source of the harrowing noise. Another croak echoed faintly from the hall, and the coroner broke free from the shadow's grasp. Gasping for air, Paolo recovered and rolled away from the quivering visage of evil.

"No, it cannot be. How?" Hissed the shadow, the voice quivering as it continued to peer down the hall.

Dark shadows of wings appeared from the end of the hall, as a third gurgling croak rang out from the stairwell. Seeing his second opportunity, Paolo dropped

250

the vial from his sleeve and rose from the blackened floor. The tenebrous pitch of his uniform blended into the surrounding darkness as he silently ascended on the shadowy figure, only the white of his mask shown through the umbrage. The amber eyes turned back to find the coroner standing between it and the Sarella, the glowing phial held outright before the amber eyes.

> "I know not what you speak of, being of the shadow. But hear me and take heed. I am Coroner Paolo Reveré, Resurrectionist of the Royal Order of Coroners. And I will hunt you, and your kind down, and send you all back to the oblivion from whence you came!"

Paolo raised the radiant glass into the air before casting the vial at the feet of the shadow-like being. The glass shattered across the stone floor, sending a wave of blinding white flame in every direction. As the eyes caught the sight of the white eosphorus flames, an ear-splitting shriek rang out from the bowels of the shadow. The flames whirled around the entity and began to consume it in a pyroclastic display of enraged turbulence.

Slowly the shadow began to sink into the ground below into the dying light of the white flames. As the umbrage plunged back into a bubbling puddle, it quickly slithered out of the decimated doorway and down the hallway. Finally dissipating into the air and out of their sight. Paolo turned to help the Sarella to her feet, the shadow of wings and the sound of croaking also receding from the hallway.

Sarella Augathina trembled as Paolo helped her up. She thanked him as she regained her strength and could finally stand on her own without assistance.

"Are you going to be all right?" Paolo asked as he helped her to the wall of the chamber. The Sarella shook her head in agreeance as she transferred her weight from his arm to the stone wall. Paolo returned to the door and observed the hallway once more.

> "What was that foul thing? Another form of these crazed beasts?"

"No, far worse than anything you have seen thus yet."

Paolo turned and spotted his cane on the floor. Picking the contrivance up from the floor, he returned to the Sarella and handed her the instrument so that she may use it for assistance. Wiping the remaining sweat from her brow with a cloth from her vestments, the Sarella spoke to the coroner.

"That being is a vile remnant from the nightmarish antiquity of our race's past. A Sklaven Wytche. They are vile practitioners of the umbryssal arts that seek to exterminate all of mankind in the name of their malevolent Drevniya. She along with the rest of her covenant, worship the six dread Drevniya from the depths of Fensylfania to the east. I feared that those of her ilk would be involved with this bestial scourge. There is much more to educate you on, Master Coroner. But I fear that after my foolish request, we no longer have the time to properly ready you for the task ahead. The wytche knows of our location and will send the Varemoden to descend upon Lethelheim to destroy us. You must make for Lazzar Perish at once, root her out and destroy her. Only then will we be safe from this blight that plagues our land."

252

Paolo's mind raced with questions but knew that time was of the essence.

"I don't understand what any of this has to do with our organizations. I have never been a pious man, nor do I consider myself a righteous one. But I swore an oath to protect and serve the people of the realm, and I am to honor my oath. If I am to understand this correctly, are you implying that this bestial scourge is the byproduct of some form of mephitic curse?"

"That is exactly what I am trying to tell you, Master Coroner. Can't you see? I had you perform the phlogistony so that you would see the truth of the matter. These poor souls, these poor guardswomen, were all infected. Their mutations were brought about by the conjured mephitic mist that rapidly encroaches upon our realm."

Paolo stood frozen, the gravity of the Sarella's words hitting him in his chest like the swift blow from a war hammer. His knees grew weak under the strain of the news and eventually took a knee on the chamber floor. Further, his mind raced on what protocol he was meant to follow considering the unraveling circumstance.

"Sarella, you must forgive me. This is most troublesome news. You are wanting me to believe that a crazed, delusional, band of women have somehow conjured something that has not happened in our kingdom for centuries. A *plague*?"

Sarella Augathina nodded her head in silence and made another sign of the Crescent Dianastic with her right hand at hearing the word plague from the coroner's lips.

> "I must send word to the Praetorium. At once. They must assemble the Coroners, in full force."

"NO! No, it's too late, Master Coroner. Your compatriots cannot come to your aid in time. You, like me, have been chosen by our holy mother to carry out her will. To save the people of the realm. You, Coroner Paolo Reveré, are the right hand of Myrina."

The Sarella approached the coroner and joined him in kneeling. Facing the trembling coroner, she reached down and took his hands in hers and began to recite a small prayer in Old Solarnian. Although he could not understand her ancient words, a sense of peace welled up from within his bosom and he felt at peace with the task that had been laid before him. As she finished, they both rose to their feet, and the coroner thanked her with a heavy sigh.

> "Sarella, what must I do? What kind of instruments or weaponry at man's disposal can be used to strike down such supernatural horrors?"

As he asked his questions, the Sarella slowly walked across the chamber and bent down to retrieve the silabar rood that lay on the damp stone floor. Turning to face the coroner, she presented him with the fetish, and he took it in his hands. The light from the hallway

254

caressed the crescent and gibbous moons that
comprised the cross-like relic, reflecting off the
vermillion crystal lenses of his mask.

"With faith, Master Coroner, and blessed steel.
Now come, there is much to do before you
make for Lazzar Perish."

The Ferrier's Forge

<u>Within the Town Square of Lethelheim</u>
18th hour of the 91st day

Sarella Augathina accompanied Paolo in his coach as he drove from the rectory toward the abandoned forge of the Lethelheim blacksmith. Gossamer fibers and dust coated the interior of the deserted building. Paolo located the forge's hearth and deemed it fit upon inspection. He searched for fresh coal while the Sarella traversed the inner walls of the forge and placed fresh candles within the hanging lanterns.

She set and lit the candles one by one while Paolo shoveled the new coal into the hearth and filled the water basin with water from the small creek behind the forge. After starting a small fire from within the cold hearth of the forge, Paolo worked the bellows to stoke the fire while the physician spoke to him.

"The fabric of your uniform is similar in make to that of my own vestments. The black dyed wool fibers are woven together with silabar thread. This reinforcement of your garb is how you can sustain blows from both blade and claw without a single tear of the cloth, keeping your skin safe from exposure.

Though your mask staves off the mephitic odors, my simple cloth covering is equally protective through silabar weaving and my devout faith in Mother Myrina. Silabar is one of the four sacred metals and is associated with the dark Goddess of the Umbral Void.

The strands of silabar were chosen by our predecessors to protect us from mephitic evil. As silabar metals repel all entities born of the Umbryss.”

The fire within the hearth crackled and hissed with each gust from the billow as they rose to lick the freshly shoveled coals.

Slowly the fire grew in intensity, and soon, a raging flame roared from within the long slumbering forge.

Paolo turned from the bellows and approached the racks of smithy tools lining the side of the forge. Spotting what he was searching for, he reached and grabbed a medium-sized, cast-iron melting pot. Sarella Augathina approached the Coroner.

From her mantle, she produced the selenestic artifact. Reciting a small incantation from the selenestic scriptures, she held the silabar rood aloft in her hands and presented the fetish to Paolo.

“This divine artifact, a gift from our beloved goddess in times lost to antiquity, is made from pure silabar. I bestow this rood upon you, Coroner Paolo, right hand of Myrina. May it aid you in combat against the forces of darkness.”

The Sarella placed the rood into the melting pot and stepped to the side so the coroner could begin smelting the relic down to a liquid state.

“You will craft silabar ammunition for your firearm, as well as your crossbow. I will bless them and bestow the sacred metal with the favor of our Selenestic Mother of Sorrows. But you will need more than ballistae in your arsenal if you are going to drive out this evil from our borders."

The Dianastic Rood

As the divine metal turned into a liquified state within the heat of the hearth, Paolo placed the bullet mold onto the rusted anvil and readied it for pouring. The coroner removed the iron pot from the heat of the hearth, grasping the handle with both hands, and turned toward the anvil. He transferred the molten material into the cavities of the bullet mold with a steadied hand, ensuring not to spill a single drop.

He opened the mold and gave the sprue plate a sharp strike with a mold mallet, dropping the freshly cast silabar bullets onto the top of a nearby wooden barrel lid. He sized and lubricated the rounds before placing them into the bandolier sleeves lining his belt and brigantine. Paolo repeated the process, but, only this time, he cast numerous silabar bolt heads to replace the steel tips of the bolts he had.

Loading the new bolts into the emptied boxed canisters, the coroner slid them neatly into the two leather pouches crafted for them on the back of his belt. He checked the cast-iron melting pot. As he tilted the container, Paolo could see there wasn't much of the precious resource remaining. He placed the pot back onto the hearth fire and walked over to the various cast molds that lined the wall of the smith's workshop. Paolo slowly perused the multiple molds. There were longsword molds, pike head molds, tong molds, and molds for farm tools.

He grew more disgruntled the longer he searched until his eyes caught a small mold hidden behind the mold for a pitchfork. Setting aside the farming tool mold, Paolo reached and grabbed the mold that grabbed his attention. It was the mold for the head of a woodsman's hatchet. He returned to the forge and dipped the dust-covered mold into the water basin before closing it and setting it upon the anvil for pouring.

The remaining molten silabar poured from the iron pot and into the hatchet mold, filling the space with the exact amount needed. Grabbing a straight-peen hammer, the coroner knocked the hatchet head free from the mold. With hammer and bits, the coroner took to shaping the hatchet head. Through a series of upsetting the metal and peining it with the straight-peen hammer, the ax head was finally quenched in the steaming waters of the basin. Inspecting his rudimentary smith work, Paolo was satisfied with the quality of the blunted-shaped metal and scratched a series of letters into the head and filled them with heated black ink.

A gnarled Turnian birch tree could be seen from the forge's window, so Paolo ventured into the adjacent field and fetched a sturdy branch. After sawing, rasping, and sanding, the birchwood slid into the ax head and was nailed into place. After placing the handle, Paolo took to sharpening the other end of the handle with his lister knife into a sharp stake. The grindstone ensured the hatchet was honed to a fine edge and, upon completion, was handed over to the Sarella. Before bestowing the blessing upon the weapon, the physician inspected the craftsmanship of the hatchet.

"This is fine work, Master Coroner. These markings, what do they mean?"

"Long ago, I was left in a basket on the steps of the orphanage in Calitoria. When the nutricas of the orphanage eventually discovered me, nothing but a scrap of parchment was left on top of my sleeping body. It bore the words, Helsingyr, and nothing more. I carried that name until my twelfth season. After passing the entrance exam and gaining admittance into the academy, the Doctorí of the Order assigned me a new one. The way all orphan candidates get their identities. But I never was allowed to forget the name, and it instilled within me the willpower to survive in this brutal world. With the task that has been laid before me, no matter how many times I fall, this weapon can be my will personified, in righteous retribution."

The Sarella smiled at the coroner's tale.

"Helsingyr must be an old Turnian surname. It is quite fitting, Master Coroner, with all things considered. May Helsingyr guide your hand as you illuminate the tenebrous Umbryss with its divine glory."

Sarella Augathina blessed the Blade and returned it to the Coroner. Paolo found a spare hammer sleeve and fastened it to his belt before sliding the newly crafted hatchet into the leather loop. With his ammunition and hatchet readied, the two departed the forge and made their way back down the village green road to the rectory. As the cart pulled into the courtyard, Paolo pulled the coach into the stable house next to the brick building. The coroner took to unfastening his horse from her harness and switching the dray horse over to a bridle and saddle for quicker travel.

He walked Konstantina from the stable to the courtyard and was met by the Sarella and, to Paolo's surprise, a familiar face. The Turnian merchant he had rescued from the windmill stood beside the Sarella, free from his madness and appearing calm and kempt. The merchant shook Paolo's hand and thanked him repeatedly for saving his life on the road. The man spoke in fluent common speech, a skill most merchants of the realm retain.

"You saved my life, Master Coroner. I can never repay you. Those fiends ambushed my wagon and slaughtered my horse right before my eyes. If they weren't obsessed with devouring my poor dray horse, I would never have had the time to barricade myself in that infernal windmill. It was the most terrifying moment of my life. But I can only blame myself. I should have known the roads weren't safe to travel, not after the arrival of those foreign men bearing foreign tabards from the east. Ever since they started riding up and down the Border Realm, nothing but chaos has erupted in the small hamlets and villages."

Paolo gave the merchant a sideways glance at the mention of the strange foreign men.

"These men, what was the color and standard of their tabards? Was it a red hexagon on a black field, bearing a six-pupil eye?"

The merchant shook his head in agreeance,

"Yes, that is it. Have you seen them as well? Led by some brutish knight who calls himself Syr *Saidach*. He and his men have taken over the old fort northeast of here, Fort Fermyre. The locals complained to the Hawkshaw about the slaving, but Lord Richten had his hands tied when confronting the deviants. They produced signed decrees from the Queen. They don't care about men at all and often left me to my business without a fuss. They only gather the women and girls from the villages and haul them off to the fort. I've seen their slave wagons head that way many a time."

As the merchant shared the information with the coroner, Paolo's hand tightened its grip on the dangling leather rein. His blood boiled as the anger welled from within at the thought of innocent women and girls imprisoned at the fortress. The Sarella placed a warm hand on Paolo's trembling and spoke to him with a gentle voice.

262

"Master Coroner, calm your nerves and
remember your purpose. You will not best these
foes with a clouded mind. These men, they are
all Rholhynian knights who have sworn vile
oaths to the dark Sycrass. To beat them, you
must keep the Mother's sorrowful mercy in
your heart."

Paolo took a deep breath and released his tension on
the reins. Konstantina gave Paolo a loving nudge on the
shoulder and nickered, forcing the coroner to reach
over and stroke her mane as he shook his head.
Clearing his mind, he raised his head. His eyes met
those of the Sarella.

"Thank you, Sarella Augathina. Before heading
to Lazzar Perish, I will first make it to the fort
to rescue the enslaved woman and children.
Merchant, make haste and find a good horse
and cart in the nearby town of Anorheig and
bring it to Lethelheim. I will send my raven
when the women and children have been freed,
bring the Sarella to the Fort Pass and help them
to safety. Do you understand?"

The man shook his head and hurriedly departed the
village green road. Paolo placed a spurred boot in the
stirrup and pulled himself up and into the saddle.
Sarella Augathina approached him. Her prayer beads
gripped tightly in her clasped hands.

"Coroner Paolo, please keep your wits about
you. Wanton violence will only bring you to
ruin. Remember the scriptures and may the

Goddess still your soul and guide your striking arm.”

Paolo adjusted himself in the saddle and flung his cloak back to reveal the holstered hamherbuss.

> “Sarella, I refuse to go into the depths of oblivion carrying the crux of zealotry upon my back. I don’t know yet what to make of this divinity business, whether Goddess or the Drevniya. But what I know is that evil deeds are not born from the wills of Gods but are born in the minds of men. We, the races of men and other beings, are the cruel monsters, Sarella Augathina. Recently, a crazed man told me that wicked men must be met with brutal fates. In this case, I would agree.”

The coroner wheeled his horse around and faced toward the road ahead.

Before departing, Paolo turned his head to the side until he could see the Sarella standing within his periphery. Having said all that needed to be said, he only bowed his head while tipping the wide brim of his capotain toward the physician.

The Sarella nodded her head in reply to the silent gesture of thanks, and the coroner turned back in his saddle. With a kick from his spurs, Paolo rode off from the Rectory road and onto the village green road before disappearing behind the ruins of the decrepit town.

"Goddess Myrina, Selenestic mother of sorrows
and Dianastic mother of mercies. Hear my
prayer and grant me courage. For your right
hand descends upon the gates of evil, and death
has risen to meet him."

The Sarella finished her final prayer as the winds
picked up around her, blowing dried leaves and dust
across the rectory courtyard. The gurgling croak of a
raven could be heard overhead. The Sarella averted her
gaze to the evening sky and beheld the beating wings
of a blackbird as it soared over the rectory.

She continued to watch as the raven flew over
the roof of the Selenestic Sepulcher, heading northeast.
Slowly she made her way up the stone steps of the hill
and into the modest-sized cathedral, to return to her
Sarella duties. As the sun fell behind the western
horizon, the arrival of the gloamhour spread darkness
across the lands.

As the light of a harvest moon appeared over
the eastern horizon, the tolling of the sepulcher bell
began to ring out over the town of Lethelheim.

Perthmyre Downs

A heavy fog rolled onto the eastern borders of the moor. The air was thick with moisture from the evenfall rain. This brought a stretching light haze that reached out toward the Perthmyre Downs. The thin clouds spanned and curled like slender fingers, grasping greedily at the land below. A low-hanging golden moon loomed over the treetops of Faynean Forest.

As the pale flaxen rays graced the stagnant fetid puddles of the moor, the dulled reflections underlined the ominous turpitude hidden within the low-hanging vapor. Paolo rode his dray horse at full gallop through the eastern road of the Fallow Field from Lethelheim. Reaching the border of the low thin mist, Konstantina reared back and squealed before letting a single hoof cross into the egregious vapor.

Paolo knew that his mount sensed the evil within the fog and respectfully dismounted from the saddle while holding onto the reins. He calmed the struggling horse, who bucked and stamped at the mist. He stroked her mane and soothed the steed, finally bringing her to a calm, stilled state. Paolo walked to saddlebags and retrieved a bundle of tied rope from within before returning to his horse.

"This is where we part ways, old girl. I promise you. I will be fine. Listen carefully, head back to the Sarella and help her get the people to safety. That's an order. I am counting on you, do not fail me."

Konstantina only gave a single snort in response before turning from the downs and galloping off toward Lethelheim. Paolo stood in the damp grass of the small knoll and watched as his horse disappeared into the twilight-shrouded horizon and out of sight.

The phage-filled mist lingered low over the moor, allowing the coroner to see far enough ahead to chart a route toward his objective. From the hillock, he could observe over the entirety of the Perthmyre Downs, his gaze penetrating the sparse border of the menacing Faynean woods. Paolo spotted the limpid outline of a singular stone fortress penetrating over the tree line ahead. Fort Fermyre sat within the center of the encapsulating xanthous gibbous moon. The coroner could see a path through the scattered tree line that led to the secular bastion and kneeled in thought.

If I were to take the shortcut through the tree line, that would bring me close to the fortress and keep me off the main road. I should go undetected until I am in a better range to assess the compound's exterior further.

Paolo hung the rope from his belt and descended into the mist below. The haze clung to the base of the small jutting hill. With each step of his leather boot, the fog would swirl and churn around him as if writhing in escape from his presence.

Paolo kept pushing forward, his vision becoming more hampered with each step. The aromatic incense began to spark and ignite as the mist graced the brass ports along the sides of his beaked rebreather.

Slowly he traversed the moor, ensuring not to make a significant enough disturbance that would warrant unwanted attention. Crossing the last set of rolling knolls, Paolo had reached the narrow dirt road that led to the fort's entrance.

He stopped and lowered himself into the receding mist, inspecting both sides of the path before crossing. The distant sound of hoofbeats echoed from the southern side of the road. Riders were approaching, and the coroner estimated three or four from the clamoring and braying of the swiftly approaching bestial coursers.

If I stay here, I will indeed be spotted. Best to make for the tree line and conceal myself within the darkness of the forest.

Paolo sprang from his crouched position and bounded across the narrow dirt road. Sprinting toward the tree line, Paolo could hear the thunderous clamoring of the coursers closing in on his position.

The small band of armored knights passed as the last of his cloak vanished within the forest's darkness. Unaware of his presence, the group continued to ride down the path toward the fortress keep. Paolo tucked and slid into the trunk of a thick gnarled tree. As he nestled into the roots, his boots disturbed the dense unnatural undergrowth of the forest floor. As the soil shifted, the unusual vegetation began to stir.

Iridescent vines of deranged sporangium slithered from under stones and moss towards the coroner as if drawn by his very presence. Paolo beheld the disturbed sporangiophores in bewilderment before pulling himself up by a large, coiled tree root next to him. The forest floor was riddled with bizarre mycotic outgrowths as if the nature of the mist had a profound effect on the plants of the forest. Peculiar molds and tendril writhing moss could be seen in every direction. Paolo stepped backward from the encroaching sporangium until he was stopped in his slow retreat by a sudden sinking sensation. A crunching noise followed by the slow pulsating sensation of throbbing ooze came from behind Paolo.

Quickly the coroner turned to find that his boot heel had sunk into the bloated stag carcass. Paolo pulled his pus coated boot from the gelatinous putrefaction in grunting discontent. Peering into the seething and gaping hole between shattered ribs, he could see the entrails were also riddled with a bubbling saprophytic soup.

Paolo remembered the words of the Sarella as he backed from both the tainted flora and fauna of the malignant woods. Heeding her warnings on the foul beasts that lurked beyond the borders of Lethelheim, the coroner pulled the silabar hatchet from his belt and continued to back away. After a safe distance, he finally turned, only to become ensnared by some violent force around his ankle.

Before he could assess the source of the attack, his right leg was pulled backward. Paolo was sent hurdling toward the forest floor by the weight of his brigantine. His momentum shifted into the air before his chest could touch the ground. His dangling torso spun around in the air. Tensing his abdomen and steadying himself, his eyes focused on the source of his capturer.

The half-rotted and bloated corpse of the stag had sprouted forth from its chest cavity a multitude of barbed tendrils that had grabbed the coroner and raised him high into the air. Paolo gripped the birchwood handle of the hatchet tightly and pulled himself up. A quick slash from the sharpened silabar ax set him free of the oozing tentacle. He turned to his shoulder in time to brace his fall with the side of his body as he crashed into the forest floor below.

A hissing screech blasted from the stag carcass as it recoiled the severed appendage. Bones and flesh alike began to twist from underneath the decaying hide violently. As the mass of decomposition rose from the ground on stilts of compound ossifications, there came a from its putrefied back a series of fungating furuncle growths. The furuncles ruptured with xanthous pus, revealing a series of cystic snouts and gaping maws from the pockets of ruptured boils.

The newly formed visages were a combination of various woodland beasts. Lynx, wolf, hawk, and bear could all be seen jutting from the back of the horrific amalgamation. The deviation rose to a bipedal stance, each face letting loose a cacophony of howls, hisses, and roars as piles of squirming maggots spilled forth from its entrails.

The tendrils lashed at Paolo as the monster stumbled forward awkwardly, learning to walk on its newly formed legs. The coroner dove to his right into a forward roll and then made for the trunk of a large tree. Diving behind the safety of the thick tree, Paolo leaned back into the bark and reached toward his vest.

While keeping a constant lookout as the monstrosity lumbered in its search of him, he grabbed a vial of eosphorus. Popping the cork stopper of the bottle, Paolo quickly coated the sharpened ax blade with a layer of volatile white salt grains.

270

*I don't have time for this sarding shit. You want to drag
me down and force my hand? Fine, let's see how you
like a little purification by fire.*

Rapidly replacing the eosphorus salts vial, he removed
the alkahest bottle and poured it over the grains.
Rubbing the salts and solution together, it quickly
began to form a sticky paste. Once the paste was evenly
applied, the coroner drew a striker from his vest.

The brimstone striker let up in an ochre flame
as he struck the tip against the back of his knee.
Bringing the striker to the silabar ax, the flame quickly
spread to the paste-coated ax head.

A blinding white flame erupted from the hastily
made quick paste as the combustion reaction of the
chymiac ingredients took effect. Paolo sprang from the
ground and rounded the gnarled oak tree, his black
cloak fanning outward behind him.

His eyes met the monster as it spun in place to
face him, its numerous eyes reflecting the light of the
roaring white flame. The coroner held the fiery hatchet
outward at his side and slowly raised the weapon
upward toward the creature. Fulminating in a state of
absolute rage at the sight of the coroner, the animal's
spine tore free from its rotting torso. The antlered stag
head slithered high into the treetops like a great serpent
before craning down towards the coroner. Paolo stood
his ground, waiting for the inevitable lunge of the
predator.

Widening its fang-lined jaw, a multitude of
barbed tongues came jutting outward from the large
primary head of the beast. Paolo stared down the stag's
head. Not a single twitch came from his fibers. The
longer he peered into the darkened pits within the
oozing eye sockets. He caught a glimpse of a familiar

sight. The amber eyes of the Sycrass stared back at him. Paolo smiled from within his mask from the discovery.

> "So, wytche. You mean to draw me into combat with this abomination. Are you hoping the flames will draw them into the forest and surround me? Well, I hope you have other means of spying on me. Because you are going to watch me butcher each and every one of the bastards."

The stag head quivered and bellowed forth an earth-shaking roar. From within the mist and spittle sprayed from its tendril-filled maw came the tumbling of a searing white flame. The hatchet cut through the head of the beast like a falling meteorite. Every portion of the flayed skull turned to ash and white embers as the ax head continued to tumble forward. Passing from gullet to sinew, the silabar blade split the entirety of the stag. Burning piles of beasts spewed in every direction from the forest as the eosphorus flames spread onto the undergrowth.

The hatchet stuck deep into the thick bark of a colossal oak tree from behind the burning remains. Paolo ran through the fire to retrieve his weapon, the flames recoiling against the insulation of his waxed cloak and overcoat. Pulling the hatchet from the trunk, the last of the quick paste remained buried in the wood. Quickly the flames spread from twisted tree to tree, and soon a roaring sea of white flames rose high above the treetops within the small projection of Faynean Forest.

Not long after the giant oak tree was devoured in a blanket of ivory flames, the alarm was raised from

272

within the fort. The sound of men hollering echoed out over the forest, soon followed by the clanging, and rattling of heavy iron.

The gate guard raised the portcullis, and dozens of armed knights poured from the western gate toward the raging forest fire. They barked orders at one another in their broken guttural language, quickly forming a line at the forest's edge. These knights bore the same sigil upon their tabard as the one Paolo had encountered before but had undergone such mutation that they were no longer recognizable as men.

Black bilious sludge seeped from the spaces of their bloated, stained, and soiled plate armor and chainmail. Each heavy breath came hissing from the pores of their pig snout helmet, lingering in the still night air as if the land was gripped in snow. Dull red eyes penetrated through the slit of their visor like the beady eyes of rodents, darting wildly around the forest in search of the source of the fire. Soon the men split up in their search by the command of the most bloated of the group. The last knight on end shook his helm in agreeance and turned a sharp left before moving around a sizeable thick oak tree.

As the knight rounded the trunk, Paolo dropped from a branch above him and buried the hatchet deep into the helm of the bloated knight. Quietly the coroner severed the head of the bloated knight, painting the bark of the tree in bursts of bile-tainted blood. Paolo returned to the shadows, leaving the butchered corpse of the monstrous man to roil in cinders from the silabar blade.

Paolo silently stalked and butchered each of the tumefied men from the shadows of the burning forest. After descending upon the second to last armored fiend from a low branch, the coroner tackled the heaving brute to the forest floor before severing the helm from the breastplate of the behemoth. Paolo reached down and pulled the rotting mound of cranial decay from the pool of viscous black blood before hurling it toward the last standing knight.

The head filled helm soared through the air and crashed into the charred forest floor with an echoing clang. The tattered cloak-adorned knight spun around and lowered his beady red eyes to the ground. Upon seeing the severed head of his compatriot, the bulging armored brute raised his double-headed battle ax into the air and let out a thunderous war cry into the void of the expansive forest.

As he continued to hold his battle cry, a searing silabar crossbow bolt pierced the visor of his great bucket helm and severed the vocal cords. As it passed through iron and bone, the bolt took helmet and head with it as it sailed onward and into the trunk of a great burning oak tree.

Rotting seepage dripped from the pinned helmet as a decapitated body dropped the heavy iron battle-ax and crashed to its knees. Geysers of blackened arterial blood spouted into the air as the bloated, headless corpse fell forward with a heavy thud. The coroner emerged from the shadows, sliding forward the slid of the hamherbuss and sending the crossbow back into its hidden housing.

> "Cruel fates for cruel men, madame Sycrass. I
> hope you bore witness to this slaughter because
> I am just getting warmed up. Do you hear me?
> There will be no quarter given to rapists,
> slavers, or warmongers. Only the swift fall of
> my gavel."

Fort Fermyre

<u>Overlooking the Faynean Forest</u>
23rd hour of the 92nd day

Thick blankets of fog quickly swept outward from the depths of the gnarled forest and blanketed the white flames. The heavy moisture of the mist soon quenched the eosphorus flames, bringing it to a slow dwindling ember. The coroner recognized the fetid mist to be the wrathful workings of the Sycrass but grew more emboldened in his purpose.

As the mist snuffed out his forest fire, it also provided him with the perfect means of maneuvering closer to the fortress undetected. The last pillars of fire died out and the fog withdrew back into the forest as the coroner slipped past the last tree line of the thicket and toward the forest edge. Paolo crept up from the forest's edge and found himself on a raised embankment of eroded worm-ridden earth. Having swiftly traveled three fathoms northeast from the flames, Paolo moved from the thick of the forest to the scarce border in hopes of climbing in elevation to obtain a better view before rushing towards the fort.

As he passed the last line of rotting oaks, Paolo crouched low to the ground to keep out of sight and found a large boulder to conceal himself behind. After pausing his movement for a moment, he peaked from around the large stone to observe the southern portcullis gate for activity. He reached into his vest and pulled out a small brass scope with a flanged edge.

The monocular device locked into place as he joined the flanged edge to the outer cusp of his left vermillion ocular. Closing his right eye, the coroner focused his vision through the monocular to obtain a closer view of the nearby bastion from higher ground. The view of the postern fortress was both a harrowing and sickening sight.

The bodies of flayed and mutilated women hung from thick ropes over the battlements on either side of the southern gate. Gibbet cages of various sizes dangled from raised beams within the stagnant fly-ridden moat. Each rusted gibbet contained the half-crow-eaten corpses of more peasant women.

The most disturbing sight was the rows of impaled, flayed women that lined the postern road leading into the fortress. Wooden signs hung from their necks from pieces of rope, each reading the words *'Take heed any who try and resist.'* Paolo shook and seethed with restrained rage at the twisted barbaric sight, his blood pressure rising as he clenched his teeth from within his mask.

If the Lord Hawkshaw of Turnia observed this disgraceful act of blatant human degeneracy and he still was dissuaded to action by a mere royal decree, I swear on the Goddess and all other Gods that I will castrate him after this is through. That sarding coward of a nobleman, what a piss excuse for a governor.

Paolo collected his addled nerves and returned to the task at hand. His observing eye spotted the postern gate and began to take count of the remaining brigands on guard.

He could see two knights standing guard outside the postern gate of the fortress. Each watched the southern pass and the blazing flames from the forest in angst as they gripped their weapons and grunted out heavy course lingering breaths. Paolo moved the monocular from the gate to the outer bailey, counting six more men walking along the battlements. Observing the courtyard, Paolo spotted three large iron cages filled with huddled women and little girls, each of the prisoner cages manned by two armed knights.

Beyond the cells was the rear entrance to the great hall and donjon of the bastion, which he spotted two more men posted on each side of the door. Inspecting the higher regions of the fort, Paolo spotted two Varemoden, perched upon the merlon of the single lookout tower of the inner bailey. Counting his enemies once more, Paolo began to formulate a plot but was interrupted in his planning by the sound of an approaching vehicle.

Moving to the other side of the boulder, he could see the arrival of a large box wagon. Four demoniac oxen-like beasts of immense size slowly pulled the iron caged cassion. Paolo could see the thin cachectic arms of captured peasant women reaching out through the narrowly spaced bars, shouting, and crying pleas of deliverance to the heavens.

To the rear of the wagon, Paolo spotted only two mounted knights as the caravan guard. They sat heavy and slouched in their saddles upon the backs of their nightmarish, crimson-eyed coursers. Seeing a window of opportunity, Paolo drew his hamherbuss and slowly slunk back into the concealing shadows of the forest.

Quickly the coroner made for the rear of the caravan. Arriving at a patch of thick trees just a half league to the rear of the riders, Paolo slid back the forearm of the hamherbuss and revealed the hidden crossbow from within. He pulled a freshly loaded cartridge of silabar bolts from the leather case and loaded them into the weapon, keeping his eyes fixed on his targets. Taking aim with his left hand, the coroner rapidly fired four bolts at both the knights and their mounts. The bolts singed and ignited their flesh upon contact, sending saddles and armor clanging into pools of vile coagulation and smoldering cinders. With the rear guard eliminated, Paolo rushed for the rear of the cart.

As he suspected, the rear door was sealed with a heavy iron padlock. The sight of the coroner roused the captured women from their exhaustive state as they began to shift and stir from within the caged cart.

"Goddess be praised, a raven! Everyone look, our prayers have been answered!"

Shouted a shackled woman to the others. Quickly they clamored toward the gate, tears of joy rolling down their sanguine soiled cheeks. Dozens of slender feminine fingers jutted from the bars and caressed the black wool cloak draped around his shoulders as he tried to calm them.

A sense of paranoia about the possibility of detection forced him to free himself from the joyous women and move to the side of the slowly creeping wagon to inspect the driver. As he returned, the face of a middle-aged peasant could be seen smiling through the bars of the door.

"In all my days. I never would have thought the sight of a coroner would bring me joy."

278

Paolo reached into his vest and pulled a small tin canister from a single leather pouch, quietly informing the women to stand clear of the door. He packed the padlock with as much saltpetyr and brimstone clay as he could before tossing the empty tin and reaching for his tinder box. He lit the striker match and raised it to the lock. As the lock blew from the caged door in small, controlled combustion, the gurgling croak of Corvax rang out from high above the southern moor.

The cart came to a sudden stop as the blast went off. Bounding down the side, Paolo raised his weapon and turned the corner. A silabar bolt pierced through the knight's thick iron helm, sending maggot-infested sludge pouring to the couch seat under a clamoring of plate armor. The coroner's raven gracefully fluttered downward and landed on his broad shoulder as Paolo watched the corpse dissipate into a pile of eroding ash.

Returning to the rear of the cart and informing the raven to scout ahead, Paolo began to help the women down onto the road. With the last of the women and children out of the wagon, Paolo raised his arm to provide a perch for his messenger raven to rest upon. The bird returned to his arm with a quiet croak. Inspecting the mask of the coroner, the blackbird gave his master three affectionate taps on Paolo's white leather beak.

"Corvax, return them to the Sarella. Take them Lethelheim. Understand? Now, go."

The raven spread its wings and took to the sky in flight. Paolo then relayed the information to the shivering and huddled women.

"Follow my raven to Lethelheim. It is imperative that you stay clear of the mist, its foul nature will bring a pestilence most foul upon you and your kin. There is a Sarella in Lethelheim that is expecting you. Inform her that I will be sending more and have her wait for them on the borders of the Perthmyre Downs. The heartiest of you must make for Anorheig and raise the alarm for the regimental guard. Have them call the banners and bring food and clothing to Lethelheim. But tell them not to march on Lazzar Perish until the fog has dissipated, do you understand?"

A peasant woman embraced the coroner and the rest followed suit. Paolo stumbled back before catching himself, slowly lowering a raised arm to embrace the woman in return.

"Master coroner, you truly are a saint. They did terrible things, awful things. My husband cut down and butchered in front of my own eyes. I prayed for justice, for what they did to my husband, and for the vile things they did to me afterward. I cannot say it enough, thank you for giving me my vengeance. For bringing all of us our divine vengeance upon these cowardly animals."

Paolo let the woman finish her embrace before warningly grasping her shoulder with his hand.

"I am no savior or saint, missus. Nor am I an agent of the divine. I am just a man, and I am only doing my job. These ravenous animals will be put to the butcher's block, I promise each one of you that. Now be gone, the lot of you. Unless you plan to take up arms, be gone with thee."

He watched as the women departed down the road in haste and disappeared around the edge of the last trees before making his way back to the front of the cart. The distance from the postern gate was far enough that the posted guards on either the ground or the battlements had been roused.

It's good to know they have piss for eyesight. That can come in handy.

Paolo reached up and grabbed the riding crop from the driver's bench and gave the first bestial ox a hard smack on its rump returning the wagon to its proper course.

Returning to the rear of the cart in haste, Paolo climbed into the back of cart, before shutting and latching the door behind him. Slowly but steadily the cart approached the fort. As the oxen approached the postern portcullis, Paolo could hear the confused guttural sputtering of the guards outside.

"Where is the driver? Where is the caravan?"

"Maybe they stopped to investigate the disturbance in the woods. Bring the wagon in and get those slaves into the cages. Move it!"

Paolo let out a heavy sigh in relief as the cart continued to roll forward. Not long after the cart was once again brought to a slow stop. He could see through the bars the shadows of moving men and hear the heavy clanking of their metal plate armor as they inspected the driver bench. He gripped the Hamherbuss and slowly cocked back on the firing hammers when a sudden hard thud landed on the roof of the boxed cart.

The cart rocked violently under the weight of the sudden collision, sending dust and debris floating from above him.

The sound of shrill scraping and the rapping of claws could be heard as the Varemoden crawled in quadrupedal posture along the roof of the wagon, the chortling snorts of its wolfish snout sniffing along its path. The shadows approached from the sides, encroaching upon the rear of the cart. Paolo lowered himself back against the hard wooden panel behind him, bringing his firearm to the ready. As the knights came into view so did the long osseous claws of the Varemoden from the gaps between the upper bars of the wagon. Paolo aimed the firearm upward and underneath the belly of the beast, hoping to eliminate the larger threat before the knights could close the distance. His finger lightly caressed the tensed trigger, and he slowed his respiration to harness his focus. As the iron-clad hand of the closest guard reached for the door, a wave of shouts erupted from the battlements that drew the gaze of the knights crowding the wagon door. A sudden sound like the singing of a bolt grew louder before a broad tipped bolt came penetrating through the wooden roof of the box cart, pinning the Varemoden down as it roared and writhed wildly above.

A second followed which silenced the beast, sending a stream of black blood pouring over the edge and in front of Paolo's view. The knights drew their swords and axes and howled at one another in a state of bewildered panic.

"Where is it coming from?"

"Find the intruders!"

As they barked and spun in the mud, an ambush of military proportions was erupting along the battlements. Paolo rose from his seated position and made for the rear bars. As his eyes glazed from the narrow gaps, he caught a glimpse of a knight along with the postern battlement point northward and shout down below.

"THERE! Intruders are over there, near the tower!"

As the knight shouted down below, a shadowy figure rose from behind him and plunged a weapon deep into his breastplate while twisting his neck within his helm. The knights below turned toward the great hall and inspected the tower, missing the execution of their compatriot. Paolo watched as the remaining five men along the postern battlement disappeared in rapid succession.

Each of the men was rapidly being pulled under the merlons with flailing arms, followed by spouts of sanguineous spray which rained down to the courtyard below. As these men were being systematically executed, sounds of further alarm came from the inner bailey. Shouts, screams, and thuds of corpses came erupting from the inner battlements behind Paolo's position. In the wake of a carefully planned and stunningly executed, pincer move Paolo joined in on the figh.

The knights standing by the rear door were quaking in their armor, spinning in every direction trying to get a lock on the invading forces. The man in the middle shook free from his fearful grip and gave the others near him a heavy slug to the chest with his spiked mace.

"Stop standing around like pansies and get up there, you cowards are acting as if we are being attacked by a…"

A bolt pierced the speaking man's helmet, splitting both metal and bone in half and sending brain matter in every direction.

The two men near his corpse dropped their weapons into the mud and made for the portcullis. Paolo slid back the latch and flung open the back door of the wagon. Two knights spun around to inspect the calamitous noise only to be met with two devastating blows from Helsynger.

As he reloaded, the two men running toward the door were stopped in their tracks by a sudden rupture of two glass vials. From underneath their feet came an insidious purple noxious vapor, swallowing the two men who had become frozen in terror. Paolo pulled up on the side lever to lock the firearm as he watched in curious horror as the two men began to melt and burn in their armor from within the malignant mist.

Their screams turned into sputtering gargles as their iron armor collided with the muddied postern road, sending acrid singed flesh pouring from the seams of their metal suits. With the last two men lying in pools of bubbling remains, Paolo's attention was drawn to the sound of a Varemoden's howl being cut short as its decapitated head soared through the air and landed at his feet.

As the tongue of the beast rolled from its opened maw and touched his boot, he caught the sound of shifting earth from behind him. As the coroner turned in place to inspect the approaching noise, he was met with a flurry of blurred strikes. The assailant placed three lightning-fast jabs into both of his kidneys before landing a hard upward cut to the bottom of his throat. As his airway closed from the traumatic blow, the shrouded individual grabbed his left shoulder girdle and dislocated the bone from the socket while striking the nerve bundle. Paolo gritted his teeth and grunted in pain as the hamherbuss dropped from his limp hand and landed in the dirt below.

Falling to his knees, Paolo struggled to regain his respirations but was sent to his back with a hard kick to his chest. His vermillion crystals had failed to spot the assailant and it was as if Paolo was being struck down by the very air itself. Grabbing his arm with his remaining functional hand, Paolo quickly forced the humerus back into the socket.

The sound of unsheathed steel forced Paolo to cease his writhing and remain still. Slowly he went to lift himself up off the ground but was stopped. Both shin and blade closed in on his already swollen neck as his attacker grabbed the badge clasp of his cloak in their other hand.

Paolo reached upward and grabbed the shrouded assailant by the leg and felt wool, leather, and cold steel. The blade slid to his hand and stopped his advancement. Paolo grunted in disbelief and refused to accept his demise. The more he struggled, the more the slender leg pressed his windpipe and pushed his head further back. As his vision darkened, Paolo finally stopped his struggling and relaxed his muscles.

As his attacker pulled his badge-clasp closer to them, there was a moment of paused silence before Paolo was released from their firm grasp and sent backward to the dirt once more. The leg was removed from his throat and the attacker rose from his chest. The sound of another broken vial rang out followed by the escaping of more vapor. As Paolo rolled over to his side and gasped for air, the view of his attacker finally became clear in his vermillion lenses.

"I know that badge. You are *like me*. One of my… brothers. But, how? I don't understand..."

The voice from within the mask was that of a distraught woman. As she held Paolo's badge in her trembling hand, she frantically rubbed her thumbs along the raised metal punches of the words across the nameplate. Paolo remained on his side, reaching into his vest for a vial of laudanum syrup and his brass syringe.

The trembling coroner reached upward to her shoulder cape and pulled her own badge from its steel clasp housing. She held them side by side in trembling hands, muttering, and mumbling a series of incoherent ravings to herself.

"I was sent. Sent out into the border realm. I was. *The Praetorium*. I don't remember. Why can't I remember? The signal fires. I lit the signal fires and no one… *no one came*. No, this cannot be. I am alone, this is my fight! AH! The voices. Make them stop!"

She began to spasmodically convulse amid her melancholy state, dropping the black steel badges to the ground and grasping both sides of her hood-covered mask. She continued to argue with the voices from within her torn mind, her voice rising and falling between groans of confused anger.

Paolo brought himself to a knee and carefully drove the hypodermic needle of the syringe through the wax port of his uniform and into the antecubital fossa of his right arm. The nerve dulling syrup rushed into his veins, sending a wave of ague through his body and towards his core. As the viscous medicine dulled the pain in his shoulder, it also ignited his senses and focused his mind.

He withdrew the emptied vial from the syringe housing and threw it aside before retrieving the blue vial of anthemene from his vest. The anthemene chaser was a fool's choice, but he had little options if he was going to recuperate quickly after the martial onslaught from the mortalist.

Paolo grimaced as the precipitate mended his broken shoulder in a series of gut-wrenching sounds and localized corporeal contortions. His mind felt like it was ablaze. As the anthemene and laudanum mixed within his bloodstream, he could feel the body-altering effects begin to take hold of his senses. He felt anger, lust, hunger, paranoia, and melancholy all at once and at varying levels of intensity. His muscles contracted like corded steel underneath his skin, forcing the surface veins to bulge and beads of sweat to form on his taut skin.

As he rode out the violently intense humoral adjustment, the sound of pleas and whimpers came from the prisoner cags within the courtyard around them. Paolo gasped and choked as his lungs expanded from within his chest before finally arriving at a stabilized condition. Rising from his knee to his feet, he glanced toward the cages toward the noise. His eyes were met by the sunken and widened stare of an exposed woman.

The white of her eyes shone like torchlight through the battered and bruised blackness of her malformed face. It was the harrowed look of every victim he had been assigned to investigate their death.

288

It was like a look of fear and agony seen on a victim's face frozen forever in time.

The moment before their vitality was drained from them, by someone they trusted. Except for this time, this wasn't a butchered victim, as their eyes blinked back at him as he surveyed her from afar. Paolo shifted his gaze from her and scanned the cages, only to find a hundred torchlight gazes peering back at him through the bars of the cells. Some were wearing scolded bridles, while others were locked into maiming boots.

All of them were as silent as the grave, save for the children, who whimpered in fear and cowered behind the adults. Paolo quickly found his footing as he momentarily stumbled toward the first cage. As he began to make his way toward the cage, he was stopped by the mortalist, who drew her blade and held it aloft toward him.

"What do you think you are doing?"

Paolo stopped in his tracks, the tip of the blade pushing against the Kreiger steel splints of his brigantine. The resurrectionist slowly looked down at the thin straight blade of the stiletto before returning his gaze back to the eyes of the mortalist.

> "Get that blade away from me and help me free these women. We need to get them out of here and to safety before more of those bastards show up here."

Paolo went to move past the mortalist, but she stepped to block his path once more.

"I can't let you do that. These cattle are infected by the scourge. They are riddled with pestilence. If we release them, they will spread their mephitic phage across the realm. The only comfort we can offer this livestock is the therapeutic purification of flame."

Paolo clenched his fist and gritted his teeth from behind his mask. Giving the rattled mortalist the benefit of melancholy, he once again tried to move past her only to be met once more by her blade.

"I am warning you mortalist, put down the blade and step aside. Do you even hear yourself? Cattle? Livestock? These are human beings. Fellow Solarians, and women of our realm. If they are stricken with pestilence, then we will have the Sarella's care for their blight. Now cease this madness and help me free them. We are bound by oath to help these people."

"*Fuck* oaths. Do you think *oaths* and *honor* have kept me alive, flay-skin? Because let me tell you something about oaths, and honor, and the Order. We are expendable assets. Sent out throughout the realm to clean up the filth brought about by these peasants. They don't respect the law. They don't respect order. If given a choice between slicing our throats for a morsel of bread, or starve while retaining their purity, these animals would cut us from tits to pubic bone. And revel in their snack."

Wilhelmina' finger trembled as she thrusted it toward Paolo's beak while proclaiming her disposition. Rising in tone, and in tambor, Wilhelmina's voice cracked

290

under the strains of her near shouting. Each melancholy filled declaration forced a twitch from Paolo's strained eyes. She paused for a brief second, to regain her lost composure. Taking a steep breath, the mortalist lowered her finger. Wilhelmina spoke with a more controlled, and softer, tone.

> "I won't risk the stability of the realm over one of these naked, quivering, cowards who were too weak to die in their fields instead of being dragged here in chains. I know what happens to them, do you? Did Galini inform you of the destiny of these meat sacks? Or did he just entice you with morbid curiosity as he did me? They are fed the rotting entrails of their sisters and daughters, fattened on the sinew of the fallen. Made plump and engorged on the pestilence so that when she sacrifices them to the maelstrom below, they stoke the flames of plague. Is that what you want? Millions will perish in the blight to come, resurrectionists. I have seen the truth, and I am prepared to do what is necessary. Are you?"

As the mortalist finished her ravings, Paolo looked down once more at the outward held blade. As fast as a serpent strike, Paolo grabbed her outward elbow and drew her arm into his elbow.

The resurrectionist drove the side of his temple hard into the head of the stunned mortalist before thrusting his knee guard into her side. As she sucked in a heavy gust of wind under swiftly contracting lungs, Paolo continued to deliver blow after blow to the side of her head until the stiletto fell from her limp hand to the ground below. Pulling her back to her feet by the throat, Paolo then sent her flying to her back into the mud below with a heavy throw.

Straddling her, Paolo pulled the twitching mortalist up from the mud by the front of her soiled shoulder cape with both of his hands.

"ENOUGH! ENOUGH OF THIS! THESE WOMEN ARE NOT ANIMALS, THEY ARE HUMAN BEINGS FOR MOTHER'S SAKE!

Paolo raised his fist once more to deliver another blow but steadily began to lower his clenched fist as the adrenaline cooled within his humors. Relinquishing the tension in his arm, he leaned his back and gazed at the looming harvest moon above.

After taking in the rays of the celestial body, he returned to the mortalist who lay nearly lifeless in between his legs.

"Enough of this. Your name is Wilhelmina Strasse, and you are mortalist. More importantly, you are a royally appointed coroner of the Kingdom of Solarno. Within the madness of it all, you seemed to forget that. If I must beat you into a state of decrepitude to remind you of who you are and what you are, I will. Because oaths and honor are what keep us from becoming like these monsters. Do you understand? If we burn these women alive in these cages, how are we any different from the beasts?"

The mortalist stayed silent behind her battered mask as Paolo finished his words and released her from his grasp.

He swung his leg around and rose from the mud, leaving the panting Wilhelmina on her back.

292

Paolo adjusted his capotain and fixed his cloak before walking over to the badges that lie face down in the mud where she had dropped them moments before. He retrieved them one after the other and polished them on his cloak before sliding his own back into the steel housing of his badge clasp.

Returning to Wilhelmina, he tossed the mortalist badge to her chest and offered an outstretched hand. She propped herself up on her elbows and reached for her badge, once again she held the metal shield and rubbed it with her thumb. The sigil of the coiled horned serpent around a stiletto blade reflected off the vermillion crystal of her lenses as she stared in silence. Finally, she looked up from the badge and observed the resurrectionist as well as his outstretched hand. Paolo helped her to her feet and bent down to retrieve her blade.

The mortalist slid the badge back into the clasp housing and took the blade from him while uttering a hushed '*thank you*' to which Paolo nodded his head. He introduced himself and held out his hand once more but this time as a gesture of partnership. The two clasped their forearms and made amends once more. Together the two coroners freed the enslaved women from their cages and provided them with fresh torches to guide them toward Lethelheim.

As the last of the slave women rounded the portcullis gate entry and from sight, Paolo then reassessed his gear and supplies as did Wilhelmina.

"You are the first resurrectionist to beat me in martial combat. Possibly the first to beat a mortalist in the history of the order."

"You made a mistake, and I seized the opportunity. It's not natural philosophy, just a mistake in overconfidence."

Wilhelmina scoffed at Paolo's reply while cleaning her blade with a torn piece of tabard from the fallen knight below her.

"Oh, really. How was I overconfident?"

Paolo holstered the hamherbuss to his side and pulled his cloak around his shoulders.

"Would you have got that close to a martial? Always keep your foe at a forced lunge length, lesson #43 in the chapter on fixed blade combat in the Coroner's handbook."

Wilhelmina paused in thought as she ruminated on the outcome of receiving her beating from a martial.

"Fair point."

Paolo began to make his way around the great hall, but Wilhelmina called out and stopped him. She had ascended halfway up the steps leading to the great hall and beckoned to Paolo to follow her inside.

He shot a final glance toward the north side of the fortress, through the opened portcullis, and beyond the final stretch of the Perthmyre Downs. Lazzar Perish sat on the hillock like a jagged and broken tombstone at the head of a freshly shoveled grave. The outline of the hamlet was obscured in a twilight opacity as it lingered in the foreground of the low-hanging harvest moon. He turned his head back toward Wilhelmina who stood waiting for him on the broken stone steps.

"Lazzar Perish is there. What is inside the great hall? More prisoners?"

Wilhelmina shook her head in disagreement,
"No. The way into Lazzar Perish lies inside the great hall."

Paolo vaulted over a small fence and caught up to Wilhelmina on the steps. The two coroners then entered the great hall of the fortress. And began their journey to Lazzar Perish.

As the two disappeared into the great hall, the fog swept through the surrounding Faynean Forest and encapsulated the fortress in a vile tenebrous tidal wave. Sealing the coroners off from any help from the outside world.

The Grand Hall

<u>Of Fort Fermyre</u>
5th hour of the 93rd day

The two coroners entered the antrum of the great hall and began to descend a small flight of stone stairs. As they rounded the stairwell corner and entered the main hall, Paolo beheld the tarnished state of the facility. Two large tapestries hung from the rafters, each bearing the family crest of the Von Eckstein family. The light blues and vibrant oranges had long faded as the banners swayed pitifully from their fastenings. Tattered and soiled, the decrepit cloth was a foreboding sight amid the abandoned structure.

The interior of the hall was of a simple rectangular design, commonly seen in border fortresses throughout the kingdom. Whereas most grand halls within the decadent and lavish castles of the Solarnian nobility served a multitude of functions, here the grand hall was merely a dining hall for regimental guardswomen. As they proceeded through the hall, Paolo stepped over and around the shattered pieces of long tables and wooden stools. Rusted iron plates riddled with mold lay strewn across the floor amidst dusty tankers and stained cutlery.

Paolo stopped at the sight and took a moment to look around and observe the hall. Wilhelmina was quick to notice his pause and turned around with a clear of her throat.

"Guardswomen skipped their meals and left the
fort in haste. Judging by the mold, this fortress
has been abandoned for some time. Those,
varemoden, bore tattered remnants of guard
uniforms. They must have been assigned here.
It explains how this cult occupied the fortress. It
explains the identity of the beasts that hunt
along the Turnian border-realm road. It explains
everything, except the *why*. What unforeseen
force is driving this natural calamity? What
kind of mephitic phage can turn a man or
woman into a nightmarish monstrosity of this
kind of caliber. There must be an answer that
the natural philosophies can help shed light on."

He bent down toward the dust-covered floor and slid
aside a cracked tin plate to reveal a weathered piece of
folded parchment. As Paolo unfolded the parchment, it
became clear to him from the faded lettering that it was
a letter addressed to one of the soldiers. It bore the
heading, *dearest sister*, and then continued describing
scenes from a warm and happy home somewhere in
Turnia. Paolo read the name at the bottom and felt a
compelling need to inform the writer of her sister's fate.
He slowly folded the letter back up and placed it in a
pocket of his vest. Wilhelmina approached him and
placed a hand on his shoulder, keeping her gaze fixed
on the northside doorway.

"The Sarella that aided me, back in Lethelheim,
she spoke of gods and wytches. But to turn to
the supernatural for justification is an easy
answer when the question becomes too
complicated. No dark force could be
responsible for this just as no celestial being has

tried to stop such atrocities from happening. Although I can say this with ease, no answers have I found when I ruminate on the logic behind the madness. Are we truly not alone in this world?"

Wilhelmina turned her head to Paolo and helped bring him back to his feet from the ground. She then walked over to the nearby stone pillar and leaned her back against the arch support.

"A season ago, if you would have said the same words to me, I would have not only agreed with you. I would have found your observations annoying. That seems almost a lifetime ago by now. From what I have witnessed from within this nightmare, I honestly don't know what to believe anymore. But what I can tell you, is that a great evil has invaded Lazzar Perish. Be it the very air, or from the strange Rholhynian woman that resides in the desolate sepulcher, I cannot say for sure."

Paolo flinched at the race of the suspicious being that the mortalist spoke of.

"Did you say this woman was Rholhynian? You are certain of this?"

Wilhelmina paused in her recanting and looked to the stiff shouldered resurrectionist.

"Well, the woman is taller than most, silver skinned with glowing amber eyes. Her feminine form is overt, if not profoundly voluptuous, in comparison to her thinned frame. Are these not female Rholhynian traits? I guess I have only seen the silver skins a few times, and nobles at that. Whoever she is, she isn't of our race. That I am certain of."

Paolo lowered his head in thought, once again returning to his head space in search of reason.

The Sycrass. A woman proclaiming to be a Sycrass. That title eludes me, but oddly also lies in reach. I have seen this word before, but I don't know where or when. Rholhynia lies to the east, and Sycrass seems an eastern vernacular. I should make note of this.

While Paolo wondered in thought, Wilhelmina took a seat on a lone stool in the grand hall. Placing her forearms on her thighs, she continued in her recollection of recent horrors endured.

"As I was saying, I hid and crept through the hollowed-out hamlet. I watched these guardswomen slowly transform into hideous unsightly beasts. It was maddening and torturous. The sensation of powerlessness was crushing, as there was nothing I could but hide in the shadows and watch. As they writhed and screamed in the scorched streets, I could see the gray-skinned woman, watching from atop the sepulcher hill. Her amber eyes pierced through the fog like hot coals as she hissed soul-wrenching incantations toward the blackened clouds above. She cried out to the fog, and the fog answered. There is no answer in the natural philosophies, Paolo, that can explain what I heard from within the mist. The wind might howl, and the seas might rage. But there is no elemental fury in our natural world that answers when spoken to. I thought myself mad, that the large dose of anthemene I ministered to myself had taken my senses. But day after day, she summoned the mist, and the mist came. I watched as she guided the swirling vapor toward those slave women and observed in silent horror as the mist entered their bodies and mutilated their anatomy. It was like watching something from a fairy-tale happen before your eyes, the stories we hear as children come to a reality. But instead of a fairy-tale, it was a tormenting nightmare."

Paolo pulled his cloak back over his shoulders and approached the mortalist.

"The Sarella performed a type of chymiac reactions that appeared magical in nature as well. I thought the same thing. She spoke in ancient tongues and summoned divine light, claiming it to be from the goddess Myrina. I took it as the ravings of a zealot, nothing more. It wasn't until I watched that Rholhynian wytche take form in the guise of shadows and smoke, that I truly began to question my own philosophies."

The mortalist quickly looked up from gazing at the floor and stared at Paolo as he told his tale. An outstretched hand from under her shoulder cape silenced the resurrectionist.

   "Did you say, you summoned the wytche? Did she appear before you in Lethelheim?"

Paolo crossed his arms and began stroking his beak in thought.

"It is what summoned the apparition, that I found most peculiar. You said the Sycrass summoned the fog, and the fog turned the people into beasts. I saw the Sarella conjure forth divine powers through incantations to the Goddess. But what summoned her wasn't an

300

incantation nor a ritual. She was provoked after I had performed the phlogistony on a sample of varemoden tissue. The phlogistic reaction revealed black bile from within the precipitate, like when we confirm a murder. The black bile then revealed the fog within the chamber. The Sarella then drove back the fog with some form of the religious act and that's what summoned the wytche. I don't know enough about Sarella's faith to deduce a reasonable answer. What I do know, is that whatever supernatural phenomenon is underway here that it is tied to the natural philosophies."

"You think we can use our chymia to fight these beings?"

Paolo nodded in silence at Wilhelmina's question keeping his eyes fixed on the floor while he continued to pontificate on the workings of a plan.

"Do you know what we use silabar for?" He asked the mortalist after a momentary pause of silence.

"The precious metal? It is used in our uniform and drives off fetid odors and infections. Why?"

Paolo reached behind his back and pulled a canister of silabar bolts and chucked them toward Wilhelmina. She caught the canister and inspected its contents.

"Are these bolt tips made of pure silabar?"

He pulled six silabar slugs from the sleeves of his vest
and handed them to the mortalist, who slowly took
them into her other hand before inspecting them.

> "375-grain silabar slugs, if that won't fit into
> your sidearm then I'm sure we can figure
> something out."

Wilhelmina reached behind her back and drew a pistol
from the holster strapped to her waistbelt. As she
moved the firearm to her front, Paolo could see that the
pistol was of a similar design to his hamherbuss. She
pushed down on the side lever and broke open the
receiver. The silabar round slid easily into the single
chamber.

> "You received a new firearm as well?"

"What. Do you think you are the only coroner sent out
on a special mission to receive an upgrade in arms? Did
Evangelo give yours a silly name as well?" She said
while slamming the receiver shut with a flick of her
wrist and returning it to her holster.

Wilhelmina then slid the silabar slugs carefully into the
leather sleeves that lined her belt.

> "I thought the name he gave mine, was rather
> clever. But I can see a Brinoan not finding joy
> in the subtleties of the job."

She scoffed at his jab, "Native Solarnians always think
they are the center of creation. Now follow me, I need
to show you something before we calculate any plan of
attack on the hamlet."

She guided Paolo to the captains' quarters on the other side of the main hall. As they entered the large chamber quarters, Paolo beheld a large, burrowed hole in the center of the room. As he approached the edge and peered over, it appeared to be a large subterranean tunnel. Wilhelmina approached the hole next to him and crouched down.

"This is how they transport the prisoners to Lazzar Perish." She said in a hushed town.

"What is the purpose of transporting them underground?"

"To avoid exposure to the fog. The Sycrass can't afford to have them turning into beasts before she sacrifices them in her nightly rituals."

"How did you discover this network?"

The mortalist grew as silent as the grave upon hearing his question. Pausing momentarily, she informed him of the truth. Recanting the tale as if trying to remember a dream.

"I, um, the night I first learned of the truth behind all this. I had snuck into an underground catacomb from within the charnel yard, below the cathedral. I watched as she turned four knights into these horrifying creatures by summoning forth insidious vapor from her hands. I was spotted and ran, but there was more. And to my horror, there were more than I had ever thought there could be. When I first arrived at the fort, I had spoken to the captain of the fortress, and we made an accord, that if I were to find myself in trouble, to raise the alarm from the bell tower. So, I did, but no answer came. I burned the hamlet down, with emerald vitriol I created from ether vapor and flint rounds. The fire melted the stone of the bell tower and took me with it. I thought I had perished. It wasn't until I finally woke that I found myself underground, beneath the monastery of the tower. For days I lay there recuperating in a feverish state, but on the fourth day, I heard tunneling on the other side of the walls of the basement. For weeks they toiled in the mud, creating crude networks of tunnels that span from the fort to the sepulcher. I waited until their toiling ceased, and after, I ascended above ground and studied their movement. I learned that they are most active in the evening and during the night. So, in the light of day, I began to infiltrate their tunnels with tunnels of my own. It's how I set the traps here at the fort."

Paolo laughed from within his mask while nodding his head, "That explains how you made those knights think they were being ambushed by an army. You had me even spooked at first."

> "I may be a mortalist, but I am still only one woman. Laying traps and setting ambushes is what how we capture assassins in the field. I only utilized my training, nothing more."

She pulled from her vest her chronorrery and checked the position of the sun from the middle dial.

"It is almost dawn. If we are to slip into the hamlet undetected, now is the time. So, resurrectionist, what is your plan."

Paolo transitioned from a squat to a sitting position, dangling his legs over the side of the hole.

"I will tell you once you get us to a safe spot within the hamlet walls."

Wilhelmina silently nodded before also taking a seat on the lip of the earthen hole. The two then descended into the tunnel and began their journey into the depths of the forsaken hamlet.

The Praetorium

<u>City of Calitoria</u>
The 4th hour of the 91st Day

Chief Surgeon Galini sits at his desk in disgruntled silence, and purposeful solitude. With eyes softly shut behind the mirrored lenses of his oculars, he searched the confines of his vast memory, lost deep in thought. Every so often The once mere pound of quivering flesh that the mortalist had sent, had now grown into something much fouler. A heavy, solution-soaked linen sheet lay over strapped mass of human remains. Every so often, the creature would writhe and try to break free from its bonds. But it was in vain.

Galini leaned forward in his seat and let out a soft sigh as the covered monstrosity gnashed its tooth lined maw against the wet fabric covering its face. His desk was covered with every text, tome, and scroll that the Archivist Luiza could find for him within the depths of the Archivum. He had spent weeks pouring over every page, every sentence, every word. But nothing leapt out at him, as the answer to the madness he was observing from the surgical table within his flesh pit.

The *Chrychoric Plague* of 332 had similar findings. But a pox would have spread at a more rapid rate, like it had done back then. Sanitation and other contrivances of an epidemiological nature had not improved since then, so why would this act any different?

A knock on his office door had forced his eyes open for the first time in hours. A gentle tone from the chief-surgeon allowed them entry. Archivist Luiza entered the room and stopped before his desk. Placing her hands behind her back, Luiza looked over at the creature beneath the sheet while she waited for the Chief Surgeon to turn and greet her.

"Luiza," Galini said in his soothing voice, "any news from the field about our dear Master Paolo?"

She lowered her head, "The last we heard, he was spotted in Oberndorf. Nothing more to report on that yet."

The chief surgeon let out a low sigh before leaning back in his chair. Pressing his fingertips together, Galini nodded slowly as he prepared an order.

"I have a feeling that Lazzar Perish being close to Fort Fermyre was more than mere happen stance. It would be wise of us to see if anything is brooding around our southern anchor. Check and see if there are any inquest around Fawrgrave Gaol. If so, send Atrionna on the case. She's already causing enough problems for me as it is. Might as well make her useful."

Luiza nodded in response and wished the chief surgeon a good day. As she turned, Galini leaned his head back and spoke her name once again.

"Luiza, don't tell her in any way that It was me who sent her out. I know you too are close, just send her out. That will be all."

Luiza left the room and shut the door behind her. Galini returned to tapping his fingers against each other, the leather of his gloves sticking to each other from the solutions used just hours ago.

> *Come on Paolo don't let me down. We are all counting on you.*

Galini turned around in his chair and looked at the single sheet of old parchment that lay on his desk before him. Picking the sheet up between his fingers, the chief surgeon read the words written on the page in black ink once again in silence. The sound of chains rattling echoing off the tall tile covered walls of his office laboratory.

"...Brothers and sisters of the Order, it is with righteous flame and a firm hand, with devout faith in our hearts, that we must purge the corrupting pestilence from the kingdoms of men. Was it not the iron will of Saint Beniamo De'Lorm, the first of our race and founder of our order, to take up arms and rise against the sklaven hordes, that set this precedence? Make no mistake, fellow Coroners, we stand upon the precipice of doom and genocide of cataclysmic proportions. If we fail in this hour of need, not even our holy mother can stop the arrival of the Temnatic Apocolites.

And in their wake, they will devour the souls of all mankind."

- *Chief Plague Hunter Muscavini de 'Calitoria*
Given at the Grand Order Convention during the outbreak of the Chrychoric Plague.

Anor 332 P.A.

5,032 coroners attended the convention and then boldly departed to face the scourge.

Only *384* returned.

In the wake of the last plague to befall mankind:
Only 65, 657 Solarnians perished by the blight.

*105, 872 men, women, and children, perished
on the pyre at the hands of the Order.*

The inflicted were given the title of Lazzarites, meaning *cursed one*, and were sent to the outskirts of the kingdom. Here they burned in barns packed tightly with the afflicted and the damned, called lazzarettos. The grandest of these sites was given a title.

Lazzar Perish.

Tens of thousands howled in horror as they burned alive in the tightly packed lazarettos. Until their suffering was silenced by the sudden disappearance of the mephitic brume that had covered the land.

*Since this horrific cleansing of their own
people, the Order has not faced a plague
outbreak in nearly six centuries...*

"We had the local guards round up the men, women, and children of the hamlet. Riddled with pustulating boils, the lot of them. Several of their women had already turned, caught consuming their own children. We couldn't risk an outbreak. The *Lazzarites* had to be cleansed. It was an order.

One by one, they were packed into that thatch roofed barn. We lit the torches and set the entire accursed structure ablaze. I watched with cold eyes, as the walls began to shake amidst the collective pounding of a thousand fists. The Lazzarites tried to break free from the cleansing furnace. But to no avail. The fire worked too quickly.

The cries of babes, no more than a season old, filled the night sky. The scent of burning flesh and the howling of the torturous screams…

It still haunts me to this very day."

-Plague Hunter Caspiañada
Last diary entry, before being
found dead in her home. Mortal
wound from self-afflicted
suicide.
Anor 336 P.A.

=Act III=

Lazzar Perish

The Bell Tower Monastery

The flaxen rays of the harvest moon's incandescence were snuffed out behind the ever-rising wall of tenebrous and ominous cumulonimbus storm clouds that swelled to cyclopean proportions as the night moved closer to the twilight hour.

The storm clouds had moved in from the eastern reaches of the forest, from the dark lands of Fensylfania, coalescing into a swirling dark convergence over the hamlet of Lazzar Perish.

Lightning lashed out, and thunder roared from the eye of the fulminating maelstrom, high above the converted Selenestic Sepulcher. As the clouds began to churn, a gaping umbral vortex began to take shape over the Bell tower of the antiquated cathedral. From this focal point, the fog poured down onto the earth, spreading its slithering tendrils of mist and malice over the hamlet and beyond.

The hamlet of Lazzar Perish had been reduced to a blackened, charred ruin, save for a handful of structures to the hamlet's east. Impaled bodies on great wooden stakes lined the muddied roads that lead from the front gate to the charnel yard. Some burning, others being fed upon by varemoden, and the rest flailing from having recently been added to the collection.

Knights belonging to the Cult of the Personiphi patrolled the charnel yard and had begun to gather within the cathedral. Only varemoden and the stumbling raving vasghuls roamed the hamlet streets under the light of the burning corpses. Paolo and Wilhelmina crouched within the rubble of the bell tower monastery and studied the hamlet.

The moon had remained low and close to the horizon, a celestial oddity that Paolo quickly noticed. Even though the wall of clouds had covered most of the skyline above and beyond the eastern horizon, the persistent presence of the harvest moon provided enough light for the coroner's vermillion lenses to see clearly through the thick fog.

Once Paolo was satisfied with his field observations, the two crept back toward the underground basement of the monastery. Descending the debris-ridden hole below the crumbled bell tower, they proceeded through a small gap space of crumbled wall and into the makeshift bunker Wilhelmina had crafted herself.

Paolo picked up a large chunk of decorative stone as they arrived and sealed their entrance shut. While Paolo sealed the chamber shut behind them, Wilhelmina took to lighting her pommel lantern and attaching it to her short coroner cane before placing it within a rusted iron torch holder in the corner of the room.

The ochre-hued brimash flame from within the lantern illuminated the entirety of the cell with ease. As Paolo finished sealing the hole with the stone, he grunted heavily while catching himself on the wall next to him.

The anthemene was still coursing through his veins. The sudden act of inhuman strength brought a dizzying spell to his mind as the blood shifted to his large muscle group and drained from his head. The rapid changes in his cardiovascular system brought him back to his normal faculties, and he joined Wilhelmina at the makeshift table of her room.

The basement of the monastery was a small square chamber. The walls had been lined with gossamer-covered barrel racks and bookshelves lined with moldy books long forgotten to time. In the corner of the room was A saddle with two saddlebags, as well as a collection of black leather cases and bags Paolo recognized as standard coroner field equipment.

The sight of the saddle brought a sudden gut-wrenching sensation from within Paolo.

As he studied the leather, he could see various punctures and serrated tears matching those of teeth markings. Dried blood outlined the damages, and Paolo knew her mount must have faced a horrendous end.

"I apologize about the loss of your mount. I can't even begin to imagine…."
The mortalist leaned over the table and cut Paolo off from his sincerities.

> "Now that you have seen the hamlet and studied
> the state of things, what do you propose we do?
> Shall we storm the sepulcher head-on? Take the
> cult on by surprise? Or would you like me to
> lay more traps?"

Paolo pulled back his cloak, unclipped a small satchel from the rear of his belt, and laid it on the table.

"What chymiac supplies do you have left?"

Wilhelmina pulled herself up from the table and approached her pile of supplies in the corner of the small room. She picked them up and placed them on the table before unpacking their contents neatly onto the tabletop. Although he recognized most of the contents, there was still a decent portion of vials and bottles that Paolo was unfamiliar with scattered amongst the equipment on the table. He reached down, grabbed a leather vial case, and held it up to the lantern light for a closer inspection. Each of the six glass bottles contained a small plant or fungus floating within a fixating solution of various hues depending on the vial he observed. As Wilhelmina finished unpacking her field equipment, she addressed Paolo in a hushed tone.

> "This is everything that I have left. Unlike you, I recycle my glassware after use. I saw the way you discarded your laudanum vial. Good glass is hard to come by, Resurrectionist. Even so, I should have enough spare containers to make whatever you plan to use against these creatures."

She paused in reviewing her inventory and eyed Paolo, who was still observing her vial kit under the light.

> "Intrigued by alkaloids, are we? Do flay-skins not keep them in their apothecarium? Huh, silly

question. I don't keep dissection instruments in mine, so it would make sense, I suppose."

Paolo snapped from his study and turned his head toward Wilhelmina while setting the alkaloid collection back down on the table.

"Alkaloids? You keep a collection of the plants that produce the raw substance?"

"How else would I create toxins and anti-toxins in the field?" scoffed Wilhelmina while crossing her arms. "All mortalists are apothicarians first and foremost. To catch an assassin, you must know their roguish arts. And no one knows more about deadly toxins and poisons than the Worshipful Branch of Shadows. So, shall I continue with my equipment inventory? Or would you like to discuss botany and other academic philosophies?"

Paolo scanned the table and observed the rest of her equipment, ignoring the snarky wit of the mortalist.

"The silabar will turn the varemoden and other vasghuls into ash. I don't know about the Urlagores, haven't faced one of those yet."

Wilhelmina cocked her head to the side as he listed the unfamiliar names of the various monstrosities.

"Varemoden? Urlagores? Have you named the creatures?"

"The Sarella informed me of them. The Sarellahood of Ecclesial Physicians apparently has antediluvian texts describing the beasts. Gave me a rough time for not being as informed of all this madness and chaos as much as she was. Said that our order sent us out here blind and ill-prepared."

"Well, I wouldn't disagree with her on that part. The ecclesial physicians have books on these creatures, which are interesting. I thought the sarellas were just a collection of virgin women who chose religious zealotry and monastic seclusion to cope with their boring nature and lack of basic feminine sexuality. I stand mildly corrected. Well, why isn't she here if she is so informed?"

Paolo sighed and shook his head, "enough. I had her stay behind and gather the freed prisoners. Those women will need medical attention and care that only she can provide. Now focus. We don't have much time."

Paolo picked a large, brown glass bottle from the table and read the label, then proceeded to inspect the other matching three.

"I can see you have almost full bottles of the archai aquas. I see the particulars. Prussych acid, alkahest, ether, and muriatic acid. The beasts despise alkahest. Although it is a base, it singes their tissues like an acrid solution. I don't travel with muriatic acid, but I have already seen what you can do with it. Can you make more of that vapor? Spirit grains are also highly volatile upon contact with their flesh. And eosphorus salts mixed with brimstone grains not only purified the beasts entirely but had even driven the Sycrass from the rectory. Is there a way we could weaponize this?"

Wilhelmina nodded, "not only could I weaponize it, but if you give me some time, I could create a quick application grease and throwable vapors. The only addition I would like to add is that vitriols would be the most potent. But I lack the ferronium clay and casings needed to craft dispatchables or rounds. The ammunition you gave me at the fort is all that I have."

Paolo reached down and unclipped the latch of his satchel. Flipping open the leather flap of the bag, he pulled from within a sealed glass jar filled with crimson earth and set it on the table. Afterward, he removed the rest of the contents, producing wooden boxes filled with various ammunition and box canisters of bolts. The last he removed was a leather purse filled with empty brass caps.

"I see you brought the armory," Wilhelmina proclaimed while inspecting the bolts and bullets. Grabbing the brass caps and clay, she returned to the opposite end of the table and began to set up her makeshift laboratorium.

> "I will craft Aiya's vitriol and jade vitriol rounds
> and dispatchables. But know this, the jade
> vitriol will be highly volatile and
> uncontrollable. It must be used as a last resort.
> Is there anything else you can think of before I
> begin?"

Paolo listed to the mortalist the rest of what he knew. Spirit grains, azotite, and the combinations he had used to slay the various creatures before arriving at the fort. Once he completed his listings, Wilhelmina began brewing and concocting the various chymiac weapons.

320

Tabletop kilns were lit, and alembics began to be brought to a slow bubbling boil as she carefully measured and mixed the particulates within thin glass tubes and beakers.

The mixtures produced vibrant purple, green, and red hues, which swirled and danced off the stone walls of the cellar like a spectacle of prismatic wonder. She ground the alkaloid plants within her mortar and set them next to a flame piston. Reaching into a pouch on her modified brigantine, Wilhelmina habitually produced her chronorrery and looked at the rotating dials and ticking hands of the brass device while stirring a boiling solution to her left.

Upon staring at the device, she paused in her laborious work and looked at Paolo, who had taken a post near the sealed exit and was keeping watch of activity aboveground through the slivers of the rubble.

"Paolo, I might have an unforeseen issue that could affect the chymia."

He turned his gaze from the wall and rose from the rubble.

"To measure the brimash reaction in the fame piston, I need to know the sun's position. Well, it's the twilight hour. There won't be sunlight for seven more turns of the heavens."

Paolo pulled his own device from his vest and briefly studied the dials. The hour hand pointed to the vacant horizon position of the middle solar dial as the thin outermost dial ticked and rotated with the passing of the seconds of the hour.

Before abandoning hope, Paolo looked at the selenestic dial between the solar and rotating dial, counting seconds with a quizzical gaze. The moon was in the waxing gibbous phase, and a harvest moon at that. Paolo pondered on this before he recanted a lesson he had learned while an acolyte in the academy.

"Are you a student of history, Wilhelmina?"

The mortalist dropped her shoulders and sighed at the question,

"no, I suppose not. What is your point?"

"Why do we carry this celestial keeper for chymiac work but only use the middle dial? If we couldn't perform chymia at night, why have the selenestic dial at all? I remember learning in our history course in the academy about how ancient coroners would combat plague with pyritic flame.

They believed this pyritic flame could burn away the pestilence and corruption from the flesh. The only stipulation was that it was most potent under the moon's light. That is why the forefathers burned the Lazzarites at the twilight hour so that the moonlight would produce a more pyroclastic flame."

"Okay, but the forefathers were as zealous as the Sarellas. You realize that they still practiced the coroner arts under the precedence of religious principles, right? Those maniacal fiends put so many citizens to the torch that, surprisingly, we are still even in order. They were blood-thirsty barbarians, not refined professionals."

322

Paolo shook his head while approaching the table,
"I would have agreed with you before today. But with
all the madness the two of us have witnessed so far,
don't you think that the past was a darker and more
barbarous place than we give them credit for. Yes, their
methodology was brutal, but if the great plagues were
symbolic of the scourge we are within the midst of,
don't you think they might have been right about it all?
You were about to burn those women yourself before I
brought you back to reality. Why did you naturally fall
on the inclination that flames purge the pestilence in
your madness? It wasn't a maddening circumstance. It
was because of our training and education as coroners.
The forefathers were trying to pass this down to us. We
just moved it to history and labeled them primitive
man, poking at the aether in desperation."

Wilhelmina nodded in thought,
>"okay, you make a point. But this doesn't help
>solve the riddle of measuring the light needed to
>produce the reactions. If the moonlight is more
>potent, how can we quantify it?"

Paolo returned to the rubble of the wall and peered
through the crack. The presence of the harvest moon
was hovering above, and the craters of the surface were
almost palpable from the surface of the land. Paolo
reached upward and could see the honeyed rays caress
the leather of his gloved hand, the speckles of dirt
particles dancing from within the gentle rays. He
averted his gaze from the moon to Wilhelmina.

>"We don't. Get me the reflective lens. Why
>measure an artificial source when we have the
>natural source at our fingertips?"

The two set up the reflective lens and projected the concentrated moonlight toward the table. Wilhelmina continued with the chymia until the time came for applying the light on the cooling mixtures. She held the vial aloft in her hand and hesitated momentarily.

"Well, we don't have an excess of supplies. I hope for both our sakes that this works."

Keeping a steady hand, the mortalist moved the vial from the shadows toward the projected moonlight that was focused on the wooden rack. As the vial slid into the rack, it seemed to remain inert. The ticking of the rotating dials of the chronorreries combined in rhythmic syncing as both coroners observed the glass tube with bated breath.

The glass slowly started to churn with latent energy before rapidly emitting a blinding aura. The eyes of the coroners beheld rays of ivory and cerulean light from within the container, which became almost unbearable to behold behind the lenses of their masks. After a few more seconds, the intensity of the reaction died down to a faint glow. Wilhelmina pulled the tube from the rack and inspected the contents with a magnifier attachment over her right ocular lens. After a closer inspection, she removed the magnifier and turned her head toward Paolo.

"I can't tell if it worked. The substance within should be an earthy crimson precipitate, but this is different."

"How so?"

"Well, quite frankly, it looks like vermillion crystal. A more reactive form, at least."

Paolo nodded and informed her to continue her labors. Paolo returned to his post and kept watch as she continued to toil. The mortalist created the various quick application greases and applied them to wax-coated parchment squares. Afterward, she started on the dispatchables. Collecting the remaining thin glass round vials, she filled each of them with swirling vermillion vapors and heavy residual liquids before placing cork stoppers on each of the containers.

Soon after, she finished crafting the vitriols and proceeded to add them to both bottles and bullets before removing her magnifier attachment and informing Paolo of her completion. The two coroners then began filling their uniforms with their arsenal's various components.

Bullet sleeves were filled, and vials were slid into their respective sleeves. Paolo picked up a stack of folded waxed parchment containing the quick-application grease, placed them in a hard leather case fixed to his brigantine, and closed the latch. Paolo ensured that his tinder box was filled with strikers and his pommel lantern contained a new brimash fuse. Wilhelmina sheathed her two short canes within the holsters on her hips and returned to her saddlebags in the corner.

The mortalist bent down and retrieved something from within. When she rose and turned toward Paolo, he could see that she was holding a wound bullwhip in her hand. Wilhelmina unwound the whip and softly gripped the black steel handle in her left gloved hand. With her thumb, she pressed a button on the side of the handle and brought the full length of the whip reeling into the thick handle and toward a hidden reel from within the round bulbous pommel.

The steel tip of the weapon collided with the blunt end of the handle and locked it in place.

> "I left this in my saddle bag the night I investigated the hamlet. It was on my horse when he was brought down by those beasts. I won't make that mistake again. My mother gave it to me when I graduated from the academy. She used it when she was a mortalist, even gave the weapon a silly name, justice, I think. She would have liked you, old-fashioned and all that. I never cared for such contrivances, but now I can see that sometimes names can have meaning. They tell stories or give your actions meaning. Well, in that case, I think it's time that this weapon receives a new name, Emilio, after my loyal steed. May his spirit guide the lash as I take my vengeance upon those who robbed me of my only companion in this isolating profession."

She removed one of her short canes and replaced it with Emilio before turning back towards Paolo and announcing she was ready. After gearing up for the battles, the two coroners prepared to depart to the street above. Paolo adjusted his brigantine and checked one last time that he had everything he needed.

He then reached into his vest and pulled his last two vials of Anthemene. Holding them aloft between his fingers, he swirled the blue viscous liquid around so that the light caught the floating crystalline particles within the glass.

"So, I don't know how you feel about Anthemene. But I think it would be wise of us to be as amplified as possible if we are going to survive the night."

Before he could finish his thought, Wilhelmina snatched a vial from his hand and pulled her brass syringe from her vest and loaded the glass vial within. The mortalist shoved the needle through the wax port and injected herself with a half dose of the altering substance before falling to her knees while the chemical took its effect.

"Okay, I see you have no objections at all."

Paolo took the remaining vial and loaded it into his own syringe and gave himself a half dose. The substance was quick to take hold of his faculties as he dropped the device and fell into the wall behind him. He had never ministered to himself such large consecutive doses of anthemene in his entire career. The side effects of the drug were beginning to precipitate. His mind was beginning to enter a state of labile instability with each dose.

Voices and visions began to creep into his faculties as he underwent the body alteration process. His emotions were also becoming more labile as well, his physiology crashing with his oscillating psychological mood swings.

I don't know how much more of this I can handle. If the beasts don't close in on me, then the tinctures will tear me a part. Even with those, there is still the wytche to deal with. Can I survive through something I don't fully

*comprehend? Can my body sustain the
inevitable? No, clear your mind and stay focus.
There is too many counting on you to just give
in. Think of the girl, dammit.
You can't abandon her too!*

His aging body was failing him. It was becoming more
and more clear to him as the nightmare of a mission
was continuing to unravel. Paolo felt conflicted about
whether he should inform Wilhelmina on the nature of
his impending fragility. He would do whatever was
necessary to save the innocent people of the realm from
pestilence and malice, even if it meant sacrificing his
own life. But someone had to care for the girl in
Oberndorf.

He hated the thought of putting that
responsibility on Wilhelmina, but there was too much
to consider when embracing the truth of his mortality.
If the time came, he would tell her the truth. Until then,
Paolo decided to keep such morbid thoughts to himself.
As his physiology and anatomy finished adjusting, he
picked his head up to see that Wilhelmina had already
lifted the large stone slab from the entrance and hurled
it to the side.

Rising from his feet, Paolo quickly joined her in
ascending from the rubble of the cellar and towards the
streets above.

Town Square

Paolo stood in the center of the hamlet, gripped the hamherbuss in both hands. In every direction were the tumbled and scorched remnants of the hamlet. To his back was the community water well. As he stared down the road, he could see through the thin veil of the mist the burning bodies of the impaled prisoners left to rot upon their stakes.

He clutched the cudwytchian oakwood comb of his firearm and grimaced in anger at the appalling sight. Behind him, the rusted handle of the wood water pale creaked as the rope-tied bucket swayed amid a light breeze. His partner had long since departed from his position, so he counted the creaks of the rusted handle, giving her the time needed to position herself before he announced their arrival. Both Paolo and Wilhelmina contemplated sneaking toward the wytche and taking her ritual by surprise.

But once the resurrectionist surfaced from the ruined monastery and beheld the cold-blooded slaughter, the downright animalistic acts of hedonistic barbarism set on display within the confines of the hamlet, he decided that the only option was to kill them all. So, he sent the mortalist off to get into a flanking position while he drew out the bestial hordes to the center of town.

Seven, eight, nine...

He counted to himself silently. As he reached the
thirty-second count. A sound rang out from atop the
sepulcher hill. A deep timbered clang of a great bell
tolled from within the tall tower of the cathedral,
reverberating across the piles of rubble and broken
planks from across the hamlet. As the vibration of the
ominous bell toll reached the coroner, the wide brim of
his black leather capotain rose upward, revealing two
blood-red lenses from beneath the shadows of the hat.

    Right on time.

The coroner raised the firearm and nestled the stock
tightly against his shoulder. He took aim and began to
count his breaths. His breathing slowed, and with each
drop in his respiration rate, he could feel his heartbeat
slow in pace.

    The immense clapper struck the side of the
great bell again, sending another toll echoing
throughout the scorched hamlet. He held his breath at
the top of an exhale and gently squeezed the first
trigger. As the trigger came back, the striking hammer
slammed into the striking plate with a heavy clank. As
the metal parts violently collided, sparks flew out in a
dazzling display. A concussive blast from the barrel of
the hamherbuss sent a glowing red orb hurtling into the
sky in an arch of smoke and flame.

    As the flint round soared through the air, a fire
and ash trail streamed across the ruined hamlet skyline
and over the muddied road. Before the streaming comet
of a shot could reach the charnel graveyard of the
sepulcher grounds, the crimson orb suddenly erupted
into a fiery explosion of smoke and flame. As brimash
particles from the flint round began to dissipate within

the mist, soon the entirety of the town was engulfed in a sea of red-hued fog.

The xanthous light of the moon once again pierced through the tenebrous clouds above. As the yellow rays caught the lingering particles, the outline of every building and feature that had become shrouded in the fog was now brought into light from behind the vermillion lenses of his oculars.

Paolo slammed down the side lever of the hamherbuss to open the falling block. As the barrel fell forward, a single empty brass shell came soaring out of the back of the receiver over his shoulder and down the water well behind him. He reloaded the top barrel with an Aiyan vitriol shot and slammed it shut, bringing the weapon to a ready position.

Only the creaking of the swaying barrel answered his firearm, as the great bell had ceased to toll upon the thundering roar of the firearm. Paolo closed his eyes and centered his mind. Slowly he focused all his faculties on his respiration and heartbeat until he had finally entered a honed state. The sound of chittering and scratching could be heard a fathom off and deep underground.

As he strained his focus on the faint, far-off noise, Paolo began to hear the booming echoes of larger predators beginning to clamor and crawl towards his position. He opened his eyes and slowly returned to the present, the expected cavalcade of noise escaping him under the influence of the anthemene.

"WILHELMINA! They are here!"

As he shouted the warning call, the ground beneath him began to tremble. Deep within the well behind him, the echo of hacking croaks and sharpened claws on stone rang out, forcing the coroner to turn his weapon around and face the imminent threat. An explosion of stone and debris sent the coroner flying backward into the air. As his back hit the muddied street, Paolo continued his momentum into a tucked roll, landing firmly on his feet.

What crawled from the well was a creature the likes he had never seen. A grotesque mass of marbled conjoined decay hanging from a bestial frame of the most perverse horror. An amalgamation bearing the likeness of a multitude of creatures. Octopi tendrils flailed and flagellated from the flesh of its back. The beast's bulk displayed deviations like that of both swine and bear, with a collection of snouts, tusks, claws, and even hooves. It wasn't the general gross anatomy of the monstrosity that horrified the coroner.

It was the bone-chilling visage of the creature's head. As it resembled that of a human likeness. Large blue eyes wildly gazed upon him through the furled rolls of the rotting flesh that hung like a marbled curtain from the bulging forehead. Sprouting from the patches of bear-like fur, he could spot strands of blonde hair. The wide-set jaw opened with a salivating grin, bearing a mixture of sharpened fangs, blunted gnarled teeth, and yellowed tusks. From its back sprouted various heads and faces, like the Rotstag he had faced in the woods before. Although instead of animal heads, these were the heads of other women. From their gaping maws rose the octopi tentacles. Rows of sharpened barbs lined the insides as they lashed out in every direction.

The unsightly beast lowered its front paw and hoof, its rows of bloated and marbled sagging breasts digging deep into the mud under its heavy frame. After sucking in a large gasp of air, the creature reared its

332

head and let out a bellowing roar to the sky above as if signaling for others.

The Urlagore.

Paolo sprang from his position and raised his weapon at the charging monstrosity. Before he could pull the trigger, the snout of the charging Urlagore struck him dead center of the chest and sent him flying once more. Paolo soared through wall and rubble before a wooden beam stopped his propulsion.

He slumped to the ground, falling from the broken wooden with a heavy thud. The ground trembled beneath him as he rolled over and let out a muffled groan. The pile of stone rubble in front of him erupted outward as the Urlagore came crashing into the room. As Paolo sprang upright and searched around frantically, the hamherbuss was nowhere to be found.

The many eyes of the monster locked on to him and prepared another charge. Paolo drew the silabar hatchet from his belt in time to sidestep the blundering creature and swing the blade toward the belly of the Urlagore.

A lash from one of the many tendrils sent the hatchet sailing from Paolo's hand and over the ruins of the hamlet. As he watched the hatchet sail from his hand, another tentacle came barreling into his chest, sending him soaring again to his back.

I can't get too close to the damn thing. Where is that mortalist?

On the other side of the hamlet, the collective howling and shrieking of the varemoden rang out in unison as the wolfish creatures descended upon the hamlet in full force.

Wilhelmina waited in the shadows of the monastery, perched atop a broken rafter of the vaulted ceiling. She kept her eyes on the convergence of streets below, waiting for the varemoden to descend upon her trap. Hearing the bellowing roar of the Urlagore had the quadrupedal beasts running on all fours into the hamlet, vaulting and leaping over rubble in a crazed frenzy. She spotted the arriving shadows of the beasts and quietly reached for the dispatchable vials lining her belt. Clutching two glass orbs in her hands, she balanced herself in a squatting stance on the beam and waited patiently for the opportune moment.

A varemoden came charging from the south, its long, forked slathering tongue flailing and sending acidic foam spraying as it ran. As its front paws passed the tumbled-down wall of the monastery entrance, the sound of a wire snapping brought the creature to a sliding halt. A crossbow bolt sailed through the air and stuck the creature right between the eyes, sending the beast toppling head over heels until it collided with a brick wall of a burned house. Three more varemoden moved in to inspect the disturbance and triggered three more hidden wires.

Hidden crossbows fired bolts in all directions at the drop of their counterweights, splitting the hide of the monsters and turning their perverse flesh into smoldering cinders. More came cautiously crawling over the rubble but were met with the shattering of glass and the spraying of burning vapors. The acidic spray rapidly ate through their flesh in a gory display of torturous liquefaction. Wilhelmina drew Emilio from the holster and pressed the release button.

The whip came plummeting from the hollow handle and dangled over the side of the broken rafter. The mortalist drew a piece of waxed parchment from her vest pocket and applied the quick grease to the steel tip of the whip. As the varemoden howled in pain and tore at their flesh, Wilhelmina struck and caught the opposite rafter and descended upon the shrieking creatures. The whip detached as she reached the end of her pendulum swing.

Transitioning into a forward tucked roll as he landed on the ground below, Wilhelmina sprang to her feet and started to twirl the whip around her. As the leather whip picked up in rotational momentum, she brought her arm down enough to allow the steel tip of the whip to scrape along the stone floor of the monastery. The sparks from the contact of steel on stone set the end ablaze with a bright lustrous flame.

The mortalist brought the whip back before cracking the whip at the nearest varemoden. The vitriol-coated tip tore through flesh and bone as it penetrated the monster's hide with a thunderous crack. As the beast fell back in a glorious display of flames, more rose to take its place. As the beast descended upon her, the mortalist met their lunging attacks with a flesh-splitting crack of her whip. One after the other, the varemoden burst into explosive flame as the steel tip tore through them like a ballista bolt, spilling their rotting entrails onto the muddied street in tidal waves.

Pirouettes and tethered leather cracking filled the hamlet's singular street as the mortalist danced her macabre waltz of death and vengeance with the burning beasts. As she planted her foot into the street after completing her twirl, two beasts came from the road ahead and the road to her right. Firing a silabar bolt from her arm crossbow at the beast to her left, she quickly followed up the attack with a spinning crack of her whip, sending both attackers to the ground in a smoldering pile of bile and blood. Finishing off the last of the attacking varemoden in front of her with a combination of a furry of lashes and a dispatchable vitriol vial, Wilhelmina was finally caught off guard by a sudden lunge from an unforeseen diving beast. She spun in place as an outstretched razor-sharp claw grazed the side of her arm. As she stopped, the beast planted itself in the street and lowered itself once more for another attack. She kicked the side of her boot with her other heel, sending a long thin, concealed blade shooting from the tip of her boot.

As the fiend sprang into the air, Wilhelmina sailed into a backward aerial leap. As she soared over the diving creature, she flung her leg around and drove the blade deep into the cervical vertebrae of the beast. Driving the blade through the bone with as much force as she could, Wilhelmina then pulled back on her plunging leg, decapitating the varemoden with a clean blow. The head sailed from her boot and landed next to the headless corpse as both skidded through mud and carnage until finally coming to a stop.

Landing on both her feet, Wilhelmina rose from the ground and returned the blade with another heel kick. The cry of the Urlagore echoed over the rubble and ruined houses, forcing the mortalist to turn her head sharply to assess the location of both Paolo and the beast. As she tried to peer through the alleyway, tendrils sprang from the oozing neck stump of the down beast.

"Dammit, where are you, Paolo?"

The tendrils writhed in the fog-shrouded air as soon as they detected her presence. Wilhelmina drew and fired her pistol at the twitching corpse as the barbed tendrils slithered toward her. She turned her head to look at the smoldering decay before reloading her firearm and sending it back to its holster. Another shrill howl from the Urlagore pierced through the fog.

Wilhelmina vaulted over the wall in front of her and began sprinting toward the great beast. Shaking her head in disappointment, she muttered silently while vaulting over another pile of rubble.

"Resurrectionist."

Paolo pulled another dispatchable vapor from his vest after rolling through a sweeping tentacle lash from the shrieking mouth from along the side of Urlagore and threw the glass vial against the monster's side. The beast bellowed and cried in agony as acrid fumes rose from its rapidly liquefied flesh. As fast as the acid would work, the mutagenic regeneration of the beast would quickly start to mend. The more he pelted the monstrosity with various chymiac bottles, the more it would send the beast into a violent rage.

If only I could draw this thing off me long enough to find my weaponry, it's not letting up.

As the Urlagore thrashed, it brought down more half-ruined structures in its ruinous wake. Paolo dove backward, seeing an opportunity to arm himself with his lister blade.

Drawing the double edge knife from his cane, Paolo quickly reached for a wax paper from his vest. He coated the blade with the sticky, viscous grease and

338

grabbed a striker match hidden from within the decorative belt of his capotain. Igniting the striker against a stone wall, Paolo set the Kreiger steel blade ablaze while tossing the spent striker to the side. The light of the burning blade caught the eye of the Urlagore and brought the beast to a standstill. As the large black pupil of the monster widened as it beheld the flames, it began to slowly back away from the burning weapon. Paolo moved the blade from his right hand to his left hand.

With each passing of the flames, the blue eyes of the Urlagore moved with it. Its heavy legs trembled as it continued to back away from the approaching coroner, spluttering and gurgling irradiating from within its colossal gullet.

"You fear the flames, beast? Interesting. Not so onery now, are we?"

As Paolo continued to back the beast out from the toppled barn, the sound of a bullwhip crack came from the opposite street.

Wilhelmina appeared through the fog, Emilio gripped in one hand, and the silabar hatchet gripped in her other. The mortalist continued to twirl the whip around her, lashing out at the gargantuan amalgamation and forcing it to hop back and bellow whimpering cries at each spark from the metal tip across the jagged cobblestone street. Paolo gripped the handle of his lister knife firmly and gave a sideways glance to Wilhelmina.

A single nod from Paolo was all the mortalist needed to initiate a frontal barrage of whips. As the whip sliced the tentacle appendages from the side of the Urlagore, Paolo ran forward and transitioned into a slide. As he skidded across the beast's side, the coroner dug the burning blade deep into the marbled belly of the creature.

As the vitriol tore into the creature's entrails, a cavalcade of partially digested remains and bubbling sinew poured onto the street below as the beast reared its head and howled in pain. Paolo turned his head and shouted at the mortalist, pulling the blade out.

"NOW!"

Wilhelmina loosened her grip on the hatchet and swung back her arm before sending the lustrous silabar ax tumbling through the air at the beast. The hatchet sunk deeply into the bowels of the Urlagore, hitting the massive pulsating heart with a precise blow.

As the glowing blade disappeared into the organ, the beast flung itself over and violently convulsed as it bellowed out its last earth-shaking howl before exploding into a maelstrom of phage-addled blood and pus. Paolo quickly pulled his wax-coated cloak over and shielded himself from the barrage of fetid bilious splatter. When the last remains fell to the ground, Paolo uncovered himself while shaking out the soiled cloak.

The rotted coagulation rolled off the wax coating of his cloak like rain droplets from a frosted glass window as he rose from the ground without a trace of bestial residue. As he shook his uniform, the coroner walked over and drew the silabar ax from where it had landed. He cleaned the blade with his cloak and inspected the edge before returning it to his belt. He faced the mortalist, who was preparing for the next wave of beasts.

"I had that under control,"

Paolo said while adjusting his brigantine and wiping the bits of entrails from the top of his capotain.

"I'm sure you did."

The bell tolled from the sepulcher again, drawing the gaze of both coroners as its mighty clang reverberated through the fog.

"We need to get to the cathedral and stop this. But I lost my firearm in the fight with that monstrosity."

Wilhelmina untangled her whip and beckoned him to follow her.

"I saw it lying in some rubble as I came to your aid. Follow me."

The two ran back through the hamlet and retrieved the hamherbuss as more creatures descended upon the hamlet in a second wave. The two stood their ground and slaughtered the attacking varemoden in a flurry of the flame, steel, and bullets. As the horde descended, the two coroners struggled to make their way up the road toward the sepulcher.

Hundreds of blood-thirsty beasts descended upon them as the great bell continued to toll overhead. Paolo swung the hatchet with a blind fury, burying the blade with an animalistic rage as his shouts rose with each swing. As he hacked through bone and meat, his vision became clouded by the overwhelming sensation of his bloodlust. A varemoden dove and tackled him to the ground, knocking loose the silabar hatchet from his hand.

The two slid in the mud, Paolo grabbing the beast by its throat and delivering a series of bone-crunching blows from his clenched fist. As the two bodies came to a stop, the varemoden reared back its head and began to undergo a mutation of its jaw. As the teeth of the creature grew in length and size, the varemoden let loose a soul-wrenching howl, sending saliva and foam spraying over Paolo's mask.

In the wake of his impending death, the anthemene hit a second stride from within his veins. Coursing with a newfound rage, Paolo answered the beast with a roar of his own making. The maw of the varemoden lashed at the coroner but was met with a heavy blow of his fist. He buried his strike into the back of the creature's throat, piercing the decayed tissue until his hand reached the tumorous bone. As he let out a second roar, Paolo pulled on the bone with all his uncaged strength tearing the top half of the creature's head clean from its body.

A writhing tongue flailed in the misty night air as the twitching corpse of the creature fell backward from him and rolled in the mud. He sprang up from his back and onto his feet, his muscles swelling and coursing with the side effects of the drug. Wilhelmina turned from her fight to view her shouting comrade. Paolo was irradiating with lingering steam, his body becoming overheated from boiling his blood.

An icy grip of fear washed over the mortalist as she viewed the blood-addled resurrectionist with her vermillion lenses.

"Oh, shit. He is crossing over into *the Dyscrasy*."

A varemoden began to charge at Paolo at full speed while he entered his dyscrastic state. Seeing the charging beast, he whirled around and grabbed an emptied wooden stake from the side of the street. Breaking the wooden pike at the base, Paolo turned and began to run at the creature to meet it head-on.

Paolo drove the long wooden stake through the beast's maw, skewering it from mouth to anus before throwing the twitching corpse over the other ones. More descended upon him as he plunged and pierced the stake into each one of his assailants. When the wood snapped, he continued to drive the sharp wood into the flesh of any beast near him. After the wood had turned to soiled splinters, the dysplastic coroner resorted to tearing the creatures apart with his own two hands. With each beast he entwined, the more lost in the emotional state he became. Paolo had become separated from his companion in the heat of his slaughtering and had become surrounded on all sides.

As the wake of carnage around Paolo grew, the beast themselves began to keep a distance from him, choosing to form a circle around his position. Grunting and screaming, Paolo beckoned his foes to come and take him. None approached. Only the bearing of fangs and the low rumbling of growls and snarls answered him.

One of the varemoden grew bold and sprang at the feral man. He caught the beast mid-air by the throat and punched through the creature's chest cavity. His hand returned with a heart clenched within his trembling fist. Throwing the organ aside, Paolo tore the arm free from the creature, holding it aloft like a weapon. As more varemoden became emboldened and enticed by his acts of barbaric butchering, Paolo continued to cut them down before him. After slaying them one at a time, they started to pounce on him in pairs of two.

Even within the heightened state of the Dyscrasy, Paolo was no match for a swarm of beasts. As they took him down to his back, the varemoden began trying to scratch and bite through his uniform.

The silabar threading staved off any puncturing of the fabric protecting his skin from contact, but it did not stop the razor-sharp teeth from tearing his flesh from within his uniform. In his pyroclastic state, he refused to stop fighting. A right hook from his fist sent a varemoden to his right, to which he followed it with a roll.

Paolo delivered blow after blow to the fang-lined maw, climbing on top of the beast. As the beast's skull caved inward from his onslaught, a multitude of varemoden swarmed him from behind. The black cloak of his uniform was swallowed in a tide of fang and claw. As the beasts toppled over one another to pull the coroner apart, a single varemoden rose to the top of the pile and bellowed out a thunderous roar as the pack tore at the coroner from underneath.

As she turned from the decomposing corpse of a beast at her feet, Wilhelmina could see the growing varemoden mound that had accumulated over Paolo. His dyscrastic state came at a shock to her. Wilhelmina cried out to Paolo, in hopes that a friendly voice would bring him back to a stabilized condition.

But her cries fell on deaf ears, drowned out within a sea of howls and the collective snarling of the hungry beasts. She threw a series of vitriol vials towards an oncoming pack and then set the solution on fire with a shot from her pistol. As the varemoden burned alive in front of her, she scanned the area to ensure she had time to assess Paolo's dire situation. Wilhelmina could see that the initial overwhelming numbers had begun to dwindle to a scarce remaining few.

A feeling of hope welled up from within her. Wilhelmina knew the time had come. She recanted on when she instructed Paolo on how the jade vitriol should not be used until the time was right.

> "Paolo, please forgive me for what I am about to attempt. Goddess, if you are truly out there. Please let this work, I can't do this alone."

Wilhelmina drew the emerald glowing vials from her belt and clutched them firmly in both of her trembling hands. As the mortalist took a moment to say her prayer, the skyline erupted with a blinding jade light from beyond the mound of varemoden in front of her.

At first, the light struck the ground like a bolt of lightning from the harvest moon above, but after the initial impact, it began to sweep across the earth like a tidal wave. As it washed over the creatures, the light set the creatures atop Paolo ablaze in a sea of jade flame. Ash and ruin blew over Wilhelmina as she covered her mask with her arms to shield her eyes from the cataclysmic light. As the dust settled, Wilhelmina fell to the ground trembling from the shockwave.

Expecting to be consumed in the natural phenomenon, instead, the emerald light felt strangely invigorating. She picked her head up from the ground and peered through the last remnants of the light to try and spot the downed resurrectionist. As her eyes grew accustomed to the light, Wilhelmina not only saw her companion but something stirring in the fog behind him.

BBBRRRRRRRRRUUUUUUUUUUUUUUUUMMm mmmmmmmm!

From the gates of the ruined hamlet came an emboldening and familiar sound. It was none other than the war horn of the regimental guard. The lingering horn blow was swiftly followed by the sound of a second horn call from further back.

As the second horn blow faded within the fog, the sound of thunderous battle cries rose from the parted fog as the Turnian guardswomen of the Anorheig town attachment poured into the hamlet. Through saturated and soaked face covers, the armor-clad guardswomen continued in their rally cry as they formed fragmented ranks in the narrow streets, holding aloft their pikes, shields, and broadswords in their hands.

Leading the regiment was not a captain, but instead, a strangely clad woman adorned in a combination of vestments and radiating cinnabarite armor. She wore a white cloth covering her nose and mouth, and the black veil of a Sarella over her head. The heater shield strapped to her left arm bore the holy symbol of the crescent dianasis in black paint on a white field.

"A Sarella? How is this possible?"

Bright emerald and white flames sprouted from her eyes as she led the regimental guard into the hamlet and towards the advancing Varemoden horde.

Before the beasts could make contact, the Sarella raised her silabar mace high above. Her very voice shook the ground as she channeled the light of the moon onto her striking weapon. As she brought it down upon her shield, a bolt of cosmic energy fired outward and incinerated the front wave of creatures in its wake. From behind the Sarella, the guardswomen advanced.

Quickly they formed ranks and files of pike women behind a wall of steel heater shields. Forming a square formation in the street, the Turnian guard commander stood by the Sarella in the center and shouted the command to her troops.

"FRONT LINES, PIKES AT THE READY!"

The call was relayed across the square. The second row of pike women braced their stance, shoulder-width apart, and placed the shaft of their lances over the shoulders of the kneeling shield bearers. The commander raised her broadsword into the air and gave her second command.

"BRACE!"

The varemoden poured down the street and collided with the guardswomen in an explosive display of bloodshed and carnage. The soldiers held their ground for as long as they could, but the monstrous abominations shook the less seasoned guards into a fear-induced panic.

As the square weakened, the varemoden broke through the lines and began to tear the soldiers apart. As the soldiers scrambled to either re-form rank or try to flee in terror, the varemoden continued in their wanton slaughter of the newly arrived reinforcements. A volley of crossbow bolts soared across the hamlet rooftops, shredding and pinning varemoden around the hamlet as a small battery of crossbow women pressed the defense.

The Sarella continued to channel as much divine might as she could, but with each shockwave from her shield, the fire within her eyes began to wane and dim. In the pandemonium and chaos of the battle, Wilhelmina made her way to the battered and fallen, Paolo. The resurrectionist lay motionless in the blood-drenched mud. Bone and entrails scattered around him and even clutched tightly within his fists.

Desperately she tried to rouse him, but no matter what she did the lifeless man would not rouse. Placing his arm around her shoulder and lifting him up over her back, Wilhelmina carried his body to a nearby vacant and half-ruined hovel. Setting him down against the stone wall, she drew her short cane from its holster and places the blunted end of the instrument against his carotid artery. She held the cane firmly against the linen covering of his neck, but no matter how long or hard she pressed, no pulse struck back against the hollow steel cane. She refused to accept his death, not after everything he had done. She drew a vile of henbane from her vest and loaded the solution into her brass syringe.

Wilhelmina then ministered the vile solution to Paolo, threw the syringe, and laid him on his back. She listened for breaths while a hand gripped his neck to check for a pulse. When neither came, she delivered two sharp blows to his chest. Upon rechecking, there was nothing. She then gave another series of blows to his chest and checked once more.

Bringing her cloth-covered ear close to his beak, she detected the faint sputtering of a wheeze from his lips. Soon after, the rhythmic pounding of a steady heartbeat could be felt on his neckline. As the blood began to circulate, she could feel the warm vitality of life radiate from his skin once more.

"Don't hit me so hard, can't you see I am dead."

The mortalist laughed at her companion's jest, holding back tears of joy.

> "You aren't allowed to die yet. We still have that bitch to stop."

Paolo groaned as he tried to move under the weight of his brigantine,

> "It's pronounced *wytche*, you imbecile."

As the two shared their moment, the body of a guardswoman came plowing through the front wall of the hovel followed by an enraged varemoden. As the beasts reared up with sharpened claws, the steel blade of a broadsword pierced through its chest.

As the beast collapsed on the floor, the guard who delivered the fatal blow pulled her sword back out and decapitated the creature with an overhead chop of her sword.

> "Come one you two, we are getting slaughtered out here!"

As she beckoned toward the coroners, a varemoden appeared behind from behind her and plunged its claws and tendrils deep into the soldier's side before tearing her body in half and feasting on the entrails.

Paolo reached for Wilhelmina's pistol and shot the beast in the head, turning it into a writhing pile of ash. His action brought on a violent meagrom from within his skull, followed by a crippling bout of dizziness. Wilhelmina took the pistol from Paolo's hand and laid him back down on the floor.

> "You are in no condition to fight, just stay here while we finish these beasts. The Sarella has arrived with reinforcements, but what hope they brought upon arriving is swiftly fading away under the weight of fear and madness."

Paolo shook his head and beckoned her to come closer.

> "Give me… my second dose of anthemene…it's the only way I can stay in the fight… and I must see this through…"

Wilhelmina recoiled in horror and anger at his request.

> "Absolutely not! Are you mad? You just barely survived the dyscrasia, if I minister another dose, it will not only kill you, but it will push you into a state of incapacitating delirium. There is got to be another way."

He shook his head once more. With a trembling hand, Paolo reached into his vest and pulled the brass syringe from its leather holster. The last half dose of anthemene swirled from within.

350

"If you don't do it, I will."

Wilhelmina took the syringe from Paolo's limp hand and hesitated momentarily. As she took her moment, he reached up and gently grasped her forearm.

> "Wilhelmina don't worry about me. I am ready to die in the field, I have come to terms with this fate. But if I am to die this night, then allow me the justice and privilege to die knowing that I left the realm a safer place."

With this the mortalist nodded in silence, and drove the hypodermic needle into his wax port, puncturing his antecubital vein.

The battle in the streets was becoming dire as guardswomen were butchered and cut down all around the Sarella. The commander of the guard stood in the street, shouting commands in desperation to rally her remaining troops around her but to no avail. Crossbow women were firing at will from atop the rubble, but their volleys were not enough to stave back the tide. The sight of absolute carnage began to take a heavy toll on the faith of the Sarella, as she began to question the will of her benevolent goddess.

Her silabar mace sang out as she bashed in and crushed the oncoming varemoden, but a pouncing blow from an ambushing beast sent her to the street. She held her shield with all her might under the weight of the varemoden, its jaws viciously snapping at her head. She tried desperately to channel her faith, to call down a divine light to save her from the impending end. But her words fell on nothing but fog-filled air. As she struggled to reach her mace, tendrils sprouted from the gaping maw of the creature.

Before the beast could take its final plunge, its head erupted from the close-range blast of a firearm. The Sarella opened her eyes after the spraying of blood and brains to witness the arrival of both coroners. Paolo stopped at the Sarella, his white raven mask staring down at her in the mud, gripping her shield.

> "That is no place for a Sarella," he said with hamherbuss in hand. Paolo then eyed her armor and vestments. "Where in the five realms did you get this outfit?"

He reached down and helped the Sarella to her feet.

> "Thank you, Coroner Paolo. I came with the guard as soon as you sent word with the prisoners."

"I said not to come until the fog had dissipated, dammit. Well, you are here now. Welcome to Lazzar Perish."

A varemoden came crawling over the fractured roof behind him and gurgled out a hissing snarl. Paolo quickly turned and blew the beast down with the second shot of the hamherbuss. After the carcass of the creature faded to dust, he turned back to the Sarella while reloading the firearm.

"We need to get to the sepulcher! The Sycrass is inside the cathedral, conjuring the maelstrom and summoning the pestilence from within the desiccated shrine. If we

352

linger here, all the fallen will slowly transform into vasghuls within hours."

The Sarella looked around the hamlet once more. Guardswomen continued to mount an offensive, but their wounded were becoming too weak to fight back. The hope of survival was quickly fading from the ranks. As the severely wounded were moved to the rear of the lines, fresh troops were being deployed into the hamlet from outside the high stone walls. But even with reserves, their numbers were starting to dwindle as well.

After assessing the surroundings, the Sarella picked up her mace and instructed the commander to call in a squad and help push towards the sepulcher. A squad of twelve women arrived through the fog and together with the Sarella and the coroners, began to push towards the cathedral ahead. Varemoden started to push in from their rear but were driven back by the pikes and halberds of the guard. A wave came from the front, but Wilhelmina stepped forward and gave a thunderous crack of her whip to bring the stampeding pack to a sudden halt. The mortalist twirled the whip and delivered an assault of both lash and vitriol as Paolo shot down beasts trying to strike in from the flanks.

As the soil became damp from the acrid solution, she drew her pistol and fired a shot through a crouching varemoden. The bullet pierced through the beast, separating the torso and pelvis. As the bullet ripped through the bone, the heat of the mord round contacted the vitriol-rich earth and set the ground ablaze. A roaring inferno engulfed the encroaching enemies, spreading a bright white flame in a semi-circle around their small band. The diversion had worked. With newfound faith, the Sarella began to entice the white flames around them. Her incantations began to hurl great pillars of fire toward the creatures until none, but few remained. As the fire died from behind them, a guardswoman turned and peered through the fog.

Turning back toward the group, she raised her hand toward the sepulcher.

"We made it! We made it to the sepulch…"

As she shouted her joyous news, her words were stopped short but the sudden swing of a great rusted two-handed sword. The blade had cut through the fog and severed her arm at the elbow, sending both arm and guard to the mud below. The sight of her pulsating arterial spray produced a cacophony of shrieks from the downed guardswoman as she clamored to cover the wound. Being pulled into the small party by fellow compatriots, her orange and blue tricorn tumbled from her chainmail coif and into the mud below her. As it came to a stop, the tricorn hat was crushed under the weight of a heavy iron sabaton as a red-eyed knight stepped out from the fog, bellowing a war-cry, and raising his great sword high into the air.

They had made it to the sepulcher, and into the vanguard of the descending waves of cultist knights. They stood their ground as both knights and varemoden descended upon them from all sides.

The Selenestic Sepulcher

The whistling of a silabar hatchet penetrated the fog as the ax blade was buried deep into the skull of the shouting knight. Paolo yelled at the commander to take the knights as the coroners and Sarella would take the remaining varemoden. As the wave of vanguard Molder Knights descended from Sepulcher Hill, the commander of the guard ordered all lances and halberds to the front and from a spear wall. The guards dug in and braced their lances deep into the mud below.

As the vanguard penetrated through the thick fog, the momentum of their charge drove the trenched spear tips deep into their bloated, rot-filled bodies. Bilious pus and maggot-ridden blood poured out over the boots of the guard women as they stood their ground and faced the initial charge. Once the initial charge was halted, the commander gave the order to charge.

The guards met the knights in the open field of the Sepulcher Green in a collision of iron on steel as the fog dissipated into a thin mist. While the regimental guard held back the onslaught of the Molder Knights, Paolo and Wilhelmina made short work of the remaining varemoden. As the final beast fell under the crack of Wilhelmina's whip, the two coroners returned to the Sarella.

"You two need to make it inside and stop that ritual. I will call in the reinforcements and distract the knights for as long as possible. Goddess, be with you both!"

They nodded in reply and advanced toward the battle ensuing on the Sepulcher green. Paolo stopped to retrieve his thrown ax before driving the hatchet deep into the chest of an attacking Molder Knight. Sarella Augathina called the commander to sound the horn and bring the remaining soldiers to their position.

The Turnian war horn rang out through the thinly veiled fog and was answered by the rallying cries of the guardswomen at the front gates. Soon the ranks of the guard swelled in numbers as they drove back the phage-addled cultist. As Wilhelmina and Paolo cut through hordes of armor-clad men, they had driven enough of a wedge through the cultists to make a run for the stone steps leading up to the cathedral doors.

Halfway up the steps, there came a rumbling from the cathedral above. Clanking armor and heavy steps came from within the double doors. Each heavy step shook the ground as the entity from within grew closer. Paolo stood his ground and gripped his weapon, awaiting the arrival of the approaching entity. The doors of the sepulcher were knocked off their great heavy iron hinges and sent plummeting to the ground below as the visage of a cyclopean man in ooze-ridden armor emerged from the entryway.

Paolo recognized the monstrosity by the shape of his eroded helm and the scent. As the wind carried the phage-ridden air towards his mask, the fetid odor ignited the aromatic incense from within his beaked rebreather. Reminding him of the repulsive knight from the Millwood Green. The grotesque being was none other than Syr Saidach, the Knight Commander of the Cult of the Personiphi. He had swelled to grotesque proportions since their last encounter, with gelatinous

356

flabs of rotting flesh pouring from the eroded gaps in his armor.

Paolo could tell that he had not only grown in girth but also in height, as Paolo estimated he had grown a full span and a half in height. His great helm was swarming with flies and insects, which were thrown from his head with each vaporous lingering breath.

As his glowing red eyes scanned the field below, he continued to widen his gaze until finally spotting the visage of the coroner below him on the stone steps. A guttural chuckle came choking through the pores of his bent rusted visor. Gripping his two-headed battleax in one hand, he pointed a swollen, half-covered finger at Paolo. The enraged knight commander spoke at the coroner in his typical guttural croak of a voice as it thundered through the visor of his helm.

> "You take OUR slaves? Little raven. You mean to disrupt the conjuration ritual. HA! You only come here to die. I have long awaited this since our last meeting. My lady has been watching you and has bestowed upon me great boons from the six to ensure she completes the ritual. Now come, little raven! And face thy doom!"

He lowered his colossal finger and swung the ponderous iron ax into his other hand. Knight-Commander Saidach advanced toward the coroners, his bloated legs bounding forward with a leaden lumbering gate. Paolo raised the hamherbuss and fired both shots at the gigantic brute, hitting the knight-commander in the shoulder with a devastating blow.

As the eroded iron pauldron splintered from the blast, his hulking putrescent arm slumped to the ground within a throng of befouled ichor. While Paolo reloaded, the knight-commander only glanced at his severed appendage briefly before raising his ax to the eastern horizon.

"KESHMATKEN LORDS OF THE EAST, OH MIGHTY DREVNIYAK! GRANT ME SUCCOR!"

His bellowing prayer echoed over the trees of the Faynean Forest, and soon a shift in the winds responded. A billow of stygian vapor descended upon the brute from the storm that raged high above the church. Bolts of calamitous red lightning scattered across the blackened clouds as the inky smog slithered into the knight commander's gaping shoulder wound.

His penetrating eyes grew more cerise from within his visor as he chortled more guttural laughter. From Saidach's gaping wound came the abhorrent parturition of a mutagenic mucilaginous growth. As a great barbed tentacle wormed its way free. Paolo finished his reloading and fired two more shots at Saidach, this time boring large holes through the center of his breastplate. The knight staggered backward from the concussion of the shots only to sprout more tendrils from his oozing wounds.

Paolo pulled back on the forearm slide of the weapon and loaded a cartridge of silabar bolts into the hamherbuss. Before he finished loading the crossbow, Wilhelmina lit the steel tip of her flog with vitriol grease and struck it against the stone to set it ablaze. She charged up the stairs in a series of acrobatics before pressing Saidach with fiery thrashes.

The flagellations from the whip stripped pieces of his decaying armor and singed his putrid flesh with tissue devouring flame and acid. As her attack stopped his advancement, it did little to damage him. The fetid monstrosity grew annoyed with the mortalist as he shifted his attention from Paolo to Wilhelmina.

"Another little raven? And by the scent, a woman. A phage brood if thou desire. Come, die in combat first. At least you fight with steel in hand. Show us how Solarnian women defend their lesser half."

He brought the colossal iron ax above his head before bringing it down upon Wilhelmina with a thunderous blow. Dodging the strike with a backward handspring, Wilhelmina sprang forward and leaped onto the ax's handle. As she advanced toward the knight commander on the handle of his lodged weapon, she delivered a series of lashes to his helmet. A blow from a chest tendril sent Wilhelmina plummeting to the ground as Syr Saidach tore free his weapon from the ground. As he lumbered toward a dazed Wilhelmina, a silabar hatchet soared over her and struck him square in the breastplate.

Piercing both iron and decaying meat, the knight commander stumbled backward with a series of deep grunts. Paolo followed his throw, charging at the knight commander with his drawn lister blade in his left hand. The resurrectionist collided with the staggering Syr Saidach, punching into the bent metal, and pulling out his embedded weapon.

A flurry of tendrils lashed out at Paolo as he hung onto the gaping hole of metal and bone. He continued to hack into the chest of the knight commander with precise blows. Each trauma delivered forced the birthing of more tendrils from his bloated marbled body. The knight commander finally toppled over from the sustained hemorrhaging of his putrescent vitality, sending a shockwave across the ground as his back collided with the stone floor outside the sepulcher. Paolo continued his strikes, determined to reach the heart of the monster.

As each blow of the silabar hatchet cut deeper, all that the enraged coroner could think about was the battered little girl he found in the Millwood Green.

> "you come here, to our lands. You enslave our people. You butcher and kill at will. You orphan children and rape their families while they watch. You and your cult are all vile abominations and pestilence upon our kingdom!"

As Paolo reached the heart of the perverse monstrosity, he tossed aside the silabar hatchet and grabbed both vials of the jade vitriol from his belt.

> "A pestilence is only cured through the purification of flame. So, Knight-Commander Saidach. As a royally appointed coroner of the Kingdom of Solarno. Both an officer of the Queen's law and a doctor of plague prevention."

The coroner then shoved the vials deep into the bored hole of the breastplate until the glass shattered against Syr Saidach's immense maggot-infested heart.

"I HEREBY PROCLAIM YOU AS LAZZARITE! AND SENTENCE YOU TO BE CLEANSED UPON THE PYRE!"

Paolo pulled his fist from the vitriol-filled cavity and dove from the twitching body to the ground below. Syr Saidach reached toward the sky and roared out to the void above as the vitriol began to ignite from within his rib cage.

"DREVKIN! I HAVE FAILED THEE!"

His blubbery, gelatinous body writhed and quaked from within his rusted iron shell as an emerald hue radiated from his gaping chest. As the cataclysmic flame welled from within him, he released one last cry of tormented pain. Every orifice of his face became aglow with searing green light before the entirety of his putrescent corpse exploded in a calamitous display of consuming flames.

Wilhelmina shielded her eyes from the blow before frantically looking around for signs of Paolo amidst the swirling acrid embers. As she rolled from her back, the mortalist slowly started to crawl forward to escape the inferno that raged around. Wilhelmina could feel the heat rising from inside her insulated garb. Sweat began to pool on her brow as she frantically gasped for air. The primal fear of burning alive forced her to feet, although it took everything she had to do so. A Sharp pain radiated from her side as she fell onto the sullied steps leading up to the church.

Gathering her wits from the haptic flight from peril, a familiar voice greeted her covered ears through the chaos that raged below. Sarella Augathina

Wilhelmina was soon joined by the Sarella, who joined her in search of the other coroner.

"Was he consumed in flames?"
Asked the Sarella as she looked through the flames around the entrance of the sepulcher.

Wilhelmina looked through the flames blocking the entrance to the cathedral and could see the movement of a black wool cloak descending deeper into the church ahead. She turned her head toward the Sarella and placed an arm around her shoulder as she began to clutch her side.

"No, he wasn't consumed in flames. He is making his way to the Sycrass. He means to finish this, and he isn't planning to return."

The Sarella helped the Mortalist to the ground and saw her side before looking back to the looming cathedral ahead.

"We can't let him face this alone. She will surely tear him apart, and then we are all doomed."

Wilhemine scoffed and winced,

"The emerald vitriol would sear us to ash before we made it to the other side. There is no aid we can offer him. We can only have faith that he will see this through."

The Sarella fell to her knees and clasped her hands,

"No, that is not the only faith we can find in this hour. We will send him aid, one way or another."

Paolo stood at the cathedral's narthex in silence and gazed upward at the cathedral's vaulted ceiling.

As he panned from the arcade and gallery of either side of the nave, he beheld unspeakable scenes of morbid corruption within the sepulcher's interior. The xanthous rays of the moon graced the stained-glass lancet windows of the cathedral and illuminated the horrors that had occurred within the mist of Lazzar Perish.

Eastern pagan symbology praising their eldritch gods decorated the vaulted ceiling, but what lay beneath these chilling fetishes truly shocked the coroner to his core. Innumerable flayed and crucified corpses had been strung up on repulsive display from the clerestory down to the arcade.

The tormented expressions on the countless faces of the dead gaze back at Paolo as he looked upon them from below. The aisles had been piled with the bones of the sacrificed. As he looked upon the mounds of the ossified remains, Paolo could see the varying sizes of the skulls from within.

These were women and children.

The coroner approached the bone pile and fell to his knees. Reaching toward the mound, Paolo clutched within his palms a small skull. The tiny teeth fell from the sockets with ease as his fingers ran across the lower mandible, and his heart plummeted from within his chest.

Looking from the skull, he could see the various adult pelvic bones. One glance at the embedded trauma of the specimens told him that these women had undergone unspeakable atrocities at the hands of their captors. He set the skull down gently and rose to his feet. Paolo's muscles tensed and quivered violently under the tormenting wave of guilt and rage.

"SYCRASS!"

His shout echoed throughout the cathedral, reverberating off the clerestory and high into the vaulting ceiling of the nave roof. His cry was answered by a series of hissing cackles from within the depths of the sepulcher. The coroner stepped from the aisle and returned to the nave. He peered toward the choir, but some force prevented his vision from peering past the tenebrous pitch of the depths of the cathedral.

"YOU WILL ANSWER FOR WHAT YOU HAVE DONE!"

As he shouted, a sultry feminine voice whispered into his ear from behind.

"Come now, Koratok. There is no need for more violence."

Paolo spun around and lunged forward with outstretched arms. But his fingers only caught dissipating mist. Another series of hissing laughter reverberated throughout the sepulcher interior, from aisle to gallery and from behind and in front of where he stood. The hair on the back of his neck began to

364

stand on end as his eyes frantically shifted around the room.

"You think your illusions will drive me from this den of atrocious pogroms. I have butchered my way through your forces, died twice, and returned. The corpse of your champion lies burning at your doorstep. I will have your head, wytche. You will answer for your crimes, the justice of the order will be brought down upon you willingly, or forcibly."

The voice returned within his ears, freezing the coroner in place as it hissed whispers with unnerving seductive undertones.

> "Crimes? Justice? These contrivances are nothing but proof that your race has chosen pusillanimity over brutality. You have stripped your creator of power and chose to be the masters of your pathetic destinies. The race of man will fall under the weight of your own self-conceit. This is fine by us. Look at you, quivering in fear."

The voice faded once more and released him from its hold.

> "I do not fear you!"

"LIES!"

A pair of glowing amber eyes rushed toward the coroner from the dark. Sharp claws and fangs materialized through a corporeal apparition. As the phantasm collided with him, Paolo braced his arms to cover his face, but it dissipated into the shadows as it touched his body.

This can't be alkaloid induced, for my mask is sealed. I would know if I was experiencing the side effects of the anthemene, yet my physiology is stable. I don't understand.

The voice from the shadows hissed once more as he finished his thoughts.

> "Yes, human. Use your reason and rely on your natural philosophies. Surely there can't be other forces at play within our mortal plane."

Paolo felt the icy grip of hopelessness for the first time in his life as the words of the Sycrass sunk into the deep corners of his unraveling fragile mind.

> "There are no Gods, wytche! The world has been quantified and studied, there must be an explanation for how you are toying with me. Cease this trickery and face me!"

Paolo spun around the cathedral, frantically following the faint sounds of mocking laughter as he shouted into the expansive darkness that surrounded him. His heart began to pound within his chest as fear and paranoia slowly took his faculties. The meagrom returned with a searing pain within his skull. As the pounding pain shot through his cerebrum, he was overcome with a torrential flood of whispering voices.

Clutching his head and writhing in pain, the cacophony of voices continued to fill his head until Paolo collapsed to his knees on the marble floor below him. Before the madness could render him incapacitated, they were all silenced at once. A pair of warm hands descended upon them from the shadows and grasped him by the shoulders from behind.

"Koratok, still your mind. You have cast out your weak goddess along with the rest of your ilk. Come with me and let me introduce you to a more benevolent force. A pantheon of celestials that will grant you, your every desire. Divines that won't enforce cumbersome rules or hold you to higher expectations. Besides, isn't that why your race abandoned Myrina in the first place. Accountability?"

Paolo sprang from the ground and spun to meet his tormentor. But it was no demoniac entity or wytche. Standing before him was a familiar face, which only brought more confusion and anger from within him.

"Sarella Augathina? I don't understand."

The Sarella stood before him, not as she was outside a moment before, but as she was at the Rectory. She strode towards him, slowly untying her vestments.

"I know what you truly desire, Paolo Reveré. And I can be whatever you want me to be."

As she pulled open her linen tunic to reveal her breasts, Paolo drew a throwing knife from his vest and threw the straight blade at the imposter.

The blade sailed with pinpoint precision but fell on smoke and shadow before skidding across the marble floor with a clamor of clanging steel on stone.

Cackles danced around him from the shadows once more.

"Reveal yourself, and face justice. I won't ask again."

"Reveal myself? As you wish, Right Hand of Myrina."

From the shadows, she came. Towering over Paolo, the Sycrass stood tall and slender in form. Her hair was as pale as moonlight, and her feline eyes a bright, radiant amber. No hair graced her almost scale-like complexion, and her nails were long and sharp. As she smiled, Paolo recognized the sharpened canines that lined her unsettling wide-set grin.

"You appear Rholhynian, but I have never seen one as tall as you appear."

The smile faded from her face, and the amber in her eyes became a paler shade of crimson.

"Don't insult me, human. There is no other blood in my veins except that of my own. That peasant filth, who has spent centuries interbreeding with your infant race, is nothing but a pale shadow of us."

"Us?" Paolo asked, confused by her choice of vernacular.

The Sycrass walked toward the choir of the cathedral, moving the window light so that it stayed focused on her as she walked. As if she controlled the very environment around them. She stopped, turning around on her long slender bare feet.

368

"Consider yourself lucky, human. You have the privilege of meeting one of the last survivors of the Eldritch Races. There were once three of us, many ages ago. That was until your kind was born from the womb of that sniveling brat, Myrina. There was balance and order, but all that went by the wayside after the firstborn of the moon wanted to play creator. But we can speak of history another time. Sadly, I have a schedule to keep and a cataclysmic apocalypse to call down. So, I am going to offer you a proposition, only this once. You are a rare specimen of your race, Paolo Reveré. You have a strong will and a stout heart. These Molder Knights and their Cult of the Personiphi bore me. I offer them what they seek, and they just take what is given, gluttonous pigs, all of them. You resisted until the end before faltering. Not by a weakness of morality, but by a weakness in a lack of truth. You might be a strong ally in the new order that will rise from the ashes of this kingdom. A noble and loyal servant to the crown, a guard hound if you will. Pledge your loyalty to me and swear fealty to my coven, and I will spare you. I will open your mind to cosmic truth and eldritch secrets you could never discover tinkering with your silly toys."

The Sycrass walked backward as she enticed him with honied words. Raising her arms upward to shoulder height, she finally revealed what lay beyond the veil at the end of the cathedral. Paolo recoiled in horror as his eyes beheld the grotesque scene in front of him.

The statue of Myrina had been toppled from the altar, and in its place stood a cyclopean pagan statue of antediluvian origins. A great six-headed beast bearing the various horned and fanged faces of Umbryssal

titans imprisoned in the deep. It sat crossed, its
anatomy that of both male and female, both rotting and
engorged. Below the statue was an entrance to a gaping
pit that bore forth hues of a ghastly shade of crimson.

The flayed carcasses of thousands of women lay
strewn around the entrance of the pit in an orgiastic
display of blasphemous and sinful degeneracy that
made even the seasoned coroner fight the sensation to
vomit from within his mask. The sight of Paolo's
detests in the primal indulgences brought a smile back
to the face of the Sycrass. As if she drew pleasure in
seeing his pain and horror.

> "Praise my gods, Paolo Reveré, and swear to
> me your undying devotion. Or I will bring you
> to ruin and make your soul watch as we destroy
> your race in a pestilence of animalistic
> perversion."

As she began to slowly cackle at her own words, she
was brought back to silence by a single uttered word
from the coroner.

> "No."

Her eyes now lit up like raging flames with swirls of
both red and black, and her frown turned into a spiteful
grimace as she gazed upon the man below her.

> "You dare deny the eldritch gifts?"

"I WILL NOT BEND MY KNEE, to you or your gods.
I came here to bring your head on a spike and deliver it
to my superiors. And I mean to do just that. So enough
of your words, wytche. You will entice me with lies

370

and deceits. You will no longer bring pain and terror upon the innocent people of this kingdom."

The Sycrass howled in rage. Paolo drew the hatchet and descended upon the Sycrass with a speed and ferocity like a trained assassin. But before he could get close enough to strike her down with the weapon, the Sycrass ensnared the coroner within a vortex of tormenting mist and shadow. She raised him high into the air, her arms moving about her frame as she hissed out incantations in gnarled eldritch tongues. Paolo writhed and struggled from within the crushing maelstrom of malicious umbrage. The more he fought against it, the more his vitality drained away.

As the Sycrass grew louder in her monotonous chanting, the energies pushing against him grew in force and intensity. His eyesight dimmed within his periphery as he felt his skin wither and decay. Paolo looked to the glass-stained window behind the statue within the choir and gazed upon the moonlit face of Mother Myrina. For the first time in his life, he whispered a prayer.

Look after little Diffynwyd and promise to keep her safe.

Paolo Reveré took his final breath. As the Sycrass sensed his demise, she released her dark vortex as his hollowed husk of a body came plummeting to the marble floor.

He woke and opened his eyes to find himself lying on his chest. The air felt odd to him as if it was both warm and chilling at the same time. Pushing himself up from the ground, he felt his hands press against damp earth and icy pools of murky water. Slowly he rose, finding himself amongst a sea of grey smoke and smog, ever-expanding as far as the eye could see.

He stood momentarily, looking around and gazing upon the hazel sky above. Something beckoned to venture into the smoke, and so he did. He walked for an unknown period until he spotted through the fog the faint outline of a singular great oak tree. The tree became his destination. Paolo walked until he had finally arrived at the tree. It bore strange fruit, the likes of which he had never seen. He contemplated picking the fruit, but before he could, his ears perceived a noise that was both familiar and foreign to him. It came from around the tree. As he came around a tree, he beheld a strangely clad person sitting upon a stump and was sharpening a bladed weapon.

Paolo approached the person from behind, but they had taken notice of him. The individual rose from the stump and turned to face him. They were donned in ornately crafted black plated armor, which covered them from head to toe. Around him was draped a heavy black cloak that had a thick blanket of black raven feathers around his neck and shoulders. His great helm was crafted in the likes of a raven as well. Smoldering blue eyes studied him from within the helmet as if studying him. The raven knight planted the tip of his colossal great sword between his legs and clutched the handle of the sword around the cross guard with his iron gauntlets. A voice rang out from the sky above, but in the language of thunder and rolling clouds.

The raven knight looked to the sky and listened to the voice within the storm. Nodding silently, the raven knight turned back toward Paolo and lifted his heavy sword from the ground. As Paolo started to ask a question, the raven knight took his sword between two hands and drove the tip of the sword deep into his belly.

Wilhelmina and the Sarella finally broke through the emerald flames blocking the entrance and entered the narthex of the cathedral. As the Sarella gasped in shock at the grotesque sights around her, she fell to her knees and began to pray for the desecration of the sacred ground. Wilhelmina frantically looked around the inside of the cathedral as she searched for a sign of Paolo within the shadows. As she walked down the nave and toward the choir, she finally beheld the corpse of Paolo and fell to her knees in defeat. The sight of his smoking, withered body strewn upon the marble floor drew a welling of tears from within her. Her training activated upon the influx of emotion, and the mortalist searched for the Sycrass so that she could translate her pain into an act of swift retribution.

Her eyes met the Sycrass at the far end of the nave, and as soon as she beheld the monster, Wilhelmina turned her tears into plots of pinpoint deliveries of death. She rose from the floor and drew the bullwhip from its holster. The steel tip hit the floor as she released the mechanism from within. Loading the crossbow on the bracer of her leather gauntlet, the mortalist progressed down the nave in a swift and silent sprint. The Sycrass was standing with her back turned to Wilhelmina, presiding over the gaping pit and summoning forth unholy mephitic entities from deep within the earth.

As the mortalist got within range, she raised her crossbow and took aim. Wilhelmina squeezed the firing lever from within her palm and sent a silabar bolt soaring through the air. To the surprise of the mortalist, the bolt sailed through the Sycrass and into the statue in front of her. She stopped in her advance, but when she tried to examine the error in her shot, the Sycrass had disappeared.

A large-scaled hand snatched Wilhelmina from behind and sent her soaring and plummeting into the marble floor.

"I grow tired of these games. You will not stop, none of your race can. Now stand aside, or else end up like your foolish friend here."

Wilhelmina sprang from the floor and drew her pistol from her belt. Taking aim, she squeezed down on the trigger but was seized by an unseen force and lifted high into the air.

"I had no quarrel with you, Koratok of Shadows. Honestly, I was impressed with how well you learned our techniques in your training. I only allowed you to live this long because I respect those who learn to master the shadows. But shadows aren't responsive to the emotional whims of the ephemeral. If you want to resort to fighting like a brutish animal, then I will rip you asunder."

As the dark magic of the Sycrass began to tear into the soul of Wilhemine, she struggled and screamed in agonizing pain. The slow banging of a mace on a shield came echoing from down the central aisle of the nave. When the Sycrass heard the sound, her crimson gaze shifted from the dying mortalist to the approaching Sarella. The sight of the armored priestess drew a smirk from the Sycrass, and so the wytche tossed the mortalist into a pile of bones in the corner of the aisle and began to meet Augathina halfway.

"Priestess of Myrina, how lovely to meet you in person. I am going to enjoy tormenting you into a slow and torturous death. Are you ready to bear witness to the dawn of a new epoch?"

As the Sarella clashed her mace against her shield a final time, she raised her heater shield toward the stained glass and caught the reflection of the moon in the radiating outline of the holy sigil painted across the front. The Sycrass dodge the moonlight while hissing before hurling a ball of tenebrous magic back. The Sarella and the Sycrass exchanged blows of both magical and martial nature as each of the women refused to give or gain ground to the other.

Sarella Augathina was caught off guard in her defense as the Sycrass teleported through gaps of shadow throughout the nave. The priestess had suddenly lost sight of her target. Once the Sycrass saw the Sarella with her back turned, she reached out her hands and began to pull the very blood from her body. Sarella Augathina fell to her knees and clutched at her chest and abdomen in choking gasps as crimson mist tore through the pores of her skin and slowly advanced toward the Sycrass. Before the sanguineous vapor could reach her fingertips, each of the lancet windows of the cathedral began to rupture in a spectacle of refracted prismatic hues. The Sycrass released her grip on the Sarella and spun around in terror at the sudden unforeseen event. The harvest moon lingered close to the now gaping windows around her, and then suddenly, a beam of radiant moonlight entered the sepulcher and fell upon the body of Paolo Reveré.

His body began to hum with latent energies before a faint glow came careening over his hollowed frame. Rapidly he began to regenerate and mend, rising from the marble floor and into the air. As he ascended, his body rolled to his back, arms and legs dangling as if being cradled by a large phantasmal hand. The Sycrass began to shriek in a combination of horror and rage as she watched the coroner become turned upright onto his feet in the air and gaze down upon her with fiery blue eyes.

"NO! THIS CAN NOT BE!"

From around Paolo, the spectral outline of the Raven knight became visible to the Sycrass. As the ghostly helmet also met eyes with the Sycrass, a pair of great raven wings sprouted from Paolo's back and began to flap in the night air. The two bodies, ancient and modern coroner combined, descended upon the Sycrass, and collided against her dark magical energies in a barrage of searing emerald and white flames. As Paolo swung his flame-shrouded fist, a delayed blow from the raven knight would soon follow.

Blow after blow, the two drove back the Sycrass toward the edge of the gaping pit of despair within the choir. Feeling the ground slide from underneath her, the Sycrass began to panic. In the act of spiteful desperation, the Sycrass chose to deplete her Umbryssal power in one cataclysmic blast. If she was going to die, then they would all die with her. Channeling one last single prayer to her eldritch gods, the Sycrass rose into the air high above the pit and erupted in a tidal maelstrom of black and crimson flames.

The blast tore through the sepulcher with a torrential pulsation, sending chunks of the very foundation soaring through the air. The Sarella dove towards the unconscious mortalist and covered both from behind the safety of her heater shield.

Paolo braced himself with crossed arms as the spirit of the raven knight fluttered behind him. As the vaulted roof began to collapse around him, Paolo knew he had to send the wytche to the pestilent acrid void from within the pit. As the thought entered his mind, the phantom hand of the raven knight grabbed his shoulder and nudged him forward, beckoning him to follow his instinct. Lowering his stance, the coroner fanned his wings and launched into the air. With the spectral armor surrounding him, he penetrated through the dark energy and soared high above the Sycrass.

With a final barrage of wings and spectral steel, the two were able to collide with the wytche in a pyroclastic eruption of prismatic energies. The spectral form of the raven knight detached himself from Paolo and continued to carry the momentum of the Sycrass deep into the phage-filled sacrificial pool. Paolo looked below and watched as her fear-filled eyes sank into the vile lake and disappeared. Landing back on the shattered marble floor, Paolo started to feel a sudden change in his humors. Staggering backward, a final meagrom washed over his mind and sent him falling to his back.

As he hit the ground, the large raven wings erupted into a pile of black feathers and were gone from his form. The ground began to quake in tectonic rumbling from underneath them after the Sycrass had perished. Both the Sarella and Wilhelmina rose from the aisle amid the destruction and rushed toward an unconscious Paolo. Wilhelmina picked up the resurrectionist, and the two ran from the sepulcher as the entirety of the building came crashing down and swallowed by the earth.

The Charnel Yard

A sharp, exacerbated gasp brought stifled air deep into his lungs. Lying on his back in wet grass, Paolo could feel the horizontal drizzle of light rain soak through his wools as he panned the sky above with widened, bloodshot eyes. Paolo woke to the dawn of the rising sun, the cloudy gray sky being the first vision of his new life. A new life he was unaware of being blessed with. Trying to recall the final moments of his twilight, Paolo went to pull himself up before a flood of bodily pain pinned him to the grass.

The very muscle fibers of his gross anatomy felt torn to shreds underneath his flesh. He recalled the battle from the night before. The irresponsible amount of anthemene he had injected. Paolo groaned in disappointment at himself. Paolo, you sarding fool. You are too old to make these kinds of blunders. He thought to himself while aggressively ventilating, working up the courage to try another attempt at rising to his feet. You should have let those creatures finish the job. Death is a better alternative to this miserable agony you now must recover from.

After a few more attempts, Paolo could roll over to his side. Sweat had begun to percolate on his furrowed brow from under his sealed mask. Reaching upward with a stiff wrist, the Coroner unbuckled the sides of his rebreather and peeled the rebreather from the lower half of his face. The cold air felt exhilarating on his bone-dry skin. It was against every protocol of the order, but Paolo didn't care. Lying on his side, drinking the cold Turnian air in, all he could do was reflect.

It was time for the old Coroner to turn in his badge. Paolo could only think of poor Diffynwyd if she had to hear of his demise after he promised to take care of her. He would apply for a position as a doctori after turning in his report and speaking with the chief. But his time in the field had finally come to an end.

Maybe I'll be remembered as the resurrectionist who served an entire career and didn't die in the field. Well, in the end, what is the life of one Coroner if it doesn't prevent the death of thousands? I guess I have some serious thinking to do on the ride back to Oberndorf.

Paolo slowly pushed himself up on his grounded forearm. Fighting through the pain, the old Coroner rolled himself over and sat upright in the grass. The blood drained from his head and neck, causing his vision to blur. The dizziness almost made him sick, but he fought through the meagrom with concentration and conviction. And even a small prayer.

Sitting upright, Paolo surveyed a sea of time-weathered tombstones. Jutting upright like small mountains were the sprinkling of ancient mausoleums, whose names they bore had long been faded and forgotten. The slight breeze blew the dried vegetation from the crypt entrances. A flurry of orange leaves rolled and tumbled over his mud and blood-encrusted boots. Paolo felt a small bump against the palm surface of his right glove hand. Looking down, he beheld a single blood-stained leaf that radiated with a bright, vibrant white hue under the focus of his vermillion lens.

Mortality is so fleeting and finite.

Paolo let his mind wander one last time, allowing his body to catch up to his ambitions of gross motor movement. He thought about a lesson he had learned long ago while only a lad in the academy. A lecture on the subjective truth born from the objective resurrection. A course every resurrectionist takes to heart as they enter the field for the first time.

Are we nothing more than blood, flesh, and bone? Who will give a subjective voice to those who lost their lives this night? Or the others. Were we able to bring that personal justice to those who were butchered and cannibalized? Violated and deprived? Who will remember those women and children of Lazzar Perish?

A single tear formed under his tired, bruised eye. A droplet born from the memory of those feral women and children he freed from the cages in Fort Fermyre. Desecrated humans who had been treated like domesticated animals. Corralled and fattened on the rotting flesh of their kith and kin. It made the taste of whatever victory gained here bitter and unsavory.

He wished he could return to the village of Glengloam. Grab the magistrate that berated him for being cold and inhuman. Drag her to Turnia and make her watch as he and Wilhelmina deliver the news to families across the March. That their loved ones were butchered, raped, tortured, and finally turned into monsters. Monsters that prayed on others. Make the magistrate watch as the coroners were driven off properties and out of homes for bringing this news. Unable to comfort those who need it. Not allowed to

counsel those who are seeking it. Not able to shed a
tear.

*These horrors. Will haunt me for a hundred days and a
hundred nights. I can never return to the man, nor the
Coroner I was before. Diffynwyd needs a father and a
parent. But at the same time, the realm needs a
protector. The Goddess has shown me as much. In my
sincere ignorance, I was blind to the truth. The purpose
of my uniform, the donning of the raven guise. But now
I see with eyes wide open. A great evil has stirred in the
umbral shadows of our Border-Realm. An eldritch evil,
long forgotten, has awoken from their slumber. If I
must sacrifice my life so that Diffynwyd can grow up
safe and sound. Indeed, she would understand.*

Paolo finished his thoughts and closed his eyes.
The parting of his cracked lips gave way to a whisper
of a small prayer.

"Reva noxam adornos requiem."

As Paolo finished his prayer in old Solarnian,
he slowly closed his hand to make a fist. The quivering
blood-stained leaf crumbled in his palm, turning to
powder under the weight of his clenched fingers.
Opening his hand once more, the crimson
powder became caught in the breeze. And sailed off
toward the open sky above. The faint howling of the
wind sounded like a relieved sigh as it soared through
the bare branches of the nearby trees. A weight lifted
from his shoulders, but a memory he would never
forget.
Wilhelmina appeared from behind a tall, half-
battered tombstone. Rolling her shoulder under her

other firmly gripped hand, the mortalist stopped to observe the state of her peer. Studying Paolo's chest's faint rise and fall from under his brigantine, Wilhelmina let out a small sigh of relief. She approached him and gave a small greeting. Kneeling next to him, Wilhelmina removed a glass vile and brass syringe from a leather pouch on her side.

"I take it you are in a lot of pain?" Wilhelmina asked candidly.

Paolo slowly nodded while letting out a bout of deep, wheezing coughing. Wilhelmina drew up the milky alkaloid solution from the thin glass vial while Paolo continued to wheeze. Each cough felt like a hoarse was sitting on his chest, driving sharp crushing pain deep into his thorax.

Thrusting the large bore hypodermic needle into the wax seal of Paolo's sleeve, the mortalist drove the plunger deep until the medicinal solution was no longer visible. The alkaloid vitriol felt like ice water as it worked its way up his venous vasculature toward his heart.

Paolo looked to his companion with a shivering spine, "Cyatric laudanum?"

Paolo asked through chattering teeth. She nodded while he continued to fight back the urge to start convulsing. The medicinal concoction violently repaired his musculature. Paolo's heart slowed to an alarming pace before picking up a regular rhythm. The warmth returned to his vessels ending the spasmodic nature of his anatomy. Paolo let out a sigh of relief as he flexed and stretched his arms and legs. Feeling like a new man, Wilhelmina helped Paolo to his feet as the Sarella arrived to greet the two coroners.

Sarella Augathina hooked her flanged mace to her belt before slinging the strap of her battered heater shield over her shoulder. Two warm, vibrant eyes peered at them over the black cloth mask that covered the Sarella's face from under the black hood of her vestments. The Sarella's raised cheekbones gave away her hidden smile.

> "You truly are the right hand of Myrina, master coroners. Mankind will see another dawn because of your strength and courage. May the Mother keep you both."

Sarella Augathina pressed her hands together and gave the two coroners a slight bow in appreciation. Muttering a prayer in Old Solarnian, the Sarella returned to an upright posture for Paolo to return a nod of his own. Wilhelmina did not, instead choosing to look off in the distance. Gazing at the mounds of burnt and rotting corpses, both guardswomen and beast alike, the Mortalist crossed her arms and nodded in the direction of the wonton death before them.

> "What does the Goddess have to say about that, Sarella? What insight does our holy Mother of merciful sorrows have on the calamity that befell those poor souls?"

Wilhelmina looked to the ecclesial physician as she lashed out her blasphemies in cold succession. Paolo lowered his head, knowing there was a sliver of truth in the Mortalist's observation. The smile faded from the Sarella's face. Replaced with a look of stern coldness equal to that which was hidden behind the Mortalist's mask. A lightning bolt lashed out across the sky as a swarm of black wings on dark skies passed over the horizon of Lazzar Perish.

The Sarella looked up at the lightning bolt before returning her gaze to Wilhelmina, "your emotions cloud your thoughts, sister."

Wilhelmina scoffed as the Sarella continued, "We are nothing, human life is nothing. We are given meaning and purpose through her grace. Her blessing. Does the Apokryphum of Sorrows not teach of pain, misery, and loss? Our existence is tragedy as we were never meant to exist in a paradise."

Lightning struck across the sky once more. The bright white and blue flash reflected off the Sarella's vibrant hues of both her iris. She continued in a somber tone,

"You hunt men, men who have wronged others of our race. You take their life in exchange for the life they took. She has allowed you these sacrifices in her name, for it completes the cycle of a path of sorrow. A Koratok, a plague hunter, has always been the right hand of Myrina. The palm of sorrow. Whereas the left hand she reserves for mercy. I am the left hand, Koratok. I know my place, so know yours."

As the Sarella paused in her sermon, Wilhelmina lowered her arms and thus her guard.

Paolo could feel the tension in Wilhelmina melt away under the comforting tones of the Sarella.

Leaning back into a tombstone, Wilhelmina sniffled back a tear as the Sarella approached her slowly. Placing a gentle hand on the mortalist, Sarella Augathina looked toward the cloud-covered heavens with closed eyes.

> "Always walk in the path of sorrow, sister. For we were born in the shadows of its wake. Her moonlight allows us to see that, no matter how dark the night we must endure."

Nodding in agreeance, Wilhelmina chose to remain silent. Neither offering apology nor verbal agreeance, instead choosing the path of pseudo-stoic reverence with a still tongue.

Paolo turned around and looked up toward the desecrated and decimated sepulcher above. Gazing at the structure in silent disbelief, Paolo tried to recall any memory of what had occurred from within its walls. The bell tower had collapsed into a pile of rubble, along with most of the walls. Broken and tumbled lancet windows with piles of blown stained glass lay strewn on the side of the black, charred hilltop. There was nothing but a few pillars that remained. Walking up beside him, Paolo could see the mortalist enter his peripheral. Her voice cut through the silence like the sharp edge of a lancet blade.

> "Do you remember anything from last night?"

Paolo only shook his head.

> "I don't remember a thing. Everything past Saidach is completely gone from my mind."

Both coroners stood in silence again before thundering boots echoed through the graveyard behind them. It was the remnants of the Turnian Guard. They had been piling the perverse remains of the butchered beasts and putting them to the torch. As the wind picked up and the fire fanned, the scent of burning flesh radiated from the town square.

The incense in Paolo's rebreather sparked and sputtered before filling his nares with the sweet scent of beach wood and cinnamon.

Shouldering their crossbows and sheathing their broadswords, the last lieutenant of the guard ordered her troops to make rank and file. Paolo and Wilhelmina made their way toward the town square to thank the remaining guard for their aid. Paolo shook the officer's hand.

"Lieutenant, thank you. We both would have been killed if not for your bravery."

The officer looked at Paolo with lifeless eyes. Her pale complexion and sunken face showed clear signs of psychological shock. Sheathing her broadsword, the officer removed her blue and orange wool tricorn hat. Pulling back the chainmail coif, she let her long curly, auburn hair down with a soft sigh.

"You are very welcome, Master Coroner. But its Captain now. See, my commanding officer is lying half over there. While her ass end is laying on that pyre over there. She was torn in half, you see. Right before my own eyes. It was my insolence and cowardice that saved my own skin, at the price of hers. How am I supposed to follow her command? After showing my sisters in arms, that I am nothing more than a sniveling weakling."

As the newly promoted field commander poured out her grief and anger onto the Coroner, Paolo could see her sword hand tremble and spasm uncontrollably.

He knew what lay ahead for the poor woman. Restless nights, waking to the sound of screams. The scent of blood and smoke was fresh in her nose as if she was there. Sweat-soaked sheets and a life of misery awaited all the survivors here.

Quickly, the Captain apologized for her rambling transgression. Putting on her coif and tricorn, the Captain turned to her horse. Paolo raised an open hand and called out to the Captain, climbing into her saddle. He approached her saddle and began to brush the lush mane of the white war horse before speaking.

"It wasn't your fault, Captain. Don't let unnecessary guilt and shame lead you to the bottle, nor the bridge."

The Captain scoffed and shook her head, "what? It's not my fault I let my commander, my friend, my sister! For Goddess's sake. It's not my fault that she died. Is that what you're saying, Master Coroner?"

Paolo moved his hand from the reins to the arm of the rattled Captain and pulled her down to his eye level. The tricorn hat slid on the chainmail coif until falling toward the muddied road below. Her wide eyes reflected off his crimson transparent lenses. Her lips began to tremble at her own visage. Paolo let her come off her saddle before placing her on her feet before him. Leaning in closer, the Coroner recanted.

"It's not your fault, for surviving."

As the words penetrated her broken mind, the young commander broke under the weight of the Coroner's message. Wrapping her arms around Paolo, the Captain wept softly on the black wool cloak draped around his shoulders.

"Why…why me and not them? I don't…understand."

She tried to reason through streams of tears, but there was no answer he could give. No answer that would take the pain away. Looking to Wilhelmina, Paolo could see that the moment was also taking its toll on the mortalist. If he couldn't offer words of reason, then a comprise would suffice. So, Paolo slowly returned the embrace and let the Captain have her moment to consolidate both mind and soul.

While the captain wept, her subdued wails carried over the burnt hovels and scorched carcasses that littered the bygone Hamlet. They were answered by the soft howls of the autumn wind. Paolo looked up and beheld a site through the vermillion lenses of his oculars that made his heart stop within his breast. For a fleeting moment, there was what he believed to be the gathering of a hundred souls. Glowing brightly like the spirit grains used on inquest. They bore the uniforms and implements of guardswomen, the very same who had fought and died here the night before.

The massed spirits began to dissipate as soon as he caught their glimpse. All, save but one. Paolo recognized her cap and coat to be that of the captain of the guard. In disbelief, he watched in awe as the ghostly shape approached the kneeling commander who clung to Paolo. Looking downward, she reached out a single hand and rested it gently on the head of the woman who bore tears of guilt and shame. The new captain ceased in her crying, and the spirit dissipated within a sudden slow passing of a frigid breeze. The captain pulled her swollen eyes from Paolo's cloak and looked around with a perplexed gaze. "*Luprisa*?" Was all that the captain could sputter out. Her hoarse voice scraping across a barren throat and out through cracked, dry lips.

Soon, the two of them were joined by the remaining members of the Turnian guard. Uniforms torn, and armored battered. Paolo could see them for what they were. That these brave women were muddied, bloodied, and battered. Each of their faces covered in torn bits of flesh, encrusted sinew, and they each bore eyes that had seen a score of horrors. Two came to the captain's side and brought her to her feet.

Through the crowd came a large statured guardswoman, donning a unique baldric of died orange leather with deep purple bordering. The insignia within the small decorative shield was that of a line sergeant. Leader of the vanguard and commander of the night watch. As the sergeant marched toward the inner cordon, the guards parted in reverence for her. A wave of echoing clanks rang out as each guard slammed their clenched fist against their steel breastplate in salute.

The sergeant approached and eyed the new commander with grim hollow eyes, absent of any humanity or remorse. She pulled a dirk blade from her baldric. The captain was brought closer with a heavy pull from the sergeant large right hand. With her left hand, she knocked the captain's hat to the muddied road and drew back her chainmail coif. A swipe of the dirk separated the captain's right ear lobe from her head, sending a stream of fresh blood down her soiled and torn orange overcoat. Paolo took a few steps back and gave the women their space, unsure of what was to come next. He took his place by Wilhelmina's side and remained silent.

The line sergeant picked the small piece of flesh up from the ground and held it out to the captain, who took it with a trembling hand. Then, the line sergeant cut off her own, which Paolo could see was also her last. The act appeared to be a ritual of sorts, as the guardswomen moved in around the two leaders forming tight rank and file. Spears or broadswords were drawn or made ready as the captain and sergeant swiped their right hands in the small river of blood pooling on their shoulders. They clasped their bloodied hands, and the sergeant spoke with a grizzled voice. Her eyes fixed on those of her new commander.

"Lieutenant Van Hern, you will take the title of captain and lead this battalion. You will protect this March from all foes. Be they neighbor, or invader. You have chosen to serve your Queen and kingdom as a guardswoman. Being high born, the rank of officer was bestowed upon you. Men fight our wars, but it is our duty as women to defend the Homefront. This is the custom of our land. The way of our ancestors."

The sergeant took a step back to give the commander room. Drawing a longsword from her waist, the sergeant waited for the lieutenant to take a knee before her. Van Hern lowered herself to one knee and held aloft her right arm bent and parallel to the ground. As if donning an invisible shield.

"Lieutenant Van Hern, will you honor the ancient traditions, and warrior ethos which has been set forth by the foremothers before you?"

The commander cleared her sinuses. Wiping her eyes with the back of her left hand in haste, she replied with a sober voice.

"Aye, sergeant."

The flat of the blade was then rested upon the commander's presented vambrace. The guardswomen lining the cordon snapped to attention, sending a soundwave of rattling metal reverberating through the still air.

"Will you proudly give your life, for Queen, for homeland, and for your sisters gathered her before you?"

"Aye, Sergeant."

The sergeant tapped the blade loudly against the steel vambrace. The ping of the metal was answered by a roar from the guards.

"Hearth and home, we shall defend!"

The sergeant continued, "will you bleed for us, as we will bleed for you?"

"Aye, sergeant."

Another pinging tap brought a collective chant from the masses.

392

"ZUSTRYRS!" They shouted sternly. A deafening clang of gauntlets upon heavy heater shields followed their cry. A Turnian word meaning *sisters*, or so Paolo thought.

"STREJDÄMP!" They shouted in unison, which was followed by another hard blow of steel-clad fist on metal shields.

The sergeant sheathed her broadsword and extended her hand to the commander.

"You kneel before me a Lieutenant. Now rise, Ada Van Hern, a captain." The sergeant pulled the young officer to her feet by her extended arm.

The newly accepted Captain was welcomed with a cavalcade of hard salutes from her remaining battalion. What should have been exceptional moment of her life, was eclipsed by the sobering vision of piled bodies surrounding the decimated hamlet. A harsh reminder of the price paid and for what was to come in our latter days. Captain Van Hern drew her broadsword and held it aloft toward the makeshift pyres which contained the desiccated remains of their fallen sisters.

"Hail our fallen! In reverent memorial, I proclaim this day! May they remain forever lionized as heroine, one and all. May their kith and kindred never weep for them in sorrow. For they fought back the nightmares of Lazzar Perish when many would have fled in cowardice. HAIL!"

"HAIL!" Swords and spear tips thrusted toward the dawning sun. The clamor of steel plate and chain mail thundered out through the hallowed grounds of the sepulcher on the hill.

"HAIL!" yelled the captain once more through gritted teeth and quivering lips. The light of the penetrating sun through thickened clouds reflecting off her watery eyes.

"HAIL!" The final response roared with a fervent proclamation so profound that it drew the attention of the guardswomen toward the sepulcher grounds. The vision of a thousand revenants stood amidst the shattered tombstones and battered mausoleums of the charnel yard. The rallied swords and spears of familiar wights could be seen through the remaining mist which hung low on the barrow ahead. No words of questioning nor of disbelief were uttered. Only one last final goodbye between the living and the dead was spoken in silence. A final salute from their hailed comrades brought forth another wind. A gust that picked up their spectral remains and carried them away toward the setting moon over the horizon of the western sky.

The haunting site brought only more silent reflection to the old coroner. He thought on happenstance and circumstance. Circumstance forges hard truth. Truth in one's mortality, and an equal truth in one's capabilities. The one thing circumstance does not encompass is the variable of chance. Unlike other virtues woven into the fabric of mankind's making, Luck is the most debilitating to accept as fact. Destiny is the chosen vernacular for the ecclesial physician and other priestesses. But Paolo had always despised the concept of divine intervention. If those who were destined to live or destined to succeed were truly divinely blessed. Then why would any woman here spend the rest of their days in crippling angst and misery?

The battered and bruised members of the Lazzar Perish excursion team left the town, their mission completed. But not even one felt a sense of pride in surviving the nightmare. As they passed through the blood-drenched hamlet for the last time, the remaining guardswomen viewed the carnage of their fallen sisters and grieved in silence before gathering the remains for the pyre.

They had gathered wood from Faynean Forest and built the funeral pyre in the center of town, the last mound built in the hamlet of Lazzar Perish. After they had burned the dead, the group slowly began to make their way back to Lethelheim. The journey was made in silence.

As they reached the Perthmyre Downs, Paolo stopped in his tracks. Sudden sharp pain in his bad knee told him the moisture in the air was shifting. Soon after, another tremble could be felt from within the earth. Turning back towards Lazzar Perish, the group watched in horror as a maelstrom of light and energy erupted from the pit within the ground and reached into the tenebrous swirling storm clouds above. Soon after the event, a giant wall of fog began to press toward their location.

As Paolo observed the fog, he scanned southward and saw that the mist was moving across the entirety of the eastern border of the realm. His raven Corvax appeared, as well as Wilhelmina's raven Vixen. The carrion birds landed on their master's shoulders as the coroners watched on in horror at unraveling the truth in their failed mission.

"Quickly, Wilhelmina we must send word to the Praetorium. Make ready a note."

Paolo quickly reached into his vest and produced his notebook and pencil. Hastily the two Coroner's scribbled words on the torn piece of paper.

Toll the Bell, A pestilence is neigh.

Paolo thought of the specimen the Chief Surgeon kept in the flesh pits. If that were to grow, and deviate into something more deadly, then there would soon be no Praetorium to return to. Paolo made haste to send his message off. To hopefully save the lives of his comrades as well as the millions of people who called Calitoria their home.

As the birds soared high into the cloudy atmosphere, they flew westward toward the capital city in unison. As the fog slowly crept in over the borders, the coroners hastily began their journey back to Lethelheim.

As Paolo spurred the side of his mount and quickly bounded down the long-muddied path, his final thoughts were of the little girl he saved along the road. Would Diffynwyd be better off in Oberndorf? So close to the source of evil? No, he had to return and ensure she was safe in the capital.

Reaching the fork in the road, Paolo guided his horse to the road on the right. And road hard for Oberndorf, toward the child that now depended upon him.

Western Turnian Farm

The 100ᵗʰ day of the Season of Empyripas
905 P.A.

A young woman sits on sturdy log out front of her family's farmhouse. Her gaze is fixed on the eastern horizon. It had been days since the sky roared, but the fear for her sister's life took precedence over any fear she found in the oncoming storm. Clutching the thin silver necklace which hung around her neck, the small peasant woman continued to look on in fright as the giant wall of fog rolled ever closer to their estate.

Her concentration is broken by the whinny of an approaching horse. Soon after, the sound of spoked wheels on the dirt road can be detected. She eyes the rows of withering wheat. The sad state of her father's crop brings a pang of sorrow through her bosom. A black boxed cart comes into view through the dying wheat. A black cart *of a raven*.

Her mind begins to race with thoughts steeped in both anguish and paranoia. *Was father murdered? Did father slay another? Why had mother been gone for days?* An ill omen brings bleak news. Death had come to their meek farm, one way or another.

The cart approached the house and brought the driver into view. She could see the all-black guise of the coroner as plain as day. As the cart came to stop, the coroner rose to his feet and revealed a traveling companion. A small girl, no more than seven or eight years of age, sat in the bench seat. She stared at the girl, who stared back with cold eyes. The coroner spoke to the girl in a strange language she had never heard before. His words forced a nod from the child. He pulled the cloak from his shoulders and draped it over the child before dismounting from the cart.

The coroner looked around the estate before his red, almost glowing, eyes met hers. The rattling of his riding spurs echoed over the half barren field as he slowly approached her. She felt a soul penetrating fear pierce her as he approached. The lack of a cloak had revealed his various instruments of butchery and savagery from under the black trench coat he wore.

Upon reaching her, the coroner stopped and introduced himself in guttural Turnian. She could tell he was not a native speaker.

"Are you the owner of this farm?" he asked softly.

She shook her head and informed him that the farm belonged to her father.

"My name is Aylanna. What business do you have on our farm, Raven?"

The coroner froze upon hearing her name. Looking to his strange vest, he reached into a pocket and produced a folded piece of parchment.

"If you are Aylanna, then it pains me to present this to you. I am sorry."

The coroner handed Aylanna the faded folded paper with a heavy hand. Reluctantly, she took the parchment from the thin leather glove of the stranger. Her eyes wildly darted from parchment to the raven. Timidly, Aylanna unfolded the parchment slowly with trembling fingers. As the familiar handwriting came into view, she let out a low gasp in disbelief. A single tear fell from her glistening eye as she read out the opening address.

Dearest sister...

REVA

NOXA

Epilogue

The sun was setting behind the Western Turnian Range when a light rainfall began to sweep across the seas of wheat within the Kreidhorn family farmlands. A windmill creaked and moaned as the wind started to pick up and drive the large sails into rotation. A farmer was finishing up the tilling of his field when the wind swept through, icy and frigid. It brought his skin to a shiver, but he had grown up in the mountain's shadow and knew to embrace the random bites of winter as they came.

This set Kreidhorn apart from the other counties of Turnia, the harshness of the biting winds. The wind came from the southern slopes of the antediluvian and pythonic Töterhorn Mountain. The cloud-piercing peak stood at the base of the eastern Birgine Mountains, and it was the largest mountain in all the continent of Vehtossa.

The mountain's peak had never been seen, though many had tried to reach the top. Local legends propagated the myth that the mountain's peak was the home to Gods, as the peak was shrouded to protect their glorious palaces.

Others claimed that a mighty beast lived at the top, and the storms that came down were due to a raging battle between the ancient local hero Syr Edmorn Van Slach and the great winged beast. Whatever myth or legend any would want to believe, the mountain had gained notoriety amongst the race of men over the centuries.

And when the wind picked up across its snow-covered slopes, the sound of cracking pine trees and the shattering of ice formations could inform any wayward traveler how the ominous mountain had earned its titular name. As the farmer finished in his toils and began to unhitch his oxen, the sound of a wagon cart came from between the gusts of wind. The farmer grew more angst as the sound of the great heavy wheels grew louder.

He dropped the reins and harnesses and began to search for safety. The windmill was too far, and what to do with the oxen? Before he could think of a plan, the wagon came into view on the road. As his eyes observed the driver's bench, he could not spot the harrowing black and red surcoats nor the red eyes of the terrifying mounts he had heard others tell tales of at the tavern.

As the chilling fear gripped him began to melt away, he returned to his labors.

As the wagon approached his location, he could hear the axels coming to a stop from behind him. He turned to inspect the scene, and the chilling fear had returned. Two of the largest persons he had ever seen sat on the wide driver's bench. They were clad in all black armor, from head to toe, with not a single part of their body uncovered in metal. It wasn't the armor that terrified the farmer. It was the shape of their strange helmets.

From under the hoods of their heavy black wool cloaks, they donned ebony iron helmets in the likeness of a crow or raven. He could not tell. The two began to speak to each other in common speech, a language he was not educated on, but their words sounded malevolent.

"Do you speak Turnian?"
Said the one holding both sets of rains on the left-hand side. His voice sounded like a man's voice.

402

"You have been my partner for six *sarding* years, Reinhorn. Have I ever spoken Turnian to you? You should be the one to talk to the sod. You ARE Turnian."

The second voice was harder to distinguish. The farmer couldn't tell if it came from a manish-sounding woman or a womanly-sounding man. He scratched his head in thought over it while they continued to bicker.

"HA! Me, Reinhorn Von Blickensdorf, second son of the great Othor Von Blickensdorf who is cousins of the Count Bismurch Van Bloedvar? I would never stoop so low. Once this man knows of my bloodline. Which, might I remind you, is distinguishable even by the tone of voice. Once he becomes aware of my pedigree, we would never obtain any information from him. He would drop to his knees and begin to grovel at my feet. It's best that you do it, Loredana."

The farmer could recognize some words the baritone driver spoke, but they only sounded like family names and none that he had ever heard of before. As the driver finished, the passenger folded her arms.

"Do you even hear yourself when you are talking? You sound like a sarding imbecile. *Oh, I am Reinhorn Von Blickensdorf, and my father married some wench who was sisters with Count Van Cunt junior, whose daddy is Count Van Cunt senior, and he runs some bumpkin farmland in Bloedvar, Turnia.* That's you, that is what you sounded like, just then."

She sounded like she was mocking him, which forced
the driver to drop the reins and puff out his large,
robust chest.

> "How DARE you besmudge the great Von
> Blickensdorf name! Lady- Martial Loredana,
> the Von Blickensdorf family has governed the
> town of Blickensdorf for time immemorial!"

"By Mother Myrina's sagging tits, Reinhorn. It's just
Martial, why are you the only sarding buffoon that adds
the lady part? And I mean that, historically. There has
never been, in the history of the sarding Order, a '*lady*'
moniker or title."

> "Well, there should be. It's only proper.
> Guardswomen are called so in their position."

The other shook her head and sighed.

"It's not used to separate genders within the same job,
you *pissmare*. There are only guardswomen. Only
women are allowed to be guards throughout the
kingdom. Are you implying that there should be Mister
Guardswomen? Or Syr Guardswomen? I swear on the
Queen's fanny that if you weren't my partner, I would
have strangled you by now."

The passenger turned her head and gazed downward at
the farmer, who had just decided she was a woman and
was smiling while staring into the dirt road.

> "You there, farmer!" she asked in common
> speech, "Do you speak the commons?"

He didn't know what she had said, and the smile dropped from his face. Panicking, he answered her anyway.

> "Reinhorn just talk to the poor bastard, we need to get going before it gets dark."

The driver gave a disgruntled huff before turning and dismounting from the wagon. As he landed on the road and rose to his feet, the farmer was able to gaze upon the enormity of his size.

The ebony-clad man stood a whole person taller than him and half a person wider. He threw back his cloak and tucked the left side around a fixated shield on his upper shoulder. It bore a strange crest that he had never seen before. The head of a raven over a shield bearing the face of a bear. The letter M was pouring from the opened mouth of the bear. Below that was the nameplate of some sort. The enormous man strode toward him and stopped.

Looking down at the farmer, he could see a pair of crimson reflective eyes staring back at him under the shadow of his large hood. Martial Reinhorn then began to speak to the farmer in Turnian. His dialect was thick, and the farmer picked up that he spoke like a westlander.

> "Man of the agricultural peasantry, I am a Royally appointed Coroner of the Worshipful branch of the Shield. My name is Martial Reinhorn Von Blickensdorf. Yes, the very same Blickensdorf family, but there is no need to bow or grovel."

He raised his hand as if to stop the farmer from interrupting him with praise, but nothing happened. The farmer had never heard of the Blickensdorf family, and he didn't seem a lord, so why would he bow or grovel? He only scratched his head in reply. Martial Reinhorn cleared his throat and continued.

"We have received reports of strange disappearances here in the March of Turnia and have been sent by royal decree to investigate these disappearances. The sheriff of Kreidhorn had reported anomalous activity of some men in the area. They wear black surcoats with a peculiar red sigil. Some other peasants claimed that these brigands had been kidnapping women and children and taking them to a nearby fortress. We believe it is the old fortress up on the Hinterland Pass. Do you know if the Hinterland Pass is open or closed currently?

"I haven't heard of the pass being closed. Although, I haven't seen a passing of the Kings men in some time, or the passing of the regimental guard. I have seen those brigands you speak of. They rode past this farm, not two days past. Had an entire cart of women folk. But if they catch the locals looking for too long, they take to dulling out beatings quickly.

I heard they even killed some men back in Leipzig for asking questions. But please forgive me, master coroner. I am just a humble farmer. If you need more information, maybe go into Kreidhorn, and then head to the Leuwenhoek estate. I heard that a coroner arrived there not too long ago. Saw them riding with the sheriff about two days past."

"What brought this coroner to your town?"

"Murder, sadly. That young squire Leuwenhoek was killed on his own plot."

Martial Reinhorn turned and relayed the information to Martial Loredana.

"He says that they passed by here two days ago, carrying a wagon of women with them. Made their way to the old fortress but doesn't know if the pass is closed or not. He also says that a resurrectionist arrived in Kreidhorn two days ago."

Martial Loredana shrugged her shoulders,

> "Why do we care about some Flay-skin? Get back up here and let's get to it."

"What if the murder is linked to our investigation?"

> "What if, it's not? You only want to go get involved so that you can pretend to be smart and play with their chymiac set. Leave the academia to the flay-skin and let's go hunt these bandits down. After arguing with you all day I need to kill someone, let me stress out."

Reinhorn scoffed and turned back toward the farmer to thank him for his help. He strode back to the cart, and the two set off. The martials took the northern road at the next fork and began to do the climb up the Hinterland pass.

The moon lingered low over the pine trees as their cart stopped at the overlook. The road ahead was too narrow for their wagon, so the martials grabbed their weapons and decided to approach the old fortress on foot.

Martial Loredana began to shiver in her iron plate,

> "it's sarding cold up here. This armor is
> leeching the heat right from my body."

She pulled the heavy ebony cloak over her shoulder as far as she could. The ecranche shield strapped to her shoulder prevented the cloak from entirely closing, but it was enough to stave off the biting winds from the mountain. Reinhorn only laughed as slivers of steaming air came slithering from the crevasses in his plate.

> "Loredana, my dear, you must focus on the
> thrill of the hunt. It gets your blood pumping
> and opens the pores up. There is no bigger thrill
> than the thrill of the hunt. And we are hunting
> the most dangerous game known, men.
> Armored men at that. Ha! Think of the tales we
> will share with the others."

Loredana scoffed and pulled her blundercanon under her cloak to warm the wooden handle.

> "All right, calm down. No need to get an
> erection over it."

They proceeded down the overpass, their iron sabatons sinking to their ankle in the snow. As they approached the tree line outside the fort, they stopped to investigate the postern gate and battlements from afar. Reinhorn took a knee and observed the main road to the bastion.

408

He shifted through the light layer of snow and felt the hardened earth below.

"This is peculiar."

Loredana walked around him, keeping her blundercanon pointed at the portcullis.

"What is peculiar?

"There aren't any imprints of wagon wheels in this path. This and the fact that those sconces are pitch black, I would say that no one has been here in quite some time."

Loredana scoffed at his assessment.

"If they were pulling a double-wide wagon like ours, they would leave it up at the overpass and walk on foot. And torch light? How many raids have we been on at bandit invested keeps where they had the front torches lit? That draws attention. Now stop mucking about. You want to blow the gate, or take the charge?"

Reinhorn rose from the ground and grabbed his canon with two hands.

"I'll take the charge on this one."

The two martials slowly approached the portcullis, eyeing the seemingly unmanned walls and postern gate with suspicion. As they approached the gate, they split apart. Each martial takes either side of the sealed portcullis. Reinhorn peered around the ancient stone wall and looked through the holes of the rusted iron

and wood gate. He reached around the wall and
checked the integrity of the wood with a firm grasp and
shake of his large hand.

"Beams are beginning to rot, but the iron is still
solid. I would use, one stone round shot."

Loredana reached behind her back and pulled a one-
stone round shot and black powder wad from a leather
satchel strapped to her belt. Tipping the blundercanon
upward, she loaded the powder wad first, followed by
the heavy iron ball. Pulling a packing rod from the
forearm of the canon, she then packed the two deep
into the barrel of the large firearm.

Cocking the firing hammer back, Loredana
nodded to Reinhorn to signal she was ready. After
loading his weapon and giving the signal, Loredana
raised the canon to her hip. The blast from the canon
reverberated through the mountain pass as the iron
cannonball blew a hole through the decrepit gate. As
the shower of shrapnel and wood settled with the dirt
and smoke of the blast, Reinhorn pulled from the wall
into a leaning jog. Barreling through the blown
entrance, Reinhorn moved his weapon to the ready and
scanned the inner courtyard for any signs of life. As
Loredana joined him, the two martials could see that
the fort lacked any armored brigands. Reinhorn moved
to the left side while Loredana moved forward toward
the grand hall. The courtyard was filled with large,
emptied cages that, upon closer inspection, looked
recently used.

Reinhorn moved around to the stairs leading up
to the battlements but was stopped by a shout from his
partner. He approached Loredana, kneeling within an
empty cage hunched over a find.

She dropped to her knee and pivoted toward him, a piece of cloth in her hand.

"Take a look at this, what could that possibly be?"

Reinhorn took the cloth and held it up toward the moonlight above. He observed the soiled cloth and found it riddled with some form of pus-ridden meat. As he rubbed it with his thumb and forefinger, he felt it exuded a sticky, viscous texture that reminded the martial of coagulated blood.

The two applied a sprinkling of spirit grains on the substance, which caused a violent chymiac reaction, even causing the meat to writhe upon the soiled cloth. At the sight of writhing cloth, Reinhorn dropped the linen and began to stomp it under his heavy sabaton.

"What in the name of Myrina was that?"

The two martials exchanged dialogue on the specimen's origin before deciding to get a better look around the fort. Loredana inspected the other cages while Reinhorn moved to the grand hall entrance. The large martial bounded up the stone steps and moved toward the door, stopping at the arch of the doorway. The inside was pitch black, with a pronounced silence that it was audibly stifling.

He poked his head in and looked around, his vermillion lenses picking up little from within. Satisfied with his initial search, the martial turned from the door and looked down at his partner, who was approaching the stairs.

"Loredana, I can't see worth a piss in this hall.
We should get some wood and make some
torches."

Loredana stopped in her tracks and braced herself as
Reinhorn spoke.

Taking a step backward, the martial pointed up
at her partner. Behind Reinhorn, a pair of glowing
amber eyes could be seen within the ebony void of the
doorway behind him.

"REINHORN, BEHIND YOU!"

The booming concussions of cannon blasts and the
harrowing shouts from the martials echoed over the
pine trees of the Hinterland Pass.

As the noise carried over the forest a fluttering
of black birds ruptured from the trees and flew upward
toward the pale full moon. Not long after the wind
picked up once again and the fading sounds of struggle
were swallowed and silenced in the gusts of wind
coming from the slopes of the towering Töterhorn.

www.ingramcontent.com/pod-product-compliance
Lightning Source LLC
Chambersburg PA
CBHW010732310726
48971CB00010B/2813